# AT THE CITY'S EDGE

Marcus Sakey

St. Martin's Paperbacks

This is a work of fiction. All of the characters, organizations, and events portrayed in this novel are either products of the author's imagination or are used fictitiously.

AT THE CITY'S EDGE

Copyright © 2008 by Marcus Sakey.
Excerpt from *Good People* copyright © 2008 by Marcus Sakey.

For information address St. Martin's Press, 175 Fifth Avenue, New York, NY 10010.

Library of Congress Catalog Card Number: 2007036300

ISBN: 0-312-94373-3
EAN: 978-0-312-94373-8

Printed in the United States of America

St. Martin's Press hardcover edition / January 2008
St. Martin's Paperbacks edition / March 2009

St. Martin's Paperbacks are published by St. Martin's Press, 175 Fifth Avenue, New York, NY 10010.

10  9  8  7  6  5  4  3  2  1

*For Matt, who gave me the Lantern Bearers, and many other things*

Mountain grog seller and river gambler, Generous Sport and border jackal, blackleg braggart and coonskin roisterer, Long Knives from Kentucky and hatchet-men from New York, bondsmen, brokers, and bounty jumpers—right from the go it was a broker's town, and the brokers run it yet.
—Nelson Algren

# *August 11, 1992*

*His heart pumps fire.*

*Jason's feet are impossibly heavy, and his world is blurring. Shin muscles stretch to snapping, rubber bands wound too tight. When they began racing, the breeze was like cool water he could melt into. But it has been an hour at least, and now the air is something to fight through, humid and thick.*

*Arms pumping, Jason risks a sideways glance at his older brother.*

*Michael catches it. His features are crinkled in effort, and sweat soaks the thin dark hairs pointing scraggly on his upper lip. His shirt is stained a dark V. But he manages to cock one corner of his mouth up at an ugly angle. "Give up yet?" he asks. His voice the same as the upperclassmen in gym, the ones who snap locker room towels, who laugh at Jason's hairless body, call him faggot.*

*Jason leans into the run, speeding up. Feet tingling. Mouth open. Gasping.*

*He will never stop running. Never.*

# CHAPTER 1
## Funny in a Dark Sort of Way

When the man pointed a gun at him, Jason Palmer was cooling down after his daily five and picturing the first beer of the day, a sweating Corona-and-lime that he figured he'd drink in the shower. Happy hour had been coming early lately, but he'd decided not to worry about it. To pretend this was summer vacation. Spend it running along the lake, scoping the bikini-girls that hit North Avenue Beach every afternoon like rent was a concept they weren't familiar with. He pushed sweat-damp bangs out of his eyes, laced his fingers overhead, and turned into the pedestrian tunnel beneath Lake Shore Drive. The change from blast-furnace sun to cement-cool shadows left him blinking, but when his eyes adjusted there the guy was, standing like he'd been waiting.

Maybe twenty, with dark skin and predator's eyes. A sharp-edged soul patch cropped the same length as his hair. A chromed-up Beretta with the safety off. He held the weapon wrong, elbow cocked out and wrist twisted sideways, but his hand was dead steady.

"Yo, I wanna talk to you." A diamond-studded Cadillac crest hung on a rope chain around his neck.

Adrenaline tingled up the back of Jason's legs. His heart, still racing from the run, thudded louder as he stared at the black hole pointed at his chest. He tried to remember everything he'd heard about getting mugged, how you weren't supposed to look at the guy, that it could make him nervous.

"Easy." Jason slowly unwound his hands from his head. "It's no problem. Take the money."

Soul Patch tilted his head slightly, the smile wider. "I say anything about money?"

Jason froze. He'd never seen the man before, and didn't suspect they had much to talk about. He stood at the mouth of the tunnel, the sun roasting his back; behind him he could hear the sound of gulls calling to one another, fighting over garbage. There were always people on the beach.

Then Soul Patch narrowed his eyes. "Further than you think." His finger curled against the trigger. "You don't want to be playing."

Reluctantly, Jason stepped forward. Soul Patch nodded down the underpass. "Slow." He draped his track jacket to cover the pistol. A tattoo curled on his forearm, a six-pointed star with letters inside, a G, maybe a D.

Jason's sneakers crunched sand as he walked toward the far end, Soul Patch falling in behind. The sound of their passage echoed in the closed space, scuffing back mingled with the faint rumble of cars above. His shirt went cold and clammy. *Keep it easy,* he thought. *Get him off balance.*

"You know," Jason said, voice light, "I like the Cadillac myself."

"What?"

"Saw your necklace, is all."

Suddenly, he heard voices. For a minute, he was relieved. Then two girls turned from the ramp to the hallway, their voices young, college freshmen maybe, laughing like the whole world was their keg party. Soul Patch stiffened at the sight of them.

Jason's fingers tingled. One thing when it was just him on the line; this was responsibility he didn't need. He had to keep the situation under control. "Yup. Beautiful vehicles." Dry tongue forcing the words. "I got a '72 Eldorado. Convertible."

"Shit, one of those old boats? I don't roll that way."

"What do you like, the Escalade?"

"I'm black, I gotta drive an Escalade?"

"I don't know," Jason said. The girls were ten feet away. "Just guessing."

"Man, I got me a XLR."

Jason looked over his shoulder. "No shit?"

"Leather interior and a DVD in the dash."

He nodded, trying to ignore the tension in his muscles. "Nice." The girls drew parallel, and Jason clenched to jump if Soul Patch even looked their direction. But the blonde and brunette passed smooth-faced and oblivious. Jason let out a relieved breath, walked another dozen feet, out of earshot, and then stopped. Enough. "Listen, I've only got twenty bucks on me."

"So?"

"So, take it." He started to reach, froze when Soul Patch shook his head slow.

"Son, I wanted your money, you think you'd still have it?"

"What *do* you want?"

"I want to talk." He cocked his head. "About what your brother's up to."

Michael.

Jason felt his fingers go to fists. He fought the urge to jump the fucker right there. But the man's gun was steady and his smile was cruel. "What do you mean?" Jason's voice thinner than he intended.

Soul Patch cleared his throat in a sticky gurgle and spat a chunk of phlegm against the wall. "Move."

He forced himself to obey, biting at his lip, limbs raw with adrenaline. Ten more steps took him out of the tunnel, the sun landing with physical force on his shoulders, the faint burn on his neck. He walked up the concrete ramp to a two-story parking deck, most of the spaces filled, the BMWs, Hummers, and Mercedes of a class of people who saw Monday as just a quieter afternoon to take the yacht out. Soul Patch followed, gestured to the stairs.

Jason climbed, mind working furiously. What could possibly connect his brother and this man with the killer's eyes? He tried and discarded a dozen explanations with every step, but couldn't make the pieces fit. It had to be a mistake. They reached the second floor and started down the row of cars. The whole thing was funny in a dark sort of way. Used to be that every time the squad hit the street, someone might have been watching, sweaty finger on a radio detonator, waiting for Jason to step a little too close to death. It was a feeling he'd grown used to, that proximity to nothingness, the way he might just disappear in a roar of flame. Now here he was, safe and sound at home, getting hijacked by somebody who couldn't tell one white dude from another. It would have been hysterical if it weren't actually happening.

*So what are you going to do about it, soldier?*

A delivery truck was parked forty yards up, the angular rear jutting out past the car beside, and he began to drift toward it, rolling on the balls of his feet to fight adrenaline-stiffness. Six cars to go: A couple of imports, a big SUV, one of the new Beetles, and then his truck. A lunge would get him behind it. Soul Patch might snap a shot off, but it would be hurried. And after that, it was just a matter of staying low and weaving. Killer or no, a man who held his weapon sideways didn't have the skill to hit a moving target at any distance. Just a few more steps, and he'd be clear.

Three cars short of the delivery truck, a man leaned out from behind the big SUV and slammed his fist into Jason's stomach.

Breath exploded from his lungs. He doubled over, hands flying out for something solid, coming to rest on the SUV. Pain blossomed in his gut, a warm and living thing. As his body fought for air, his mind raged, telling him to take the pain. He struggled to straighten, one hand against the rear door, the other up in a clumsy defense.

The man who'd hit him stood five and a half. Elaborately muscled shoulders tapered directly into his shaven head. He wore a spotless white T-shirt that hung almost to his knees and ornate gold rings on every finger of his punching hand. Soul Patch stood beside him, chuckling, the gun steady on Jason's heart.

Every breath was razors in his belly. Slowly, he forced his shoulders back, took the hand off the SUV. He glanced at it as he turned away, did a double-take, then looked at Soul Patch.

"I thought," Jason said, "you didn't like the Escalade."

The man smiled, his tooth gleaming. "I was just playing."

"No DVD?" He struggled to stay cool, to show that he wasn't panicking, that they didn't need to jump him.

"Oh, I got the DVD. You can watch it in back."

A shiver ran through Jason's belly. This couldn't be happening, not really. "Listen man, you've got the wrong guy."

"I feel you. Hop in, we'll discuss." He gestured, and the wrestler stepped forward to open the back, standing like a limo driver on the other side of the car door.

Jason could feel the blood vibrate through his palms, pound in his neck. In the truck he'd be trapped. That action-movie stuff about people rolling out of moving cars and walking it off, that was crap. Bail out of a car going faster than twenty miles per, you weren't walking anything off. Plus, here, in a public parking lot, he had some hope. A single bullet might be dismissed, but a firefight would attract attention. He hesitated.

"I said get in." Sun made Soul Patch's eyes glow yellow.

"Okay." Jason held his hands up. "Easy. I'll come." Electricity burnished his skeleton as he started for the car.

Then, for the first time, Soul Patch made a mistake. He stood still.

It was as much of a window as Jason could hope for. Continuing his forward motion, he stepped into Soul Patch like they were dancing, right hand closing on the guy's wrist to lock the gun in place. But instead of grappling for the weapon, he spun, planting his back against the man's chest, the gun arm now in front of both of them. The wrestler startled awake with a snort. Soul Patch gave a surprised yelp, struggled to free his hand. Jason continued his spin, remembering this fucker talking about Michael, threatening his brother. He yanked, and as he felt the man come off balance, he kept turning, transforming the fall into a throw that hurled the gangbanger against the half-closed car door. It flew open and slammed into the wrestler, the frame catching him square in the face with a meaty thump. The double impact knocked the wind out of Soul Patch, and the gun clattered from his hand.

The moment it did, Jason shoved away. Two awkward steps and he had his balance. His heart screamed to run, but his head was cool. They were enemy combatants. He didn't want to leave them armed. The grip of the pistol was warm and slightly sweaty as he snatched it from the concrete.

Then he took off in a sprint, knowing that he hadn't incapacitated either man. His legs pumped clean and strong. He crossed the open asphalt to the next row, then planted his left foot and lunged behind a car. A window exploded with a sharp crack. All the old energy came back. He jerked to the side again and broke from the row, then poured it on in a straightaway to the boundary of the lot. Leapt for the concrete abutment, planted one foot, and sprang off the second-story parking deck.

In the endless instant he floated through the air, Jason Palmer realized he was smiling.

Then he hit the soft earth of the park. He kept the fall going, tucking one shoulder and rolling it off the way he'd seen Jump School candidates do it. He was back on his feet and moving in a fraction of a second, knowing he was clear but running anyway, loving the rush, the gun part of his hand. A copse of carefully arranged trees lay twenty yards away, and he angled for them. The wind on his face cooled the sweat, and as he dodged branches he could smell the fetid dampness of the earth, a good clean scent like sex. After another thirty yards, he risked a glance back.

Soul Patch stood at the edge of the parking lot, his face twisted into a furious snarl. The wrestler leaned beside him, chest heaving, a pistol in one hand, the other clutching his nose. Blood seeped between his fingers.

Jason couldn't resist. Smiling, he stood at attention and threw them a salute. The pure hate on Soul Patch's face was the most beautiful thing he'd seen in days.

With a laugh, Jason tucked the pistol into his pants, dropped his shirt to cover it, and set off at a gentle jog. Just another guy working out on a beautiful day. When he reached the edge of the grass, he crossed the street and cut into the neighborhood.

He knew a bar two blocks away, thought about heading there to call the cops, decided against it. If he'd had his cell on him, maybe; those two stood out in white-bread Lincoln Park. But by the time he reached a payphone, they'd be rolling down Lake Shore Drive.

Anyway, there was Michael to think about. Jason turned right, digging for the keys to the Caddy. Forget the police. He had to check on his brother, just to be sure. No way this had anything to do with Michael—you could take the boy out of the choir, but never the reverse—but no harm in being certain. They'd probably share a laugh about the absurdity of the thing, a gangbanger tying to hijack him. But Jason doubted he'd ever know what it had really been about.

He was wrong.

# CHAPTER 2
## Sinking In

It was funny how something inanimate could become the focus of your whole damn day.

Michael Palmer stared at the phone resting on the end of the bar. Standard-issue pub telephone: Scuffed black plastic, cord a snarled mess, a chunk broken out of the handset where it had hit the floor two years ago. *Funny thing is, I don't know if I want it to ring or not.*

"Dad?"

"Huh?"

"What's a," Billy hesitated, then took the plunge, "tay-vurn?"

"Tav-ern."

"What's a tavern?"

"I'll give you a hint. You're sitting in one."

Billy glanced down. "A stool?"

"Not *on* one. *In* one."

His son looked at him, looked around, then smiled like a burst of sunlight. "A bar?"

"Bingo."

Billy gave a little nod like he'd known all along, he'd just been asking to test his father, then returned to the newspaper spread out on the counter. Eight-year-old fingers choked all the way down the base of the pencil as he scratched the letters. As he hunched over to read the next clue, his lips mouthed the words. His mother had been the same way. Michael used to find Lisa in bed with a novel, lips moving as though reciting a spell. How many nights had he stood in the doorway and watched her, just watched, entranced by the rise and fall of her breath, the curve of her shoulder, the smiles and frowns she gave her secret world?

He shook his head to clear the memory, counted how long since the last time he'd thought of her. Pretty good—not since lunch yesterday. Peanut butter and bananas cooked up like a grilled cheese, crunchy outside, gooey in. Lisa had always called it "De Elvis Especial," saying it in a bad Latin accent, and that was how Billy asked for it now, though Michael doubted he remembered much of his mother but auburn hair and love.

Michael, he remembered everything.

He glanced at the phone, then moved to the sink, started dunking dirty pint glasses: soapy water, clean water, stack to dry. A nice, easy rhythm, solid and steady.

"Dad?"

"Hmm?"

"What's another word for 'lucky'?"

Michael thumbed something sticking to a glass. "What can you think of?"

"Ummmm . . ." Billy's eyes unfocused. "Happy?"

"Well, somebody lucky would probably be happy. But do they mean the same thing?"

His son chewed his lip. "Guess not." He twiddled the pencil with his fingers, went back to staring. After a moment, he sighed. "Can I have a clue?"

"How many letters?"

Billy hesitated, then ran his finger along the crossword. "Seven, eight, nine."

"Got any of 'em?"

"It starts with an 'F.' "

"Nine letters and an 'F.' " Michael straightened. His feet ached like carpet tacks had been driven into the heels. Occupational hazard. Picking up a rag, he dried his hands. "Okay, if I'm rich, what do I have?"

"Lots of money?"

"Yeah, but what's another word for that?"

"Ummm . . . a 'fortune'?"

He nodded. "And what's a word like 'fortune' that means—"

*RING.*

It wasn't loud. Not any louder than usual, anyway. It just seemed that way.

*RING.*

The back of his neck tingled. Outside, a truck rumbled past, weight shaking the front windows. The towel was old and threadbare, worn soft on bar and glass, and every nerve of his fingers registered it.

*RING.*

He saw motion out of the corner of his eye. For a moment he stood rooted while his brain processed. Billy. Moving to answer the phone, a chore he delighted in.

That tore it.

Two quick strides brought Michael to the corner of the bar. He reached out and snatched the handset just before Billy reached it. "Mike's Place."

"Mr. Palmer." The voice was soft and precise.

Billy stared with his mouth open like he'd had his ice cream taken. Michael turned, phone cord wrapping around his side as he spun to face the mirrored wall of bottles, bourbon and scotch and whiskey bathed in the reflected glow of afternoon. "Yes."

"You know who this is?"

"Yes."

"Are you okay?"

He smoothed one palm against the leg of his pants. "Just a little nervous."

"Has something happened?"

"No. I just . . ." Michael squeezed the bridge of his nose between his thumb and middle finger. "It's sinking in, you know? What we're doing. The consequences."

"If you're careful, there won't be any consequences."

"Yeah, well, easy for you to say. You're staying out of sight."

A long pause. "Are you having second thoughts?"

The liquor was arranged in stepped rows, three of them. Sunlight threw spectrums against the mirror. The expensive bottles had dust on them. Why had he even bought the Balvenie? Who in Crenwood wanted seventeen-year-old single malt? His customers were Beam-and-a-Bud guys, payday drinkers, not connoisseurs.

"Mr. Palmer?"

But then, shouldn't there be something to aspire to?

"I'm here."

"Listen, I know this is hard. I understand why you're nervous. But so long as you do just as we discussed, you'll be fine. You haven't told anyone, have you?"

"No," he lied.

"No one?"

"I said no."

"I don't mean to tell you what to do. It's just the people we're dealing with . . . anyone you tell you put at terrible risk."

"I understand."

"Good." There was a pause, and the rustle of papers. "The usual place?"

Michael looked over at Billy, who leaned halfway across the bar, stretching for the soda tap. His stool was canted backwards on two legs. "I've got my son."

"Just half an hour."

"It has to be right now?"

"Michael . . ." A dignified sigh. "There comes a time when you have to decide whether you're in or out."

He closed his eyes. "I'll be there." The bell gave a little ding as he hung up the receiver.

Billy had hooked a knee onto the bar and was leaning forward at a precarious angle.

"Hey."

His son froze, tilted his head to look up.

"How many of those have you had?"

"One?"

Michael raised an eyebrow.

"Three." Billy leaned back onto his stool and dropped his chin in one hand, then gave a theatrical sigh.

Michael laughed. "I guess one more won't kill you. Ginger ale, though, not Coke, and that's it, okay? Plus you brush your teeth when we get home."

He set the drink on the bar, then opened the corner cabinet. His wallet was brown leather, mottled with stains, the seams a mess of loose threads. Lisa had given it to him at their last Christmas together. Almost three years now. He slid it in his back pocket, grabbed his phone and keys. Straightened.

The tremor started in his belly and worked out through his whole body. He heard the words again. *The people we're dealing with . . . anyone you tell you put at terrible risk.*

He looked at Billy leaning into the crossword with the intensity of a scholar studying an ancient manuscript. His son took a sip of the ginger ale as he puzzled out a clue, lips moving. Michael fought an urge to sweep him off the stool and clutch him tight in his arms, tight and warm and safe.

*This is crazy.*

It wasn't too late. He hadn't done anything that couldn't be undone. Hell, not even undone—it hadn't gone that far. All he had to do was not take another step. Blow off this meeting, and when the phone rang again, say that he had changed his mind.

"Dad?"

"Hmm?"

"What's a four-letter word for 'obligation'?"

Michael laughed. Sometimes that was all you could do.

# November 13, 1995

*The machines do not beep, not like medical shows on TV. Mostly, they hum with soft fans. There is a faint suction sound from the one helping his mother breathe.*

*Jason sits on the monkey bars and watches the sun set the city on fire and thinks about that suction sound. The sky is crimson and gold; the metal is cold through his jeans.*

*She has been in Cook County for weeks, and every day he and Michael have gone to visit. They sit on opposite sides of her bed—her body—slumped in comfortless chairs. Sometimes they talk, but not for long. She is tired, and drifts away in the middle of senseless sentences. The pills. But without them, the lines of her jaw draw tight and her eyes glisten with moisture.*

*Jason sits on the monkey bars and thinks of driving Michael's car late at night on the Kennedy, pedal to the floor, the old Chevy rattling like it wants to come apart, the rush of daring it to. He thinks about Terry O'Loughlin, Sweet T, about her long brown hair and lean thighs, and the smell of the back of her neck and the sound she makes when he kisses the spot between her breasts. He thinks about screaming guitars and Pequod's pizza with hot peppers and the high that shivers up his thighs when he runs for an hour. He thinks about swimming deep into the lake, the water colder with every stroke until he's sure his chest will shatter in the frigid blackness.*

*None of it drowns out the suction sound. None of it helps him forget that he and Michael should have left thirty minutes ago if they wanted to make visiting hours.*

*When his older brother finds him, the sun has fallen too low to see, though the sky still glows. Jason watches Michael draw steadily closer. He wonders what his brother will say. He wonders if today is the day his mother will die, and if he will forever regret not going to see her. He wonders if life will ever seem like it belongs to him again.*

*Michael stops in front of Jason's dangling feet. He sighs.*

*Then he reaches for a grip and pulls himself up to his stomach, spins, and drops down next to Jason, the impact making the cold metal vibrate.*

*Together they watch the light fade.*

# CHAPTER 3
## Ancient Fucking History

The door to his brother's bar was unlocked, and a stool lay on the floor like it'd been knocked over.

Jason had blitzed to get here, the sun streaming in the windows as old Gordon Downie sang that he didn't have no picture postcards, didn't have no souvenirs, that his baby she didn't know him when he was thinking 'bout those years. He'd swung onto the shoulder when the Drive jammed up, then jumped to the Dan Ryan, slapping the steering wheel. Riding south in the express lanes, skyline in his rearview, the corporate monstrosity that had replaced Comiskey Park on his right.

Even after he'd pulled off the highway and into the sweltering decrepitude that was Crenwood, he'd barely touched the brakes. Just let the tires squeal as he rounded corners where hard-eyed boys in long white T-shirts postured before crumbling storefronts, gang tags and liquor stores and rusted fences sliding by in a blur of heat and failure. And all the while, Jason told himself that this errand was nothing. Mistaken identity. No way could Michael really be in serious trouble.

But the door to his brother's bar was unlocked, and a stool lay on the floor like it'd been knocked over.

Jason slid into the cool of the interior. The silence wasn't reassuring. Hiking up his T-shirt, he eased the Beretta from the waistband and disengaged the safety. Leaving the door open and holding the weapon low, he moved in. The animal part of him wanted to sprint. But he didn't know the situation, and a soldier didn't run in blindly blazing. He placed his feet gently, glad for his running shoes. A newspaper was spread open on the bar, the fallen stool in line with it, like someone had been dragged away while reading. Broken glass winked from a pool of dark liquid on the floor.

"Freeze!"

Jason's heart shot into his mouth. The voice had come from behind and beside him, and he whirled, pulse-pounding, pistol up, finger on the trigger, staring down the barrel—

At his nephew.

Billy stood behind the bar, arms braced and pointed like Starsky, fingers curled into the shape of gun.

"Jesus!" Jason jerked the Beretta downwards, then blew a breath as his heart hammered his rib cage. Sweat slicked his armpits.

Billy stared at him wide-eyed. "Uncle Jason."

"You scared the *crap* out of me, kiddo." He held a hand to his chest, made himself take slow breaths. The image of his nephew lined up dead between the pistol's rear sights burned on his retinas. "Where's your dad?"

"He's not here. Why do you have a gun?"

"Did he say where he was going?"

"Nuh-uh." Billy stared at him. "You're not in the Army anymore, right?"

Jason fought a grimace, knowing his nephew didn't mean any harm, but still feeling the Worm twist in his belly. His wet-palmed panic and greasy shame had built every day for months now. He'd named it just to have something to hate. "No."

"So why do you have—"

"Your dad left you alone?"

"Mrs. Lauretta was here for a while. But she had an appointment. Besides," Billy straightened, "I'm eight. I'm not a little kid. Can I hold your gun?"

"No," Jason snapped, harder than he intended, and he saw Billy recoil. "Listen, this isn't a toy. And your dad would kick my butt if I let you touch it." He cocked his head. "Actually, your dad would kick my butt if he even knew I showed it to you."

Billy sucked a bit of his lip between his teeth. He seemed to be weighing something. After a moment, he nodded solemnly. "Okay."

"Okay?"

"I won't tell."

"Thanks, buddy. I appreciate that." Jason forced a smile, then tucked away the pistol. He closed the front door and bent to retrieve the stool. The broken glass lay in a pool of what looked like soda. "What happened here?"

"Oh, I knocked it over when I was reaching for . . . ummm . . ." The boy rocked from foot to foot and stared at the floor. "I just knocked it over."

Jason laughed. He went around the corner of the bar and ruffled his nephew's hair, then took two pint glasses. Filled the first with Coke, then pulled Bud into the second, the beer splashing sweet and cool as a memory of swimming, a lake he wanted to throw himself into. "Tell you what," he said, and handed the soda to Billy. "I won't rat on you if you don't rat on me. Deal?"

"Deal."

They clinked glasses on it, and Jason took a long open-throated swallow. The first hit off the first beer of the day was always the best, a deep and satisfying shiver of relief. Budweiser wasn't his favorite, but cold beer was cold beer.

He helped Billy clean up, gathering the big chunks of glass by hand, then sweeping the rest into a metal dustpan. His nephew bounced around like a cat with its tail on fire, and part of Jason was wondering whether another soda had really been a good idea.

But most of him was thinking of Soul Patch, the steady gun hand, the look in his eyes when he had said he wanted to talk about Michael.

He finished two Buds quickly and poured a third, let it set-tle on the counter while he went to the stockroom. The dim space smelled of stale beer and wet cardboard. Jason had just returned the broom and dustpan to the rack when he heard the front door open.

He stepped out of the back, hands at his side, alert.

Michael froze like a convict in a spotlight. His eyes darted in nervous circles. "Jason. Jesus." He wore khakis and a faded oxford, and carried a soft leather briefcase, tapping absently at the handle. "You startled me."

"Lot of that going around." Jason walked past his brother and shut the open door, then locked it. "I need to talk to you."

"Sure. Sure. Let me just," Michael hoisted the brief-case, then lowered it quickly. He turned to Billy. "Hey kiddo. Everything good?"

"Hi Dad." The boy waved, then went back to working on his crossword puzzle.

"Where's Lauretta?"

"She had an appointment."

"Ahh, right." Michael winced, glanced at his watch. "She said. Guess I ran a little long." He walked behind the bar, opened a cabinet and put his wallet and keys inside. Lifted the briefcase up, started to slide it in, stopped. He looked around, then set the case at his feet, beside the cooler. "Beer?"

Jason gestured to the one he had going, then pulled out a stool and sat down in front of it. "Where you been?"

"Errands. Nothing exciting." Michael held a pint glass under the tap. When it was finished, he set it down, picked up the briefcase, frowned, then spun in a circle and set it against the back counter. "Cheers."

They tapped glasses.

"So. To what do I owe the pleasure?"

Jason looked at Billy, then back at Michael. Gave a little jerk with his head.

Michael got the point. "Hey buddy, your uncle and I have a few things to talk about. You mind finishing your cross-word over there?"

Billy sighed. "I am eight years old."

"And you know what? When you're nine years old, I'm *still* going to want to talk alone some times." Michael smiled, then jerked his thumb toward the tables. "Git."

Grumbling, the boy collected his newspaper, slid off the stool, and moved in front of the window. A beam of afternoon sun set the paper on fire.

"So what's up, bro?"

"I was going to ask you that."

"Huh?"

"Are you in any trouble?"

"Trouble?" Michael took a sip of his beer. "Well, I haven't won the Mega Ball yet, but other than that, I'm fine."

"You're sure?"

"Sure. Why?"

"A guy tried to hijack me this morning," Jason said, then took a long slow swallow of beer. "I was jogging, this guy with a soul patch and a Cadillac necklace jumped me in the pedestrian tunnel, said it had something to do with you."

"A Cadillac necklace? He have a tattoo on his arm, some letters?"

The muscles in Jason's back knit tight. "You're kidding me."

"What?"

"He didn't have the wrong guy. You *do* know him."

"I know him."

"Who is he?"

Michael shrugged. Jason stared at his brother. "What are you mixed up in?"

"What're you, Jimmy Cagney? What am I 'mixed up' in? Gee willikers, little bro."

"Fuck you."

Michael laughed. He glanced at the briefcase, picked it up, then put it back down in front of his legs. With a worn rag he began wiping the bar. "Listen, it's nothing to worry about."

"Yeah, well, you weren't the one had a gun pointed at him."

The cloth stopped. "He pulled a gun?"

Jason nodded. "Said he wanted to talk about what you're doing."

For a moment, there was a flash of something that could've been fear in Michael's eyes. It went fast, and then he was back to wiping the bar. But he kept running the rag in the same circle over and over. "What else did he say?"

"Not much." Jason leaned back. "He and a buddy of his, short guy looks like he's auditioning for the WWE, tried to muscle me into their car." He ran Michael through the whole story, enjoying telling it, the way he'd once enjoyed telling war stories. "You shoulda seen it, bro. The two of them standing there trying to murder me with their glares. The short one's nose is broken, and Soul Patch, he looked like his head was about to explode."

"You call the police?"

"Nah. After my heroic escape, I figured it made more sense to see if my big brother needed any protecting."

Michael smiled. "Next time I hear this story, there are going to be four guys, right?"

"Only if my audience is cuter than you. Want to tell me what's going on?"

His brother shrugged. "You know the neighborhood."

"Not really. Not anymore." When Dad had lost his job, they'd moved from Bridgeport to Canaryville; when he'd started drinking at breakfast, they'd moved from Canaryville to Crenwood. When he'd run off with the waitress from his off-track betting house, Mom had taken a third job, but never made enough to climb back up the ladder. It'd been an interesting place to grow up, white in a black and Latino neighborhood with a high school dropout rate of fifty percent.

"Things are getting out of hand," Michael said. "You remember, it used to be manageable—the gangs drew up lines and mostly respected them. Did a lot more posturing than killing." He shook his head. "These days, though, if somebody gets killed on Monday, Tuesday his boys ride around till they find somebody from the other side to shoot. Wednesday, it's the reverse."

"So?"

"So, this my neighborhood, man. I'm trying to raise my *son* here. Right now, I can't even let him play in the front yard."

Jason groaned. "I get it."

"What?"

"You're at it again, aren't you?"

"At what?"

"You're running some kind of crusade."

"I got involved." Michael shrugged. "After Lisa died."

Jason softened. "That was an accident. This is different."

"Is it? My wife was killed by a thirteen-year-old in a stolen car. He was running from the police. That sound like the sign of a healthy neighborhood to you? And things get worse every day. Why shouldn't regular people fight back?"

"Because . . ." Jason held his hands open, all the reasons in the world between them. "These guys are dangerous, for Christ's sake." Behind him he heard a faint rumbling, something rhythmic. He spun to look past Billy out the window, where a shiny drop-top with four men drove by, music trailing behind them like a bad smell. "What exactly are you doing?"

Michael shrugged. "Everything I can. I work with Washington Matthew's gang recovery program. I talk to local business people. I organize community-watch groups. I even met with the cops, not that it did much good."

"You talked to the cops?"

"Sure."

"You mean you informed on a gang?"

"Don't be so melodramatic. I just talked to the police."

Jason stared across the bar, his mouth open. Growing up here, you learned certain things. The cops were good guys. They fought for the real people, the ones with jobs and homes and children. Some innocent kid got killed for his sneakers, they rolled in hard. But sooner or later they rolled out again.

The gangs lived here. They were eternal.

"Why haven't you told me any of this?"

"I don't know." Michael sipped his beer, looked out the window. "I didn't want to burden you with it. I mean, I know you're dealing with your own baggage. From whatever happened in—over there."

"You can say it. Iraq."

"Okay, tough guy, Iraq. After everything there, I know it's been bad for you. Besides," Michael shrugged, "you've made it pretty clear how you feel about taking responsibility." He said it in the older-brother tone of voice he reserved for Jason, like he was a puppy that might piss the rug.

"What's that supposed to mean?"

"Let it slide."

"No." Jason set down his glass. "You got something you want to say?"

Michael sighed. "Brother, you were always the smart one. You could make something of yourself. Put down roots. Fight for something."

"Like you?" The anger was quickening in Jason's chest. "Pretending you're Charles Bronson?"

"Keep it down." Michael nodded to where Billy sat.

Jason lowered his voice. "And that's another thing. It's not just you. You're putting him at risk, too. Do you know what you're doing?"

Michael hardened. "I'm trying to make a better place for him to grow up."

"Bullshit." He shook his head. "I've tried to save the world, okay? It doesn't work." The Worm looped another knotted segment around his ribs. Jason looked at his hands, the wrinkles that lined the flesh between thumb and forefinger. He could almost see his pulse jumping there.

"Bro," Michael spoke softly, "I know something happened, and I know you blame yourself for whatever it was. But this is different."

"You don't know shit, *bro*."

Michael ran his tongue around the inside of his mouth, making the cheek bulge. He just stared at Jason. "I know you could have been the first of us to get a degree, until you blew your scholarship. I know your longest relationship lasted three months, and that you got busted for stealing televisions when you were twenty." Michael snorted. "I know that if it weren't for Washington, your ass would be in jail."

"That was kid stuff. And ancient fucking history."

"Kid stuff? You haven't changed."

"I was in the Army for seven years," Jason hissed.

Michael shrugged. "Sure."

"What's that supposed to mean?"

"Never mind."

"No," Jason said, feeling sweat in his palms, "what does that mean?"

"You really want to know? It means you're twenty-seven years old and only qualified to flip burgers or carry an assault rifle. It means you're willing to fight for something, you just don't want to decide what, or have to stick to it. I think you enlisted so other people would do that for you. And when that didn't work out, you fell back into what you knew. Drinking at noon and trying to get laid."

Jason stood up, his stool scraping across the floor. "Fuck you, man."

"Yeah, fuck you too."

Their voices had risen, and Jason saw Billy staring at them from the front table, his mouth wide. He felt bad about that, his nephew seeing them this way, but it wasn't his fault. It was the old dynamic, Michael pushing that same old button, and Jason blowing up over it. Shaking his head, Jason hip-checked the stool and headed for the front door. Behind him, he could hear Michael sigh, and he knew if he stood there for three seconds his brother would apologize, but he didn't have it in him.

The bell on the door tinkled, and the sun hit like a slap. He kicked at a chunk of broken glass, sent it skittering to break against the plywood facing of a burned-out store. The Caddy was parked with two wheels up on the curb; he'd been in such a hurry to make sure Michael was okay.

Brothers. Shit.

He fired up the engine and cranked the radio, then stomped

on the gas. He needed a shower. And then a drink. Several drinks.

Michael saw him as a flake? Fine.

Jason could play the part.

# CHAPTER 4
## Single Malt Heaven

During Prohibition, the bar had been a speakeasy. The real estate agent who had sold Michael the place had known the whole story, told him about the hidden nooks and crannies, the safe concealed behind the radiator. She'd called the narrow basement steps "Navy stairs," and the phrase fit: narrow, steep metal that would be at home on a cramped battleship. Standing on them and looking up through the ancient trap-hatch, Michael could almost feel the basement roll with the waves. "Come on," he called. "Time to go."

"One sec." Billy was lost in a stack of cardboard boxes. The air smelled of dust and time, of the junk piled against crumbling retaining walls: a piano with keys like nicotine fingers, a sofa with cushions worn thin, his own stuff mingling with the detritus of a dozen previous owners. Someday he meant to go through all of it, figure out what was worth giving away. Meanwhile, the basement was Billy's favorite haunt. What was it about dark places packed with sharp rusting junk that so fascinated boys?

"Let's move, kiddo." The bar would open in less than an hour. Given the contents of the briefcase, it seemed ridiculous that he had to spend the rest of the day pouring boilermakers for municipal workers and construction guys, but at least he'd taken care of business down here. All he had to do was get through today, then tomorrow he could do some real work. "Now."

Billy emerged smiling; something clutched in his hand. "Check it out, Dad! Was this yours?" He held up a laser gun.

Michael squinted, recognized it as a Transformer, a toy robot that origami'ed into a purple pistol. "Would you look at that." He reached for it. The plastic felt oddly familiar, comfortable, like some part of him had been yearning to hold the toy again. "I used to *love* this thing." He turned it over. "See, I even carved my name on it."

"It's crossed out."

"I know. Uncle Jason won it from me on a dare."

"What did you dare him to do?"

Michael remembered just fine, but no way was he planting ideas about sprinting across the El tracks, so he just shook his head and handed the toy back. His son took it, stared at like there was a message written in invisible ink. "Dad?"

"Hmm?"

"What's wrong with Uncle Jason?"

The question brought him up short. "How do you mean?"

"He doesn't seem like when he used to visit." Billy stared at his fingers tapping the pistol grip. "He's sad, and you guys fight more."

Michael opened his mouth, then closed it. Truth was, he didn't know what had happened to his brother. The week he returned he'd stayed with them, sleeping on the sofa, drinking most of a case of beer during the day and bringing home a different girl most every night. When Michael had broached the subject, Jason had said he was fine. The next week he'd moved out.

Michael looked at Billy waiting for an answer, his eyes the same brown his mother's had been. The truth seemed the best way. Never could lie to those eyes. "You know your uncle was a soldier."

"Uh-huh."

"Well, sometimes when soldiers go to war, they get hurt. Wounded. Sometimes it's on the outside, like—"

"Getting shot?"

"Sure, like that. But sometimes it's not that simple.

Sometimes they're hurt on the inside." He paused. "Sort of like getting sick."

"And that's what happened to Uncle Jason?"

"Yeah. He got sick, and so they sent him home." Not perfect, maybe, but not bad.

"Will he get better?"

"Of course." Michael smiled softly, and set his hand on the boy's shoulder. "Of course he will. But it might take a little while, and we have to be here for him."

Billy nodded thoughtfully. "Okay."

"Okay. Now," Michael gestured for the stairs, "what say we get out of here?"

"Can I bring this?" Billy held up the Transformer.

"My friend, you can have it."

They climbed back to the world. Billy immediately sat at the scarred desk in "his" corner of the stockroom and began playing with the Transformer, figuring out how the thing bent, which parts twisted to convert it back to a robot. Michael watched the boy work with that familiar feeling in his chest, a sort of liquid bursting. *That's my son.* Like always, the thought seemed both novel and ancient, a profound thing that could be taught only by the wet-lipped intensity of an eight-year-old boy.

Funny. The toy had been his, then Jason's, and now Billy's. Just plastic and metal, and yet it bound them all together, tied the present to the past. Michael found himself remembering another trip to the basement, years ago, he and Jason clearing space, hauling loads of sweating junk up the narrow stairs. When they were finished, they'd dropped into folding chairs, and Michael had opened the safe, taken out the Black Label he'd stashed. He could still remember the smile on Jason's face.

He smiled himself, then ruffled his son's hair and left him at work. Behind the bar, he finished washing glasses, then checked the supplies of Beam and Jack. As he did, his eyes fell again on the rows of bottles, the dusty bottle of Balvenie he'd noticed earlier.

What the hell. The cork twisted free with a pop. Holding

the bottle under his nose was like dissolving in a river of warm caramel. He poured two fingers, took another long inhale, sipped with his eyes closed.

*Damn.* Something to aspire to indeed.

The thought came with a stab of guilt. The words had come out all wrong, again. Hell, he'd damn near called his brother a coward. Michael sighed, reached for the phone. If he could get Jason back down here, he could apologize with a glass of single-malt heaven, try again. He'd dialed the first couple digits when the front door opened, the bell rattling. The brilliance of afternoon framed a silhouette, big, balding, another man behind him.

"Sorry," Michael said, setting down the receiver. "We're not open yet."

The men stepped inside and closed the door.

"I said, we're not—" But as they blotted out the light burning behind them, Michael Palmer saw who had entered his bar.

The highball glass slipped from his fingers to spin, glinting, until it passed into shadow and shattered.

# CHAPTER 5
The Sexiest Porn in the World

The girl was up, bustling around in the kitchen. Jason could still smell her perfume on the pillow beside him, something fruity and strong. Nice, though. His head ached a little with the remnants of last night's bourbon, and he toyed with the idea of rolling over, grabbing another hour of sleep.

But the sheets were muggy and close, and a fat-bellied fly buzzed around the room, dodging between the blades of the ceiling fan. Forget it. He pulled himself upright, leaned against the bare wall and watched the girl make coffee in the studio kitchen.

She still looked good in the morning sun, a long, toned body. Pixie hair. A curvy faux-tribal tattoo led into pale blue panties that fit well, no droop. She opened one cabinet and then another, searching with quiet efficiency.

Her name was . . . Jackie. Yes.

"Filters are in the drawer." He rubbed his cheek, the skin sticky and full.

"You're up." She turned to smile.

"Yeah." He pulled the sheet off and spun to the edge of the bed. The hardwood felt nice, cool. As he started to rise, pain spiked his belly. The muscle had a purple and yellow bruise, courtesy of the wrestler's rings. He winced, then smiled, remembering the rushing air as he'd jumped off the parking deck. With one hand on his gut and the other on the bed, he stood, glanced out the window. *Morning, world.*

Clark and Division. A weird-ass place to live. Lincoln Park to the north, all that prosperity: Tree-shrouded sidewalks, little dogs yipping in graystone windows, the streets safe at three A.M. And south of him, the Loop, bristling with skyscrapers where the Lincoln Parkers made their inexplicable livings. Then here, smack in the middle, his corner. One block of ghetto-light carved out of the otherwise pristine Gold Coast, courtesy of the #70 bus connecting the Red Line and Cabrini Green. Twenty-four-seven, guys hanging out by the Currency Exchange, the sandwich shop. Late some nights he'd hear the hookers fighting, hollering the way only pissed-off black women could. But the studio was cheap and month-to-month, and that was about all the thought he'd put into it.

The smell of coffee pulled him from his reverie. The girl had found two mugs and was pouring carefully. Jason never knew how to handle the morning after, if they were supposed to hug and kiss like a real couple. Her eyes were blue and steady, but she didn't make any moves. He opted just to squeeze her arm as he took a cup, and she smiled, then pulled a chair out from the table and sat down. "I'll just have one before I go."

"Take your time." The coffee tasted great, strong and bitter.

She smiled again, then glanced around the kitchen as if she looking for a topic of conversation. There wasn't much—a pantry with folding doors, a couple of dishes in the sink, a bottle of Jim Beam on the counter, grade-school analog clock on the wall. Finally her tour brought her full circle, her eyes back to rest on his. She hesitated, then said, "Were you really in Iraq?"

"First Brigade, Twenty-fifth Infantry."

"Can I ask you something?"

He said, "Sure," but sighed inwardly.

"What's it . . ." She paused, stared down at her cup. "What's it like?" When she looked back up at him, it was with something like lust in her eyes. He recognized the look, saw it all the time. Like pulling back a curtain, you could watch people change. Their inner darkness hungry to know what it felt like to get wet. Wanting him to tell them horrible, delicious things. The sexiest porn in the world.

"Hot," he said, then stood and opened the refrigerator. Leftover Thai. When had he gotten it? He opened the container and sniffed. Seemed okay, though how spoiled curry would smell different from regular curry he couldn't say. He found a takeaway packet with a napkin, chopsticks, soy. He split the chopsticks, rubbed them together, then scooped up a mouthful of noodles. Tasted fine.

"That's it?" she asked, turning to look at him. "Hot?"

He shrugged. "Noisy."

"You don't want to talk about it?"

"Want some?" He offered her the takeout container. She stared at him, and he sighed. "Look, it was hot, it was noisy. I was there, now I'm back."

"Okay," she said.

They small-talked through the rest of the coffee. After about twenty minutes, she made a point of looking at the clock, and he smiled to let her know it was no problem, that he was easy. He washed the mugs, then leaned on the counter to look at her. Watching a woman get dressed had always felt nearly as sexy as the opposite. She scrunched up her face at a rip in her stockings, decided to do without. Covered the blue panties with a black skirt and pulled on a fitted shirt that clung to her body.

"Listen," she said, moving to him, "About what I said—"

"Don't worry about it."

"It's just, I was curious. I didn't mean to go to a bad place or anything."

He shook his head. "It's fine."

"Okay." She took one of his fingers in her hand, played with it idly, eyes down. For a moment she looked like a little girl. Then she straightened and said, "So, good-bye."

"You're not going to leave your number?"

She smiled. "Any point?"

He laughed, and for a moment, wanted to say, *Hell yes*. She was sexy and smart and self-possessed, and he ought to consider himself lucky for the chance.

Then he thought ahead to the way it would end. The way it always did.

She saw his hesitation, shook her head. "It's okay. It was nice to meet you." Then she opened the door and stepped out, giving him a little wave using just her fingers. The walls were thin, and he could hear her heels click all the way down the hall.

"Shit." Jason scooped the container of noodles from the table and tossed it in the trash.

He made his bed, pulling the sheets tight and tucking the corners. Ready to bounce a quarter off. Then he stretched, and hit the deck for push-ups. Normally he did a hundred neat snaps with hands beneath his shoulders, followed by fifty arms-wide. But he thought of Jackie, the way he hadn't had the balls to tell her yes, and forced himself into another fifty of each, no break. He was panting by the end, shoulders and chest sore, the mop of bangs he'd let grow since his return sticky against his forehead.

Standing, he spotted his cell phone. He thought about dialing Michael, apologizing for getting worked up. Guy was an asshole sometimes, but they were still brothers.

Instead he went to the bathroom and showered off his sweat and the smell of the girl's perfume.

The chrome on the Beretta was shiny, but the works were filthy. Besides not knowing how to hold a weapon, Soul Patch obviously didn't have a clue how to maintain one. Jason ejected the magazine and set it on the table, then checked the chamber for rounds. When he was sure it was clear, he held down the disassembly latch and removed the slide, then the recoil spring and barrel. He set each piece on the kitchen table, enjoying the feeling of the routine. Maintenance was a simple, methodical process. It was something you could do without thinking, the way some people painted models or knit sweaters. Just a way to defocus the mind. And it felt good to hold a weapon again. After years of having one in arm's reach every moment, he felt naked without. Silly, really; his need to be armed had died months ago, when he walked out of the Administrative Discharge Board.

The thought made him grind his teeth.

Enough, he thought, and blew at a speck of dust. So his old life was over. So it had ended badly. So what? People moved on. They forgave themselves, rebuilt their lives. Managed, somehow, to be happy again. It happened all the time. Right?

Jason gave the barrel another buff with the cloth, then slotted it back in place and tightened it with the spring. Fit the slide back on, then inserted the magazine.

It was no wonder he pictured his guilt as a Worm, thin and segmented, blind and pale. Like some foul eel from the ocean's darkest chasm. With razor teeth it was slowly eating him, a bite at a time. Would it eventually die?

Or just feast until there was nothing left?

He hoisted the Beretta and reversed it. Pointed it dead center of his face, in that spot where his eyes fought for focus. A shiver ran down his thighs. It would take so little. Just the smallest squeeze of his thumb. A short dance of muscles and a fire exploding in his brain, and then gone. No more Worm, no more memories. Just blackness cool as the shadow inside the gun barrel.

There was a knock at the door.

The sound jerked him from his trance. In the two months he'd lived here, he couldn't recall anyone knocking. He was halfway to the door before he realized he still had the Beretta in one hand.

What was he, the freaking Unabomber? Moping around alone and cleaning a gun?

The knock came again.

"Just a minute." He looked for a place to stash it. Furniture hadn't been a top priority. He grimaced, then locked the safety and tucked the gun in his pants like a Tarantino gangster. At the door, he peered through the peephole. Nothing but the neighboring door.

Then he heard something that stopped his heart.

"Uncle Jason?"

# CHAPTER 6
## Business As Usual

The dead boy wouldn't shut up.

So far, Officer Elena Cruz's day had been lousy, and she didn't have a sense it was likely to improve. She'd spent a good chunk of the night trying to tune out the thumping music of the club downstairs. By the time her radio kicked on with the latest casualty figures from Iraq, news of a bombing in a mosque, and the President's monotone promise to stay the course, she'd managed barely three hours of sleep. Mint Nicorette tasted better than the regular stuff, but couldn't compare to that first drag off that first cigarette.

And now the dead boy.

Talkers drove Cruz crazy. In the movies, victims whispered a crucial clue, gasped out a name. Then they coughed two dots of blood and politely rolled back their eyes.

Her years on the street didn't match. Instead, mostly the talkers wanted to tell you how much they loved they mama. Twenty minutes ago, she wouldn't have heard anything about his mother. She'd have gotten cold eyes and hard posture. A glance fixed on her crotch, maybe a lick of his lips.

To transform him into a good civilian and dutiful son, all you had to do was kill him.

Of course, he didn't realize he was dead. But Cruz knew better. After five years in a South Side beat car, another three kicking in doors on the tactical team, and eighteen months with Gang Intelligence, she'd gotten pretty good at reading the faces of the paramedics. This had been called in as a shooting, but she gave it ten minutes to graduate to a proper homicide.

"Can you hear me?" She leaned over the boy. Judging by the zits pocking his face, he was about seventeen. She repeated the question in Spanish, and his eyes focused. *"¡Como te llama?"*

"Teo." His voice was faint.

Not Six-Pack, or Choco, or T-Dog, or whatever his street name was. Now that it was too late, his name was Teo. She'd've laughed if it were funny. "Teo, I'm here to help." She put a little extra accent into her Spanish, let him know they were of the same blood. "Who did this?"

He stared back. "Where's my mother?"

"She'll meet you at the hospital. Right now, I need you to tell me what happened."

He shook his head and coughed. A lot more than two drops of blood spattered his lips, the copper smell strong.

"Officer." The paramedic was young, his hands fast on the gurney straps. "We've got to roll."

She nodded and stepped back, took in the scene.

A typical Crenwood corner. Rows of sagging two-flats dotted with brick bungalows, metal security gates covering the front doors. The sign for the elementary school on the corner read "Believe and achiev !" People gathered on the stoops and porches, enjoying the show. Business as usual in the 'Wood.

"You know what I'm thinking? Suicide." Sergeant Tom Galway ran his hands through his neat salt-and-pepper hair. "I'm guessing our boy had been pondering the inequities generated by geopolitical gamesmanship, got so depressed he went and shot himself in the back. Four times."

She rolled her eyes at her partner. "Geopolitical gamesmanship?"

"Heard it on NPR this morning." He looked over her shoulder. "Uh-oh."

"What?" She glanced, saw the detective in charge of the scene walking toward them. "Shit."

"Go easy, partner." Galway put a hand on her shoulder. "Don't be starting anything."

"*Me?*"

Galway shot her a look that said, *yeah, you.* Then he straightened and smiled.

The detective was a veteran with a gut and too much aftershave. He stepped around a pool of Teo's watery vomit, folded his arms, and looked at her coldly. "Aren't you supposed to be driving a database?"

She decided to take it in good humor, pretend he was being playful. "I wanted to get some air. What's the story?"

He shrugged. "Victim was walking with his girl, kid rounds the corner, opens up. Weapon's a nine-millimeter. Nineteen shell casings, clustered, with four hits."

"Four for nineteen?" Galway shook his head. "Lousy shooting."

Cruz ignored him. "*Nineteen* casings from one weapon? Somebody's got an Uzi."

"Or an MP-5, or a MAC-11, or Christ knows what else." The detective dug in his ear with one finger. "Remember the good old days when kids killed each other with knives and baseball bats?"

"The girl have anything to say?"

"Nah."

"Neighbors?"

"I've got uniforms knocking on doors. But you know," he made the hand signal for jerking off. "Nobody—"

"—saw nothing." Cruz finished the mantra. Old story. If Teo had gotten popped in Lincoln Park, they would have had twenty-five people lining up to share every detail. But down here, everybody had vision problems. "You mind if I look around?"

"You mind blowing me?"

Her eyes went wide, and she felt her pulse kick in her chest. "Excuse me?"

"I said," the detective curled one lip, "go back to playing with your computer, and leave case work to people who earned their jobs without spreading their legs."

Fire flowed up her neck, and her fingers bit into her palm. Unthinking, she started forward, cocking one hand back, ready to lay this tubby chauvinist flat on his ass.

Galway moved fast, stepping between them and grabbing her shoulders. "Easy, Elena. *Easy!*" Over Galway's shoulder, the detective winked. She bucked against her partner, knowing he was right but not caring, just wanting to deck the guy so badly she could taste it. But Galway's grip on her arms was steel. "You're already in the shit." He hustled her back, met her eyes. "Hitting him isn't worth losing your job over."

He was right, and she knew it, but that didn't make her like it more. Cruz shook her arms free, then spun on one heel. Behind her she heard the detective laughing, but just squeezed her fingers into her palms until her arms trembled. Galway followed her.

"Goddamn boys club *bull*shit," she said, stomping toward the car. "One mistake, *one*, and ten years don't mean anything. Like I'm some secretary who got promoted."

Galway sighed. "You don't make it easier on yourself."

"Whatever." She patted her pocket for her smokes, remembered she'd quit. Cursed and tore open a piece of gum, flicked the wrapper to the curb. "He's an asshole."

"That comparison," Galway said dryly, "is unkind to your average asshole."

She snorted and dug for her keys.

"Listen," he said, "don't let it bother you. It'll pass."

"Easy for you to say." She glanced down the block to where a ghetto-roller vibrated with bass. "It's been a year already."

Galway shrugged, smiled at her. "It'll pass when somebody *else* gets caught doing something stupid."

He was right, as usual. Cruz took a deep breath, then shook her head and laughed through her nose. "Tell them to screw up quickly, would you?"

"You got it, babe. Need be, I'll do it myself." Galway took a napkin from his suit pocket and mopped the sweat on his forehead. He folded the tissue, then squinted up at the sun. "You saw Teo's ink?"

She nodded. "Latin Saints." The set had been feuding

with the Gangster Disciples for a long time now, with bodies dropping on both sides.

"You know who didn't?"

It took her a minute, but when she got it, she smiled. "A certain overweight detective."

"Yep. A day late and a dollar short. Close the case out from under him, it'll hurt more than your right hook."

Her smiled broadened. "I feel like chatting with the Disciples. You want to come?"

"This one is all you. I got a date." Galway patted his stomach. "Pompeii, bowtie pasta with garlic." He made a pistol of his right hand and shot her.

The department's Ford smelled of cigarettes. She rolled the windows open and jammed the AC on, hot breath blasting in her face. What she *should* do was go back to the station and put in another couple hours of data crunching. This was only a gang-on-gang shooting, and closing it wouldn't matter enough to anybody to get her out of her chickenshit assignment. But revenge was its own reward.

She turned up her police radio as she pulled away from the curb. There was something comforting about the steady tones. It felt like the voice of Chicago itself, like the city was speaking to her. Cruz sometimes left it on in the background at home, when she was reading or making dinner.

Right now, all Chicago had to say seemed routine: a domestic call where a woman was threatening her husband with a broken bottle; a noise complaint from Oak View Terrace; an accident at Halsted and Sixty-fourth.

Then, just as she was about to turn it back down, another item came on. The voice didn't change, spoke in the same measured voice as always.

But before it had finished, she'd spun the Crown Vic in a squealing turn and jammed on the gas.

# January 22, 1993

*Eddie Murphy is killing him.*

*On the screen, the comedian is talking about grandmothers, how they're always cold, always asking what time it is. This may be the funniest thing Jason has ever heard. He's only met his grandmother once since he was old enough to remember, on a trip to Spokane, two weeks of Mom and Dad fighting in the car. But he can picture her crabbed up in a shawl, telling him he's nasty, then asking what time it is.*

*There is sick fire in his belly.*

*Michael nudges him, passes the near-empty bottle, red label with black domed buildings, somewhere in Russia. Jason wonders if the vodka actually comes from Russia. Wonders if there really even is a place called Russia, if there's anywhere but fucking Crenwood. Crenwood and Spokane. This strikes him funny too.*

*He twists off the red plastic cap and drinks. The liquid is warm and thick, and scours his throat. Acid curdles in his stomach. He fights a grimace, fakes appreciative noises. Turns to hand the bottle back to his brother, feeling a strange lightness inside.*

*Turning, he explodes.*

*Fire pours out of him, bile spilling up through his nose, a spray of wet heat across Michael's chest and lap. It spatters and soaks and drips. The sick is bloody with the fruit soda they used to chase the Popov, and as he looks at it, Jason thinks of the old expression, puking your guts out, and then the world tilts to black.*

*He wakes in bed, in a beam of sweaty sun.*

*At first there is only the throb and ache of the room, but then memory hits, and shame runs through him like warm water. His dirty clothes are gone, his mouth is clean. Somehow he doesn't smell like vomit.*

*Michael.*

*Jason groans. Hating the humiliation he knows will come, hating himself for failing this test of manhood. Hating that his brother witnessed it, saw him for a baby. Knowing that he will never hear the end of it, that every friend will laugh, every girl will giggle.*

*But he's wrong.*

*Michael never says a word.*

# CHAPTER 7
## Clear As Broken Glass

Traffic on the Kennedy was steady, so Jason fumbled his phone out and tried all of Michael's numbers again. The same thing—voice mail, voice mail, technical difficulties. He cursed under his breath, then shut the phone. Beside him, Billy stared out the window.

"Kiddo?" Jason tried for a gentle, avuncular voice, the kind that belonged to someone who hadn't woken with a hangover and a woman whose last name he didn't know. "You feeling any better?"

The only response was Billy's fingers tightening on the armrest.

Twenty minutes ago, when Jason had yanked open his apartment door, he'd found his nephew trembling, clothing filthy and torn. A small leaf hung orange in the tousled mess of his hair, and it made him look like a corpse, some broken thing washed up on the banks of a desolate river. The boy hadn't said a word since, not as Jason took in the enormous pupils and shaking hands that meant his nephew was in shock, not as he'd run his hands over Billy's thin limbs to check for wounds, not even as Jason had gathered the boy into a bear hug and told him everything would be all right.

It was nothing, Jason told himself for the hundredth time. Some sort of kid stuff, some miscommunication or accident. Maybe Billy had been with a friend and they'd gotten in a fight. Or maybe he'd somehow gotten lost. Chicago would seem an enormous and scary place to an eight-year-old alone. Hell, sometimes it seemed that way to him.

*"I met with the cops."*

*"You mean you informed on a gang?"*

Jason heard Michael's words again, clear as broken glass, but pushed the thought aside. Michael was fine. He had to be. Everything had to be.

He turned onto Damen, driving through déjà vu. Not twenty-four hours ago he'd ridden this same route, past the same closed shops and narrow crooked houses, the same boys on the corner daring him with their eyes. Cracked pavement and exhaust haze, broken glass firing glints of too-bright sun. Damen Avenue, just like yesterday.

Then he reached his brother's block, and realized that it was not at all like yesterday, that everything was not fine.

Everything was a thousand miles from fine.

Over there was the extensions place, Lauretta's, the African queen on the sign slightly darkened. Lauretta who babysat Billy from time to time, who liked Jason because both her boys were Army, too. Then, on the other side, the little storefront diner, one of the front windows spiderwebbed so that you couldn't read the specials, something about two eggs and ham on the bone. Michael's bar was supposed to sit between them.

But somehow it had been exchanged for a reeking ruin.

Timbers twisted and scorched into bubbles of ash lay amidst bricks licked black by flaming tongues. Fire had eaten everything, left behind only a charred carcass. A twisted gothic cathedral decorated with spires of cinders and rubble. Firemen moved through the debris like acolytes of flame.

Some part of Jason expected to hear foreign tongues, the alien wailing of the women. He'd lost count of how many burnt-out buildings he'd seen, of the missions to secure-and-contain, of triaging tiny broken bodies and calling for the medics. For a moment he found himself back in it, boots on the ground in the desert's wrathful heat. Sulfur in his nostrils and sweat in his eyes. That was the world to which this kind of destruction belonged. Half a world away amidst people who spoke a different language, worshipped a different god. That was where buildings burned out, where survivors were left to gape at the ruins of what had been real.

Not here. Not *his* brother.

And on the heels of that thought, another. Billy.

*Idiot!*

He jerked to the curb, screeching to a halt in front of Lauretta's shop. Scrabbled at his seat belt, then unbuckled his nephew. "Don't look." He pulled the boy out of his seat, dragged him into an awkward embrace. "You don't have to." Billy was light as rags, warm and shuddering rags. His breath came heavy and wet, spit and snot and tears soaking the shoulder of Jason's T-shirt. They sat in the rattle of the air conditioning, Jason holding his nephew, stroking his hair. Telling the boy not to look even as he himself stared.

The tattered heap of dense charcoal running down the center must have been the bar, where yesterday he'd shared a beer with his brother. The ash sparkled, and it took him a moment to realize it was shattered glassware. And there, in the back, he could make out the brick wall, now half demolished, that marked the storeroom. Somewhere back there was the trap-hatch that led to the basement, from the days of bootlegging, when the place used to be a speakeasy. He remembered sitting in that basement after a day's work hauling shit out of it, Mikey pulling out a bottle of Black Label and toasting—

The rap on the window threw him into combat mode. He spun with one arm up, the other tightening protectively around his nephew.

A woman, big, in a sundress of turquoise and bright orange. Lauretta, owner of the salon and part-time babysitter. She was squinting, her face drawn with concern. He shook his head to clear the memories, his own traces of clinical shock. Understanding could wait. Now he had to act. He rolled down the window.

"You all right, honey?"

His head felt light, like it might float away. "What happened?"

She gestured at Billy, and then shook her head. "Why'n't you come inside?" She gave him a sad smile. "Get William here a Coke."

He nodded. Sunlight splashed like molten iron as he stepped out, hoisting Billy with him, careful to keep his nephew's face buried in his shoulder. Inside the shop, barber's chairs ran along a mirrored wall. On the other side there were tubs that looked like you might put your feet in them. A customer relaxed while her stylist wove extensions into her hair.

Lauretta led him through a curtain to a narrow room where a couch faced a television, the sound on mute. Jason lowered the boy, Billy's grip on his neck tightening at first and then loosening as Lauretta came alongside. Billy sat upright, the muscles of his body rigid, his eyes darting. When they settled on Lauretta, he seemed to relax.

"There you are, baby." She changed the channel to the Cartoon Network, opened a minifridge and came up with a can of soda. "You just watch the cartoons, okay?"

A sudden look of terror swept across his face, but she spoke immediately, her voice honey. "Don't you worry. We'll be right here." Jason followed Lauretta to the curtain, marveling at her ease, how in control she was. He was Billy's uncle, supposedly a guy who could take care of him, but she was the one who knew what the boy needed. Jason wanted to thank her, but what he said was, "What happened?"

"I don't know," she said, her voice low. "Po-lice wouldn't tell me much."

"Is . . ." He hesitated, afraid to ask the only question that mattered, terror slopping like water against a weakening dam. "Is Michael okay?"

She stared, her eyes soft and sad, and he knew the answer. The levees inside him broke. He heard a faint whimper and was surprised to realize he had made it.

His brother was dead.

Michael had needed help, Jason hadn't been there, and now his brother was dead.

The world tilted. He felt dizzy, put one hand against the doorframe. An iron voice sounded inside of him, a voice he hadn't heard in months. Telling him *straighten up, soldier.* Telling him this wasn't the time. He took a deep breath, and wiped at his eyes with the back of one hand. "Will you . . . can you watch Billy for a little while?"

She gave him a look that made him wish he were five again, could hug himself to her dress and feel safe. "Of course."

He knelt beside the couch, his face level with Billy's. The boy was obviously still in shock, but his pupils seemed a little less dilated, the tension in his shoulders a bit looser. Familiar surroundings.

"Buddy, I'm going to go out for a minute. But Lauretta's going to sit with you. Is that okay?"

Billy looked at him, then up at Lauretta. He nodded. Jason squeezed his shoulder, stood up and stepped through the curtains.

"Jason." She fiddled with the belt of her dress, then raised her eyes to meet his. "Your brother, he was a good man, and careful. It don't seem right that he'd have fallen down drunk in his own bar, let it burn around him."

A chill ran down his spine. Again he heard the words in his mind.

*I met with the cops.*

*You mean you informed on a gang?*

"No ma'am," he said, his hands clenching to fists. "It doesn't."

# CHAPTER 8
## Dark Spots

She hated when the good guys died.

Cruz had driven over cop-style, stopping at red lights only long enough to check oncoming traffic before rolling through. Parked the unmarked across the street, behind an ambulance where bored EMTs sipped coffee. A couple of beat cops were interviewing bystanders. It was just past noon, the air still and sticky. Blast-furnace heat.

On the ride down, her main emotion had been concern for a guy she knew, a real person in a neighborhood of assholes. Now, nostrils burning with the stink of ash, the anger was starting to come as well. Michael Palmer had been a good man.

She rearranged her cuffs so they didn't dig into her back and crossed the street. The responding units had taped off the sidewalk, and she ducked under it. Men in bunker pants and jackets sorted through the rubble with shovels. The reflective stripes on their clothing shone bright. One held what looked like a portable radio with a wand that he ran above the wreckage, eliciting clicks like a Geiger counter. A tall guy held a hand to his mouth, shouted. "Behind the tape, lady."

She pulled aside her suit jacket to show the star on her waist.

He nodded, gave her a *one-second* gesture, and started threading his way through the blackened rubble. Each step kicked up a puff of smoky dust that hung in the still air.

"You the fire investigator?"

He nodded, pulled off white latex gloves with a snap of soot, held out a hand. "Tom Huff. You?"

She introduced herself, told him she was with Gang Intelligence, that she knew the owner. "What's the story?"

"It was set last night, late, maybe three or four. Took us a long time to get the flames knocked down."

"Somebody set it? You're sure?"

He pointed to a patch where rubble had been pushed aside to reveal flooring scarred by a large spot that was darker even than the charcoal around it. "You see?"

"Pour pattern?"

He nodded. "When it's that precise, it always means accelerant. Lab'll say for certain, but I'd bet gasoline. Wrong color for butane or charcoal fluid."

Accelerant. Which made this arson. At least. "You find a body?"

He nodded. "One adult male, well-done. On the way to the Medical Examiner now."

Which made it homicide. And the victim had to be Michael Palmer. Who else would be in his bar when it burned down?

*Damn it*, she thought, remembering his handshake, firm but not out to prove anything. And *damn it* again for his son. And one last hearty *damn it* for the neighborhood. Somebody tried to do some good, this was what happened. No wonder the police were always short of witnesses.

"Just called it homicide, so a detective should be here soon." Huff paused, looked to her right, gestured with his chin. "That one with you?"

Cruz turned, saw a man walking down the sidewalk. "No." She moved to intercept him. "Sir, you see the tape?"

He stopped, met her eyes without cruising her body first. Blonde surfer hair. Nicely built. Good-looking in a white sort of way. There was something in his face that was very familiar, and she figured it out just as he said it.

"I'm Jason Palmer. This was my brother's bar."

* * *

He'd started in with a bunch of questions, but she'd told him to hold on. Asked him to wait on the other side of the tape, and then gone back to Huff and given him a card. "Can you give me a call, let me know if you find anything else?"

"It'll all be in my report."

"This guy was a friend of mine." She smiled at him. "Do me the favor?"

He shrugged. "Sure." Tucked the card away, pulled a pair of clean latex gloves from his pocket, and went back to work.

She turned to find Jason Palmer at her elbow. "I thought I asked you to wait outside the tape."

He stared at her. "My brother. Is he . . . was he . . ." He looked at the wasted bar, back at her.

She opened her mouth, ready to go into her all-business rap—*sorry for your loss, but I need to ask you a few questions*—and instead found herself saying, in a soft voice, "I don't know for sure. I'm afraid so."

He seemed to droop, something giving way in his shoulders and neck. "They killed him." His voice thin. "Mikey, they killed you."

Cruz looked at him sharply. "Who killed him, Mr. Palmer?"

He put the back of his hand to his mouth like he was trying to keep from vomiting. "Those gangsters."

"Who?"

"I don't know. Soul Patch. The guy from . . . oh, Jesus. Michael." His face was pale. "I should have been there." He had the faraway look of a man seeing ghosts.

"Mr. Palmer." She put a hand on his arm. "I need you to focus."

He looked at her. Blinked a couple of times, shook his head. "Yeah. Okay." Blew out a breath, took another one in. "You were a friend of my brother's?"

She thought of sitting in Michael Palmer's bar with Galway, she and her partner listening as Palmer said that there were things going on in the neighborhood that were worse than anybody guessed, that the gangs were the tip of the iceberg. Saying that he would have proof soon. Calm and logical, with a polite kid and a history of community service. Not seeming even a little crazy.

But what she said to Jason was, "I knew him."

"So then you know about him and the gangs. That he was fighting them."

"Yeah."

"Good." His jaw set and posture grew rigid as he came into himself. "Good."

A thought occurred to her. In the mathematics of a crime scene, if spots equaled accelerant, and accelerant equaled arson, then accelerant with a body equaled homicide. Which meant she had no place here. Technically, her job was just to baby-sit Palmer until the detectives arrived, at which point they'd tell her to head back to the station and work on her damn database.

On the other hand, if this was a gang matter, no one could say it wasn't her case.

"You mentioned gangbangers." She jerked a thumb at a JJ Fish across the street. "Why don't you let me buy you lunch, tell me about them?"

"I . . ." He paused, looked back toward a storefront extensions place. "No, I can't. My nephew is here, and I'm worried."

She said, "You know how I made it sound like a choice?"

He said, "Yeah?"

She said, "It's not."

"This is the name of a doctor at UC Hospital, the ER." Cruz wrote on the back of her business card. "Tell him I sent you, he'll make time for your nephew today."

Jason reached across the table for it. "Thanks."

"No problem. You mentioned someone named 'Soul Patch'?"

"That's not his name. I mean, I don't know his name. That's just what I called him."

"Who is he?"

"I don't know. Some sort of gang member. Gangbanger, I guess you call them."

"How do you know him?"

"Yesterday he tried to kidnap me."

She sat quiet as he told the story, how he was jogging when a banger came at him with a gun, had tried to force Palmer into the car. How he'd gotten clear, and then come to make sure his big brother was okay. "You a martial-arts guy, take a lot of self-defense classes, that kind of thing?"

"Huh?"

"Well, I mean, you scuffle with two men, both of them armed, you get away . . ."

"I'm a soldier." His voice steady and maybe a little proud.

"What did these guys look like?"

"Black," he said, not African-American, and she liked that he didn't try to put on a show of how racially sensitive he was to impress the Latina. "One was maybe five and a half, stocky, weighed one-eighty or so. Wore a lot of gold. The one I called Soul Patch was about two inches shorter than me, and thin. He had tattoos on his arms and, well, a soul patch," holding his thumb and forefinger up to pinch his chin.

Which, between the two, described about half the boys in the Gang Intelligence files. "Anything notable about the tattoos?"

"I didn't get that good a look. A star with letters inside, maybe 'GD'?"

Gangster Disciples. She felt a quickening in her stomach. She had pictures of a lot of them. If he could ID the men who came for him, she could shut this thing fast, maybe earn her way off the database and back on the street. Plus get a little justice for Michael Palmer, with his good kid and his good handshake. "Would you recognize them?"

He nodded, looked out the window at the fire investigators picking through the ruins of the bar, lawnmowering back and forth like they were searching for a lost contact lens. "I never expected to see this again." His voice low and soft, like he didn't realize he was speaking.

"Again?" She looked up.

"I was in Afghanistan, and then Iraq." He picked up a fry, swirled it in ketchup like he was mixing paint on a palette.

"When I first got there, I couldn't believe the destruction. Whole blocks of apartment complexes where the walls had been knocked out, you could see right into people's homes, their kitchens. A lot of the Humvees have mounted Mark-19s, that's a grenade launcher, and they just demo the shit out of a building. And these beautiful mosques. Once the insurgents figured out we were trying not to damage mosques, they started sniping at us from the towers. So we had to light them up too." He shook his head. Dropped the fry, picked up another, poked listlessly at the pile. "Everywhere you went there were these piles of rock and ash. Something was always burning. Always. IEDs, insurgent mortars, trash fires." His eyes seemed clouded. "I expected everyone would just, I don't know, drop to their knees. Stare. But they didn't. They went about their business while the world burned around them." He shrugged. "Get used to anything, I guess."

"You mind if I ask where you were last night?"

Palmer looked up, and she saw surprise in his eyes at the change of subject, but no flash of fear, no game face. "I was with someone."

"Girlfriend?"

"Just someone I met."

"You have a phone number?"

He shook his head. "Her name was Jackie. She said she was a hostess at Spring. You know the restaurant, North and Milwaukee?"

"Out of my price range." She sipped her godawful excuse for coffee. "Your brother have life insurance?"

"I don't know."

"You know it doesn't pay out on homicide?"

Palmer set down the fry he had been playing with, wiped grease on a napkin. Stared at her, unblinking. "I understand why you're asking. But I didn't kill my brother."

He wasn't the bad guy. Half her job was instinct, and she knew. Of course, it would be worth running down the girl to be certain. First thing you learned was that *everybody* lied. But he wasn't the bad guy.

Which left her with the gangbangers. "I need you to come to the station with me, look at some pictures. See if you can identify Soul Patch."

"Okay."

She nodded. "You drive, or you want to ride with me?"

"You mean *now*?"

She cocked an eyebrow.

"I can't." He leaned back. "My nephew. I told you, I want to get him out of here."

"Perfect. I want to talk to him, too."

"No way. He's in shock. No way."

"Mr. Palmer, I'm trying to solve your brother's murder. You can help. Don't you think Michael would want you to?"

He stared at her, jaw clenched. A long moment passed. Then he said, "You know what my brother would want, lady? He'd want to know his son was okay."

She leaned back, feeling like a bitch.

"Look." He set his napkin atop the uneaten fries. "I loved my brother. I'll do anything to get the fuckers that killed him. I just want to take care of Billy first. Please."

She could compel him, but that didn't make for the best witnesses. Besides, she liked his insistence on taking care of the kid. Too rare in the people she dealt with. "Tell you what. How about you come see me first thing tomorrow morning?"

"Thank you." He started to scoot out of the booth.

"Meantime, if you or your nephew remember anything else, call me right away."

"Yeah." He stood. "Can I go?"

Cruz took a sip of coffee. "Sure." Watched him turn and push through the door, back ramrod as he strode broken sidewalks. Good-looking guy, seemed smart, cared about the kid. There was definitely something off about him—the way his eyes had gone all thousand-yard when he was talking about Iraq—but she still didn't like him for the murder. He was hurting too much. Tough to lose someone like that. One day there, the next, poof, gone forever.

She thought again about the afternoon last week, when

she and Galway had sat down with Michael Palmer. Things were bigger than anyone realized, he had said, and worse. And she'd humored him. Said if he had proof, she'd act on it. She'd said it the way she said a lot of things on this job, a voice aimed at calming people, at mollifying the crazies. Not really believing.

And then someone had killed him.

She sipped her coffee and gazed out the window, wondering if that counted as proof.

# CHAPTER 9
## Dog Days

In the dream, Washington Matthews was back in his cell. Bare concrete floors and the scarred metal of the open toilet. History books from the prison library stacked neatly on his desk. Pharaoh snoring in the rack above, that wet choking gargle bouncing off lonely midnight walls. Washington thought of getting out of bed, and then in the way of dreams, he suddenly was, just standing barefoot in the dim light of lockdown. The air was thick and humid. He stretched his body, prison muscles and bruised knuckles, and in his chest that old cold feeling, the song of twisting metal.

Pharaoh snored louder, and Washington went to bump his cellie, tell him to roll his ass over. Only as he got closer, he realized Pharaoh wasn't alone. He had his arm around a thin figure, a slender black boy with a cauliflower ear spooned up against him. The boy was eight, and the thick wet gurgling was coming from the bloody ruin where his throat used to be.

Washington tried to run. His limbs were bound with sticky ropes.

Then he woke to find himself bound with sticky ropes.

It took a moment to realize that it was his sheets that tied him, sweat-soaked from the heat. August. The dog days of summer. He'd read somewhere that the phrase came from Sirius, the Dog Star, whose conjunction with the sun used to mark the hottest months of the year. In modern times the conjunction is slowly coming earlier each year, something to do with the Earth wobbling. He struggled free of the bedding, wobbly himself. His hand hit something heavy and smooth, and in the sharp sunlight he just had time to recognize the highball glass before it dropped to the hardwood floor.

"Shit." He stopped thrashing, gently worked his arms loose, and patted around until he found the Beefeater. Empty. He set the bottle on the nightstand, then extricated his legs. Sallust Crispus's "The Conspiracy of Catiline" lay open on the bed, the pages wet. The book was ruined, but at least he hadn't finished the whole bottle this time.

Washington swung his feet over the edge of the bed. The dream muscles were gone, replaced with droopy man-breasts and a forty-three-year-old paunch. His temples were sore and his eyes spiked. A vision of the boy with the cauli-flower ear was painted on the inside of his mind.

In the shower he danced as the water flickered hot-cold-hot. Trimmed his mustache in the mirror, thinking how his days of looking like Richard Roundtree were over. Now it was more like James Earl Jones, and that on a good day, which to-day wasn't.

There was a racket through the floor. Something metal gonged. A pause, and then the sound of yelling in two lan-guages. Washington grimaced, yanked his pants on and ran for the door, struggling with his shirt as he went. Took the stairs in a rumbling plunge.

In the kitchen, Oscar and the new boy—Diego?—were screaming at each other and bucking against the arms hold-ing them back. Silverware gleamed on the counter, and a bag of groceries had been knocked over, spilling oranges across the hardwood floor. Two boys had a solid grip on Diego, while Ronald's monstrous arms wrapped around Oscar from behind, nearly lifting him off the ground.

"Let me go, *putas*!" Diego's face burned scarlet as he tried to shake free.

Washington stepped into the kitchen. "Gentlemen." He didn't yell, but everyone's head cut sideways. A guilty look crept into Oscar's eyes. "This dude," he started, "came at me outta nowhere."

"That's a fucking lie, you piece of—" Diego bucked and struggled.

Washington sighed. His head hurt too much for this right now. He took a saucepan from the drying rack and stepped in front of Diego. The boy saw the heavy pan and threw himself harder against the arms holding him, fear flashing in his eyes. Washington drew his arm back and grit his teeth, feeling that old cold song of twisting metal.

Then, hard as he could, he slammed it down on the counter.

The impact was shockingly loud, and everyone froze. "Gentlemen," Washington said again, looking back and forth, decided to start with Oscar. He should have known better; he'd been coming here for months. Washington stared, taking in the rage in Oscar's eyes, the pits in his cheeks, mementoes of a driveby. The boy was alive only because the shooter hadn't known the difference between birdshot and buckshot, and yet here he was, falling back to the old ways.

"You can leave," Washington said, "anytime you like. No one is forced to stay. You can go back to the street, back to putting your work in. I know you're strong enough," glanced over his shoulder, "both of you. I respect your strength." He set the pan down. "But is strength enough?" He paused, nodded at Ronald, who unwound twenty-inch arms from Oscar's chest. "What did strength get you, Ronald?"

"Four years gladiator school." The man spoke quietly, his voice at once rumbling and soft. "Me shot three times. My l'il brother dead."

Washington nodded. "That's right. And you know why?" He gestured at the two boys holding Diego. They slowly released him, but stayed close. Diego puffed out his chest, kept his face hard, but didn't make a move. "Because that kind of strength isn't enough." Washington stepped forward, put a hand on the boy's shoulder, feeling the play of muscles beneath. Looked him in the eye. "You know that. That's why you're here.

"The street says stand up straight. Take shit from no man, right? Murder if you got to." He shrugged. "That's a start. But when everybody gets that same lesson, what happens?"

Washington scanned their faces. Other than Ronald, not one of them was over nineteen. Most had been banging since they were shorties, twelve or thirteen years old. Children of single mothers, never knew a father figure. That they were listening at all was a miracle, a testament to how badly they wanted out of the life. Even Christ hadn't been able to sell salvation to contented sinners.

"Everybody here came on their own. Left their set and came to me for help. Climbed past the sign says Lantern Bearers, knocked on my door. Said, 'Dr. Matthews, I'm tired. There got to be more.'" He paused. "And I said, 'Son, there is.'"

"That *vendejo* disrespected Vice Lords." Diego turned his head and spat. "Shit don't go unanswered."

Washington shook his head. "You leave that behind. No street names, no flying colors. If you're out, you got to get all the way."

"I want out. But he don't get to piss on my people."

"I understand," Washington said. "They're your friends. *Su familia.*"

"That's right."

"You were with them years, they looked out for you."

Diego nodded at him, wary.

"So why are you here?"

"Huh?"

"Why come here?"

"Because . . ." Diego struggled. "My girl, she *embarazada,* right? Six months. And I don't want my baby growin' up to be no—"

"Gangster?" Washington asked.

Diego shrugged, looked away.

"Coming here, son, that took strength. More strength than the street." He stepped closer, locked eyes with Diego. "I respect that." He held the gaze for a few more seconds, let the boy see he meant it. "Nobody is forced to stay. You want to go," he gestured down the hall, "door's over there. Go back to banging and hustling and always looking over your shoulder. But if you stay, you leave the rest behind. You hear?"

Diego left his killer face on, but nodded. It was a start. Baby steps.

"What are we about?" Washington threw out the call.

"Respect," the response came back.

"What are we about?"

"RESPECT." The voices rang together.

He nodded. "All right. Now let's eat." He bent and began picking up oranges and scattered silverware. And felt that familiar thrill of pride when ten hands joined his.

The day would be a busy one. After the meal, while Ronald oversaw the cleanup—wisely separating Oscar and Diego, no point rubbing flint and steel—Washington retreated to his office. Lousy day to sleep late. One of his boys had a job interview and wanted him along. He had a shift at the library later. Plus a pile of paperwork, forms that declared the Lantern Bearers a 501(c)(3) organization, stated that he was not-for-profit.

Shit, he hadn't been for profit since he was seventeen. Only the government would need a form to prove it.

He settled into his chair with a sigh, laced his hands across his belly. The half-empty bottle of Beefeater on his desk caught the light, split it into slow-dancing rainbows. A couple of swigs would ease the pain in his head, the burn in his belly. He looked away, closed his eyes, watched patterns of red and black as he searched for his own strength. When the phone rang, he answered half-alert.

"Dr. Matthews, it's Adam Kent." The voice harried.

"Mr. Kent." Washington jerked upright, eyes snapping open. "How are you?"

"Up to my ears. I've got a shipment of parts two weeks overdue from South Korea and four separate inspectors asking for bribes." The man sighed. "How's life in the gangster-reform business?"

"Oh, we're fine here." He put on his whitest voice, trying for a tone appropriate for dealing with a millionaire entrepreneur and philanthropist. "One day at a time."

"Don't I know it. Your party's in three days. You rent a tux yet?"

*Shit.* "Yes."

"Good. Listen, the alderman just called. He wants to meet again. Some last details he's worried about, something about your history?"

Talons seized Washington's belly. "My history?"

"Yeah, I don't know. I'm sure it's nothing. Tomorrow afternoon?"

"Ah . . . of course."

"Good. I'll bring a check."

"A check?"

"You didn't think I was going to give you five hundred thousand dollars in a duffel bag?"

"No, I just . . ." Washington sighed. "Honestly, Mr. Kent, I'm not used to dealing with this kind of thing. Parties and politics and big donations. Tax forms. I just . . ." He rubbed his aching eyeballs with his thumb and forefinger. "I help kids."

"I know." The voice warm. "Don't worry about it. We'll get it cleared up, whatever it is, and let you get back to the important stuff. Okay?"

"Okay."

"Good. Tomorrow."

Washington hung up, head buzzing, the way it did every time he thought about the money. Half a *million* dollars. Enough to build out the basement with bunks and a bathroom. Buy computers and training manuals. Pay for certification classes. Tattoo removal. Transit cards so the boys could find work. Hell, maybe even hire a full-time tutor. Plus food, utilities, and maintenance for years. Enough to turn the house his mother had left him into a proper gang-recovery center.

His eyes fell on the silver picture frame on the desk, a faded Sunday portrait. A woman with ink-dark skin, her hair pinned primly beneath a hat with a spray of black lace. Gloves, and her blouse buttoned to the neck. Her lips were smiling, but at the same time she squinted against the sun, and it played like a battle on her features. Beside her stood a boy of twelve, thirteen, wearing a Salvation Army suit and a sullen expression.

Photos had strange power. A moment frozen in silver and

paper. The way the sun fell in the woman's eyes, the blurred motion of summer trees, those things would never come again.

The boy in the photo didn't know that in four years he would kill a child half his age. The woman dragging her son to church didn't know he was already lost to her. These things hadn't happened yet. Had they been inevitable, even then? Was it just a matter of waiting for the world to catch up?

He didn't know. The world had kept turning, and things had happened. The relationship between the two, he couldn't say. All he knew was that thirty years ago, Sally Matthews had forced her son to go to church for what had turned out to be one of the last times. And all that remained of that lost moment was a piece of paper.

*I'm trying, Mama. Every day, I'm trying.*

There was a knock at the door, and it pulled him from his reverie. He started to tell whoever it was to come in, but the door was already opening. Something must be wrong. Washington straightened, expecting to hear about Oscar and Diego, their feud continuing.

Then he saw Ronald's face and realized something much worse had happened.

# CHAPTER 10
The Good Life

Jason couldn't remember ever being so uncomfortable in a place he knew well.

They'd ordered a couple of pizzas, light sauce and extra cheese for Billy, pepperoni and double giardiniera for him. Sat in Michael's living room and watched the first *Star Wars* movie on DVD. Not the *true* first *Star Wars*, but the one Lucas made later, with the fart jokes and the long-eared alien. Jason felt the man should have left well enough alone, but the movie was one of Billy's favorites, and that was doctor's orders.

"Shock wears off. Don't pull at him. Just take him somewhere he feels safe and make sure he gets some rest." The doctor, a wiry Asian guy not much older than Jason, had written a prescription for Valium, warning not to give more than half a tab. Then he'd left Jason alone in the too bright hallway, forced to face the fact that the place Billy would feel most comfortable was the last place on earth Jason wanted to be.

"How's the pizza?"

"S'okay," Billy said around a mouthful, eyes on the screen. The familiar surroundings did seem to be helping. Which was something of a mixed blessing. The physiological purpose of shock was to help you operate through pain. Right now, he suspected Billy wasn't even thinking about what had happened. His mind was protecting itself by screening out the day. But sooner or later, he'd have to deal with it.

*So will I,* he thought, and then leaned back on his dead brother's sofa and forced himself to chew another bite of pizza.

Later, Jason walked Billy up to bed, feeling like an imposter, like at any moment the curtains would pull aside and Michael would step out with an accusatory expression, a look that said *I'm dead because you weren't there, and by the way, you're a lousy uncle.* He sat on the edge of the bath and watched Billy brush his teeth. Fought to conceal his animal panic at the thought that he was somehow supposed to know all this stuff now. That he had to be responsible. Last night he'd taken home a girl he'd just met and screwed her against the wall of his shitbox apartment, her moans hot in his ear as he buried his fear in sensation.

Today he was supposed to be Daddy?

In his room, Billy pulled off his clothes and tossed them on the floor, then crawled into bed and pulled the covers to his chin, leaving the lamp on. Jason didn't really know the bedtime protocol—was he supposed to read a story? His nephew looked so vulnerable, so tiny, that something in Jason's chest tugged sideways. He wanted to promise that everything would be all right, but he didn't even know what that meant, so he just stood and stared, taking in the boy's long lashes, the white spot where toothpaste had crusted on his lip. Through that doughy unformedness of children, Jason could see the beginnings of the man Billy would become. Shoulders just beginning to broaden. Michael's strong chin—a lot of Mikey, actually, in the nose and eyes, too. For a moment Jason felt an odd lightness, like he was untethered to the planet, but then the boy's small fingers curled around his callused hand.

"Would you stay?" Billy tugged at his hand. "Till I fall asleep?"

"Sure thing." Jason tried a smile. "As long as you want." He sat awkwardly, butt on the bed and back against the wall. Reached out and tentatively stroked Billy's hair.

His nephew let out a long sigh and closed his eyes, scrunching them hard enough to carve little crow's feet. He wrapped the blanket tight and flopped on his side. Through half-closed lips, he mumbled, "G'night, Uncle Jason." Yawned. "I love you."

The words hit like blows. Not the declaration of love— Billy was a sensitive kid, said it all the time—but the recognition that he was the only one to whom Billy could say that now. Panic flooded Jason, and he wished with everything he was that the world would go back to making sense. It wasn't supposed to be *Michael* who died. Fate had tagged the wrong Palmer brother.

"I love you too, kiddo." Iron fingers squeezed his chest as he stared down at all that remained of his family. "You sleep now."

He switched off the lamp and eased himself to lay on the mattress beside Billy, feet sticking off the end of the twin bed. The ceiling was dotted with glow-in-the-dark stars, the whorls of fake constellations and plastic planets forming a canopy above. Wide awake, Jason counted his nephew's soft breaths, counted and stared up at the false sky, stared and wished he knew what he was looking for.

Oh-one-hundred hours. Back in the living room, the only light was the TV, the DVD menu for *Star Wars* still up, bright colors showing the Jim Beam was half gone. He poured another two fingers into a juice glass, threw them back in a gulp.

They'd played at Star Wars when they were little. One of the games they could agree on. Michael always wanted to be Luke, the responsible farm boy who saved the world. Jason preferred to be Han, the pirate who saw the galaxy and got the girl. He remembered the broken concrete and brown grass behind the closed meat packing plant, throwing rocks through the window and pretending they were blowing up the Death Star. Sometimes the police would come, and they'd run away, scampering over wrought iron fences and down the river bank, pleased to be chased, knowing the cops didn't care enough to catch them. Luke Skywalker and Han Solo, shoulder to shoulder.

*Except in the movie, Han came back to save Luke's butt. And you let Mikey die.*

The Worm twisted, stronger and crueler than yesterday. He took another gulp of the bourbon, knuckles white on the glass. Grabbed the clicker and changed the channel to CNN, watched armored M113's, "Hatewagons," roll through Fallujah. An Iraqi in a striped shirt pointed out where small arms fire had chipped chunks off a concrete wall.

His brother was dead.

He tried to grasp the thought, but it was like throwing his arms around smoke. Nothing made sense. Ever since Soul Patch stepped out of the shadows, letters tattooed on his forearm and a chromed-up automatic in his hand, the world had stopped following rules Jason understood.

No, not yesterday. Before then. It had stopped making sense when Martinez died.

Martinez, who'd once stuffed sock tits under his fatigues and painted his lips cocksucker-red, then paraded around the FOB with his rifle at his shoulder, a ghoulish, heavily-armed cheerleader. Even the LT had hidden a smirk and turned away, let the grunts have their fun.

One more brother he'd let down.

Seemed like every time he dared to care for something, it went away. First Dad, the fucker, and later, Mom. He'd found a home in the Army, and a new set of brothers. But that ended when Martinez died. He'd lost his friend, and then he'd lost his second home, and now he'd lost Michael. If there was a rule to life Jason understood, it was that he was poison.

The bourbon cut, but he poured another, drank it fast. Conscious of the pulse in his forehead. On the television, a lonely building burned, black smoke bruising the sky.

*Cry. For Christ's sake,* cry, *man.*

He remembered sitting in the basement of Michael's bar. A tinny radio in the background. The old safe behind the fake radiator, Michael explaining they'd kept money there in the Prohibition years, when the place had been a speakeasy. Michael opening it to get a bottle of Black Label, taking a pull and passing it to Jason. Smiling at him, all arguments forgotten.

Saying, "To the good life, bro."

*Cry, goddammit!*

He slammed a fist on the muscle of his thigh, then again, feeling the meaty thwack of it. The dull rippling pain that didn't change anything. What was he? How many times since his return to the States had he sat in the dark and tried to cry, and yet the tears never came. No tears for Martinez, and none for himself. And now, none for Michael. What kind of man couldn't cry for his brother?

Jason remembered the morning, cleaning the Beretta. The strange trance he'd felt as he spun it around and pointed its lethal eye at his forehead. The siren call of gleaming metal, his thumb on the trigger, the urge to squeeze it. He was tired of failing people, tired of infecting them. Tired of moving weightless through the world.

And inside, the greasy twisting of the Worm.

Jason leaned forward, his hands clenched on his stomach, fighting the urge to wretch. Gulped deep breaths, then took the bottle by its neck, wrapped his lips around it like he was sucking redemption through the rim. Tilted it and opened his throat, the liquid splashing hard and hot. He breathed through his nose as he swallowed and swallowed, picturing the Worm drowning in it, writhing and screeching, its sick flesh slapping waves of amber.

He swallowed until the bottle was empty, and then he let it fall numb from his fingers. CNN had switched to talking heads, Rumsfeld spinning vagaries into rhetoric. Jason remembered years ago, shortly after he'd first arrived in country, hearing Rumsfeld's famous line about known-knowns and known-unknowns and unknown-unknowns and thinking that crazy as it sounded, he knew exactly what the guy meant, only it wasn't the war he was talking about, it was life, at least life the way Jason had always seen and never understood it, and for a while he sat and stared at the television, let the light wash over him without touching him, trying to see a way to make sense of things, to knit the world together.

By the time he gave up, his mouth was dry and he had the beginnings of a head-splitter. The clock on the cable box read two twelve. He reached for the clicker and fumbled around until the television snapped off. Dropped the remote to the table with a thud. Unlaced his tennis shoes, pulled off his socks. Rack time. For a moment, he thought of going upstairs to his brother's bedroom.

No. No way.

Jason pulled the blanket off the back of the couch, curled his legs under, and put his head down. A long, terrible day. A day with no sense to be found. Maybe sunlight would make things clearer.

He was almost asleep when he heard glass breaking.

## July 2, 2005

*Billy's tongue is between his lips. He's gripping the hammer wrong, little fingers clenched too far up, and though he whacks the nail again and again, it never goes in. On the ground beside him lay five mismatched two-by-fours and a tangle of rope.*

*He's building a treehouse, he explained to Jason earlier, and his uncle laughed, and ruffled his hair, and went back to the house for a fifth beer. That one is gone, and his mouth is dry for a sixth, but Jason lingers on the screened porch, watching his nephew. Billy winds up and swings wildly. The nail pings free and leaps away. He drops the hammer and kicks the tree, then hops around on one foot.*

*Instead of going to the kitchen, Jason opens the screen door and steps out.*

*He shows Billy how to grip the hammer, hand at the base. Drives one ten-penny to demonstrate: Two taps to set, three blows to finish. Then he holds the board and hands his nephew the hammer.*

*When Michael gets home, he finds them in the tree, each to a branch, legs dangling. An uneven ladder runs up the side of the trunk. He takes it in silently.*

*"We're out of wood," Billy explains.*

*Michael sighs and walks away.*

*"What's wrong?" Billy looks suddenly nervous.*

*Jason shakes his head. "I don't know."*

*A moment later Michael returns carrying two pine deck chairs. He sets one upside down, reaches for the hammer, and snaps the leg off.*

*"Can't stop now. Look how much higher you could go."*

*He winks as he hands up the plank.*

# CHAPTER 11
## Shades of Red and Blue

Jason's eyes snapped open. He sat up, shadow-boxing the boogeyman. Raw adrenaline trampled his bourbon haze, fight-or-flight pushing everything else aside.

The sound had been unmistakable, but a little muted. In this neighborhood, the breaking glass could easily have been a drunk throwing his last bottle, or kids smashing a car window. There was no reason to panic yet. He tried to attune himself to the house, to stretch his perception into every corner, to make the place an extension of himself, as personal as limbs.

Glass shattered again. Louder. Inside the house.

Then he was moving, bare toes tracing the grain of the hardwood floor. The room went wobbly for a second from a rush of blood. He stepped past the armchair into the darker shadows, heart thumping against his ribs. Another crisp crack, like someone snapping off the glass in a windowpane, followed a second later by a thump that could have been the piece hitting a rug.

His mind raced, assessing the battlefield. The living room where he stood was in the front of the house, next to a small foyer and the front door. An open arch led to the kitchen and dining area. Off the back of the kitchen was the three-season room, a screened porch where they ate in the summer. That would be it. A lock snapped open.

His jacket was flung over the armchair. Moving lightly,

he slid one hand into the front right pocket. The gun was gone.

Shit. The hospital. He'd taken the gun out of his jacket and stuck it in the glove box, betting correctly that the emergency room would have metal detectors. Afterward, he'd been preoccupied, and forgotten it. From the other room he heard a sound like someone banging into a table. "Quiet," a voice whispered. Not intruder, then; intruder*s*.

Jason inched along the wall, pulse racing and mouth dry. A shaft of yellow light cut through the air, veering crazily before settling on the floor. A second beam came on, this one more careful. Jason flattened his back to the wall, the arch to the kitchen a few inches to his right. Dust motes danced in the light as the beams pulled inward. He pictured the kitchen —breakfast table near the arch, black-and-white linoleum tiles, counter and sink along one wall. The sudden illumination from the flashlights would have cut their night vision. He had to know what he was facing. Fingers tingling, he peered around the arch.

Three men stood in the kitchen talking softly. Two had little Mag-Lites they pointed at their feet, minimizing the splash of light. They wore loose dark clothing and tennis shoes so bright they had to be fresh out of the box. All three had pistols in their hands. Why would thieves have pistols out?

Then the third man twisted on a flashlight of his own, pointing it at his chest as he tightened the beam, the light spilling up to reveal his face. For a moment Jason thought his heart had stopped, then realized he was just holding his breath.

It was Soul Patch.

His first reaction was pure energy. He thought of the ruined bar, the wood twisted and bubbled with heat. Thought of his brother's body, lying in some morgue somewhere, still to be dealt with. His heart pumped rage and his veins carried murder. Soul Patch wanted to dance? Bring him on.

Then he remembered Billy.

Jason eased back from the door into shadow. He had to find a way out of this that didn't risk Billy. Maybe he wasn't much of an uncle. Maybe he wasn't ready to play Daddy. But he sure as hell wasn't going to let anyone hurt his nephew.

There wasn't much time. He scanned for weapons, eyes falling on the fireplace pokers, then the coffee table with the television remote and empty Jim Beam bottle, on to his brother's desk, a box cutter sticking out of a jar of pens. Nothing he saw was a match for one pistol, much less three.

Then he looked at the coffee table again.

Move.

Staying on the balls of his feet, he quick-stepped over, grabbed the remote, then crept to the front door. From the other room he heard the faint sounds of footfalls, the men splitting up. He had a few seconds at most. He grasped the deadbolt key and began turning, body screaming for speed, mind fighting for stealth. He eased it open one slow degree at a time, and when he felt it seat, reached for the handle. He said a quick prayer that the hinges wouldn't squeak.

The door swung open silent as a ghost.

Jason stepped outside, the August humidity cotton-thick after the air-conditioning. He turned and pulled the door shut, closing it just as a dark shape stepped into the living room, swinging a flashlight beam across the floor. Jason spun, ducked down, and hurried across the front of the house.

The neighborhood was quiet, the small slumbering houses leaning against one another. Most of the streetlights were broken, but the remaining few lit the yard more than he'd have liked. He kept low as he moved. When he reached the living room window, he eased himself against the wall next to it, his feet moving from grass to the sharp wood chips lining the empty flower bed. Something jammed into the soft portion of his foot, but energy was slaloming so hard and fast through his body that the pain seemed muted as distant thunder. Rocking his head sideways, he looked in the window of his brother's house.

A man stood in the center of the room, holding the flashlight in one hand and pistol in the other. Six-foot-plus, with heavy-lidded eyes and cornrows. He had the gun loose and low, not tracking with the beam the way he should have.

Jason raised the remote, pointed it through the window at the television six feet away and pressed the button. The set sprang to life, screen brightening. The gangbanger whirled. His gun flew level as he gave a short little yelp.

Jason pressed the volume button, turning the TV louder. CNN still on, the sounds of a Blackhawk rotor beating through the glass. Inside, the banger moved toward the TV, then spun again, the flashlight beam dancing crazily across the room. Jason smiled, dropped the clicker, and sprinted.

The Caddy was parked down the street, and he thought of going for his gun. But as diversions went, this one wouldn't keep them occupied for long. He had to get Billy out. He raced across the yard, sucking hot air into his lungs. Between Michael's house and its neighbor was a thin walkway, and he dodged down it, feet slapping splintered concrete. The house next door was in lousy shape, chunks of siding missing, the holes like sunken eyes watching his progress.

Fifteen steps took him to the backyard, and he paused in the darkness, peering at the three-season room. As he'd expected, one of the panes of glass in the door had been broken. The door swung open at his touch. Thin traces of light coming in the windows highlighted the sparkling edges of broken glass on the floor, and he stepped carefully.

He paused, heart racing, blood thrumming through his system. The television in the other room was still blaring, Arabic with a translator overdubbed, talking about an ambush that left three Marines dead. The insurgents had come out of the alleys with RPGs and Kalashnikovs, a man was saying. Jason stepped through the kitchen door on the balls of his feet. The room was dark, the air-conditioning cold and stale. A bead of sweat made the long slow run down his side. His hands were shaking. He ignored them, taking one cautious step after another, moving toward the stairs.

"Man, shut that thing off." The voice was loud, way too loud for an ambush, and Jason recognized it. It had once told him about a DVD in the dash of his imaginary Cadillac XLR. Under other circumstances, if his life were the only thing at stake, he might have smiled to think of Soul Patch coming back for another try.

The TV snapped off, silence dropping like an echoing curtain. Damn. The audio had provided good cover for his movement.

"What you doing, dog?" Soul Patch sounded irate.

"Shit came on by itself."

"Maybe Trey-Ball stepped on the remote."

Three men, three voices. That meant the stairs were clear. He kept his pace steady, lifting a foot, moving it careful, setting it down fully before picking up the other. He reached the counter, noticed the telephone on it. Why not. Picked up the receiver, dialed 911, then gently placed the handset on the counter and moved on.

"Man, I didn't step on shit."

"Well, somethin' happened."

Soul Patch's voice cut off the bickering. "Shut your damn mouths. Find this kid and let's take care of business."

The words yanked Jason's head sideways. His hands trembled as he processed the meaning behind the words. He'd assumed that Soul Patch had held a grudge from the other morning, had come back to try and finish him off. But that wasn't it at all. They weren't after him. They were after Billy. For some reason, they wanted to kill his nephew.

Not on Jason's watch.

He started up the stairs, moving along the outer edge, never putting his full weight down. Like all the houses in the neighborhood, Michael's was old, but where half the owners let them crumble, Michael had cared for his. The stairs were covered in new carpet, and the heavy weave muffled sound. If all went well, he could get Billy, head back down and out the way he'd come before the gangbangers realized they were gone.

Then a light went on in the hallway above him. "Dad?" Billy's voice was sleepy, confused, heartbreaking—and loud.

So much for stealth. Jason's heart jumped through his chest and he lunged forward, pounding up the steps, hearing the pursuit focus behind him, the squeak of sneakers on hardwood, something falling over with a crash.

At the end of the hallway, Billy stood in the crack of the doorway, framed in yellow light, tiny in his tighty-whiteys. Jason sprinted down the hall, passing the doors to Michael's room and the bathroom, then scooped his nephew under one arm, stepped into the boy's room, and kicked the door closed. His eyes danced fast: posters, NASCAR clock, pile of dirty clothes, writing desk with a ladder-back chair. It would do. He set Billy down, grabbed the chair and jammed it under the door handle, then flipped off the light.

He knew better than to think they were safe, strode across the room to the window. The roof of the three-season room was a few feet below them. He tugged at the window. Nothing happened. Footsteps slammed up the stairs. Jason cursed, wrenched the lock open, then threw the window up. "Come here!"

He turned to find Billy already standing beside him, eyes wide and skin pale by the glow of the streetlight. Jason pushed aside the stab of guilt at the boy's panic. No time. Chalk up one more reason to hate Soul Patch.

He heard a door slam open down the hallway, imagined the men sweeping flashlights across Michael's bed. Jason leaned forward to fumble with the latches of the screen. They were ancient, the plastic tabs sticking, the springs long rusted out. Fear coursed through his veins. He had to get Billy out of here.

He grimaced, then drove his right foot into the edge of the screen frame. The cheap assembly ripped off the window, falling out to clatter on the roof below. "Come on," he gestured to Billy, then half-helped, half-tossed him out the window. Behind him he heard the rattling of the door handle, heard it open a half inch to where the chair blocked it.

Jason crouched on the edge of the sill, threw one leg through, then pulled the other out. Billy stared at him, eyes wide as moons. A ripping crack, and behind them the chair gave, the door flying open. Someone yelled.

Jason grabbed his nephew, slung him over one shoulder, and ran to the edge of the roof, the tar sticky on his bare feet. Didn't even hesitate, just jumped to the grass below, the impact ringing electric in his knees and ankles. As he hit, he noticed the crooked two-by-fours laddering up the backyard's single tree to the wobbly treehouse he and Michael and Billy had built together, not two months ago.

There was a crack and an explosion of glass, and then he was running, mind automatically cataloguing gunfire, two, then three shots, he'd guess nine-millimeter. He dashed down the thin walkway between the houses, Billy's weight riding like a rucksack, the boy's arms around his neck, what was left of the childhood he'd known receding with every pounding panicked step.

Lights began to blink on in the houses around them, people who were awakened by gunfire more than they'd like, who knew to turn on their lights but never step out on the porch. The Cadillac was thirty yards down, and he sprinted as best he could, fumbling for his car keys with one hand. Ran to the passenger side and opened it, then climbed in that way, using the car as cover from the house, pulling Billy after him. Jason cranked the engine and jerked it into drive before the engine had finished firing.

The front door to Michael's house yanked open as they squealed away, and Jason half expected Soul Patch to run down the sidewalk, blasting away at them like some action movie bad guy, the back window blowing out. But mingling with the tires and the engine was the sound of sirens, loud wails coming from more than one direction. The call to 911 paying out. The figure in the door raised his gun, hesitated, then turned and vanished into the house.

His heart was racing, and Jason wanted to mash the gas and tear ass for miles, but he made himself slow down, turning off on the first street he saw, keeping his speed an even thirty. A police car screamed toward him, and he pulled out of its way, every bit the good citizen.

As he did, he looked over at his nephew, his little-boy

body all but naked, lit up like a bruise in shades of red and blue, and he wondered who could be so messed up they'd want to murder an eight-year-old child.

And whether they'd try again.

# CHAPTER 12
## Menace

Anthony DiRisio was bored. He couldn't see how the police did it, sitting on stakeouts for hours and hours. In the movies, they always made it look like the cops had just enough time to share a war story before something went down. But he'd been waiting half a block from the niggers' house for two hours, and the only thing that'd happened was he really needed to take a piss. He sighed and stretched, the shoulder holster riding up on his ribs.

He was parked far enough away that nobody would notice the van, but still had a good angle on the front porch, where homeboys sipped bottles of Eight Ball. They were clowning and posing like the lords of all creation in the midst of a neighborhood that looked like the Lebanon. Crumbling bungalows with steel cages over the front doors, tiny yards grown to shit. No respect for their environment. Graffiti on the billboards, graffiti on the lampposts, graffiti on the goddamn street in front of the house.

A muscular guy stepped outside, his body silhouetted. Bass-heavy rap flowed out from the open door like theme music. Dion Williams, called himself "C-Note." Anthony called him "C-nappy-ass nigger." He bumped fists with one of the brothers, and the jig got up and followed him back inside.

He knew it wasn't fashionable to call them "jigs" anymore, but it was the word he'd learned as a child growing up south of Taylor, and it stuck in his mind.

He reached down beside the seat to the recline control, eased back a notch, trying to take some pressure off his bladder. Waited.

Ten minutes later, two of the guys on the porch stood up. They gave elaborate handshake-hugs to the others, then pimp-rolled down the steps. The one they called Brillo stopped at the bottom and tilted his forty back in a long swallow. When he'd finished, he tossed the bottle on the grass. No respect even for their own things.

The two climbed in a 1970 black Monte Carlo, a lot like the one Denzel Washington drove in that cop film. Denzel, he was all right. Anthony didn't expect Denzel threw empty beer bottles on his front yard. Chaser lights circled the license plate, and bass rattled the frame. Sounded like something locked in the trunk trying to get out.

"Can't spell crap without rap," Anthony said to himself, and started the van.

He hung back and let them have plenty of room. They passed a Currency Exchange lit up like Vegas on one corner, a couple of storefront businesses with hand-lettered signs on the other. Waited for drive-through at McDonald's, then turned down a neighborhood block fronted by a sign saying it didn't tolerate drugs or gangs. A Gangster Disciples tag was sprayed right across the sign. The Monte Carlo pulled up next to an abandoned lot, and the music cut off abruptly.

He drove past. When he came to a stop sign he paused, glancing in the rearview. Brillo and his boy walked across the street, the greasy white bag dangling. Anthony circled the block and found a parking place. Spent a moment listening to the engine tick before he took his case and got out of the van.

First thing he did, he went alongside the house the two jigs had gone into, fished out his dick, and tagged the house Anthony DiRisio–style. Felt like a new man once the last drops splashed down the mortar.

Back at the Monte Carlo, he took a thin metal strip from the toolbox. He eased the slim-jim behind the window seal until he felt it seat against the control arm, and then pulled over and up. The lock popped.

Inside, the air was heavy with weed and the cheap scent of evergreen. The windows were tinted so dark that he could hardly see the street. Anthony pulled the air freshener from the mirror, clicked off the volume knob on the CD player, then took a thin screwdriver from his case and wedged it into the ignition. He used a hammer to tap it further, tightened a wrench on the blade, and then cracked the hammer down to snap the mechanism. The whole assembly came out in his hand.

One twist of the rotary switch, and the engine woke with a sexy purr.

Anthony smiled. Any car built past about 1985 wouldn't have been so easy. And most from the last decade had an RFID engine immobilizer to keep them from starting without the key. Bless the homeboys for choosing style over substance.

He turned the radio back on, the volume at a Caucasian level. A CD started immediately, and he punched the button to eject it. Checked the title out of habit—know your enemy—saw it was DMX, "It's Dark and Hell is Hot."

"Amen, brother," he said to himself, and chuckled.

He tossed the CD in back with the air freshener, spun the radio dial till he found real music, Phil Collins singing how he could feel it coming in the air tonight, hold on. The shoulder holster dug into his side, and he removed the pistol, a Swiss-made SIG-Sauer P-226, and lay it on the seat next to him.

Out on the city street, he leaned back in the leather, feeling good. Always struck him as funny, the things gangbangers cared about. Their sneakers couldn't have a speck of dirt. Their rides had to be pimped and shining. But they'd happily live in crumbling shitboxes, the kind where when you moved the furniture, a colony of roaches scattered for the walls. In a drug crib, they might have forty grand in cash stacked beneath a fifty-inch flat-screen TV, and a bucket half-filled with piss by the end table, because the toilet didn't work and they couldn't call a plumber. Anthony hated going into the houses, hated the stink of them. Hated the posturing of teenagers who hadn't put in their work and become affiliated, hated the attitude of the O.G.'s that ran the set. Hated the monikers and dope and rap and bling and bandannas and brutal rivalries none of them could explain and demand for respect none of them had earned.

Nights like this were more fun.

He rolled west, watching the numbers climb and the buildings change. Bodegas began to crop up, little urban markets with bright fluorescent light spilling into the night. The graffiti changed, too, crowns and stars, the occasional number thirteen. In the parking lot of a taquería, the cars had Latin beats playing and *cholos* leaning: the men in chinos and work shirts, the women with that full-to-bursting lushness. Say what you like about the Mexs, and Anthony could say plenty, but their senoritas did have something.

He slowed to a crawl, letting them get an eyeful of the Monte Carlo. Menace coalesced. The men straightened, and a few stepped forward. Most were beefy, their shirts ripped to show muscles ringed with tattoos, some the faded black of prison tatts. He wondered if any of them knew the car belonged to Brillo, or if they just saw a ghetto roller that wasn't theirs. Either way.

Two minutes later, he'd reached the street. Tract houses ran down both sides, a few abandoned, all looking like shit. The night was hot, and people sat on porches. "Angel of the Morning" came on the radio, the original Merrilee Rush version. He turned it up a little, liking the way her voice rang out clear and strong. Halfway down the block he killed the headlights, the car a black shark, a predator in dangerous waters.

To an untrained eye, the house looked the same as all the rest. Chipped brickwork, faded siding, metal gates. But every window had a security screen, all of them welded or secured with case-hardened locks. The front door was dented above the handle, where a police ram must have tagged it at some point. The yard was bare, not even the scraggly bushes that fronted the other houses. Thick shades masked all the windows.

Anthony put the car in neutral. Play time. He took the SIG

from the passenger seat, the black plastic grip made for his hand. Merrilee was getting into it, singing she was old enough to face the dawn. Anthony hummed it with her, rolling down the window and aiming along the barrel, the SIG's white dot-and-bar sights clear.

*Just call me angel of the morning, angel.*

A blast of fire spat from his hand, the crack rolling out across the darkened street. The upstairs corner window exploded in a sparkling rain.

*Just touch my cheek before you leave me.*

Down the street someone screamed. Anthony moved to the next window, squeezed again. He'd blown a third window before the glass from the second hit the ground.

*Just call me angel of the morning, angel.*

He shifted down, the pistol an extension of his arm. Exhaled and then squeezed twice, blowing out the porch lights in a shower of sparks. He paused, forearm resting on the window, waiting.

*Then slowly turn away.*

Someone yanked at the front door, and before they'd cleared it by more than a couple of inches, Anthony triple-tapped it, a nice cluster near the handle that kicked it all the way open. A silhouette suddenly exposed jumped back into hiding. Anthony heard cursing in Spanish, someone calling him a son of a whore.

Not a wise thing to say to a guy who grew up south of Taylor.

He swiveled half an inch, bringing the SIG to bear on the left side of the door frame. Squeezed twice. The 123-grain full-metal-jacket rounds punched through the tired siding and rotting wood like they weren't there. There was a difference between yelling and screaming, and the man on the inside demonstrated it.

Anthony grinned, tossed the gun on the passenger seat, then neutral-slammed the Monte Carlo, sending it lurching forward, the engine revving crazy as he squealed away.

In the rearview, broad figures boiled out of the house, guns in hand. Anthony whooped and mashed the accelerator. Sharp cracks sounded from behind. He reached the corner and jerked the wheel without touching the brakes, tires squealing, and then he was in a long clean straightaway, and he let the Monte Carlo run, the roaring engine mimicking the roaring in his ears. He cranked the radio as he wove back and forth, pops and screams dying in the background.

And as the good burned smell of gunpowder filled the car, and Merrilee screeched over the speakers in full ghetto bass, Anthony DiRisio burst into laughter, and leaned forward, beating the wheel like a jockey whipping his horse to death.

# CHAPTER 13
## Slam Dunk

Cruz had woken from a dream of fire. She'd wanted to slip back to sleep, and had tried a cop version of counting sheep, trying to remember as much as she could of various arrest sheets. Street tags and priors were easy, but height, weight, addresses, those were tricky.

She'd gotten up to the gangbanger from yesterday's shooting—eighteen years old, two priors for assault, known affiliation with the Latin Saints, street name *Ratón,* a Crenwood address that was probably his mother's—when she gave up. She wasn't any closer to sleep, just more depressed. After a while it got hard to think of bangers as people. One went down, another was always ready to step up. Shorties recruited out of junior high, a ghetto assembly line. Each model younger and nastier than the last.

She rolled out of bed, pulled on sweats and socks. Darkness pressed the glass to the east, and the skyline blazed to the south. Might as well do some work, make up for the time she'd spent yesterday talking to Jason Palmer. As she booted the computer, Cat jumped purring into her lap. She scratched his ears, then sighed, opened the topmost of a stack of manila folders, and started typing.

The Gang Intelligence Unit was the CIA of the CPD, their mandate to track the gangs, their members, alliances, and rivalries. Information came in a hundred different ways: street interviews, graffiti, suspects that flipped on friends for a lighter sentence, arrest photos, tips from confidential informants. When combined, the information was invaluable not only for closing cases, but also guiding decisions on beat-car rotation, preemptive arrests, even budgetary discretion. Gang Intel was a special unit, a plum assignment, and she'd worked her ass off to be the first woman to make it.

The only problem was that instead of gathering info, she'd been saddled with inputting it.

It hadn't started that way. For the first ten months she and Galway had ridden hard, leading the south side in the development of CIs and the amount of useful tips. Even the boy's club had started to accord her a certain grudging respect.

Then the thing with Donlan last year, and it all went to shit.

How everyone came to know, she wasn't sure. But it started with jokes—condoms left on her desk, advice columns about interoffice affairs tacked to the bulletin board. Then some clever prankster had called IAD and suggested her position had to do with favoritism. Total bullshit that they had no choice but to investigate. And it hadn't helped when she found out who the prankster was and took him apart in the boxing ring. So now here she sat, on a "temporary assignment" any secretary could have handled, inputting data other cops collected.

It was the kind of job meant to suck, and it did. But knowing that there were a lot of people who wouldn't shed tears if she quit gave her the strength to stay. Besides, lemonade from lemons. She now knew more about what was happening in Crenwood than anyone. Every tip, every scuffle, every murder, if it had gang overtones, she knew about it. Like a spider in the center of a web, aware of any twitch. The strands ran out in all directions, and every now and then she felt she could see the larger pattern.

It helped a little to think that way. But only a little.

When her phone rang, she answered without looking at the caller ID. "Morning, partner."

"Rise and shine," Galway said. "There's bad guys need busting, and huevos rancheros that need eating. You up for breakfast?"

"Can't."

"Hot date?"

She sighed. "Donlan called last night to schedule breakfast."

There was a long pause. Then Galway said, "You and he, you're not—"

"No." She spoke fast. "Definitely not."

"So what is this?"

"I don't know. Sounds like something is seriously chapping his ass. I gotta tell you, breakfast with him is about the only thing sounds worse than the data entry I was doing."

"I hear you." He sucked air through his teeth. "Look, be careful, all right? Things are bad enough for you as is. Don't need Captain Hollywood messing with your head."

"Sergeant Galway," she said, smiling. "Are you trying to protect me?"

"Hell no. I just don't want to have to listen to you whine anymore than I have to."

Cruz laughed. "Who says chivalry is dead?"

The restaurant off the lobby of the Peninsula Hotel was done rustic European style, like the kitchen of somebody's grandma, provided Gramms lived in a five-hundred-dollar-a-night hotel. Donlan looked right at home, sitting at the antique table in a tailored suit and knockoff Rolex.

"Elena," he said, flashing teeth like a Crest commercial. "Good to see you."

She felt that weird ripple, remnants of attraction mingling with anger and shame. They had agreed to be adult about the whole situation, which meant that she usually felt anything but. "Morning, Chief. How's your family?" She sat carefully, straightening her skirt and her smile.

He looked like he was deciding whether she was insulting him. "When it's just the two of us, you can still call me James."

"I don't think that's a good idea."

"Why not?"

She was saved from answering by the waitress. They ordered, a danish for him, a quiche for her, the closest she was getting to huevos rancheros this morning.

She'd come to Donlan's attention six years ago. An offender had been strangling prostitutes, leaving the bodies in burned-out buildings and abandoned parks. Whore murders were notoriously hard to solve: no fixed address, few close relationships, plenty of opportunity. Nobody else was excited about the case, but she'd seen it as a chance to make her name. Worked it off the clock for months, finally catching a break when a Forty-seventh Street 'tute she'd given a card called with the license plate of a suspicious john. Cruz had asked what she meant by "suspicious."

"White," the girl had replied.

"Lots of white johns."

"Not on Forty-seventh Street, sugar."

When they busted him, Cruz had earned her first newspaper ink, a commendation for her file, and the friendly interest of then-Lieutenant James Donlan. He was a politician, with a spotless record and a bright future, and Cruz knew the score. As a Hispanic woman, every success of hers translated into good PR for him. In return, he could give a little guidance, a reference when she needed one. In the CPD, it never hurt to have friends in high places. Everything was clean and above board.

For a while.

"How have you been?" His voice soft.

"Fine, Chief. Just fine. You?"

"You don't sound fine."

"How do I sound?"

He shook his head. Brushed a piece of dust off his shirt, starched white broadcloth that shone like armor. "What are you working now?"

She picked up her coffee, leaned back. Through the haze of steam, his features warped and shifted. "You don't know?"

"I asked, didn't I?" He spread his hands in exasperation. "Can't we just have breakfast?"

*No. No, we cannot.* Adult, she reminded herself. They

were going to be adult. She sighed. "I'm the official typist of Gang Intelligence." She told him about IAD's investigation, about getting pulled off the street to work the database.

He winced. "I heard about the IAD thing, but not about the demotion. I'm sorry."

"Me too."

"Anything I can do?"

"No." At this point, nothing could hurt worse than help from him. She sighed. "You know the frustrating thing? I just want to do the job. These guys, it's like they think I'm after their livelihood or something. Which is crazy. It's not like I have political aspirations."

"Elena, this is Chicago." He shrugged. "Everybody has political aspirations."

She started to laugh, then saw he wasn't joking.

"Don't worry." He adjusted his watch. "It'll be forgotten before you know it."

She stared at him. Wondered if he could really be that dense. "You know what somebody asked me the other day? This beat cop trying to impress his buddies?" She leaned forward. "He asked if now that you'd been promoted you ranked a bigger desk, or if I was still banging my head against the bottom of the old one." Coffee slopped over the rim of her cup as she set it down hard. "Don't tell me it'll be forgotten, okay, *Chief*? You're not the one who has to listen to that and pretend it's a joke. You're not the one who got fucked here."

The waitress arrived with steaming plates, one eyebrow just slightly cocked, like she'd caught the end of the conversation. Cruz ignored her, picked up a fork, and cut off a bite of the quiche. Chewed without tasting, her pulse racing.

"You know," Donlan said, gaze steady, "no one forced you into that hotel room."

"I'm not pissed about the hotel room. I'm pissed about what happened afterward."

"We've been over this. I'm sorry it got out, but I didn't tell anyone."

"Neither did I."

"Elena," he shrugged. "Cops talk. They hypothesize, they

bullshit each other, they gossip like old ladies. You know that."

"Is that why we needed to have breakfast this morning?" She felt sweat under her arms, set her fork down to hide the anger shakes. "So you could remind me cops talk?"

Donlan finished chewing, used the corner of his napkin to wipe his lips. "No." He straightened, put on his official face. "I heard one of your CIs bought it yesterday."

Her head jerked up. "What?"

"Somebody Palmer, died in a fire?"

"He wasn't a confidential informant," she said slowly. "Just a citizen I was working with." She paused. "That's a little small to make your radar, isn't it?"

"You like anybody for it?"

"Palmer was being taxed by the Gangster Disciples. And he volunteered with a community anti-gang group, the Lantern Bearers." What was this? Donlan had recently been promoted to Deputy Chief of the Area One Detective Division, the latest step in a meteoric rise. Him taking an interest in this case was like the mayor worrying about a broken stoplight.

"So it was a gang hit," he said.

"I'm not sure."

"Why not?"

"It's too simple." She hesitated, trying to choose her words. "I met Michael Palmer at a CAPs meeting. He came up afterwards, asked to talk with me later. When I came by his bar, he claimed he had some info on the gangs. Said it was something big."

"That sounds like motive."

"I know, it's just . . ." She shrugged. "He was really hush about it. Wouldn't even tell me what exactly he meant. But he said that it went beyond the gangs. That other people were involved." She paused. "Then his bar burned with him in it."

Donlan sighed, shook his head. "And you think it's a conspiracy."

"I'm just being thorough." Under the table, she laced her fingers and squeezed until the bones ached. "I knew the guy."

"You making this personal, Officer?"

She straightened. "No sir."

"This case is a heater. As long as the bangers are shooting each other, nobody gives a shit. But when they kill citizens, we act."

"I agree. I just want to make sure—"

"Enough," he said. "This was a gang hit. Homicide is going to wrap it fast. You want to be thorough, help us with intel. Don't go playing detective and screw up a slam dunk." He set his fork down precisely beside the plate. "You get me?"

She got him, all right. Donlan had knocked more than one person off the ladder to clear his own path. "I get you, Chief."

He nodded, stood up. "You're a good girl, Elena," he said, peeling a twenty from his money clip. "If you're careful, you'll go far." He dropped the bill and walked out without a backward glance.

Leaving Cruz sitting in the restaurant of a hotel where a room cost a week's pay, wondering what exactly she'd just been told.

# *July 11, 1975*

*"Sun Zoo? Who dat?"*

*"Sun Tzu. He a brother wrote a book called* The Art of War." *Swoop leans back, elbows flung on the step behind. "Chinese brother, long time ago."*

*"So?" Washington can't believe Swoop is talking about books at a time like this.*

*"Man said 'War is deception.' You feel that? War is deception." Swoop gestures out at the sunlit street. "See, that 'Rican dropped Eight Ball, and he your boy, so you wanting to go gunning for them, right, cuz?"*

*"Straight up."*

*"But you run up in their hood now, what you think gonna happen? You all alone, they know you coming. Shit, they gonna kill your ass."*

*"I'm bringing Crazy Dee."*

*"Dee don't belong to me. He do as he like. But you ain't going nowhere." Swoop stares hard.*

*"Aww, c'mon man—"*

*"You ain't going. You gonna let them think you too scared." He pulls at his beer. "Then when they let their guard down, next week, next month, you and I, we roll over there together and do some damage." Pauses. "War* is *deception, yo." Then Swoop stands, nods at the sun, and vanishes with a squeak of the screen door.*

*Thirteen years old and hurting, Washington starts to rise. Then sits down again.*

*That night, Crazy Dee opens fire on a chili dog joint in Latin King territory. He gets off three rounds and breaks a window before soldiers in the neighboring houses blow his chest onto the street.*

*When he hears, Washington locks himself in his bedroom and sobs his throat raw. Beats the pillow and thinks about how when he'd told Crazy Dee he wasn't going, Dee called him a pussy and a bitch and stormed away. And about how when they were seven he and Crazy Dee, who was really Dennis, and Eight Ball, who wasn't Eight Ball yet but William, how they'd made up a game all their own. Started as handball but got complicated enough they named it, DWW or WDW or WWD, dependin' who was throwing. How they played it all summer long, the three of them laughing and loud.*

*And he thinks how war is deception, and how strange it is, that the power of a long-ago book by a Chinese brother is the only reason he is still alive to cry for his friends.*

# CHAPTER 14
## Scared

Jason woke with the sun in his eyes and the Beretta in his hand. The first thing he did was disengage the pistol's safety. The second was check the room.

Billy lay tangled in the sheets, one pasty leg sticking off the edge of the bed. He was face down, shoulders in and arms tucked under as if trying to fold inside himself. "Peaceful" wouldn't have been Jason's first word for the boy, but at least he looked unharmed. Physically.

Jason clicked the safety back on and set the weapon on the floor between his thighs. He rolled his head to either side, vertebrae creaking and popping. After putting Billy to bed last night, he'd triple-locked the front door and slept with his back against it. The position had taken a toll. His body felt thick and heavy. Flaming ants marched up his spine, and his legs had gone numb.

He stood slowly, the world sliding in funky circles as the blood drained from his head. A rush of nausea pole-axed him. The room throbbed in time with his pulse, and he could still taste the Jim Beam, gone foul now. Adrenaline had pushed aside his drunkenness during last night's excitement, but it wasn't doing shit for the hangover.

In the bathroom Jason stared at the toilet until he felt the bile rising, then pinched his nose and vomited. Twice. Spat and flushed, gargled Listerine. Set the pistol on the counter and splashed double handfuls of cold water on his face, the streams running down his neck and into his shirt, icy rivulets that counter-pointed the needle-tingling of his legs. When he began to feel his strength returning, he dried his face on the hand towel and tossed it on the counter.

His brother was dead. The thought hit as he caught his stare in the mirror. Michael was dead. No. Murdered. And it was about time he found out what was going on.

Jason tucked the gun in the small of his back, straightened, and left the bathroom.

The apartment was a studio, one mid-sized room with a tiny kitchen at the end. He started making coffee, not trying to be loud, but not being quiet either. Wanting Billy to wake up to regular sounds. Before the gangbangers had arrived last night, the boy had started to seem better, and Jason needed that to continue. He poured Corn Pops in two cereal bowls, set spoons in with a clank. What did kids drink in the morning? Juice? He had some lime juice for gin and tonics, but that was about all. He figured what the hell, poured two cups of coffee, one black, one beige with milk and sugar.

The boy's eyes were open when Jason turned to set everything on the kitchen table.

"Morning, kiddo." He kept his voice light, hoping it didn't sound too fake. Billy yawned and sat up; then, spotting his bare chest, lay back down and pulled the covers to his neck. Jason smiled. "There's a T-shirt on the edge of the bed. Why don't you put that on and come have breakfast?"

Billy seemed reluctant until he saw that it was a gray shirt with ARMY emblazoned in black. His eyes bugged, and he grabbed the tee and pulled it over his head, then came to sit at the other end of the table, rubbing sleep from his eyes. When he saw the coffee, he looked questioningly at Jason, then took a sip. His lips contorted like worms.

Jason covered his smile with one hand. "Dig in."

They ate in silence, just the sound of metal clanking against plastic and the crunch of cereal under a play of soft gold sunlight. The coffee was strong and sharp, and Jason could feel it spreading through his belly, reviving his weary cells. When he couldn't delay any longer, he asked, "How you doing?"

Billy looked up from a spoonful of yellow milk. "Okay." His voice sounded a little trembly, but his eyes were sharp and undilated.

"Good." Jason sipped his coffee, thought about what to say next. "You know you're safe now, right?"

Billy nodded.

"I'm not going to let anything happen to you." Jason bent forward, put his hand over his nephew's. "I promise."

The moment held for what seemed like a long time, and then Billy smiled. It was a quick thing, there and gone, but the sight of it went a long way toward easing the muscles in Jason's body. "But I need your help, okay? I have to know what happened yesterday. Before you came."

Billy stiffened, but didn't seem to be retreating into zombie mode. "Do I have to?"

"I'm sorry, buddy." He put as much comfort into his eyes as he could. "But I really need to know. It's important."

Billy pushed sodden cereal back and forth with his spoon. "I didn't want to run." He mashed a Corn Pop. "I got scared."

"That's okay," Jason said. "I've been scared before. I know what it's like. It makes you do things you don't want to."

His nephew nodded vigorously. "I wanted to help, but I couldn't move."

"Help who? Your dad?"

"They were hitting him." The lower half of Billy's face scrunched up, his chin quivering. "Dad told them to get out. They laughed, and then one of them grabbed a bottle and hit him in the head with it. And I didn't mean to, but I . . ." He trailed off, pushing his head deeper into his chest. "I peed myself."

Jason slid out of the chair to crouch beside his nephew, one arm around his shoulder. Fury tightened the muscles of his jaw.

"When I felt it, I moved, and I knocked into one of the shelves. I was in the back room, and they both looked up, and one of them walked toward me. I was so scared, I just stood there, and then Dad climbed over the bar and tackled the guy. He was bleeding, and the other one started kicking him, but Dad didn't let go. He yelled for me to run." He looked up in Jason's eyes. "He *told* me to. I didn't want to."

Jason nodded, understanding blooming bitter in his chest. "You did good." He squeezed his nephew's shoulder. "You did exactly right."

Billy straightened like guilt had been a hand pressing him down. "I ran out the back, and I kept going until I couldn't anymore. I was in a park and there was a big bush, and I crawled under it and hid. One of the men looked around, but he didn't see me. I waited there for a long time, and I guess I fell asleep." His words spilling fast, a poison he wanted to be rid of. "When I woke up it was morning, and I didn't know where I was, but there was a train station, and I remembered the stop where you lived, so I snuck on."

He thought of Billy alone, sleeping under a bush in Crenwood Park, the kind of place cops wouldn't go into alone at night. Dealers slinging dimes and quarters, ragged whores giving ten-dollar blowjobs. Waking up to morning mist and daddy-long-legs crawling on him. His father already dead.

"The guys who came into the bar," Jason asked, his voice calm as he could make it. "Can you tell me what they looked like?

Billy nodded. "One looked normal. He mostly watched. The other was taller and really strong. He looked a little like the man in *Who Framed Roger Rabbit,* only he was bigger and meaner."

Jason almost smiled. The tape was one of a handful Michael kept at the bar for Billy. God bless popular culture.

Then it hit him.

"Wait a second. Which guy?"

"*The* guy," Billy said. "The guy with Roger."

Jason thought back to the movie, saw the actor's face. An Italian-looking dude. But—

"Billy, what color were these guys?"

"White," his nephew said. "The big one was bald, and the plain one had black and gray hair. They were wearing suits."

Jason stood up, walked to the window, stared outside at

the corner below, where even at ten in the morning, a couple of slow-eyed men hung out. The sun fell hot against his face. The beginnings of another scorcher.

He'd been expecting to hear about a black man with a soul patch and a diamond necklace. Instead, Billy was telling him that two white men in suits had beaten and murdered his brother.

*Mikey, what the hell did you get into?* He felt a cold shiver up the back of his legs, a hollowness in his falling stomach. Recognized it.

Fear.

If it wasn't gangbangers that killed his brother, then who was it? And why? And what did that have to do with the gangs?

What in God's name was going on?

"Uncle Jason?" Billy sat on the edge of the chair, swimming in the Army T-shirt, his thin legs barely touching the floor. He looked like he was about to cry again.

"Hey, it's okay, buddy." Jason walked back across the room. "I'm sorry. It's not you. I'm just . . . sad." *And confused. And totally out of my depth.*

*And God help me, scared.*

He knelt down beside Billy, put his hands on the boy's shoulders. "Thank you for telling me. I know it was hard."

Billy nodded solemnly.

"I want you to know something." Jason looked him in the eyes. "None of this is your fault. You did everything right. Everything." He smiled. "Your dad would be so proud of you."

Billy's lip trembled, and then he began to bawl, the tears streaming down his face. Jason leaned forward and took the kid in his arms, Billy hugging his neck like it was all that was keeping him from tumbling over a ledge.

"It's okay, buddy. It's okay." Jason stroked his back. "Go ahead and cry." He held the boy in his arms, feeling the warmth of his rag-doll body. And as he did, it hit him.

He'd been adrift. A soldier without a cause, which was no kind of soldier at all. Ever since he'd lost his Army, he'd been looking for something to fight for.

Now he realized it sat in his arms.

"Billy." Jason leaned back so he could meet the boy's eyes. "I don't know what's going to happen. But I want you to know that you're safe now. I'll protect you. Whatever I have to do."

Billy looked at him, salt smell and wet lower lip, and nodded.

And for just a second, Jason felt the Worm cower.

# CHAPTER 15
Debts

The base of the toilet was coated in hair. As he mopped at it with a paper towel, Washington tried not to think about where the hair came from. Not like they had a cat.

"What next?" Ronald leaned in the doorway, the motion popping muscles that strained the seam of his shirt. "Garage?"

"Leave that be," he said. "They'll park on the street. You could get a couple of the boys to tidy up the office, though."

"What about all your books?"

"My closet?"

Ronald laughed.

"Right." Washington stretched, feeling his back twang and stab. Grimaced, looked around. Gestured to the shower. "Stack them there." So much to do. In fifteen minutes, Alderman Owens and Adam Kent would arrive to discuss whatever was troubling the alderman. Washington had a pretty good idea about the subject, didn't really believe a clean house and a sparkling toilet would make up for it. But you had to try. "Ronald!"

The big man poked his head back around.

"Put a plastic bag down first, hear?" Then he concentrated on scrubbing the damn toilet.

When he was done, he dumped the used paper towels in the bowl and flushed, then put his hands on his knees and pushed himself to his feet. The house was abuzz with activity, former gangbangers grudgingly helping him clean. But what

Washington saw was fire. Flames dancing like djinn, wrapping sinuous fingers around old wood and ragged stone. And two bodies, blackened and ruined, nothing but teeth and horror.

*Stop that, you fool. You don't even know it was Michael, much less the boy. Just because folks saw a body taken out doesn't mean it was your friend.*

Who else would it have been, though?

A knock at the door broke the train of his thoughts. He glanced at his watch, winced. Brushed dirt off his knees, then straightened and went for his office. Ronald bumped into him, asked, "That them?"

"We're not ready," Washington said. "So of course it is."

"Want me to get it?"

He nodded, then said, "Wait." He stepped closer, glanced around. "Have you heard anything else?"

"About—"

"Yes."

Ronald shook his head. "Got the word out. I hear anything, I'll let you know."

Washington nodded, forced a smile. Went to his office and sat at the desk. His mother looked at him from the silver frame, that war between smile and frown warping her features. Down the hall, the door opened, and he heard the muffled sound of voices. Took a deep breath, closed his eyes, and sought comfort in his Cicero: *Rational ability without education has oftener raised man to glory than education without natural ability.*

Then he opened his eyes and saw the Beefeater bottle still on the desk. *Shit!* He grabbed it and yanked open a drawer, hearing footsteps draw closer, the click of dress shoes on tile. He dropped the bottle and was just closing the drawer as the door to his office opened and Alderman Owens strolled in, followed by Adam Kent.

"Fast" Eddie Owens was the sort of trim, sharp-looking black man for whom single-breasted suits were conceived. His shirt was a subtle cream and his shoes shone like still water. Beside him, Adam Kent seemed underdressed in khakis and a light sweater, salt-and-pepper hair neat, nothing in his manner suggesting he could write a six-figure check. Despite their smiles and extended hands, both men looked like judges to Washington. Or maybe executioners.

"Gentlemen," he said, and stood. "Welcome."

They shook hands, and he gestured them to the couch that had once been the crown jewel of his mother's living room. "Can I get you anything?" he asked, hoping one of them would ask for a drink so that he could have one himself. Neither did.

"Good to see you both again." He smiled as blandly as he could, pretending he couldn't hear his pulse. "Any trouble parking?" Kent shook his head, and the alderman played with the zipper of a leather portfolio. Washington tried again, going for hearty this time. "Going to be a heck of a time Friday night, huh?"

His guests looked at each other. Something had changed; the last time they were here, it was all toasts and promises, discussions of how much good they could do together. Now neither seemed sure how to look at him.

*They know.*

His hands trembled and his heart seemed loud. He had that little-kid sense of being caught. Maybe it was better this way. He was a lousy liar. "Something on your mind, gentlemen?" He leaned back in his chair. "Maybe something about me?"

Owens shot his cuffs, then opened the portfolio. "Actually, there is." He took out a sheet of paper, glanced at it. "It was a surprise, let me tell you." He set the paper down on the coffee table. "You know what this is?"

Washington couldn't see the details, but he could make out enough. His chest tightened as he nodded.

"So it's true."

"Yes," he said. "It's true."

"You spent twelve years in prison." Lawyerly, confirming the facts.

Washington nodded. "Most of it in Danville. July 19, 1979, to May 12, 1991. Missed the whole eighties."

"For murder."

They'd pled for manslaughter, but no point quibbling. "That's right." He leaned back, lips set hard. Trying to ignore his mother staring at him from the desk. Trying to forget the plans he'd had, the good that half a million dollars could have done.

A long moment stretched. Then Kent bent forward on the couch, his expression earnest and curious. "Jesus, Washington. Why didn't you tell us that?"

Now it would come. The lecture, and the disappointment. There was no point in explaining. It didn't matter how many books he read or boys he helped. He'd learned the same hard lesson as every other felon—once people knew that much, they didn't want to learn anything else.

Then he heard Cicero in his head again, talking about how it was ability that raised men to glory, not paltry circumstances like education or whether they'd been to prison. Better to try.

He sat up, put his hands on his knees. "I didn't tell you because that wasn't me."

The alderman started. "Wait a minute, you just—"

Washington waved his hands. "I'm talking about who I *am*. The man I am, not the stupid boy thirty years ago. That boy, he was damaged. He was confused and he was dangerous and he was high most of the time." He sighed. "That boy died in prison.

"Before I went in, banging was my life. That was my whole purpose. Didn't know anything else. No bigger world. In the ghetto, life is counted in dog years."

The alderman straightened. "Dr. Matthews—"

"You know damn well I'm no doctor," Washington interjected. "I let the boys call me that because it's a title they understand for a man with some education, even self-education, and it's a title they don't know many black men that have. But it doesn't mean the same thing when you say it."

"*Mr.* Matthews, then. It's not that we don't sympathize with your upbringing. I grew up on the South Side, too."

"Sure." Washington snorted. "Bronzeville, right?"

Owens gave him a cool glare. "Still not Lincoln Park. I had my share of troubles. But just because you came from an underprivileged neighborhood—"

"See, right there, that's part of the problem. You aren't even using the right language. An 'underprivileged neighborhood' you can ignore. A *ghetto* you have to do something about. This here, this is the ghet-to." Washington turned from the alderman to look at Adam Kent. The man held his gaze, though it was hard to read anything in his eyes. But at least he hadn't walked away. "When you came to me, you said that you had pulled yourself up from nothing. That you wanted to make it easier for others to do the same. You said you needed someone who knew the way the street really worked." He shrugged. "What did you expect?"

Kent nodded barely. "I suppose that's fair." He folded his hands on his knees. "Still, you have to understand. This is half a million dollars we're talking about."

"I *do* understand." Washington fought the urge to use his preacher voice. "That money can buy food, education, and support for the boys in this neighborhood. It can give these kids something. Teach them that the world is bigger than Crenwood. I had to go to prison to learn that."

Kent chewed on his lip. "Tell me about it."

"What? Prison?"

"Why you went."

*A roar, and a hot punch against his hand. Blood spatter like a red mist.*

"I killed a boy." He felt stiff, his eyes far away. "I didn't mean to, but I did. Wasn't even an enemy of mine. Just somebody's little brother, got in the way."

"It was an accident?"

"I was in a gang, I carried a gun." Washington shrugged, his shoulders heavy. "Accident isn't the right word."

"What happened?"

*The boy with the cauliflower ear spinning, slow, a last pirouette. Falling. A pause while the whole world drew a breath.*

"It . . . doesn't matter."

"It might."

Washington sighed, shook his head to clear visions of that long ago day. "You know what happened? I picked up the gun. Ten years old, I swore myself to the Blackstone Ranger Nation, and I picked up the gun. Once you do that, life is just a clock ticking away. And before I put the gun down, I killed a boy and cost myself twelve years." The room felt claustrophobic, and he fought the urge to stand. "The specifics don't matter. What I did, it's done. It was real. I can't take it back. There's only two things I can do. I can promise never to pick up the gun again, not for anything. And I can help other boys put it down. Which is what I've done for fourteen years. It's why I came back." He stopped to gather his thoughts, realized he'd said all he had to say. "So it's up to you, Mr. Kent, and you, Alderman Owens. You're both good men. You make the decision."

For a long moment, the two of them stared. Washington sat straight, kept his eyes level, fought to the urge to beg, to say again how much good the money could do, how his boys were counting on it, knowing that anything he said now would be a waste.

Then the alderman looked at Kent, and raised an eyebrows. Kent shrugged. "Well, I guess if you're running a long con, it's the longest one in history." He smiled, then laughed. "Maybe I'm crazy, but I'm still going to give you the money."

Washington only realized his mouth was hanging open when he tried to speak. "Thank you."

"Two conditions." Kent counted them on his fingers. "First, I get veto power on expenditures over, say, a grand. Second, I want to be on the board of directors."

"The veto's no problem. But we don't have a board of directors."

Kent opened his briefcase and removed a ledger. Scribbled with a silver pen. "You do now." He tore off the check and handed it to Washington with a smile. "I made my money because I educated myself on every aspect of the business, and then went and fought for what I wanted. And I don't see why this should be any different. Because you're right. This isn't an underprivileged neighborhood, is it?"

Washington stared at the check. A five, followed by five zeroes. Jesus wept. Five zeroes. Half a *million* dollars. More money than he'd make in fifteen years at the library. Something bloomed in Washington's chest. "No sir." All these years, all the evil he'd seen, and people still could manage to surprise him with the good. "It's not."

They chatted for a few more minutes, details for the party on Friday night, logistics. The check lay on the table right beside the sheet with his prison record. After a few minutes, Kent looked at his watch, and Washington walked them to the door.

"Mr. Matthews," the alderman said, "so you know, this wasn't personal. I wasn't looking for that information, and it, well, it took me by surprise when I found it." Owens hesitated. "I'm very glad of what you're doing. No hard feelings, I hope?"

Washington supposed maybe he should be angry with the man, but couldn't find it in himself. "No hard feelings." Some debts weren't paid in money, and some were never truly paid at all. The boy with the cauliflower ear would walk with him for the rest of his life. And when he died, he expected to find the boy waiting.

Couldn't blame him, either.

He stood at the door and watched the men walk to a Lincoln Towncar, handmade Italian dress shoes crunching broken glass on the sidewalk. After they pulled away, he walked back to his den, dropped in his tired chair. Feeling worn but good. The war he fought had no end, and he knew he was on the losing side. He'd known that going in, but it was never easy to fight when victory was impossible.

But at least every now and then he won a battle.

# CHAPTER 16
Derailed

"*White* guys?" Cruz leaned forward, stopped twirling her pen.

"Yeah," Palmer said. He looked ragged, dark pits blooming under restless eyes. "That's what Billy said."

"He's sure?"

Palmer shrugged. "He's eight, not color blind."

White guys. Another piece that didn't fit. Something was wrong here, and it had her stomach knotted. First, Michael Palmer's assertion of a conspiracy and his promise to deliver evidence, only to end up murdered less than a week later. Then the warning from Donlan. And after that, she'd arrived at work to hear about the attack at Michael Palmer's house the previous night, the 911 call, and report of gunfire.

Hence her stomach. "Where's Billy now?"

"In the breakroom. I wanted to spare him as much of," Palmer waved his hands in a gesture that took in the whole station, "*this* as I could. It's been a rough couple of days."

"Yeah, I bet." Cruz leaned back. "These white guys. Any idea who they are?"

He shook his head. "Not a clue. I only saw the gangbangers. The one I'd been calling Soul Patch, that you say is named Playboy." He nodded to the stack of photos on her desk, shots of known Gangster Disciples members and associates. Playboy glowered a *Fuck You* from the top of the pile. "What's with these guys' names?"

"Monikers. Like nicknames. Usually they pick ones that

make them sound tough. We had a guy in here last year called himself Anthrax." She cocked her head. "I thought you Army guys had them, too."

"Only in Vietnam movies."

"You recognize anybody else?"

"No. I didn't get a good look at the other two last night, and the short one, the wrestler, he's not here."

The hit on Playboy was something, at least. Playboy, real name Louis Freeman, was a good lead—Gangster Disciples number two, a couple of priors for assault and weapons charges, suspicion of involvement in a stack of shootings. She'd spoken to him before, and he was smarter than a lot of his boys, which meant he might have had the initiative to pull something like this.

Only problem was, he wasn't white.

When the pieces didn't fit, you had two choices. Look for a new one that did, or push hard on the ones you had. "You still have no idea what they want with you?"

"Like I told you. They were after Billy."

"Uh-huh." She squinted. Paused. "It's just that I don't understand how all this fits together. I mean, your brother being killed by gangbangers, that would make sense. But if it was white guys, then why were the bangers after you? And why would they come after his *kid*?" Her gun was weighing down the side of her slacks, and she shifted. Clicked the pen. "See what I'm getting at?"

Palmer kept his hands in his lap, a wary expression on his face. "Not really, no."

"There has to be something else, some connection." Click-click. "I understand protecting your brother's memory, but if Michael was into something shady, I need to know about it."

"No way." He shook his head. "Not my brother."

She switched tacks. "Jackie says hi."

"Who?"

"Jackie." Click-click. "Your girlfriend from the other night? She confirms you were with her all night and yesterday morning. But when I mentioned to her that you'd left the Army, she seemed surprised to hear it."

He leaned back, crossed his arms over his chest. "Yeah."

"Mind if I ask the circumstances of your departure?"

"Actually, yeah, I do."

She cocked her head. "Was that some sort of a sore point between you and your brother? Did he disapprove?" Following it out of habit, digging.

"Why are you going after me, lady?" He stared at her. "You *know* I didn't do it. Are you trying to prove something to yourself?"

She started to snap at him. Then wondered if he was right. "I'm just being thorough."

"What you're doing is hassling me, when you should be out arresting Soul Patch. I mean Playboy. Whatever his fucking name is."

Cruz leaned back. "I'm looking into every angle."

"Including him?"

"Yes." She gave him a steady gaze, waited for him to ease up. When he did, she reminded herself to do the same. Yes, something strange was going on, and no, she didn't have any idea what it was. But she didn't believe he was involved. "I've spoken to some of my informants already. And I'll visit the bangers this afternoon, both Gangster Disciples and some of the other sets."

"You can do that?" He seemed surprised.

"Talk to bangers? Of course. I'm police."

"But, I mean—they tell you things?"

"They rarely give up their crew. But it's a small world. And they're cagey, but not rocket scientists." She leaned forward. "Now, what did these white guys look like?"

He took a deep breath, then rubbed the back of his neck with one hand while he told her. She scribbled notes. Not much to go on—one thin and plain-looking with dark hair going gray, the other a scary-looking Italian, muscular and balding.

"Should Billy talk to a sketch artist or something?"

Cruz smiled. "That's cop show stuff. People don't really see each other—how big was the nose, how high was the forehead. Sketches end up looking like a composite of everybody in the room. And that's when it's an adult doing it. With a kid . . . ."

He pursed his lips. "So how are you going to track these guys down?"

"From a description? No names, no license plate, no fingerprints?" She laughed. "I'm not."

"But—"

"The point of this is that if we can get suspects, Billy will be able to identify them. He can put them at the scene where your brother died. But *finding* them? Nine million people in the Chicago area, a lot of them white."

"That the best you can do?"

She hit him with the stare again.

"I'm sorry. I'm just—" He slumped back, brushed bangs from his eyes. "I don't understand this." There was a weird, appealing combination of strength and vulnerability in his pose, part soldier, part schoolboy, and she found herself wondering what it would be like to have a drink with him. Maybe one of those sexy River North lounges, both of them on a second martini. It was an odd thought, out of left field, and it annoyed her, so she pushed it aside and spun it into concern. "I'm sorry about your brother. He seemed like a good man."

He nodded, then a darker expression came across his face. "Do I have to . . ." He stopped. "Do you need me to—"

"No." She spoke softly. "We've identified him from dental records. You can see him if you want to. But I wouldn't recommend it."

"Should I be planning something? You know, for his . . . body?"

"He's with the medical examiner now," she said, choosing her words carefully. "They're trying to see what we can learn about how he died. In a couple of days, they'll release him to the funeral home of your choosing. You should start thinking about what kind of service to have."

"How can I?"

"I know it's a lot to deal with, but the funeral director will help—"

"No, I mean, how can I have a service? How do I know a group of gangbangers won't show up for Billy?"

Cruz opened her mouth, closed it. After a moment, she said, "I'll be there."

He nodded, eyes panning the room, falling across the cramped desk she shared with another officer, the good-enough-for-government fluorescent lighting, the ancient computer. He said, "I need your help. We need some sort of police protection."

"Police protection?"

"For Billy."

She winced. One of those moments when the realities of the job were disappointing. On television, they'd have a safe house guarded by snipers, a fifty-inch television on the wall and ice cream in the fridge. "I can ask patrol cars to spin down the block more often. The Crenwood rotation is pretty heavy, so you'd see a lot of them. Once or twice an hour, maybe more."

"Once an *hour?*"

She raised her shoulders, held her hands in front of her. "There's not much else I can do. You're welcome to stay here until this is settled."

"Here."

"Yes."

"In the police station."

She shrugged.

"Unbelievable." He shook his head. "He's eight. You know that? Eight."

"I'm sorry."

He stood up. "If you're not going to protect Billy, then I will."

"Mr. Palmer." She stood, too, put steel in her voice. "Don't do anything stupid. Leave the criminals to us."

"You think I'm out to solve a crime, lady?" He looked ragged and tired, but his eyes blazed. "I'm trying to protect my family. That's all I care about."

"Jason." She said it softly, hoping to defuse this, to keep

him compliant. She could stuff him in a holding cell, but didn't want to. "I care about that, too."

His hands squeezed into fists, and his lips went white. He stared at her for a long moment. "Terrific," he said.

Then he turned on his heel and stormed away, back straight and shoulders clenched. She thought about calling after him, telling him to stay. Ordering it. Instead, she flopped down in her chair. The star on her belt felt heavy.

"You know what I blame?" Tom Galway rocked his chair back on two legs. Between the neat suit and the salt-and-pepper hair, her partner looked more like an orthodontist than a Gang Intel Sergeant. "*CSI.*"

"Huh?" Cruz looked up from her laptop.

"All these cop shows with elaborate plots. You know, the vic is killed with a potato masher, fashion models with badges talk to twelve people, shine that mysterious blue light all over, it turns out it was the guy's scoutmaster he hadn't seen in ten years."

She laughed. "So you don't buy it?" Cruz had filled him in on all the weird vibes from the case. "You were there, you heard what Michael Palmer had to say."

He snorted. "Yeah, and I liked him, too. More polite than most crazies."

"All that stuff about the gangs being part of a larger problem, his claim there was evidence. You think he was making that up?"

"No, he was one hundred percent correct. The gangs *are* part of a larger problem. It's called being dead-ass broke. Evidence of that ain't hard to see." Galway shrugged. "Look, your victim spoke against the gangs. He lived in a gang neighborhood, and died in a bar in gang territory. A Gangster Disciple went after his brother and his son. And not just any Disciple, but Playboy, a shithead we *know* has dropped bodies. Why make this complicated?"

He had a point. But still. "What about the kid's description?"

"A day late and a dollar short. What is he, eight? He's scared out of his mind, probably remembering something from TV. And you can't put an eight-year-old on the stand. Public defender would tear you a new orifice. Besides," Galway looked around, then leaned forward. "I was talking to the lieutenant earlier."

She set down her pen, prepared herself.

"Palmer was an activist," Galway continued. "The press hasn't picked up the story yet, but they will. The chief, the superintendent, they're getting crazy pressure. Hell, Alderman Owens called to say he wants a gangbanger in cuffs on the evening news."

"*Alderman Owens* is involved?" This case just got better and better.

Galway nodded. "He won on a promise to fight gang violence. This doesn't make him look good." He gave her a look that wasn't hard to read. It said, *Danger.* It said, *Cover your ass.* She flashed back to breakfast with Donlan, his none-too-subtle warning. Telling her that this was a heater, not to mess it up on some half-ass theory. Telling her she'd regret it if she did.

She felt a vein pulse in her forehead. "So what you're saying is we're in the middle of a shitstorm."

"What do you mean, 'we,' white girl? It's your case." Galway winked as he stood up. He took his vest from the back of the chair and put it on. "Look, jokes aside, can I give you some advice, partner-to-partner? The powers that be want to clear this quick. This is a chance to earn their gratitude. And Playboy would look awfully good in handcuffs. Maybe," he said, tightening the straps on his Kevlar, "good enough to get you off database duty."

As he walked out, she fought an urge to sweep the stack of folders off her desk. Instead, she leaned back, stared at the ceiling tiles. Picked up a pen and clicked it open, closed, openclosed. When had things gotten so complicated? Criminals were usually stupid, generally arrogant, often drunk or high. They loaded their weapons barehanded, leaving casings with fingerprints. They smoked two seams of dust and shotgunned a liquor store owner to get money for a third. They murdered each other for spray painting on the wrong wall.

What they didn't do was operate in elaborate plots.

Still, something was going on. Michael Palmer killed after talking to her about a gang. Apparently, killed by white guys, even though black gangbangers had later gone after his kid. And add to that the warnings from Donlan and Galway, the political pressure.

Cruz opened her bottom desk drawer, took out her vest. Put it on, checked her pistol, her star. Hesitated, then dug out her backup piece, a "mini-Glock" in an ankle holster. Going through the motions, preparing herself to hit the street and look for Playboy. All the while inhabited by a weird nervousness, a sense that things were moving beyond her control. It was starting to feel like she was on a train that had derailed, left the tracks to hurtle through space.

True, she hadn't felt an impact yet.

But that didn't mean it wasn't coming.

# CHAPTER 17
Tumors

They were on their own.

Goddamnit.

Outside the police station the sun beat on Jason's back. Cars hummed by on the Dan Ryan. Billy looked up, his eyes wide, and in them Jason saw that fear was only barely restrained, and felt the weight of that.

The cops couldn't help. He was all that stood between his nephew and the men who wanted to kill him.

*First things first, soldier. You need a place to go.* Where, though? If the bangers had found Michael's home, they might be able to find his apartment. He needed a place where no one would look for them. But what were they supposed to do, live out of hotels for the rest of their lives?

The answer came like a smile. "Billy," he said, "let's go see an old friend."

The drive was short, but rife with weird milestones. Jason hadn't been back to the street where he'd grown up in years. He passed his old house, still leaning like a drunk about to fall off his stool. Siding spotted yellow, concrete crumbling, but the flowers tended. He was glad to see that. Someone making a go of it.

"You'll like this guy," he said, glancing over at Billy. "He was really important to me when I was growing up. To your dad, too. His name is Washington."

His nephew looked at him like he was crazy, said, "I know Uncle Washington."

Somehow that made things worse. Michael had been gone a day, and Jason was already realizing that as well as he'd known his brother, he hadn't known him at all.

Washington's house was as he remembered it, a three-flat with a fading wrought iron fence and tired curtains in the windows. But beside the steps to the porch there now hung a sign that read "The Lantern Bearers," and under that:

**R**espect
**E**mpowerment
**P**ride

He led Billy up the steps, feeling like he was walking through an old dream. A stringy kid with pocked cheeks answered the door, listened dubiously, and then told them to hang on. Jason ruffled Billy's hair. The screen door dimmed the view into the house. He saw a figure moving, and his head went light. It hadn't hit him until this moment who he was about to see, or how long it had been.

Then the door flew open. "Oh, thank God." Washington dropped to a knee to wrap Billy in an embrace. "I was worried."

"I'm okay," Billy's voice was muffled by Washington's shoulder. "Uncle Jason has been taking care of me."

Jason shifted on his feet, strangely nervous. It had been years. And the moment felt awkward; he hadn't expected Washington to go straight for Billy. He hesitated, then smiled. "Hello, old man."

Washington straightened, squared himself off in front of Jason. "So." He wore a beard now, and the lines around his eyes were a little deeper. "The prodigal son returns."

For a long moment, they just stared at each other. Then Washington broke into a wide grin, his eyes bright. He spread his arms, and Jason stepped into them, the two of them grinning and clapping each other on the back.

"Welcome home."

Jason closed his eyes and hugged him harder. Then stepped away, one hand on the shoulder of the closest thing he had to a father. His lips pinched in a solemn frown. "You've heard?"

Washington nodded. "Word on the street goes faster than light. You all right?"

"Yeah. I don't know. I should have been there." He paused. "We need to talk."

"Yes." Washington cut his eyes to Billy. "Later, though."

They stood silent for a moment. Jason wanting to ask for something, but not sure what. Help? Forgiveness? For Washington to make it better? He looked away. Then he felt something warm tugging at his arm.

Billy looked up at him. "Can I go inside and see Ronald?"

"Who's Ronald?"

"He's my friend. He can pick me up with one hand."

Jason looked at Washington, saw the nod, said, "Sure thing, kiddo." Billy grinned and dashed inside, his heels flashing. It stabbed Jason's chest. For a moment, Billy had looked just like any normal kid.

"So," Washington made the word sound like a grunt as he settled back in his chair and put his feet up on the porch railing.

They'd arrived in late afternoon, but now, nearly eight o'clock, was the first chance to really talk. Jason hadn't seen the old man in years, and in that time Washington had transformed himself from a librarian who tutored local kids into a full-fledged activist. The house Jason remembered visiting as a teenager had become a cross between an afterschool center and a clubhouse, with former gangbangers washing dishes in the kitchen and studying for the GED in the living room. Washington seemed to be everywhere at once, talking to "his boys," taking meetings, spending hours on the phone.

The delay had turned out to be a good thing. It gave Jason a chance to hang with Billy, to distract the boy from the rest of the world. He'd taught his nephew all the jokes he knew, the clean ones at least, and the two of them had spent the afternoon getting schooled in basketball by teenaged killers.

Now though, with Billy tucked in early and the sky fading to purple, Jason couldn't avoid his own mind anymore. "So."

"Are you okay?"

Jason shrugged. "I don't know."

"He was a good man."

"Yes." Jason felt a buildup of electricity. He still hadn't cried for his brother, and he was starting to hate himself for it. He took a belt of gin, watched bugs loop the streetlights. Tried to think of something to say. "You still working at the library?"

"Not much longer."

"Better job?"

"This one, actually." Washington took a sip of his gin. "You heard of a man called Adam Kent?"

"Nope."

"Started an import business out of his garage twenty years ago, now he's a multimillionaire. Night after tomorrow he's hosting a benefit dinner for us, and he's giving half a million dollars from his own pocket."

"Half a million?" Jason whistled. "Jesus."

Washington nodded. "Going to make a world of difference. Right now, we're running on scraps and prayers. I lose a lot of boys could be helped."

Jason took another sip of the liquor. Felt that male discomfort, wanting to say something but the words weird. "You helped me."

"You didn't need much. Just a little direction."

"Still. I was sliding. I mean rebellion is one thing, but stealing televisions?" He shook his head. "If you hadn't kicked my ass, I might have gone the wrong way."

Washington leaned forward with the bottle and refilled both their glasses. Somewhere a siren screamed.

"I should have come before," Jason said.

"I was wondering if you would. Your brother told me you were out of the service."

Jason grimaced, stood, walked to the porch railing. Opposite the house was an abandoned lot. When he'd lived down the block there used to be an old playground carousel out there, a rusty metal circle that spun on a central point. He and Michael would grab hold and run as fast as they could, then jump on, watch the world blur around them. "I thought about it." He closed his eyes, saw Martinez, opened them fast. "Just that things . . . haven't worked out so well for me."

"How do you mean?"

"I didn't *leave* the Army. I was discharged." The sky had grown too dark to show whether the carousel still sat amidst the weeds. Jason tried not to think about the words. " 'Other than honorable,' they call it. For 'patterns of misconduct.' It's a pretty common way to drum somebody out. They do it to a lot of guys who admit to having PTSD. Not the same as dishonorable, but not good."

"You want to talk about it?"

"No." From a distant car he caught a snatch of music, something Latin and pretty, appropriate for a night so thick with heat. He sighed. "I made a mistake."

"What kind?"

"The kind where people die."

Washington said nothing. The old man had always been good at that.

"I disobeyed an order," Jason said. "I was a sergeant, and I ordered my men somewhere they weren't supposed to be. One of them got killed."

The Worm slid between his ribs and his heart, a nauseous slippery feeling.

"That's a hard load, son."

Jason sipped his gin, stared into the darkness. "Harder for the guy who died." So much had happened in so short a time, he felt battered, like a heavy bag worked over by a boxer. He blew a breath, brushed the bangs from his sweating brow. Turned and leaned back against the railing. "You see Michael a lot?"

"He brought Billy over plenty of weekends. Helped out, threw us a fundraiser once a year in the bar. But he always wanted to be more aggressive. Wanted the community to fight back, to go after the gangs directly. And he didn't like the politics and fundraising. Said people just gave money so they felt okay about ignoring the problem."

"Is that true?"

Washington shrugged. "Son, I don't much care. Kids are dying out here. The money helps."

Jason nodded. That sounded like Michael, to draw a line in black and white, not be able to see the shades of gray between. It was one of the things that had always made it difficult between them, the way Mi—

*Crack!*

The sound was loud and sharp, and Jason acted without thinking, body moving to a combat stance, jerking the Beretta from beneath his shirt, his eyes wide, searching for motion or muzzle flare, ready to spring in any direction. Neck tingling, senses raging, palms sweaty but sure against the grip.

Nothing

happened.

It took a moment of standing weapon-ready before Jason remembered where he was. How often he'd heard that sound as a kid, always far enough away that he could never be sure if it was a gun or a car backfiring or a cherry bomb. It was a city phenomenon, especially on the South Side, just one of those things you got used to. He felt a flush of heat in his face, a vein in his forehead. He stared into the darkness, afraid to turn around.

Then, from behind, "You want to tell me why you brought a gun to my house?"

Jason sighed. Snapped on the safety and tucked the pistol away, still looking out into the twilight. "I'm sorry."

"Sorry's no kind of answer." The softness was gone from Washington's voice.

Jason nodded. Turned slowly, pulled out a chair, and told the man the whole story, from Playboy on. It took nearly an hour, and Washington didn't say a word until he was done. Just sat stonefaced and alert. When it was all over, he said, "I don't like guns."

"I'm sorry."

"I won't have it in my house."

"I'll leave it in the car. I'll take it there now, if you want."

Washington stared at him. "You do that before you walk through my door. And lock it in the trunk, you hear?" When Jason nodded, Washington leaned back. He took a slow sip of gin, stared into the distance. "You said it was Playboy come after you?"

"You know him?" After the afternoon he'd had, Jason supposed he shouldn't be surprised. Washington obviously knew most everything going on in the neighborhood.

"He's a Gangster Disciple, a soldier. Second in command."

"Second in command? He was like twenty-three."

"Gangs recruit young. A thirty-year-old thinks before he pulls the trigger. A fifteen-year-old don't."

"Is Playboy somebody who might come after Michael for talking to the police?"

"Sure. But you said the men Billy saw were white."

"Yeah." Jason put his feet on the railing. "I don't know who they were." He rubbed his eyes, black stars popping. "Hell, I don't even know what's going on out here."

"What's going on?" Washington shrugged. "Things are getting worse. That's the nature of things. You know that nearly *fifty percent* of black boys drop out of high school? I'm talking city of Chicago. A whole generation, and we're failing them."

"Who's failing them? I didn't force them to drop out of school. And I sure as shit didn't ask them to come after my family," Jason said. "What about their parents?"

"Parent, son. Usually just a mom alone, working two minimum-wage jobs, bringing in maybe four hundred a week. Can't afford daycare, can't afford books or a computer, and she ain't never *there*. Kid doesn't have a home, school is failing him, the streets are rough, what choice he got but to pledge a set?"

"Bullshit." He was a guest, but he couldn't let that go, not after the last days. "I grew up down the block. You know my dad split. Mom had *three* jobs. Michael and I both worked, bought our own clothes from when we were twelve. Everybody's got a choice. They join because Tupac or Snoop Dogg or whoever else says it's cool. Join a gang, you get to ride around with a gun, women falling all over to climb in your Benz."

Washington shook his head. "You know how much a kid makes slinging rock? Nine, ten bucks an hour. Suburban kids make that at Starbucks, don't have to worry about nothing but burning their fingers. They don't join up for the money."

"Lemme guess. They join up for their community, stand against the white man."

"There's a black-white thing, sure, but not the way you mean."

"So why then?"

"For respect," said a low voice from behind them.

Jason whirled. The man in the door was menacing as hell: two-fifty, six-something, with arms of carved granite and hair tightly braided to his skull. "Got nothing, goin' nowhere. But if they join a crew, then they famous. Rising ghetto stars. Nobody can mess with them, 'cause they belong."

"Jason Palmer, Ronald Wilson." Washington gestured from one to the other.

Jason stood and they shook, Jason expecting the guy to crush his fingers, surprised to find the grip firm but not macho. "You're Billy's friend."

Ronald broke into a smile. "Bills is fun. Hold him upside down for an hour, he still wants more." He stepped onto the porch. As the light fell across his forearms, Jason jerked backwards. He bumped the chair, and it teetered, then fell with a crack.

"Easy." Washington was on his feet and between them.

Ronald's gaze was calm. "Problem?"

"You tell me." Jason pointed at Ronald's arm, where a six-pointed star writhed in flames, surrounding the letters GD. The same tattoo Playboy had, or damn close.

Ronald nodded, lifted his arm and rolled it back and forth in the light. "My set mark. I was Fifty-fourth Street Gangster Disciples."

"You were."

"Yeah."

"Not anymore."

"Left almost four years ago." He tilted his head sideways. "Dr. Matthews helped me. I'd like to get rid of the ink, but can't afford it yet."

Jason blew air through his mouth. "Sorry, man." Shook his head. "Been a long couple days."

"So Bills said."

Washington eased out from between them, his eyes on Jason. "Ronald is my right hand. He's an example of what can happen if we work with kids instead of ignoring them. Helps me in a hundred ways, and even the new boys know not to mess with him."

"I can see why." Jason bent down, picked his chair up. "So, respect? That it?"

"Pretty much."

"Doesn't seem like enough."

"Why? It's not that different," Washington looked at Jason, "than finding a family in the Army."

He flushed. "It's goddamn worlds different."

Ronald spoke, his voice sounding like it came from a cavern a thousand years undisturbed. "I don't know 'bout the Army. But grow up around here, sometimes a set seems like all there is. I did my first shooting at thirteen, started selling dope about that time. Had a son when I was sixteen. His mama took him when she left. Back then, I didn't care. Just banged harder. I didn't need a son. My crew was my world. Till somebody gunned down my little brother. Took that for me to start seeing different." He fell silent, leaving just the night and the heat and the sound of men breathing.

"You see what I mean?" Washington finally asked. "Life for these kids is accelerated. Their whole world, it's burning."

"So what's the point?" Jason may have grown up a block away, but this wasn't his world. Never had been. Maybe because he'd never really considered the neighborhood home. Maybe something in the way he'd been raised, or the way he and Michael looked out for each other, or simply that his mother's white skin had helped her get jobs above minimum wage, even if she still needed three of them. Whatever the reason, somehow he'd sidestepped all of this. Teenagers killing each other over pieces of colored cloth, pretending bandannas were uniforms. "Why not just get out? Both of you?"

Washington stared, a long gaze that made Jason uncomfortable, like the old man was seeing through him. Jason took a slug of gin, his head throbbing heat and booze. The moment dragged on. When Washington finally spoke, his voice was soft. "You ever hear the story of the Rutupiae Light?"

"That a gang?"

"History, son." Washington shook his head. "In the fourth century, Britain was one of the most civilized places in the world. Culture, literacy, medicine, social rights, all the things we think of as advanced. There was a huge lighthouse at Rutupiae, where Dover is now, and every night they lit it. Mostly to guide ships, but it was symbolic too. So long as that lighthouse burned, Britain's enemies knew Rome protected the country.

"But it was hard times for the Empire. The glory days were behind, and they had enemies of their own. Eventually, they ordered their troops out, left Britain at the mercy of the Saxons. Barbarians. Painted their faces blue, drank blood, raided and raped and enslaved. That bad. Without the Legions, Britain was doomed.

"But there's a story says that the night the Legions sailed for Rome, a group of soldiers deserted. It was suicide. They were vastly outnumbered, couldn't possibly win. But they stayed, and they lit the Rutupiae Light."

"Hoping to fool the Saxons?" Jason snorted. "They couldn't've pulled that off for long. What, they died to keep a lighthouse going for a night or two?"

"That's one way to look at it." A gentle smile tugged at the edge of Washington's mouth. "Another is that faced with the end of a dream, they chose to stay and fight. To hold the darkness back. Even if only for a night or two." He glanced at Ronald like a professor calling on a student. "Know what they were called?"

The big man nodded toward the sign. "The Lantern Bearers."

Jason felt a wave of self-contempt. What an asshole he was. The Worm writhed within, its teeth pulling hunks of him. "Yeah."

Washington smiled, lowered himself into the chair next to Jason. Patted his knee. "People always talk about the 'Fall of Rome,' like one day there was a thud." Shook his head. "Didn't happen that way. Empires die slow and from the inside. Like cancer." He gestured at the darkened street, gin slopping inside the glass. "Like here. At the city's edge. We're covered with tumors, but nobody's looking."

Jason ran a hand across the back of his neck, massaged the sticky flesh. A breeze had picked up, warm and sweet with lilac and a hint of rotting trash. He thought of Billy, asleep with his thumb in his mouth, still wearing the Army T-shirt. Helpless. Trusting. Hunted. "Would it be okay if Billy stayed with you for a little while?"

"Of course." Washington stroked his mustache. "Why?"

Jason stood up and leaned against the railing, his back to the night. "I need to know everything you can tell me about the Gangster Disciples."

Washington's eyes narrowed. "Community interest?"

Jason smiled. "Recon." It felt right to say it. If Washington could rage against the darkness, if Ronald could, then he damn well could, too. "I'm going to stay and fight. Like you said."

Washington stared up, his face expressionless. Calculating. The smile withered on Jason's lips. A long and pregnant pause fell, just the night sounds and the blood in his veins and the booze in his head.

Then Washington stood. "You disappoint me, son."

The words hit like a slap. "What? Why?"

"When have I ever been about violence?"

"I'm not asking you to be. But you're the only one who knows all this stuff, all about the gangs, the neighborhood. I need to know what I'm up against."

"No," Washington said. "You're just acting a goddamn fool. You think that story is about fighting? You think I was trying to inspire you to march up to Playboy, pull your gun, prove how tough you are?" He shook his head. "Maybe your brother was right. Maybe you shouldn't have joined the army, that's all you learned."

Jason blinked, held his hands open at waist level. Watching Washington walk away. The man took three heavy steps, then pulled the old screen door, its hinges screeching. There was something in the way he turned his back on Jason, dismissed him, that made his anger flare, made words spill out. "That's it? You're not about violence, and that's the end of it?"

Washington pivoted, one hand propping the door open, eyes burning in the dim light. "That's right, son. I've been down that road. You know I have. I'll never do it again, and I won't help you do it."

"Somebody murdered my brother. Tried for my nephew. But I should just turn the other cheek." Jason shook his head. "You know the problem with that? Christ got his ass *beat,* old man. So forgive me if I want to fight back." He set the gin glass down hard, and warm liquid splashed onto the railing. "I'm asking for your help. If you don't have the guts, fine, bury your head in the sand. But I'm going to fight for Billy. He's all I've got and I'm not going to let anyone hurt him."

For a long moment they stared at each other, Jason and the closest thing he had to a father. Then Washington turned away. "Don't bring that gun in my house." He stepped through the screen door and let it slam behind him.

In the sudden silence, the insects seemed very loud.

Jason spun, anger already turning to something uglier, something the Worm liked. Took the rest of gin in a gulp. Fuck it. All of it. If it was him against the world, so be it. Maybe that was the way it had always been, and only now was he seeing it clear.

He'd forgotten Ronald was even on the porch until he heard the voice. "You know, my mama used to read me the Bible." The big man moved over to lean on the railing. His arms were knotted cordwood.

Jason sighed. "Yeah?"

The man nodded. "I liked the Old Testament. Isaac and Abraham. Moses."

"I never actually read it." Through the open window of a neighboring house, Jason heard angry voices, a man and a woman bitching with the casual anger of habit. He was back to nothing. The cops wouldn't help him. His friends wouldn't help him. His brother was dead. He was alone against enemies he didn't even understand. Hell, enemies he couldn't even identify.

"Never cared much for the New Testament, though." Ronald's voice was calm. "Mama was always on about Jesus, but I felt like you. Easy enough to turn the other cheek when your father's God, right?" He shrugged. "Me, I never knew my daddy."

Something in his tone caught Jason. He turned away from the darkness. "Ronald, there something you're trying to tell me?"

The big man smiled. "Just that Dr. Matthews isn't the only one knows the neighborhood."

# CHAPTER 18
## A Thousand Murders

There was parking closer to Dion's ratty-ass excuse for a headquarters—clubhouse was more like it, teenaged bangers sprawled all over the crumbling porch—but then Anthony DiRisio would have missed the march of a thousand murders.

Just past noon, and the brutal sun had driven the monkeys out of their shitboxes. They lounged on steps, stood on street corners with their shirts off. Musclebound homeboys flying colors openly, blue bandanas in pockets, baseball caps twisted to the right. Ten-year-olds trying out their war faces, baby fat and killer's eyes. And through it all, that hate, a burning black thread that stunk like sewage.

Anthony smiled, put all his contempt into it. Skydiving was for wimps. He measured his dick in hatred.

He walked slow, met stares. Some of them knew who he was, gave a grudging nod. The others read him for a cop, a detective, untouchable. Most just saw others give way and so they followed suit. Herd reflexes.

Anthony strolled along, knowing that his car would be untouched, that none of them would make a move on him. Buoyed by hate, he floated from the end of the block to the sagging bungalow. Greasy hip-hop flowed like smoke from the windows. Kids on the steps passed a thick blunt, the sweet tang of dope rising in the summer heat. Two OGs stood under the porch roof and watched him come, and he held their gaze every step, body alive, cells vibrating.

"To-nay D." The guy managed to make a Northern Italian name sound black. His eyelids drooped low, like Anthony wasn't worth the trouble of really seeing. "C-Note's waitin'."

Anthony smiled without using his eyes, climbed the steps, making the kids get out of his way. After the brutal sun, the interior was dim, and he paused for his eyes to adjust. Blue sheets had been nailed over the windows in lieu of curtains, and combined with the smoke, they gave the air an underwater feel. What light made it through seemed disappointed to spill on the battered couches and tattooed gangsters. A sudden silence met his entrance, just the music in the background. Then someone spoke, he turned, saw Al Pacino sitting behind a mound of cocaine.

"Lemme ask you," Anthony said, voice conversational. "You ever get tired of that movie?"

One of the kids on the couch lifted his forty, took a long pull, eyes on Anthony's the whole time. "Naw, *Scarface* is *tight*." He smiled a player's smile. "You ever get tired of those cheap-ass suits?"

That broke the boys up, and they bumped fists.

Anthony smiled. Walked over to stand in front of the kid. Waited for the silence. This close, he could smell the monkey's rank sweat. Let the tension draw out slow, then smiled, reach down slow, took the beer. Tipped it back and poured, the liquid warm and foul, but he kept his throat open, swallowing and swallowing till the bottle was drained. "No," he said, and handed the empty back. "I don't."

The banger laughed, tossed the bottle across the room, where it hit the carpet with a thump. "Don't bother me none, dog." He reached over to the table, grabbed another bottle. "I got plenty more."

"Big Anthony, my nigga." The voice came from the kitchen, where Dion Williams stood with his arms braced against the doorframe.

Anthony nodded, but didn't look away from the kid on the couch. "Hello, Dion."

"This way."

He held the stare for one more moment, then turned and

followed Dion. The kitchen was filthy, every surface covered with bottles and takeout containers, blunts and menthols stubbed out on the counter. A fly buzzed lazy circles over a sink piled with plates. Anthony chose his steps carefully, hands at his sides, not eager to touch anything. Dion opened a door in the back wall, and the two of them stepped into his office, a Chicago-style second bedroom with barely room for the big desk and padded chairs. Anthony always had to fight laughter at the setup, like something bought off the floor at OfficeMax.

Dion settled behind the desk, his palms out on the table, fingers drumming. The motion caused the muscles in his arms to swell and ripple. Anthony sat and stared at him. Waited a long moment. Finally said, "You fix your screwup?"

Dion's eyes narrowed. "We been over that. You brokered that through Playboy, not me."

Anthony shrugged. "Thought he could take care of business. Didn't know you let faggots on your crew, Dion."

The gangbanger's nostrils flared, but he sat silent for a moment. Then said, "First off, you're talking about my boy, so you best ease up. Second," he said, "my name is C-Note."

"Whatever." Anthony let a little contempt into his tone. "You didn't answer my question."

"I sent some of my dawgs over to the address you gave us last night."

"So it's done?" He relaxed a little, leaned back in the chair. "The kid is dead?"

"Nah." Dion fixed him with a hard stare, as if daring him to do something. "Cops came."

Anthony felt that pain in his left temple, fought the urge to rub it. Took a deep breath. "What you're saying, then, is you fucked up again."

"You got one freebie on that tone. Don't try for two." Dion's voice was low. "You in *my* house now."

The threat hit Anthony right in the spine, that sweet tingle, and he almost told "C-Note" to suck his ropy white dick. The man's hands were on the table and even if he were strapped, no way he could pull as fast as Anthony could, his

SIG in a quick-release shoulder holster. But Dion was still useful, at least for now, and so he just smiled, and pictured a bullet taking him in the eye, tearing away half of his head.

The right half, he decided.

"So the boy is still alive."

The gangbanger nodded, then leaned back, his hands behind his head, evidently satisfied at his dominance. "Yeah. But," he drew the word out, "now I'm taking a personal interest, he ain't going to stay that way. Not if you tell me where to find him."

Anthony snorted. "What do I look like, the Yellow Pages?"

"Told us where to find him so far."

"That was before." He tried not to show it, but his mind was racing. The situation had spiral potential. He'd wanted to handle the boy personally, but there were advantages to having the bangers do it, and he'd allowed himself to be convinced. And now the little shit had gotten away—again— and might be talking to who knew which cops.

And there was only one way that could have happened. "Jason Palmer," he said.

"Who?"

"The uncle." It made sense. With his father dead, where else would the kid go? And as a former soldier, Palmer'd have the training to protect him. "The one Playboy screwed up on. You find him, you'll find the kid."

"White boy and a kid somewhere in Chicago?" Dion shrugged dismissively. "I mean, you got a picture or something? I don't even know what this dude looks like."

"Playboy does." Anthony smiled. "And I know where Palmer lives."

"'Aight," Dion said. "I'll hook Playboy up with a couple of soldiers. Your dude won't hardly know what happened to him." He started to rise.

Anthony sat still. "I don't think you understand. You fucked up." He paused for a beat, leaned in. "You need to make it right. I'm not talking about sending a couple of retarded teenagers." He met Dion's glare, still picturing half his head gone, a raw and ragged mess. "Put everything you have on it. Scour the goddamn city. Palmer goes golfing, I want his caddy ready to draw down. I want every nigger here looking for Palmer and the kid."

C-Note's eyes narrowed at the word. But before he could respond, Anthony continued. "You're not my only client, Dion. Hell, I've got a meet tonight." He adjusted his tie. "If you mess this up, I'll hold a fire sale. Dump my supply to your enemies. Your homeboys won't know what hit them. Your crew will be a remember-when." He smiled, his lips tight. "You feel me, boy?"

For a long and happy moment, Anthony thought the jig was going to make a move. Then it passed, C-Note leaning back in his chair like an executive, his face a model of calm. "Disciples finish what they start. I'll get my club rolling."

Anthony nodded, stood up. "Good." Straightened his jacket, shot his cuffs, all business. "Find Jason Palmer and the boy, kill them both." He walked to the door, opened it, then turned. "Dion? This time get it right."

And smiled to see the hate ripple across C-Note's face.

# CHAPTER 19
Alien Cities

Jason had to admit that it was starting to feel like a bad idea.

Tactically speaking, the strongest position was the offensive. So long as your enemy was defending, they couldn't be working toward their own goals. It kept them off balance, kept them reacting to you instead of acting themselves.

That's what they, whoever *they* were, had been doing to him for days. But in the rainbow haze of last night's gin, Jason had thought he'd seen a chance to turn that around. With Washington watching over Billy, Jason could go on the offensive, starting with the only lead he had: Playboy. If Jason could figure out how he was involved, it might lead to the guys who killed Michael.

What he was going to do then was a little murkier. Confront them, look for regret in their eyes? Call Cruz, have her arrest them?

Pull the Beretta and waste them?

If he'd had the gun when the bangers came after Billy, no question. That was combat. He'd been at war before, walked point through alien cities. He'd called the locals Hajji and Ali Baba, same as everybody else, even as he'd tried to do good, same as everybody else. He'd sighted down the length of his M4, remembered his training—exhale, hold, squeeze—felt it kick and watched men fall.

But to hunt a man, touch a pistol to his temple, and blow his world apart? That wasn't soldiering. That was murder.

*One step at a time.* Right now he had to find a way to get to Playboy. Last night, when Jason had suggested he might just stake out the house until he found a chance to hijack Playboy, Ronald had only smiled. This morning, Jason understood why.

This wasn't Lincoln Park, where he could have slept on the sidewalk. It wasn't Clark and Division, a one-block melting pot where he wasn't out of place. It wasn't even the Crenwood he knew, underprivileged and ruined, but largely filled with families struggling to make a go.

It was a war zone.

They weren't all gangbangers, of course, he reassured himself. Not every kid on every corner, every shirtless man glaring at him. The hard stares, daring him to meet their eyes, daring him to look away, it wasn't about him. It was about crushing poverty and four hundred of years of repression. About patrol cars circling like the tanks of an occupying army. About a neighborhood without jobs or opportunity, where college was as accessible as the moon. He'd listened to too many of Washington's lectures, spent too long in a largely black high school not to get that.

But it still felt like mostly they'd like to watch him die.

Jason stopped at a red light alongside a cell phone store, one of the few thriving businesses. A car pulled up next to him, bass throbbing, an angry voice rattling his windows. He didn't look over, but tried not to tense up, just stared at the stoplight.

Ronald had talked for a long time. His knowledge was exhaustive: The leaders of the gang, how it was structured, how they made their money, who they were feuding with, where they were based. That this particular set was run by a guy named Dion Wallace, nicknamed C-Note.

Ronald might not bang anymore, but he clearly remained in touch with the world. Which made Jason wonder why he was helping. After an hour, he asked.

The big man had paused, then nodded up at the window of the room where Billy slept. "I'm helping you help him." He hadn't said anything else, but Jason could see the man was thinking about his own brother, murdered young.

The light changed. It was decision time. Turn right and face his enemies on their turf, or turn left and go have a drink, think of a new plan.

A car honked. He turned right.

At first glance, the street looked like any other. Broken pavement, heat ripples off the brick. A lot of activity for a weekday afternoon, folks lounging on steps and posing on the corner, drinking from paper bags.

Then he pretended he was back in the desert, and looked again, and everything changed. The two shirtless dudes at the end of the block were bullshitting casually enough, but their eyes were active, and each faced a different direction. They had Nextel phones, the ones you could use as walkie-talkies. Lookouts. A couple of little kids hung nearby, lounging against a fence and posturing. Probably runners.

The house sat in the middle of the block, a rundown brick bungalow with a large open porch. A shiver ran down his calves. Five, no, six men on the porch. Four in their late teens, but hardened and staring. The other two were older. They stood with the posture of casual readiness he'd seen in Special Forces boys, men who'd been in Somalia and Afghanistan and Iraq One, who had enough experience with mayhem to think of bullets and blood sprays as simple facts of life, part of the way the world worked.

Screwing with men like that got you killed, that simple.

His stomach felt greasy, and his fingers tingled. Viewed as a soldier, it was a goddamn nightmare. Enemy territory. Guards and watchers. Complicit citizens. Numerous combatants, many armed. Few of them, if Washington was right, expecting to see old age. Street soldiers in a rag-tag army.

He kept the car rolling, trying not to acknowledge the looks. Wanting to slow down, to take mental pictures, but not daring. Mouth dry, palms wet.

March in and try to hijack one of them?

Suicide.

Jason gave the Caddy a little more gas, locked his eyes forward, did his best to look like a civilian who'd gotten lost.

His fingers tapped the wheel, the pulse loud in his throat. Finished the block, turned right, rolled another couple, turned again, found himself back on Halsted, back in the real world. Same neighborhood he'd been circling for an hour, but after the gang block, it seemed tame.

"Jesus," he said to himself, wiping his palms on his jeans. The sun burned through the windshield, sparkles of heat spots on the dusty dashboard. The sinking in his gut was replaced by an acid burn. Those men had been involved in the murder of his brother, had tried to kill his nephew. Now they strutted in the sun of a weekday afternoon, and there wasn't a thing he could do about it.

He realized his teeth were clenched, his jaw sore. A hundred yards ahead lay a corner market, the glass front covered with metal screening. He parked the Caddy in front of the door. Two kids who should've been in school hit him with murder eyes, but he glared back, chest forward. Held the gaze as he stalked past, daring them to move.

The market was dirty linoleum and fridges of beer. A sign on the inch-thick Plexiglas protecting the counter read: LOOSIES, 50 CENT, with a drawing of a cigarette. The back cooler had Coke and Pepsi but also orange and grape pop, brands he didn't recognize. No Gatorade, so he settled for a Mountain Dew.

Back in the sunlight, the kids stood where he'd left them, one on the payphone, the other beside, a wooden match clinging to one moist lip. The sun felt good on Jason's back and neck, so he leaned against the side of the car and stared down the road, watching cars come and go.

Sweet as the soda was, it couldn't wash out the bitter. With Michael gone, he was protector and maybe—Jesus—father to Billy. That last was too scary to contemplate. Better to focus on the first part, on dealing with the people hunting them. The Worm laughed from his belly. Some protector he was turning out to be so far.

A police car pulled into the weed-cracked parking lot. Jason glanced over, then at the two kids on the phone. Their shoulders were up, necks rigid with the stiffness that came of trying to act calm. The one on the phone hung up, and they started to strut away.

"Hey." The cop spoke through the open window, his voice commanding, a practiced tone. "Scooby, right?"

The boys froze, then slowly turned. Hesitated, then strolled over to the squad car like they were doing a favor. "Yeah."

"How's it going?"

"S'aight." Scooby slid the matchstick from one side of his mouth to the other. His friend kept glancing around, like he was hoping they weren't being seen.

"You know we found Li'l Cisco out back of St. Francis's?" The cop cocked his head. "Somebody shot him in the face."

"Ashes to ashes."

"Yeah." The cop smiled. "You hear anything about who was gunning for him?"

"Nah, man."

"Come on. He was your boy, right? Help me out." The cop glanced around, gestured Scooby closer. The kid looked back at his friend, then put his hands on the car, and leaned in. The other cop, a square-jawed woman with the placid expression of someone who did this every day, sized Jason up through the windshield.

She reminded him of Cruz, the way she'd interrogated him yesterday. Just as he'd been about to lose it, she'd eased up. Told him she would work all the angles, talk to the gangs, try to pick up Playboy. It'd surprised him, the idea of this five-five Latina questioning gangbangers on the street. She had some fire.

And then, as he watched Scooby listen to the cop, saw the way his buddy rocked from foot to foot like he needed to piss, an idea hit Jason square and center, made him almost drop his drink.

It was more than a long shot. It was pretty well preposterous.

Jesus, what a ballsy play that would be.

And realized he was smiling.

# *January 11, 1988*

*She knows her body will never be long and willowy, knows she will never have shampoo commercial hair. But it doesn't matter, because now, a month past her fifteenth birthday, Elena Cruz is a woman of the world; she is dating a high school senior, and tonight her mother is out of town.*

*She does not write "Elena Vaughn" on scented paper, or draw crabbed hearts with EC+ EV scrawled in the center, but her dedication is complete. She has tracked Eric Vaughn's slouch through gray hallways, thrilling in his surliness, in his unkempt clothes and his crude tattoo.*

*That he demands they keep their love a secret she chooses to find romantic. It's not that he's cold; he is just wounded, in a way only she can heal. True, he is in a rush that makes her nervous, always trying to put his hands where she isn't ready to have them. But that's proof how badly he needs her.*

*This is love, and love triumphs. Every story says so.*

*And she reminds herself of that when she opens her front door to find not only Eric, but his friend Steve. Reminds herself again when she realizes they are drunk. She even tries to believe it is love that makes dark fire flash in Eric's eyes.*

*But it isn't love that tears her sweater. And it isn't love that laughs as Steve yanks at her belt.*

*And as she watches beautiful Eric Vaughn unbuckle his pants while his best friend holds her from behind, she sees that he knows he has already crossed a line and is determined to make the most of it, more drunk on the moment than the stolen booze. That she is no longer even a person, but merely something he wants.*

*And so she stomps on Steve's foot and twists free. Grabs the cordless phone and dials the police from the bathroom. And waits, shivering, in her panties—the pretty pair she had worn special, that she wanted him to remove for the first time, when she planned to give what he only wanted to take.*

# CHAPTER 20
## Dead Grass

Her mother, with a look of bone-weariness, had once told Elena Cruz that one thing she'd learned was that you should never have more children than arms.

Now, as she watched Keanna bounce a baby on one leg, use her free hand to undo her middle son's jacket, and simultaneously yell at her oldest to leave the dog alone before he got himself bit, it occurred to Cruz that Keanna might have benefited from that same advice. Of course, looking at the blasted park where the nineteen-year-old sat with three other baby-mamas, there were probably a whole lot of things that the formidable Dulcinea Cruz could have passed along. Most likely accompanied by a lecture, several pleas to Jesus, and a paddling with a wooden spoon.

"I don't know nothing about no bars burning," Keanna said, and then held her baby up to the sky, making cooing noises.

Cruz glanced at Galway, who rolled his eyes. She said, "Mind if I sit?"

"They say it's a free country."

Galway chuckled at that, crossed his arms in front of his chest. As Cruz sat on the cement bench, the middle kid, maybe four years old, looked at her with huge eyes. She waggled a finger and he smiled, a sudden devious thing like he'd stolen it, and then turned away quickly and buried his face in his mother's knee. "How you holding up?"

"The phone got turned off." Keanna smiled at the baby. "Ain't you just perfect," she said, and the baby made a gurgling sound. "Mama lost her job."

"Rondell isn't giving you anything?"

Keanna looked at her balefully. "Rondell was daddy to Lawrence." She jerked her head toward the fence where the oldest boy was petting a dog the wrong direction. "He ain't been around since Spider an' me got together."

Cruz nodded, said sure, sorry, she'd forgotten. Hard to keep up sometimes. A low-rider rolled down the block, music pouring out, and one of the mothers hopped up and ran over to it, looking like the seventeen-year-old girl she was.

"Anyway, what you care? You gonna pay the bills?"

"Spider went down on a possession charge, right?" Cruz shrugged. "I could talk to the board for him. Make sure he gets a parole hearing soon."

"Ain't that the Po-Po." The girl snorted, shook her head. "Lock him up, then offer to set him free."

Cruz smiled. "Like I said before, Keanna. A bar. On Damen."

"Lawrence!" The girl twisted all the way around. "Why'n't you leave that dog alone?" She turned back to Cruz. "I told you, I don't know nothing about no bars catching fire."

Galway interrupted. "How about Playboy?"

"What about him?"

"He know anything about it?"

"Ask him."

"Where's he crashing these days?"

"Don't know."

"You don't know?" Cruz added a little edge to her voice. "Disciples number two, and you don't know where he sleeps?"

"I ain't close to it no more. Not since Spider got hisself locked up."

"What about the bar?"

The girl sighed. "Man, y'all is tiresome, asking the same question over and over like this time the answer's gonna be different. I don't know nothing about no bars burning up."

"Think hard." Cruz took her sunglasses off, blinking in

the scorching light of late afternoon, hit the girl with her earnest look. "This is important. We've got the juice. We could help you, help Spider."

"I don't *know* nothing. And besides slinging dope, only thing Spider's good for is making me a baby-mama." The girl looked up at Galway, back to Cruz. "You wanna help?" She shook her head. "Buy groceries."

Cruz snorted. "All right. Thanks for the time." She stood up, put her shades back on. Adjusted her handcuffs. Galway started out of the park, and she fell in beside him.

Behind her, they heard the girl's voice. "Shit's burning down in Crenwood all the time, anyhow. How come y'all so interested in this one?" Keanna raised her voice. "Belong to a white guy or something?"

Galway laughed. Cruz flipped her a wave, walked to the unmarked they'd left at the edge of the park. As Galway opened the passenger door, he said, "So I saw my son last night."

"The Bitch let you visit off schedule?" Cruz had heard so much about Galway's divorce, she sometimes felt like she was the one who'd been left.

"Miracles never cease, right? Anyway, I pull up to her house. Schaumburg. Nice house, nice neighborhood. Aidan mopes out, mumbles hello, starts messing with the radio. His hair is gelled up in different directions, and he's wearing jeans that have holes at the pockets and ragged bottoms. Bleach stains. So I ask him, I say, 'Aidan, what's with the jeans? Won't your mom buy you new jeans?'" Galway paused, stared at two men exchanging an elaborate handshake on the opposite corner. They wore bright sneakers and long white shirts.

Cruz turned up the air conditioning. "What did he say?"

Galway spoke without looking at her. "He said I didn't understand *fashion*. That it was the style, jeans being all torn up and shitty looking."

"He's right," she said.

"Yeah, well, I never claimed to be Mr. GQ. But doesn't that seem weird?"

"What's that?"

"His new dad is a lawyer, six figures. Aidan dresses like he's about to paint the house, but he's got a car, an iPod, mutual funds earning interest toward college." Galway gestured out the window. "Those guys, they don't even have a *bank* account. Probably don't have anything in the fridge. But their shoes are spotless, they got gold chains around their necks, and I couldn't get my shirt that white if I tried."

"So?"

"So it's weird, is all. The ones with nothing are flaunting all they have; the ones with everything are trying to look like bums."

Cruz laughed. "You should quit this cop gig, get a job teaching philosophy."

"I could never let go of the glamorous lifestyle." Galway leaned back. "Drop me off at the station, would you? I got a stack of paperwork."

She smiled and spun north.

Afterwards, she went back to the 'Wood. She didn't have a goal in mind, just wanted to feel the street. Anything was better than working her goddamn database. Cruz drove past sagging row-houses and crumbling bungalows, dead grass, signs tagged with graffiti. Many of the houses had been boarded up, dark V-patterns from old fires marking the exterior walls. The plywood windows were covered in posters: The new 50 Cent album, ads for *Hustle & Flow,* election flyers for Alderman Owens. Each block, one or two buildings had been knocked down as if in preparation to build a new house, but few had any progress. Mostly the bare lots were just fenced off and left to rot. Blank holes in the block. Missing teeth.

Her phone rang, the caller ID showing a number from the Area One police switchboard. "Cruz."

"This is Peter Bradley. You asked me to—"

"Yeah, I remember. Did you find anything?"

"We rolled by Playboy's last known address. An apartment off Racine."

"And?"

"It's a real shithole."

"Surprise. Was he there?"

"No. Talked to the landlady, she said he left months ago. Skipped on two months rent."

It wasn't a surprise, really. It would have been too easy to expect him to be sitting around waiting for them. Though it would have been nice for something to go right for a change. She sighed, then thanked the beat cop and hung up.

How to find Playboy without sending him running? The Gangster Disciples would know, but they were his crew, and if they told him she was looking, he might bolt. Which would leave her in a tough spot. Galway was right—Playboy *would* look good in handcuffs. Whatever the truth might be about Michael Palmer, picking up Playboy was a smart first step.

Best to continue looking for him quietly, working her informants. Cruz was the only reason a lot of them stayed out of jail; hopefully that would keep them from warning him. She swung onto Sixty-third, the paint on the buildings fresher, fewer windows busted as she neared the El stop. In Chicago, prosperity followed the trains, even in Crenwood. There was a cluster of small businesses: a party store on the corner, a Popeye's beside it. Even a coffeehouse, not a Starbucks, but the kind with purple couches in the window and a chalkboard listing sandwich specials named after movies. Somebody's dream, something they'd scrimped to own, had probably hoped to put in Wicker Park or Lakeview, but couldn't afford the rent.

She wondered where Jason Palmer was now. He'd been pretty steamed when he stormed out yesterday, had that vigilante eye. There was something about him that she liked, but something damaged, too. She remembered his distant stare in the fish shop, the way he'd talked about the devastation he'd seen in Iraq, all the buildings burned out. How people just got used to it, didn't even see them anymore—

She almost rear-ended the car in front of her.

Holy shit.

Keanna's voice rang in her ears. *Shit's burning down in Crenwood all the time.*

Cruz spun toward the Dan Ryan. Had to get back home. She needed her computer, the spreadsheet of crime data. Her head felt light, that beautiful rush that came of being onto something. When her phone rang again, she was so lost in thought she answered without glancing at the caller ID. "Cruz."

"Officer. Are you somewhere you can speak?"

The voice wasn't familiar. "Umm . . ." She took a second to check the number, but didn't recognize it. "Sure."

"You don't know me, but I'm a friend."

"Uh-huh." She leaned back in the seat. A crazy, then. How had he gotten her cell number? "What is this about?"

"Michael Palmer's death."

She pulled the car over, right up onto the curb, tires crunching on sun-scorched grass. Flipped her hazards as she threw it in park, and said, "What do you mean?"

"You're working on his case, aren't you?"

"Yes. But I'm not a detective. You should talk to—"

"And you're also in Gang Intelligence."

"Yes."

"Have you discovered that this was more than a simple gang retaliation?"

Who was this guy? "I can't discuss that."

"Sorry. Let me be more direct. The Gangster Disciples didn't kill Michael Palmer."

Streaks of sunlight prismed on the dashboard. She stared at their liquid pattern.

"Officer?"

"Okay," she said. "I'll bite. Who did?"

"I wish I could tell you." His voice had enunciation perfect as a news anchor. "But you wouldn't believe me."

"You know, for a mysterious caller, you're not much help."

"The burnt child fears the fire, Officer."

"And a rolling stone gathers no moss. What the hell does that mean?"

"It means, Officer, that I know who killed Michael Palmer. And I'm going to tell you how to find out."

# CHAPTER 21
## A War Goin' On

He took a deep breath and another look at himself in the rearview. His heart felt flittery and his fingers tingled. Bar none, this had to be the craziest thing he'd ever done. Jason smiled a grin tight enough to make his teeth ache.

The suit fit well, but looked a couple of years out of style, just as he hoped. It'd caught his eye the moment he stepped into the used-clothing store: double-breasted brown fabric with the faint sheen of too many wearings. A blue tie, Windsor-knotted, and a silver tie clip he'd seen beside the register.

"You're going to be fine," he said to his own reflection. Then he took the Ray-Bans from the passenger seat and put them on, the oversize lenses flashing back a sunset.

He was only three blocks away, but felt every inch of them, the pressure and pop of cracked blacktop beneath the wheels. The breeze stale and warm as someone breathing in his face. The reactions as he turned down the street, the way one of the men at the end of the block glared as he unclipped a phone from his belt and spoke into it. The way things seemed to swirl and resolve, a spiral with himself at the center, the eye of a human hurricane.

He had a moment of panic in his belly, and then he was putting the car into park, and it was too late, the point of no return, and that gave him the energy he needed, just like it always had on patrol, when they left the relative safety of the FOB and went into the streets. Jason moved deliberately, trying not to show hurry or nerves. Just another day, another item on his list. Shuffled papers, took one last breath, then opened the car door and stepped out.

He could feel the stares pressing down. A handful of younger gangbangers sat on the steps of the sagging porch, a radio at their feet spilling hip-hop like fog. He glanced at them, then casually further up, to the two men who stood in the bungalow's doorway. Early twenties, faces composed and steady, poker masks sheened with sweat and hatred.

His veins pumped panic, but he met their gaze, nodded slightly, turned to close the car door. Adjusted his suit jacket as he did, pulling it up enough that they could see his purchases.

The holster was soft brown leather, stained dark down the center with traces of Hoppes #9. He wore it on his right hip, not low-slung like a gunfighter, but high on his slacks. He'd left the Beretta cocked, a subtlety he doubted would be noticed but that might buy him a half second if things went wrong.

He almost laughed. Like he had a prayer of walking if things went wrong.

The handcuffs hung on his belt behind the holster. The Army surplus store had a bunch of different kinds, most of them for sex play, with quick releases and padding. He'd gone for a classic nickel-finish pair, heavy and shiny. Beside them, where his coat would cover it most of the time, hung a silver star on a black leather square. He lingered long enough at the car, retrieving a notebook he'd set on the roof, for the kids on the porch to get a nice long look. Counting on them seeing it.

At a distance.

Because if anyone saw it up close, he was a corpse. He hadn't held a police badge, but he felt fairly sure they didn't have the words "FBI: Female Body Inspector" etched across the face.

*It's in the attitude,* he thought. That sense of unquestioned entitlement police had, the way they walked the street like they owned everything on it. The pads of his fingers were numb. He pocketed the car keys and turned slow, jacket falling back to cover the gear on his belt, leaving only the butt of the pistol still in sight. Notebook in his left hand, fighting the urge to flex the fingers of his right. Felt a mad urge to run, to just jump in the car and go, knowing he could be back in safe territory in twenty minutes.

Then he thought of Billy, asleep in an Army T-shirt.

He walked over, trying for swagger. Hit the boys on the porch with his Ray-Bans and a stern expression. Showtime. "Which one of you is going to tell Dion Williams I need to talk to him?" Jason asked, and flashed a thin smile that said he didn't have a worry in his life.

The afternoon sun lay on his shoulders. His demons raged, screamed, sent electricity crackling up and down the lengths of his nerves. He stood still.

Then the taller of the two in the doorway nudged one of the teenagers with his foot. "Bounce on in, tell C-Note a detective wants to see him."

Jason tried to look bored, tapping his notebook. Tried not to run the odds on whether or not Playboy would be here, knowing that if he was, it was certain death. One of the guys on the steps turned up the radio, the music saying there was no such thing as halfway crooks, scared to death and scared to look. Jason glanced down the block and pretended to stifle a yawn while fear hollowed out his body.

"Don't remember calling no police." The man in the doorway wore a striped button-up with a Sean John logo, the lines stretched across the muscles of his chest and arms. The two bangers stood beside him like bodyguards.

Jason smiled. "You don't call us, Dion. We call you."

One of the bangers stepped up, head cocked and chest forward. Jason met his gaze. Knew the game, one he'd played plenty of times in the Army. No weakness, no fear. "Best control your boy. Hate to search him, find something that violates his parole."

"Go easy, cuz." Dion kept his voice level, and the banger stepped back. "Who the fuck are you?"

"Detective Martinez." The real Martinez, crazy mother that he'd been, he would have approved of this stunt.

"You don't look like no Martinez."

Jason shielded his eyes from the sun, drawled, "Get that all the time."

"How come I ain't seen you before?"

"Because I only come when shit's about to get out of hand. We need to talk." Gestured to his car. "Let's take a ride."

Dion's eyes narrowed. "Since when the police drive Cadillacs?"

*Shit.* He'd wondered about that, but hadn't seen a way around it. He controlled his expression, said, "That's my personal ride." Smiled. "Car's the Virgin Mary. You like the classics?"

"They 'aight. My boy Brillo used to have an old Monte Carlo, till that shit got disappeared the other night." He paused. "Why'n't you make yourself useful, find Brillo's whip?" The boys on the steps laughed at that.

"Hop in, we'll go look." Waited a beat, saw the hesitation in the other man's eyes. "Unless you want the whole block to know your business."

"You come here to arrest me?"

"Nope. To invite you."

"I ain't going nowhere."

Jason shrugged. He felt like his stomach was being slowly tugged away from him. "Trying to do you a favor here. You know Cruz, from Gang Intelligence?" He waited for the faint nod. "She and the lieutenant, they wanted to send in the cavalry. I said no. Said C-Note's a smart guy, that we should try to talk to him first." So much came down to the gang leader buying this, getting in the car with him. Taking a drive around the neighborhood, talking as they went, the Caddy giving Jason a tiny edge in enemy turf. Mobility and security.

A long moment. Then Dion turned and opened the door. "My office."

Jason's hands went swampy, his heart thudding against his ribs. If he went inside, he was a whisper away from death.

One wrong move, and the gangbangers could do whatever they wanted to him, do it safely and in privacy.

Take as long as they wanted.

Under his jacket, the sleeves of his Oxford were soaked. Dion watched him, measuring. The look in the man's eyes lit a cold flame in Jason's belly. This lowlife had sent men to kill Billy, maybe Michael, too. Was he going to walk away from that?

Jason curled his lips in a sneer, shrugged. "Lead the way." Stepped up on the porch, brushing by the bodyguards, the skin on his neck tingling as he passed into the monster's lair. A strange déjà vu, the same combination of terror and exhilaration he'd felt every time he cleared a house with the squad, not knowing what he was walking into. A soldier's rush, the fear present but controlled, mastered. Except that then he'd been wearing body armor, slinging an M4, and representing the strong arm of the United States Army.

It was dim inside, and reeked of weed and sweat and Chinese takeout. A constellation of cigarette burns scarred the carpet. A girl reclined on one couch, a baby asleep on her chest. On the other, two shirtless teenagers were leaning forward, each furiously punching buttons on a controller. Jason looked up, saw a big plasma TV where the two were storming a dusty city block under an orange sky. A voice yelled, "Fire in the hole," and a grenade blew on screen, tossing a digital body like a rag doll. One of the gangbangers hooted. "Like that?" he asked, and then leaned forward to grab a beer from the table, exposing the gleaming handle of a pistol tucked in his back. "Want a little more?"

The office was a small bedroom. Enormous particle-board desk, pleather wing chair, green banker's lamp. A junior-executive rig in the middle of a gang house guarded by teenaged killers playing videogames about soldiers. The only things that kept Jason from laughing were the fear he wouldn't be able to stop and the knowledge that every step he'd taken forward was one he might have to fight his way back.

"All right, Po-lice." Dion turned and offered a grin laced with menace. "Now we're all alone. Now we in *my* house."

A muscle in Jason's thigh jumped, but he kept his face straight and stepped closer, his chest inches from the other man's. They were about the same height, but Dion had an easy thirty pounds of muscle on him. Jason stared, unblinking, feeling the wetness in his armpits, the tremor in his fingertips. From the moment he'd stepped inside it'd been play hard or die. He had to make the man believe completely. "You think I'm alone?"

"Don't see nobody else." Dion's voice had a sort of restless craziness to it.

"'Cause you ain't looking. It's like cowboys and Indians. I'm the scout. You only see me, but the whole tribe's waiting just over the hill."

Dion's eyes narrowed. "What you want?"

"I want to know why you sent Playboy to kill Jason Palmer."

"Don't know anybody by either name."

"You sell crack out of houses on Eggleston and Ross. You run a basement club in a warehouse up on Hooker. You got a baby-mama named Cherise." He saw the reaction in Dion's eyes, and silently thanked Ronald for the details. "We're always watching. I know more about your business than you do." Jason made himself wait a beat, then put a little steel in his voice. "You *really* don't want to piss me off. Now, why did your boys try to hit Jason Palmer?"

Dion shrugged. "That was Playboy's deal. He was just supposed to pick him up, wait for a call."

"And what about the bangers you sent to kill his nephew the other night?"

"I don't know nothing about that." Dion had a decent poker face. If Jason hadn't been there, he might have believed.

"We've got a witness that ID'd three members of your crew, including Playboy." He was starting to feel the part. The lingo may've been pulled from television and books, but the attitude was familiar. In this part of the city, being a cop wasn't that much different from being a soldier, just as in Iraq, being a soldier had been a lot like being a cop. "You're saying they acted without you?"

"Could be. Players got minds of their own."

"Maybe I ought to talk to them." The air conditioner in the window hummed to life. "Let them know you're washing your hands. Maybe they'll remember it differently once they know you're going to let them face murder on their own. Now why did you kill Michael Palmer?"

"I don't know what you're talking about," Dion said. "And even if I did, I wouldn't tell you shit."

Jason shook his head. "You aren't giving me much choice. It's one thing to do a little business, keep it reasonable. But hijacking civilians? Breaking into houses, chasing little kids? I can't have it."

"Ain't a crime till the victim's white, huh?"

"You sent men to murder an eight-year-old. You want to see how it plays on the news? They'll bring the death penalty back just for you."

Gun blasts sounded in the other room.

Jason whirled, one hand reaching for his weapon. A second shot, and a third. Then, timed with the fourth, a wicked bass beat, thick with anger.

Music. He turned back to Dion, saw the banger smirking, wet-lipped and arrogant. "Pretty jumpy, Po-lice. You scared?"

Jason's tongue was a dry beast flopping in the desert of his mouth. He eased his hand off the Beretta, his fingers reluctant to move. "Nah." He forced himself to smile. "I just don't want to have to fill out the paperwork for shooting you."

The muscles in Dion's neck bulged, and he stepped forward. "Oh, you fucked up now."

"I don't think so." Jason's bowels went warm and loose, but he stood his ground. "Like I told my lieutenant, you're a smart man. You know no cop is going to walk in here all alone, no backup. So you know what will happen if you make a move." He held the moment like it was nitroglycerine: one wrong move and everything would blow. There was only so far he dared bluff. But he had to get something out of this for Billy's sake. "Besides, I'm here to do you a favor."

Dion had stopped moving, looked at him suspiciously. "Yeah?"

"Truth is, we know you didn't kill Michael Palmer. We've got a witness says it was two white guys. But since Palmer was such an upstanding citizen, we have to lock somebody up fast. Ideally, that would be the guys who actually did it, probably the same ones that hired you to grab Jason. Problem is, we don't know who they are." He paused, let his words sink in. "But we do know who *you* are."

Dion shook his head. "Po-lice."

"Just telling you how it is. Fact that I know you didn't do it doesn't mean I won't arrest you for it." He paused. "Unless you got a better name."

"Black man can't get no break."

Jason shrugged. "Has more to do with you being a gangster and a killer. But whatever you like."

Dion turned to the window, set his hands on the air conditioner, fingers drumming idly. Stared out the dirty pane above it. The moment stretched.

Then he turned back. "Playboy was hired by a white dude, name of Anthony DiRisio."

Relief washed through Jason's body. "Who is he?"

"Wait a second. If I give him up for the shit you're looking for, will any, you know, previous dealings he and I have had come back to bite my ass?"

"No way." Jason smiled. "My word, as a cop."

"I feel better already." Dion shook his head. "Guy's a dealer."

"What, drugs?"

"Naw," Dion said, and smiled. "He's specialized. He sells hardware."

"Guns."

"Nigga, please. I want a gat, I pick up the phone, have boys here in half an hour with a trunk full. Anthony sells *hardware*. Military shit. MPs, AKs, those big-ass combat shotguns. Ain't cheap, neither."

Jason stared, his mouth hanging open.

"Been selling for about a year now. Sells to anybody, which is the only reason you and I is talking, 'aight? That boy don't have *no* loyalty."

Jason blinked. "So this guy, he hired you to hijack—" almost said *me*, caught himself at the last second—"Jason Palmer? Why?"

"Like I said, that was Playboy's deal. All's I know is he was supposed to grab the dude and wait for a call."

"And what about the other night, breaking into Michael Palmer's house?"

"After Jason got away, DiRisio wanted Playboy to make good. He called, gave us an address."

"And you sent people to kill everyone there."

Dion shrugged. "I didn't say that."

Jason smiled, a thin expression, his heart raging. Wanting to tear Dion apart, even knowing he wasn't the real problem. "I need to find DiRisio."

"Who you really after, cop? You trying to arrest a couple of brothers, or you want the dude who gave the order?"

*Both. I want all of you rotting in the depths of the earth for a thousand years.* "All I want is the man who gave the order."

"DiRisio was in here talking like a punk this morning." Dion shrugged. "Said he's got a deal going down tonight."

"Where?"

"Don't know for sure," Dion said. "But our last couple meets were downtown. Wacker Drive."

"Upper or Lower?"

The man smiled. "*Lower* Lower Wacker. The drive under the drive, down on the bottom level where they was filming that Batman movie. There's a spot there by the loading docks for the Hyatt. That's where we done it."

Jason nodded. He didn't know the specific spot, but knew Wacker. A three-level artery for the city, following the river's curve from Lake Shore Drive to the highways. The top levels were fairly busy, but the bottom was mostly used by service vehicles and delivery trucks. Smart. Private and easy to secure, but with plenty of exit options. It was the kind of location a trained soldier might choose. He felt twisting in his belly, acid in his throat. What in the hell had Mikey gotten himself into?

"Now, Po-lice." Dion glared at him. "How about you get the fuck outta my house."

Jason nodded. He'd gotten as much as he could expect. More. Time to go, before some stupid mistake gave him away. "All right." Jason backed away, eyes on Dion. He risked a quick glance to find the doorknob, then turned back.

"One more thing." He paused. "You said this guy sells submachine guns, military hardware. What do you need fire-power like that for?"

"Ain't you noticed, cop?" Dion's voice was soft, his gaze weary, and for the tiniest second, Jason almost felt sorry for him. "There's a war goin' on."

# CHAPTER 22
Netherworld

"I'm kind of busy," Jason said, cell phone pinned between ear and shoulder as he glanced back. An SUV pulled past him, and he switched to the right lane.

"Doing what?" Washington's voice was ice.

"You don't want to know."

There was a long pause. "You're right."

"Look, just tell Billy that I love him and that I'll call him later."

"He wants to talk to you. Boy's scared."

"I know, it's just that—look, I left him there so that I could be a soldier instead of an uncle."

"Only one of those things is worth a damn." The disapproval couldn't have been clearer if Washington had been shouting, instead of speaking in measured syllables. "But if you have to be both, be an uncle first."

"Jesus, we been friends how many years now? You can't just do me this favor, take care of my nephew for a little while?"

"Play soldier all you like. But you can't park Billy in his foxhole and expect him to keep his head down. Maybe you forgot, but that boy lost his father."

Guilt fed the Worm, always. "I didn't forget."

"So act like it."

"All right. All right, old man, I get you." Jason sighed. "Put him on."

The exit from Lake Shore Drive swung him onto the far north end of the Magnificent Mile. Tourist heaven, the shop windows bright against the twilight, a slow tide of women in shorts and men with sunburned faces. He turned onto Oak before he got lost in the crush of cars, double-parked in front of a designer boutique and flipped on his hazards. Took a breath and tried to gather his thoughts.

Combat he could handle. An eight-year-old he was less sure about.

"Uncle Jason?"

"Hey, kiddo."

"Where are you?"

"Nowhere, buddy." A breeze came through the open window, and Jason closed his eyes, smelled the lake on it. "I'm just out taking care of some things."

"What things?"

"Just, you know, errands." *Errands?*

A sigh came over the phone, long and theatrical.

"What?"

"You can tell me the truth. I'm not a little kid, you know."

Jason started to laugh, caught himself just in time. "You know what?" He bit his lip. "You're right. I'm sorry."

His nephew sounded properly mollified. "That's okay."

A long pause, and then Jason realized that it was his turn to talk. Only, what was he supposed to say? *Well, earlier I pretended to be a cop to bluff my way into a drug house, and now I'm on my way to ambush a meet between gangbangers and an arms dealer. And neither one scares me half so much as the idea of suddenly being responsible for someone else.* "I'm downtown."

"What are you doing?"

"I'm . . . well, I'm trying to find out what's going on, buddy. I need to know why those guys came into your house."

"Oh." His voice sounded faint and far away.

"But," Jason spoke quickly, "it's going good. I think I'm starting to figure it out."

"Have you found the bad guys?"

"Some of them. Not all yet, but I will."

"What are you going to do then?"

He rubbed at the back of his neck. "I'm not sure."

"Are you going to kill them?" Billy's voice hard to read, a mix of sincerity and fear.

Jason had felt bullets chip cinderblock above his head, heard the ragged screams of wounded men, the raw prayers of desperate mothers. But he'd never heard anything quite so horrible as that question falling from eight-year-old lips. And all the worse because he didn't know the answer.

Did he want revenge? Oh, *hell* yes.

Would he murder for it?

He flashed on a class room in Basic, a lecture from a soft-spoken captain with sharp features. He had been talking about what defined a soldier, and a line had stuck in Jason's head even then. The difference between a thug and a soldier, the guy had said, was the moral courage of his cause.

"No," he said. "I'm not." He paused. "But I'll make sure that they can't hurt you ever again. I promised you that, and I meant it."

There was a long pause, and then Billy said, "I believe you."

Water spattered down the wide pipe, a constant chattering like autumn rain, like the dripping of ancient stalactites. A ragged man with dirt-pocked skin stooped, cupping his hands to catch the dark liquid. Splashed his face, moving calm as a suburbanite preparing to shave in the comfort of his own bathroom.

Jason slowed the Caddy, rolling down the ramp at a bare crawl. He'd never been down here before. What most people thought of as Lower Wacker was actually the second level, a throughway that wrapped along the river and provided a shortcut to dodge the traffic lights and gawking tourists of the surface streets. Everybody knew *that* Wacker, but he doubted many had taken the ramps down one more level, to the bowels of the city, a bleak lost place where service trucks moved between exhaust-stained roll doors under the timeless haze of yellow sodium light.

This world belonged to people the one above tended to forget. Garbagemen, repair crews, delivery drivers. Scores of homeless huddled under iron girders. They all had the same blanket, which baffled Jason until he realized where the blankets came from. They were hotel linens, grown too ratty for paying customers. Tossed in the Dumpster and re-purposed by an army of the forgotten that slept shoulder to shoulder in the street beneath the Hyatt. The lowest tier of hotel guest.

It seemed like a beautiful, terrible symbol, though he couldn't have said of what, exactly.

Jason coasted to a stop where Stetson intersected Wacker. Felt that tingle in his fingers. He didn't know exactly when the meet would take place, but probably not till closer to midnight. It was eight now; he'd come early to see how it looked.

Lousy.

To the right, the street continued into darkness marked by signs indicating the city impound lot. The other direction dead-ended in a broad cul-de-sac of dingy concrete, wide enough for a mid-size rig to turn around. The roll doors were closed, but a faded sign marked the loading dock for the Hyatt. Crayola-orange shipping containers partly enclosed the area. A fence ran parallel; beyond it, a thin strip of grass led to the river, inky water sheened with reflections of convention hotels on the other side. Those glowing windows seemed a million miles distant from this misplaced netherworld, where the hum of cars and the fall of water swallowed sound, and the dingy light stole color. No security cameras, no traffic, and the only witnesses homeless men a block away, men who survived by not getting involved.

You could do just about anything down here.

Jason tapped a fingernail against his front teeth. There was no way to stay in his car without being spotted. The area was simply too vacant. Which meant he'd be on foot, out-numbered, and if what Dion had told him was true, dramatically outgunned.

He felt a pull for a drink, the desire to forget it, put on a nice shirt, hit a club. Find a girl who got wet at war stories,

bury his troubles in booze and sex and the sweet forgetful-
ness of those moments before sleep, when everything washed
away, and he didn't have to think about what came next,
about owing anything to anybody.

Then he thought of the trust in Billy's voice. *I believe you.*

He parked the car in a delivery zone, hood up and hazards
on. It took less than a minute to jog back, and he took the
metal-slat fence like an obstacle at Basic, a sprint that culmi-
nated in a lunge, planting his toes against a post and shoving,
letting momentum carry him up and over. Twenty feet of dry
grass separated the river from the road. A bike path bisected
it, but this late, in this dark place, he didn't anticipate any
foot traffic, and the men coming shouldn't have any reason
to look here. Jason checked the Beretta, then settled in to
wait.

He'd lost friends in the dust of a foreign land. His Army
didn't want him. His brother had been murdered for reasons
he didn't understand. And now someone stalked the only family he had left.

If a cause was what separated a thug from a soldier, then
he intended to be a soldier.

The time passed slowly, but he'd learned all about waiting in
the Army. The trick was to find Zen, to not rush the moment,
but simply to know that the moment would eventually come.
He lay on his back, staring up at the skyline, listening to the
buzz of cars, watching lights blink on in the high rises, normal people going about normal lives.

Across three hours, headlights flashed across the cul-de-
sac only a couple of times. A few taxis and a low loader tow-
ing a BMW. The truck didn't hesitate, just made for the
impound lot, and Jason flipped back over and tried to pick out
stars through the city glow. Remembered the desert night,
rolling from Baghdad to one of the settlements that dotted the
landscape, how they'd stopped halfway and turned off the
Humvee headlights, his team standing in the darkness with
heads craned upwards, bad-ass soldiers reduced to marveling
boys by the majesty above. Stars like holes poked in the

night, like the sky was a blanket and just beyond it was some great and glowing thing, a radiant world where everything was full of light.

He was wondering if Dion had lied to him when he saw a slim shape moving beside the river.

Adrenaline sang in his blood. Still forty yards away, nothing but a cutout against the gentle lapping of the water. But even from here he could see that the guy was dressed in black and staying low. This wasn't a citizen out for a walk. It was someone trying to be stealthy. And headed right for him.

He cursed silently, feeling the sweat in his palms, the muscles in his legs. If he moved now, he gave away his position. He could flatten himself to the ground, turn his face away. The guy might walk right by.

*And if he doesn't?*

The space was barely twenty feet wide, just dry grass and scrawny trees. Too big a risk. Jason eased the Beretta out, the grip warm from his skin, and clicked the safety off. He didn't intend to shoot anyone. But it wasn't murder if he was defending himself.

He took thin, shallow breaths. Watched the figure grow closer step by step. Counted down the feet. Twenty. Fifteen. At ten feet he couldn't stand it any more, and threw himself upwards, lunging forward and bringing the gun to bear quick. The figure reacted fast, one hand flying to a shoulder holster.

"Don't move!" He stepped closer, weapon ready, willing the guy not to draw, not to make him do anything he didn't want to. And as he did, he caught the cinnamon skin, the eyes wide with panic, and realized who the figure was, and then they both said it at the same time.

"What the *fuck* are *you* doing here?"

# CHAPTER 23
## Crossed a Line

Jason lowered the weapon the moment he realized the slender guy was actually a woman, the moment he recognized her. His pulse pounded in his throat, panic and power mingling to make every breath surreal. Cruz stared at him warily, her hand still on the pistol in her shoulder holster.

"You're part of this?" she asked, her voice incredulous.

"Part of what?"

Her eyes narrowed. "What are you doing here?"

"I was wondering the same thing about you," he said.

"I'm the police." Her voice firm, a brook-no-bullshit tone.

"Yeah, but *why* are you here?

She hesitated, then said. "I got a phone call. Anonymous. He told me there was something going down I would want to see." She took her fingers off the butt of her pistol. "Do you know what that is?"

"One of the men who killed my brother is coming here tonight. But who would have called you?"

"How about you put down the gun, we figure that out together?"

Jason looked at her, looked at the Beretta. He'd crossed a line when he'd pointed at her—shit, when she saw it. Still. "I'm sorry I scared you. But there's an explanation. Let me get through it, okay?"

She shrugged. "Mr. Palmer, you're holding a gun. I'll agree to pretty much anything you say."

This wasn't how he wanted it to go. He bowed his head, rubbed the back of his neck with his free hand, the muscles taut and hard. "I know how this seems." He looked up at her. "But will you just hear me out?"

After a pause, she said. "Okay. Who's the guy coming here?"

"His name is Anthony DiRisio, and he sells weapons. Military hardware. He's been selling to the gangs." He saw the confusion on her face. Spread his hands at his side, palms up. "Best I can guess, maybe Michael found out about it, and DiRisio killed him for it."

He thought he saw something pass behind her eyes, but all she said was, "How would the owner of a bar be mixed up in something like that?"

"Mikey was a crusader. Trying to save everyone," Jason said, remembering that last view of Michael, his brother's face angry and red. "Maybe someone he worked with told him, or maybe he just stumbled on it. But if he did find something like this, he wouldn't have been able to ignore it." He paused. "Wait a second. You said you knew him, that he'd talked to you about something. Was this it?"

Cruz shook her head. "He never said anything about weapons." She glanced around. "So. You're planning on shooting DiRisio?"

"No." He hesitated. "I don't know what I was going to do. I'm figuring this out as I go. All I know is that someone killed my brother and is trying to kill my nephew, and I'm not going to let that happen."

She nodded slowly, her forehead wrinkled, like she was thinking carefully. He let the moment stretch. Heard a car and glanced back at Lower Wacker, but didn't see anything. A soft wind carried a whiff of her perfume, something spicy and good, over a faint clean smell of sweat. "So now you know everything I know." He stared at her. "Thanks for hearing me out." She nodded, and he locked the safety on the Beretta and slid it into the back of his belt.

The moment his hands left the gun, Cruz kicked him in the balls.

He saw the move late, managed to shift position a little, but her foot still hit hard and square enough that the bottom fell out of his stomach and he gasped for breath, living that quarter second when his brain knew what was coming before his body felt it, and then *wham!*, ice-cold nausea flamed through his whole body, and he cupped his hands on his testicles and dropped to his knees, thinking *shit, oh shit,* and it took all his strength to process what he saw, her pulling her own gun, a businesslike automatic.

"Put your hands on your head."

He sucked air through his teeth. His last second shift in position meant that she hadn't connected fully, and he knew the worst of the agony would ease soon, but that was small comfort now.

"Hands on your goddamn head!" Cruz had the cop voice down: Firm, commanding, a weapon. His hands moved without him meaning for them to, the left and right finding each other, interlacing and squeezing hard to block out the pain. Cruz stepped behind him, gun never wavering.

He turned his head to look at her over his shoulder. "Jesus *Christ,* that hurt." Gasping the words.

"Shut up." She moved, and he felt his gun tugged away from his belt, heard it clatter against the earth. "Face forward."

He obeyed, his eyes on Lower Wacker, vision blurry. Knelt there, waiting to feel the cuff snap on his wrist, angry and frustrated and aching.

Which was when he saw headlights coming down the ramp.

# CHAPTER 24
Dark Brown

Jason turned his head as best he could, fighting through the icy core of pain from his testicles. Cruz stood behind him, her gun holstered now, cuffs in one hand, the other reaching for his wrist. He could see that she was staring over him, past him, to where a black Odyssey was pulling down the ramp to the cul-de-sac. It was hard to tell from this angle, on his knees with his balls on fire, but she looked kind of spooked.

"Get down," he hissed, and pulled his hands from his head.

She saw him move and reached for her own gun. He froze with his hands up. "Look, arrest me later, okay?" He met her eyes, pleading. "That's the guy who killed my brother." Jason heard the engine grow closer, saw the sweep of head-lights moving across the dead grass. "Get *down*."

She narrowed her eyes, and for a moment he thought she was going to refuse. Then she drew her pistol, and, training it on him, dropped just as headlights washed above them. The guard rail and fence on the side of Lower Wacker cast enough shadow that he doubted they'd been spotted.

The van was a couple of years old, dusty and dinged up in the way city cars tended to get. The driver pulled it in a circle, the front facing out, engine running. Ready to bolt at a moment's notice. Tactically sound. The windows were smoked, and he couldn't make out anyone inside.

Jason looked over at Cruz. "Now do you believe me?"

She glanced back at him. "All I see is a van," she said, but her voice had lost its gruff edge.

"Wait."

"For what?"

As if on cue, a second set of headlights bounced off the drab concrete. "The buyers."

A lowered pickup, bright purple, with a spoiler, rolled next to the van. Two men got out, the echoes of the car doors hollow and flat. At this distance, he couldn't make out much about them beyond Hispanic coloring, shaved heads, and tattoos.

Cruz turned, her gaze appraising. "How did you find out about this?"

Before he could answer, the door to the van opened, and the world stopped turning.

The man stood six-two, with the stocky build of a dockworker, heavy slabs of muscle that came from labor. Balding and in need of a shave. The unmistakable bulge of a shoulder holster. Carriage at once rigid and languorous, the way career soldiers could make standing at attention look as comfortable as a sprawl in a hammock.

His were the last eyes Michael had seen before he died.

Jason knew it, knew it beyond doubt. It wasn't just that the guy looked the way Billy described him. There was something elemental, something that shivered the air between them. He tasted bile, a dark brown that burned his mouth. His brother was dead. Michael, with his good laugh and bad temper, who had bought Jason his first beer, who had told him what to expect under Mary Ellen Jabrowski's bra, and what to do with what he found there. Murdered and burned and his son hunted, and this man, standing right here, was responsible.

"Anthony DiRisio?" Cruz whispered.

Jason nodded. Reached for the gun. His hand found nothing but belt and shirt, and he remembered she'd taken it off him. He looked over, found her watching, eyes narrowed and weapon ready.

"Don't make me regret not cuffing you," she said.

He took a deep breath, blew it through his mouth. Fought a wave of nausea that was only partly to do with her kick. Turned to look at his enemies and tried to steady his thinking.

The two gangbangers headed for the rear of the Odyssey. DiRisio waited like they were gardeners he was ordering around his yard, acknowledged them with a nod and a smile that looked fake even from here, then turned and opened the back of the van. Inside, Jason could see what looked like wooden shipping crates. Then he realized what had to be in those crates, and ice chips flooded his veins.

The taller gangbanger, a mustachioed muscle-boy with a barbed-wire tattoo, hooted and slapped his partner on the shoulder. Looking like a kid on Christmas, he stepped toward the van.

DiRisio casually put a hand against his chest and shoved.

The guy flew, all stunned expression and swinging arms. The other banger yelled, reaching behind his back. He froze when he saw what DiRisio had taken from the van. Jason had never carried one, but knew it on sight. One of the world's most recognizable weapons, preferred by military and special ops teams in Christ-knew how many countries. Two feet of blued-steel capable of firing eight hundred rounds a minute.

A Heckler & Koch MP5 submachine gun.

The passenger door of the van opened, and another man stepped out, sighting down the barrel of another MP5. A trim suit and a stern expression beneath neat salt-and-pepper hair.

Cruz gasped, cut the sound off with one hand over her mouth. Jason felt his fists clench. Even knowing what this was about, it wasn't something he'd been ready to see. For some reason, he thought of the gang house earlier, the kids playing video games.

Under the threat of 1,600 rounds a minute, the standing gangbanger had taken a step back, raised his hands. His partner on the ground had the dazed expression of a a kid who'd fallen from his bike.

"Money first," DiRisio said. His voice bounced oddly off the concrete.

The gangbangers nodded, began moving slowly toward the pickup. Jason turned to Cruz. She stared straight ahead, her face slack.

"This is why Michael was killed. Those have to be the guys Billy saw in the bar."

She nodded numbly.

Suddenly an idea occurred to him. A beautiful, simple, perfect idea, and the weight of the world lifted off his back. This was the perfect opportunity. He couldn't have planned it better: Gangbangers, arms dealer, and weapons all in one place. No need for personal campaigns, and he'd be able to keep his promise to Billy. Both his promises.

"You're a cop," he said. "Call for backup."

But Cruz turned to look at him, shook her head. "No."

"Why not?"

"Because," she said, her voice matter of fact but her face slapped, "one of those guys *is* a cop."

# CHAPTER 25
Firecrackers

It couldn't be.

It just couldn't fucking be.

Cruz lay on the ground, the sun-baked dirt painful against her pelvic bone. Stared at the scene, something from a movie, men with suits and submachine guns doing deals in the ghastly yellow of sodium lights. Only it wasn't a movie, it was real, and one of the men was Tom Galway. Her partner.

Earlier she'd had the feeling that this whole case was like a train off the rails and hurtling through space. Now she felt the impact.

Then from behind came the most precise sound she'd ever heard. Perfect and sharp and clean, like God snapping his fingers.

A pistol cocking.

The veins in her neck throbbed, and the skin on her face seemed to tighten. She looked back, the move pure reflex. A man's silhouette blocked the glowing lights of the convention hotels on the other side of the river. She could only make out one detail, the only one that mattered, the gun held in both hands.

Beside her, Palmer had rolled up on his shoulder, bracing himself against the ground with his knuckles. He looked like coiled springs about to snap. It reminded her that she had a gun too, and she started to raise it. Not really thinking, just not wanting to die right here, on the shitty banks of the shitty Chicago River.

The silhouette said, "Don't."

She froze. The voice had been cool and unemotional, the kind of voice that belonged to someone comfortable dropping the hammer on his weapon. Her palms went dry. How deep had she gotten herself in here?

"Lose the gun."

She grit her teeth, looked around.

"Damn it, you stubborn cunt, drop it." By the reflected light she could almost make out his features, cruel lips with a white ridge of scar tissue cutting across his cheek from the corner of his mouth. If he was a cop, she didn't know him.

She set the Smith down on the dead grass, feeling her whole life falling away with it. Like the earth was tilting and she was unable to hold on. Arsons. Conspiracies. Mysterious callers. Gangbangers with submachine guns. Dirty cops and deadly voices.

Cruz looked over at Palmer, found him staring back at her. Cursed herself for taking his gun. She'd yanked it from his belt and tossed it, intent on getting the cuffs on, and there wasn't enough light to make out where it had fallen.

"I'm police," she said, pleased to hear her own voice come out steady. "No matter how bad you think you are, believe me, you don't want to be pointing a gun at a cop."

Scarface snorted. He cleared his throat with a long gargle, then leaned forward and spat phlegm on the grass between her feet. "Be quiet, cop." He straightened, raised his voice. "Hey." The sound was lost in the traffic noise from above. "Hey!"

"What?" Oddly, she could hear the response clearly. The concrete of the cul-de-sac must have bounced and amplified his words.

"Company."

"What?"

"*Com-pan-y.*"

Cruz risked a glance back. The Italian-looking bruiser in the cheap suit, the one Palmer had said was named Anthony DiRisio, had the two gangbangers in the killing arc of his submachine gun. His stance was perfect, his posture calm. He reminded her of a cobra, hood flared, gentle rhythmic sway, ready to strike faster than you could see. Staring down the barrel of all that death, the gangbangers were posturing children.

Galway, meanwhile, had walked toward the fence, the MP5 still dangling from one hand, the other up to shade his eyes. "What have you got?" He reached in his pants pocket, then slung the submachine gun over his shoulder by its strap. Fumbled with something in his hands. A flashlight, a mini Mag-Lite.

The beam lanced out through the fence to stab Scarface in the eyes. He winced, raised one hand to block the light.

Cruz glanced at Palmer, saw the same thought in his face, and then they were scrabbling for their feet. Scarface whirled, his gun swinging over until she could see right down the black barrel, but she kept moving, twisting her body as she stood. The roar surprised her, the gunfire much louder than the muffled crack she heard through ear protection on the firing range. A gout of orange flame tore a chunk of turf not two inches to the right of her thigh. She froze, fear and sounds and revelation all combining to crush her, saw the gun coming up, this time the man aiming at her chest, a kill shot, no way he could miss. She watched his finger tighten on the trigger, knew she was dead.

Then Palmer hit Scarface in a rushing tackle, his shoulder driving hard into the man's gut, the guy gasping, gun flying wide, Palmer pushing like a linebacker on a tackling dummy, driving him back ten feet to the river's edge. They hit the railing, and for a second Galway's flashlight held them both in its beam, Palmer jumping back as the gunman flipped over the railing, arms pinwheeling like he was trying to swim upward through the light.

The drop to the river was only about five feet, but it seemed to take a long time for the splash.

The beam of light swerved crazily, spinning off of them, and Cruz wondered why that would be. Then the answer occurred to her, Galway probably reaching for his MP5 with both hands. She couldn't believe he would shoot her, that her partner and friend would fire on them, but didn't want to find out. She started running, yanking at Palmer's arm. He turned away from the water, and she could smell his panic, feel the tension in the muscles of his arms, and then they were sprinting, her leading the way and him fast behind, pounding up the bike path toward the Michigan Avenue Bridge.

There was a cluster of explosions behind them, like firecrackers.

Jesus *Christ*.

No pain. Her breathing came hard, pulse slamming in her wrists and neck, skin tingling. Her footsteps fell firm and true, and she heard Palmer's echoing behind her. Another set of firecrackers, but the bike path was good footing, and ahead of them loomed a stairwell up to the bridge. She took the stairs three at a time, one hand on the railing yanking herself up, knowing they were safe now. That there was no way their pursuers had been able to get around the fence fast enough to chase them. Michigan Avenue lay two flights up, and even at midnight, there would be people on the street, cabs prowling. She didn't slow, kept pushing, and from behind she heard Jason Palmer, his footfalls heavier, and above the ringing of the breath in her own ears, she heard him laugh, the guy somehow enjoying this.

"I guess," he said, panting, "you won't be arresting me tonight."

# September 23, 2003

"So these three kids, Mexicans, they get it in their head to start robbing nail salons." Tom Galway sips his beer and shakes his head. "Fucking nail salons. They come in waving shotguns, clear the register, grab jewelry, purses, cell phones from the customers. In and out. Smart. No security, no cameras, and it's all women, so they scare easy—right, Cruz?"

There's laughter, but there's more when she tells her partner to check out her manicure and flips him the bird, so it's all good, just cops on their sixth pitcher of Budweiser laughing at the whole goddamn world.

"Anyway, these innovators, they're hitting two places a week, but it's Chicago, so no telling how long that could roll. Except they have the bad luck to pick the salon where the wife of the state congressman gets her mani-pedi, poor bastards. She wasn't even there at the time, but word comes from on high, these three have got to go down, top priority, bar none. I'm not kidding. Whole area is on the lookout for the goddamn Pedicure Bandits." That breaks them up, and Galway pauses to drain half his beer in a go. "So one evening we get a tip that they'll be in a bar down the West Lawn. We roll in, but we don't know what these guys look like, right? They've been wearing masks. So my partner and I, we're in this dump Mex bar, and we're thinking what, we're supposed to search all these steroided cholos? No thank you."

"Pansy," she says, and the table erupts in laughter, and Galway flashes her bird back.

"So my partner, he asks the bartender, can we borrow the phone. He takes out a list of the numbers of the cell phones stolen that afternoon and starts dialing. And I'm standing there trying not to crack up at the sheer brilliance of the Chicago Police Department, when lo and behold," Galway's voice getting louder, coming to the punchline, "but the guy I'm standing behind, I mean right behind, his pocket rings." The table breaks into laughter. "And you know what this guy does?" Galway spreads his arms as if measuring stupidity by the foot. "He fucking answers!"

The laughter is an explosion, an upswell of love, love of the job, love of each other, love of the sheer lunacy of the world, and as she joins in, as loud and hard as all the rest, Cruz thinks to herself that this is it, this is all she wants, just to run with these men and chase idiot criminals and wear a star, and at the end of the day to drink Budweiser and tell stories, and then get up the next day and do it all again.

# CHAPTER 26
## Black-Eyed Dreams

Cheap paneling ran between a carpet dotted with stains she chose not to look too hard at and a ceiling smoked beige. Cigarette ghosts soured the air. The smell tugged at Cruz; right now, she'd have dug butts out of a bar ashtray. "Classy place."

"It'll do." Jason closed the door, flipped the deadbolt, and slid the chain across. Pulled the blinds, concealing the rusting Dumpster and mismatched junkers in the motel parking lot. He moved with an economy of purpose, and she found herself watching him with appreciation. The emotion of someone far away. Adrift from the real.

She wandered to the bed, looking at the grungy pillowcases with distaste. Above the fake headboard hung a print of a lily painted by someone who'd once heard flowers described. She brushed at the mattress, sat on the very corner. "You ever listen to Tom Waits?"

"Huh?" He looked away from the break in the curtains.

"This place reminds me of a song of his, I forget the name. 'The rooms smell like diesel, and you take on the dreams of the ones that have slept there.'"

He smiled. "'9th and Hennepin.' From *Rain Dogs*."

"You're a fan? Me too. I used to date a guy who got me into it. He'd fall asleep to it."

"Jesus." Jason laughed. "Must've made for some black-eyed dreams."

She nodded. "The guy was a waste of time, but at least he introduced me to Waits." There was dirt under her nails from laying on the ground. A memory hit, and she chuckled. "One time he played it while we were, you know, in the middle of things." A flash of rumpled sheets and the smell of bourbon. His tattoo, dice showing sixes and a ribbon that read *Its all good,* just like that, no apostrophe. "So we're going, and Waits sings 'I knew him when he was nothing, and he hasn't changed a bit,' and I burst out giggling. I mean one of those can't-stop, hurts-too-much fits. Right in the middle of things."

Palmer laughed through his nose, eyes alight. "Was he pissed?"

"What do you think? One minute he's king stud, the next I'm laughing so hard I can't breathe." She smiled to think of it, then shook her head. "Yeah, he was pissed."

A loud rumbling from outside caught both their attention, and they sat frozen and listening as it grew louder and passed, an anonymous semi headed for the freeway.

"You know the one I love? 'Christmas Card From a Hooker in Minneapolis.' It's got this line, 'I wish I had all the money that we used to spend on dope—' "

" 'I'd buy me a used car lot and I wouldn't sell any of them,' " Cruz said.

Jason smiled, stepped away from the curtain. Pulled a ladder-back chair with a broken slat and sat down. Facing forward, which she liked. She said, "How'd you get into him?"

"My brother."

The real world flooded in like they'd broken a levee. She winced, crossed her arms. Realized she still had her shoulder holster on, though her gun was back by the river. Shit. Her gun. "I guess we can't trade song lyrics all night."

"No." He sighed. "Too bad, though. First normal conversation I've had in days."

She looked him over, cop instincts taking in detail. Dark circles and needing a shave. His back straight, a lot of strength, but also that haunted look she sometimes saw flickering through the eyes of men living under the Stevenson overpass. "So."

He nodded, ran a hand through his hair. Straightened. "So the guy by the back of the van was Anthony DiRisio. You said the other was a cop?"

"Tom Galway." She sighed. "My partner."

"Your *partner*?"

She nodded. "Yeah."

He stood and went to the window. Glanced out. Checked the door again. Turned to her. "You remember what Billy said? He told us that the guys who killed my brother wore suits. One was tall, balding, and muscular. That's DiRisio. And the other was thin with black and gray hair."

It shouldn't have surprised her after what she'd seen, after her former partner had fired on her, but it still did. "Jesus. Galway." A thought struck like a shaft of light through a cloud. "Wait a sec. What if we're reading this wrong? What if it were someone else in the bar, and Galway was only pretending to be in on it tonight? What if it's some kind of sting?"

He shook his head. "He shot at us."

"Maybe he missed on purpose." It sounded thin even as she said it. A cop firing a submachine gun in the heart of the city? A ricochet could have bounced anywhere. And if it was sanctioned, where was the backup? There should have been thirty men, tactical teams, a chopper, the works. No way they'd let bangers roll away with live SMGs. "Okay. So Galway and this DiRisio guy are selling weapons to the crews." She sighed. "How'd you find out about it?"

He stiffened, then gave a little laugh, rubbed his neck. "I guess it doesn't make any difference now." He sat down. "I went to see a guy named Dion Wallace."

"The Gangster Disciple leader?"

"Yeah. I pretended to be a cop, and convinced him I was going to arrest him if he didn't give me a name."

"You *what?*" She was on her feet. Unbelievable. The *arrogance* of this guy. "That's a felony."

He looked at her with a sarcastic smile. "Well, seeing as how actual cops are selling heavy weapons, let's put impersonating one on the list of things you can arrest me for later, okay? Besides," he said, "if I hadn't been there, you'd be lying beside the river now. Remember?"

Her reply died in her throat. She saw the shadow of Scarface's gun, the way she'd stood frozen as he lined up for a kill shot. Macho asshole or not, Palmer had saved her life. She sat, stared at the pattern of stains on the carpet.

He sighed. "Look. I'm a very normal guy. This is all new to me. But this thing, it's real, and we're in it together." He paused. "We're going to have to trust each other."

"You say that like it's nothing."

"I was a soldier, remember? I know what it means to trust someone. But whatever is going on, it just keeps getting scarier. We need to help each other."

She blew air through her lips. "You're right."

Palmer nodded, rocked the chair back on two legs. Laced his fingers behind his head and stared at the ceiling. A TV turned on in the room next door, cartoons playing too loud through thin walls. "You know what I still can't figure? Why Michael? Why would these guys go after my brother?"

The muscles in her back clenched. She'd asked the same question of him earlier. But after what she'd seen, she realized she knew the answer. "Because of the mysterious caller."

He cocked an eyebrow.

"Remember I said someone called me? He wouldn't tell me his name, but he knew who I was, and said he was a friend of your brother's." This afternoon seemed a thousand years ago. Strain had been showing at the seams of the world, but at least a semblance of normalcy had remained; amazing what a few hours could do. "This guy, he told me to go to Lower Wacker and look for a black Odyssey. That was why I trusted you—I saw the van."

"Hmm." Palmer leaned forward with his elbows on his knees. "So someone else knows what's going on."

"There's more." Cruz massaged her temples. "He

said . . ." She sighed. "He said that he had given Michael something that had gotten him killed. Some sort of evidence."

Palmer stared at her, rubbed his chin hard enough the five o'clock shadow grated. He looked like he was considering putting the chair through the window. She waited. Finally, he said, "The briefcase." He leaned forward, buried his head in his hands, groaned.

"What briefcase?"

He spoke through his fingers. "When I saw Michael the other day, he had this briefcase, just a regular leather case, but he kept fidgeting with it. Set it down one place, talked for a minute, moved it somewhere else. I didn't think anything of it at the time. But whatever was in that briefcase is the reason my brother was killed." He looked up. "I was three feet away, and I didn't know a goddamn thing about it."

"Where is it now?" If they could get hold of that, everything could change.

He smiled grimly. "They have it. Galway and DiRisio. Don't you see? That's why they came to the bar, for the briefcase. It must have evidence about what's going on, dirty cops selling weapons to the gangbangers. If Michael had gone public with it, they'd have been ruined."

Cruz nodded, the pieces clicking into place. "And after they got what they came for, killing your brother would have been the best way to cover it. Kill him and burn down his bar, and everybody blames it on the gangs."

It was such a simple thing, once all the facts were in place. Simple and ruthless and terrifying.

"Any idea who the caller was?"

"Not really, no. He knew a lot about the department. Could be a cop." She concentrated, trying to think of anything else that could help them. "By the way he talked, I'd say he's educated. He spoke precisely, like a news anchor. And he used some weird expressions."

"Weird?"

"I pointed out he wasn't giving me much specific information, and he said something like 'the burnt child fears fire.'"

"The burnt child fears fire? What does that mean?"

"Apparently," she said, "it means his way or the high-way."

He looked like he was doing long division in his head. "He told you not to tell anyone."

"Yeah," she said. "Actually, more than that. He told me not to tell any of my colleagues." She thought back, remembering the play of sunlight through the window, the feel of the phone in her hand. Felt a shiver down her core. Jesus. Oh, Jesus. She looked up at Palmer. "He specifically said not to tell a guy named James Donlan."

"Who's he?"

Her body felt heavy. "He's the head of the Area One Detective Division."

Palmer's mouth fell open. "My god."

"Yeah."

They sat for a moment and listened to the cartoons coming through the wall. Her shoulder holster pinched, and she undid it, set it on the bed beside her. Rubbed at her eyes, remembering Donlan as she used to know him, a friend, then a confidant, then a lover. "It might not mean anything. The guy could just have been making a point."

"Hell of a point."

She nodded.

"What about calling Internal Affairs? Couldn't they help?" Palmer said it like a civilian, somebody who'd watched cop shows but never worn a star.

"IAD?" She winced. Coming out against another officer was betraying the brotherhood. Besides, it wasn't that simple. "We've got no evidence."

"We'd tell the same story, though."

She laughed. "Sure. It'd go like this: 'While neglecting my assigned duties in order to work a case I'd been ordered off, I had an anonymous caller tip me about a secret meet where I saw my former partner, a decorated sergeant and twenty-year veteran, sell submachine guns to gangbangers. No, I don't know where he got them, or where they are now.

No, I don't have any pictures or physical evidence of any kind. On the up side, I did manage to lose my service weapon—does that count for something?' "

"We know DiRisio's name."

"You extorted it from a gangbanger. Not too useful. If it's even his real name."

"We'd have Billy. He could identify them."

"Our ace in the hole is the eyewitness testimony of an eight-year-old?"

"So what, you want to just quit?" His voice had that tone men only got when speaking to women.

"No, coach," she said. "Stay in my face and I'll win the big game."

He stared at her, anger in his eyes, and then something broke, and he ducked his head and laughed. "Right. Sorry." He blew a breath. "Been a long couple of days."

"Yeah." She paused. "Look, you're right. Your nephew's testimony is something. But it's not enough. Not nearly."

"So where does that leave us?"

"I believe the technical term," she said, "is 'up shit creek.' "

Their TV had a porn channel.

They'd talked round and round until they were worn out. No evidence, and no way to know who was clean and who was dirty, so they couldn't go to the cops. No lead on DiRisio. Working Galway was their best bet, but he would know that. He'd surely protect himself. And the mere thought that Donlan might be involved was enough to make her consider fleeing the country.

Finally, in frustration, they'd decided to take a break, clear their heads. He was in the shower, and she'd flopped on the bed looking for local news, see if by any chance there was mention of automatic weapon fire in downtown Chicago. A deep exhaustion had begun to settle, a hollowed-out feeling from the spent adrenaline. The dingy mattress felt better than it had a right to, and she was channel-surfing, the volume muted. Click, sports. Click, sitcom. Click, two blondes with fake tans and fake tits doing unlikely things to one another with an enormous pink dildo.

It was like a nature film, bugs filmed in extreme close-up. This turned men on?

She shook her head, clicked again. The water stopped, and she heard the curtain slide and a towel pulled from the rack. It was a strangely intimate sound, and put her back in another hotel bedroom. Cramped and dim, a threadbare robe and the smell of red wine spilled on the sheets. Burning shame as she listened to James Donlan in the shower, whistling as he washed her off his body before going home to his wife.

*Stop,* she thought automatically. But it never worked.

She remembered their awkward breakfast. The pressure he'd put on her, telling her not to screw this up. Was it a message that he was involved? Or was it exactly as it appeared on the surface, a politician's desire not to see a simple case get complicated?

No idea. She sighed and rubbed her eyes. Her mother had warned her not to be a cop, said that it would only lead to trouble. Lately it seemed like she was right. Cruz had loved the first nine, ten years, being on the street, running down bad guys. Sure, over and over she'd needed to prove herself, but over and over she had managed to. But ever since her mistake with Donlan, things had gone downhill. First the respect she'd fought to earn had disappeared like smoke. Then the order had come to tie her to a desk, and she'd spent month after endless month working the database, entering reports and interviews other cops gathered. Seeing the street from a distance, a collection of stats. Just a secretary of horror, a reporter of gang crimes and murder scenes and arsons—

Cruz was on her feet before she realized she was moving. She rounded the bed, hit the closed bathroom door, didn't even hesitate. Shoved through.

"Whoa!" Palmer was bent just inside the door drying his legs, but as she came in, he jerked upright, yanking the towel in front of him. His body was tan, his chest lean and muscular, spare, with the puckered ridge of a scar trailing down his left pectoral to where metal dog tags dangled. "What the hell?"

She smiled. "I know what we need to do."

# CHAPTER 27
## Custodian

Goddamn amateur.

Anthony grit his teeth, the line of his jaw hard, that muscle jumping. He had the windows half-open, and a warm breeze blew through the car, tugging at his tie, rifling the *Sun-Times* on the passenger seat. He'd brought it thinking he might read a little to calm down, but the paper lay untouched. His SIG sat on top of it, an ugly suppressor screwed onto the barrel. In the movies everybody had a suppressor, like you could buy one at the corner store, but he'd never had any luck getting a line on them, even with his contacts. Had to build his himself: Steel tube, drill-pressed holes, springs and washers. Used a metal lathe to machine a threaded bit that matched the SIG, then silver-soldered the pieces together. He'd heard you could buy suppressors over the counter in Finland, have to get there someday.

But tonight the SIG was just in case there were any more surprises.

The thought set his jaw jumping again. Galway. Amateur. First he wouldn't acknowledge what had to be done to silence the Billy Palmer brat. Anthony had been forced to plead the case like a first-time triggerman, and Galway had still found a way to screw that up, using gangbangers to do the deed. And tonight, when Jason Palmer delivered himself up dead to rights, Galway managed to let him get away.

So now here Anthony was, two in the fucking morning,

sitting in this fucking jig neighborhood like he had nothing better to fucking do. A fucking custodian, just mopping up the fucking mess.

Headlights glowed in his rearview. About fucking time. He wriggled low in the seat, took up the SIG, held it close to his chest, barrel up, just in case. But the Jaguar passed, the engine smooth and soft as it paused outside a garage, the door rolling up. The garage was surprisingly orderly, no clutter, clean swept, even a pegboard with tools neatly hung. The guy had probably never used them, bought them out of a catalog 'cause that's what you were supposed to have in your garage.

Anthony smiled. Felt that tingle in his bladder that meant play time.

He counted one hundred, then got out of the car, leaving behind his SIG in favor of the cop's Smith. He'd busted the porch lights when he first arrived—it took three shots for two lights, which pissed him off a little, but the suppressor threw off accuracy—and so he walked tall to the front door. He wondered idly if the guy would have company tonight. Galway wouldn't like that. Weakling amateur, no stomach for the work at hand.

Two locks, one an up-model Schlage that cost an extra twenty seconds, and he was inside, mouth open, listening. A hunter. Let his mind feel his way through the dark as his eyes adjusted. Sleek furniture coming into focus, a black leather couch, a low glass coffee table, a painting of an African woman fighting a tiger, only her head tilted back and her tits exposed, like maybe they weren't actually fighting, maybe the tiger was tearing off a piece. It wasn't clear, let you decide. He kind of liked it.

Thick white carpeting covered the floor, and he moved easy, his passage barely a rustle. Eased up the steps as music started above, something softer than Anthony would have expected. Brown sugar beats and a woman's voice, singing how when she first met him, he was the sweetest thing, a Sade tape in the cold of spring, and then Anthony kicked the door open, the wood swinging fast to crack off the opposite wall, Dion Wallace frozen in tableaux in the middle of his bedroom, perfect, no cover, no weapons, a snifter in one hand, a bottle of Courvoisier in the other, paisley silk robe open and his junk exposed.

"Hiya, C-Note. I'd ask how it's hanging, but I can see for myself." Anthony smiled, stepped in. "You know, I'd always heard you boys packed extra weight. Must be cold in here, huh?"

Dion had the panicked look of an animal surprised, eyes darting left and right, like he wanted to dive back in his hole. "Man, what you about?"

"Figured I'd drop by, see how things were going. You know, shoot the shit. See if you'd finished the assignment I gave your black ass."

The gangbanger straightened, narrowed his eyes. He poured cognac into the snifter, threw it back, poured another. "You want one?"

"Sure."

Dion turned the bottle upside down so the brown liquor poured out in a ropy stream, glug glug. Smiled. "Just ran out."

Anthony shook his head. "See, that's what's wrong with you people. Trying to come off hard, but all you did, you poured booze on your nice white carpet."

"Carpet don't mean shit to me," tossing the empty bottle aside. "I got the bank, have new stuff down before I'm even home tomorrow."

"Yeah, but see, it didn't do any *good*. You ruined your carpet for nothing. I mean, if wanted to use the bottle as a weapon, that I could understand. Of course," gesturing with his left hand while his right jerked the Smith, like a magician distracting his audience, "a bottle would be a little outclassed. But at least it would suggest some, what do you call it, proactivity."

Dion glanced at the pistol, then into Anthony's eyes. "What you want?"

"I want you to close your damn robe."

The man moved slow, insolent, his eyes heavy-lidded, showing this weren't nothing but a minor annoyance. Anthony waited till he had the sash tied, then holstered the Smith, smiled like they were buddies. "Now, tell me what's happened with Jason Palmer."

"I got crews out all over the place. His crib, his brother's, even watching the bar y'all burned down. He pops his head out anywhere, I got a hard-eyed brother ready to take care of business. Boy's a corpse, he just don't realize it yet."

"That so?"

Dion nodded, took a sip of cognac.

"So then, I gotta ask, how did he and his little cop girlfriend show up at Lower Wacker, screw up a deal I was making?"

Dion coughed, lowered his drink fast. "What?"

"All of a sudden, there he is, like he don't have a care in the world. Not acting like a man got a hundred angry niggers on his tail."

"Lower Wacker." The drink slipped, spilling a few drops before he caught it. "You're shitting me."

Anthony felt his eyes narrowing. This wasn't the reaction he'd anticipated. Something unexpected was going on here. "That ring a bell?"

"Motherfucker." Dion drank the rest of the cognac. Shook his head. "Martinez."

"Martinez?" What was this? DiRisio replayed the conversation in his head. Lower Wacker. The jig had reacted to Lower Wacker. Now why would that be?

It hit. "Oh, you stupid monkey. You made a deal."

"Shit no." The words coming too fast.

"Yes, you did." Pussy-assed *amateurs*. "You talked to Palmer, didn't you? He offer you money or something?"

"Nah, man, I ain't seen him." His eyes edgy, glancing at the night table. That would be where he had a weapon.

"So who's Martinez?"

"Just some cop, white dude. Came into my crib running game, you know? Said it was like cowboys and Indians."

Anthony stared at him. "I don't speak Ebonics."

"This Martinez said the cavalry was waiting, gonna roll us all up unless I gave him something. I didn't have no choice.

But I didn't give up shit he could use, no names or nothing. I figured you're a man who can take care of business. Handle hisself, you know?"

Who was this Martinez? He could be a friend of the woman cop's. But why bring Palmer? And why hadn't Galway heard about it? It didn't make any sense. If the police had known about the buy, they wouldn't have sent just Cruz and Palmer. It would have been a circus of red and blue lights. But if Martinez hadn't told them, how else could Palmer have gotten there? Unless . . . "You said this cop was white?"

"Yeah, just had a Latin name."

"Was he by any chance about six foot? Built, surfer hair, drove a Caddy?"

Dion stared. "How you know?"

Oh, the fucking humanity. Anthony laughed. Jason Palmer had some sack, no doubt about it. Some serious swinging sack.

Good. Better that way. More fun.

"This Martinez, what did he do to get you to talk?" Savored that sweet tingle. Spoke slow, contempt in his voice. "He get up in your grille? He dis your hoopdy?"

"Man, what you talking about?"

"Nothing, Dion. I'm talking about nothing at all." He did his magic trick with the cop's Smith again.

The first shot hit just above the cheek, ripping the skin up and back, and for a split second, just before it tore off a sizable chunk of his head, the bullet made it look like Dion Wallace really got the joke.

# CHAPTER 28
Everyday People

Jason hadn't realized how hungry he was until they'd walked in the diner and the smells hit, bacon and coffee and grease.

"The X-Factor," Cruz said.

"Yes." He spoke around a mouthful of tuna melt.

"I entered a lot of data. I mean, you wouldn't *believe* how much data I've entered. And every now and then, it started to seem like there was a pattern. You know, something moving behind the scenes. Only I could never put my finger on it."

"Right." He gestured at her untouched fries. "You going to eat those?"

She pushed the plate across the Formica tabletop. "And then yesterday, something you said made me look at it differently."

"Something I said?"

"Yeah. You said something about how in Iraq, people just got used to living in a world that was burning. It made me think, shit, sounds like Crenwood. The arson stats are really high—much higher than they should be. I'd noticed that before, just in the course of entering data. But I didn't realize what it meant, because I hadn't found my X-Factor."

"Galway and DiRisio."

"Exactly." She held a fork in both hands, spun it, staring at the tines. "It's funny."

"What?"

"I hated this assignment. The database. You know, I

thought, this is no kind of work for a cop. They put it on me to keep me off the streets. Only it turns out that the cops working the streets are bad, and that the database is the weapon we need."

He nodded. "I think they call that irony."

"Yeah," she said and stiffened.

Jason followed her gaze, saw the blue-and-white out the window. Two men inside. She turned to face him, put a hand up to play with her hair, hiding her profile. Her eyes darted. "Are they watching?"

Jason popped a fry in his mouth, looked out the window, just a guy having breakfast. Ready to move if he had to, thinking a sprint through the kitchen and out the back exit would probably be the best route.

The light changed, and the cruiser pulled away.

"They're gone." He reached for the Tabasco, shook till the fries turned crimson.

She glanced out the window, glanced back. Shook her head. "I still can't believe this is happening."

"I know that feeling." Thinking of Michael, of Billy. This dirty little conspiracy had cost his brother's life, had saddled him with responsibility he wasn't prepared for. That he hadn't even had time to think about. But now wasn't the time either. First he had to make sure his nephew was safe. Then he could figure out the rest of his life. "You're sure it will have what we need?"

She nodded. "My computer at work is basically an abacus. You wouldn't believe the equipment we have to deal with. So I always work on my personal laptop, then just upload the database to the CPD system every day. I've got data on every recent gang incident, from graffiti to homicide to arson. Somewhere in there we'll find what we need. Then when we go in to IAD, it's not just us talking. We've got facts and stats. Maybe not exactly proof, but enough to get a good cop's attention."

"Sounds pretty thin to me."

"That laptop is the closest thing we have to evidence," she

said. He started to argue, but Cruz cut him off. "Look, you know how you were talking about trust? Goes both ways."

He sighed. "Yeah."

The waitress came by with the check, telling them to stay as long as they liked, no rush. Jason nodded, took a slug of the coffee, lukewarm now, forked a Tabasco-soggy fry. Chewed slowly, trying to steady his tingling nerves. For the moment they were all right, but he knew it was a temporary respite, like ducking under an awning against a storm. It didn't stop the rain.

Cruz reached for her tea, took a sip, set it down with her lips curling. "I don't know how you do it," she said.

"What?"

"Eat. My stomach is completely off."

"First rule of soldiering. When there's food, eat. Never know how many miles you'll have to run before chow."

"I wouldn't make it. I need food every two hours or my body shuts down." She paused. "Did you like it?"

"Being a soldier?" He thought of the feeling of pride he'd had when he made sergeant, the thrill of walking with his unit, the camaraderie and faith. "Yeah. I liked it a lot."

"So why leave?"

He wiped his lips with the napkin. "What about you, you like being a cop?"

He could tell she noticed the evasion, but she didn't call him on it. "Yes, I like it."

"Good at it?"

Cruz opened her mouth. Closed it. The condensation from her water glass had dripped into rings on the table, and she dipped a finger in one, traced wet lines. "I used to think so."

"Hey," he folded the napkin and laid it atop the remnants of his meal, "don't let this get to you. There was no way you could have guessed what was going on."

"It's not that."

"What then?"

She paused. Said, "No one trusts me."

"Why not?"

"They think that I got assigned to the squad as a PR move." Her cadence slow, like she were picking her words. "Or that it's favoritism. No one believes that I belong there. How can I be a good cop if no one trusts me?"

"Prove them wrong."

"It's not that simple. There are a lot of . . . issues." She sighed, shook her head. "Can we talk about something else?"

"Sure." He waited a beat. "Cubs or Sox?"

Cruz looked surprised, and then laughed. She had one of those honest laughs, rich and good, and he grinned back at her. Realized he didn't think he'd heard her laugh before, and liked that it was his doing. It felt normal, a man and a woman sitting in a restaurant booth, talking, joking. No guns, no gangbangers.

"I didn't leave the Army," he said, the words just kind of coming out. "I was discharged."

She cocked her head, but didn't say anything.

"They call it an 'other than honorable' discharge. What they give when you don't merit a formal court martial."

"What happened?"

He looked out the window. Everyday people, coming and going. The sun shivering the concrete. Girls on blankets in the park. In all, a perfectly normal morning in Chicago. Even now, months back, he still sometimes had moments when he couldn't believe it existed. Bikinis and billboards, neon and green grass.

"We were on-mission, guarding a house. The brother-in-law of somebody's nephew, one of those things. There was a lot of that stuff there. Still is. Anyway, it was just another mission, nothing special."

The squad bulky with body armor under desert gear. The acrid smell of sweat and the way the clinging dust itched. A silent head count, his hundredth of the day, terrified, always, of leaving a man behind: Jones, Campbell, Kaye, Frieden, Crist, Flumignan, Borcherts, Paoletti, Rosemoor, and Martinez, ten men. His ten men. Martinez clowning, saying that to really guard the house, they ought to be inside, where the owner was watching the Red Wings on his satellite television. Joining in the laughter, feeling good, the air soft with the approach of sunset, already tasting the ice-cold Gatorade that would be waiting in the chow hall.

Then the sound of the engine. The joking vanishing instantly, replaced by operational paranoia. They'd moved as a team, weapons fixed, positions good, covering the entrance to the courtyard. He'd led from the front, the first to step onto the winding alley that fronted the place.

"It was an ambulance, an old diesel job with black smoke coming out the back," he said. "I heard a loud pop, sounded like a blown tire."

More real than the street outside the diner was his memory of that moment. The comforting weight of his weapon against gloved palms. The taut pull of the chin strap of his helmet. Dinner smells, cumin and black pepper and smoke.

The ambulance had stopped a hundred yards north, in the center of the alley. Jason could see the doors wing open. Two dark-skinned men looked around edgily. One vanished around the back, then returned with a tire iron, squatted beside the front right of the truck while the other kept a nervous watch. Knowing, as Jason did, that in the center of a back street in insurgent territory, with no protection, with medical supplies and possibly drugs on board, they were only one thing.

A target.

Jason's orders were clear: Guard the house. Stay put until relieved. But there could be wounded in back. Maybe women, or children.

"You never know, is the thing. Over there. One minute somebody is smiling and waving, the next they're aiming an AK-74." He shrugged. "But it was an ambulance."

He'd ordered the squad to stay put, taken Paoletti and Martinez. Moving carefully, not hugging the sides. In a firefight, bullets rode the walls. Dark eyes watching from windows, always gone when he turned to look. The ambulance drew nearer a step at a time. A long hundred yards. He watched the men working on the truck, saw one of them stop, shade his

eyes with his hands, wave them forward. Yelling something in
Arabic, fast and guttural. Jason ignored him. The previous
week a truck disguised as an ambulance had been loaded with
bathtub-brewed dynamite and detonated amid a crowd of men
applying for positions in the Iraqi National Guard.

"Funny, but you remember the littlest things. The sun was
setting, and I remember thinking how someday I would miss
those sunsets. It's all the dust. Makes it look like heaven is
on fire."

The man squatting beside the tire had a thin dark mustache. A perfect bead of sweat hung at one end. He'd looked
up and smiled, pointed to the spare beside him, said something unintelligible.

Jason signaled Paoletti to watch while he and Martinez
moved to the rear of the ambulance. His heart pounding. Not
something you ever got used to, the realization that if things
went wrong, you could suddenly not be there any more. Not
be, period.

At the rear, he'd leveled his weapon as Martinez put one
hand on the handle. Nodded to him, ready to fire, thinking
*short, controlled bursts,* thinking *don't let this be the moment,* and then Martinez had yanked open the rear door and
raised his own rifle, both of them yelling Arabic phrases
they'd learned phonetically.

A wide-eyed boy about five years old stared at them from
the floor of the ambulance. A man knelt over him, crimson
fingers moving in his chest. The doctor glanced at them,
turned back to the boy without a word. Didn't ask what they
wanted, who they were, just worked to save the life of a child.

"It'd been a shell, a mortar shell. Insurgents lob them all
the time, and their aim sucks. No training and old Soviet
hardware smuggled in from Afghanistan. This kid had been
playing with his brother a mile from our FOB. The shrapnel
tore him to ribbons."

"Jesus," Cruz said. Her voice quiet. "What did you do?"

"We set down our weapons and cranked up that ambulance like we were swapping a tire at the Indy 500."

When they were finished, the little man with the driver

had shaken Jason's hand, then put his right hand over his heart. Jason had repeated the gesture, feeling good. Watched them start the ambulance, black smoke farting out the exhaust, and stood aside to let them drive away. He and Martinez and Paoletti had smiled at one another. Started walking back beneath the burning sky. He remembered the warmth in his chest, the sense that he loved these men and would do anything for them.

And when they'd gone about thirty feet, Jason heard a distant crack. His mind classified it, medium-caliber rifle fire, single shot, and then Martinez said, "Oh."

Just that, "Oh," no scream or cry or curse, and then blood began to pulse from his neck, a thick, ropey flow, not spraying like an arterial hit but pouring fast, the top of his desert camos staining dark, no, no, Martinez, the nicest guy you'd ever meet, blood everywhere, Martinez with his hands at his throat like he could hold it back, his whole life pulsing through clenched fingers.

Christ save him, Jason's first thought was relief that it wasn't him. And the Worm had been born in his chest, filthy greasy contemptible cowardly pansy useless outsider waste that he was.

"A sniper shot one of my men," Jason said, and stared at the pattern of divots in the Formica table. Traced shapes with a rough fingertip. "I haven't talked about it with anyone since I came home, not even Michael." He scratched at his forehead, closed his eyes, able to see Martinez passing around pictures of Scarlett Johansson and claiming she was his fiancée, Martinez crying with laughter as he pummeled Jones with a chair in their X-Box wrestling game, Martinez who died before they could even get him in the Humvee, who coughed and clutched at Jason's arm and left fingerprints black and ragged. Just a boy. "I don't know why I'm telling you."

Cruz reached across the table and took his hand. The move surprised him, brought him back to the moment, to the simple pleasure of human contact, a living woman touching him. He looked up, met her eyes, watched her bite her lip like she was picking her words carefully.

Then she said, "I slept with another cop. A married one."

"What?" Confused.

"That's why no one trusts me. He was a superior, a friend, and one time things got out of hand. Just one stupid time. But after it got out, everybody figured it was how I'd earned my place in the unit." Fire in her eyes on that, angry pressure on his hand. "So now no one trusts me, no one believes I have what it takes. And no matter how hard I work or how many cases I close, I can't go back and undo it."

He didn't know what to say, just looked at her, felt her fingers warm and soft in his.

"I know it's nothing like what happened to you," Cruz said. "I'm not comparing it, my problems at work to your war. I just . . . I don't know, wanted to tell you something. Tell you the thing that I didn't tell other people, the way you hadn't talked about what happened in Iraq." She stopped, started again, stopped. Looked at him. "Does that make any sense?"

"Yes," Jason said. For a moment he let himself just meet her eyes and pretend that they were two normal people sharing secrets amidst the clatter of silverware and the burnt smell of coffee, like this was the morning after a date that left the world ripe with possibility. Then he sighed and took his hand from hers.

"It's time."


The street was wide and lined with trees in summer bloom. A gentle breeze set branches rustling, their shadows shifting liquid. Cars were parked along both sides, and well-dressed women with expensive hair drifted among the small shops. The fresh smell of bread rose from a bakery.

"Looks clear," Cruz said.

He nodded. "Hurry."

They moved north on the sidewalk with the fastest walk that wouldn't draw attention. A car rounded the corner from Lincoln, and Jason tensed. "I wish we had a gun."

Cruz didn't reply. Her apartment tower was born of the seventies, a plain, blocky structure with broad windows bouncing sunlight. From the lobby an elderly doorman smiled

at her and touched a button on his desk, and the entry unlocked with a buzz.

"Mr. Thomas," she said. "How are you?"

"Fine, Ms. Cruz." The man nodded as they walked past.
"You have a good day now."

A hallway led off the lobby to the elevator bays, four
shining doors. Cruz thumbed the call button while he rocked
on his heels. His shoulder itched and his neck was sore from
tackling the guy last night. Behind him, he heard the buzzer
sound again, but couldn't see the lobby door from this angle.

An elevator arrived with a soft ding, the doors opening as
it settled. They stepped in and she hit the button for fourteen.
The floor was soft carpet, and a polished brass rail ran along
the back wall. Not showy, but definitely nice.

"This isn't where I'd have pictured you living." Talking to
fill the silence.

"Whiter than you expected?"

"No, just more, I don't know, poodle-owning."

Cruz laughed. "It's not what my mother pictures either."
The doors opened on a decorated waiting area, a side table
with fake flowers and a mirror above it, like people were often choosing to hang out by the elevators instead of in their
apartments. "Police have to live in the city. There's a joke,
neighborhoods like Beverly and Garfield Ridge are called
'My Blue Heaven' because of the number of cops that live
there. Nice enough, but it never appealed."

"Why does this?"

She shrugged. "Maybe because my mother can't picture
it." They reached her apartment, a door at the end of the hallway beside the stairwell. She dug in her pocket for the keys.
From down the hall came a chime, another elevator arriving at
her floor. Cruz slid a key into the top deadbolt. "It's not that
I'm not close to my mom, it's just that it's better when she's
far away."

Jason started to reply, then it hit. Another elevator.

He spun, looked down the hall. The space was narrow and
constrained, a long row of staggered doors with the elevator
lounge halfway down and around a corner. Nowhere to hide.

A male voice drifted down the hallway, the sound muffled. "Which way's her place?"

"Over here."

Cruz froze, her key in the deadbolt, her eyes mirroring his panic.

He tried the door opposite hers. Locked. Glanced around. The stairwell.

Jason pulled her after him, key ripping out of the lock. He fought the urge to throw open the door, stepped through quickly, then spun as she passed and caught the handle to ease the door closed so the spring-hinges didn't slam it.

Bright sterile light, cigarette butts and gum stains. There was a small window in the door, and Jason flattened himself along the wall, Cruz close enough he could smell her perfume. Maybe he was wrong. Could be a neighbor. Hell, could be a pizza delivery guy.

"—can't believe this shit." The gruff voice grew closer through the door.

"Don't surprise me at all. You got the key from the doorman?"

"Here." Metal tickled metal, and then the clean snapping sound of a deadbolt opening. "Ready?"

"Go."

Jason tensed, then heard a door slam open, the one to her apartment. He heard the men rush in, shouting *Freeze!*, their voices growing muffled by the walls of her apartment. Only cops yelled like that.

He pointed down the stairs. She nodded, moved on the ball of her feet, lithe, one step at a time but quick as an aerobics routine. He followed, wanting to glance back up at the door but not daring, knowing if the police stepped into the hallway, the gesture could give them away.

More dirty cops. Cold fingers closed on his heart.

His fingers traced the chipped metal railing. Taking three steps at a stride, more jumping than running. The sounds of their footfalls echoed up the shafts. He watched the numbers drop on the fire doors, eleven, ten, nine. His breath came harder, not the effort but the suddenness of it, dead stop to mad hustle. Six, five, four. Cruz spun around a landing, and he focused on her, watched her body move, spare and economical. On the third floor, he stopped, said her name. "Finish up slow. Can't burst out panting."

She nodded, started down again at a walk. One flight, a landing, another flight, and then the exit came into sight. He felt an urge to call Billy, promised himself he'd do it if they made it out.

"Ready?" she asked.

He nodded, and she stepped into a carpeted hall. Easy, confident, the kind of fine-looking woman who belonged in this building. He fell in beside, willing his pulse steady. Just stroll thirty feet of hallway, clear the lobby, and they'd be out. He concentrated on the little details instead of thinking, tracing the patterns in the carpet, counting the sconces in the hallway. His reflection distorted as they passed the bronze elevator doors. Almost there. He could see the sunlight spilling in the lobby windows.

"Motherfucker, I *look* like I'm playin'?" The unseen voice from the lobby was familiar and filled with menace. Jason grabbed Cruz's arm, stopped her just before she stepped into view. Shook his head, listened.

"You see this?" A whimper came from the front. "That's right. You right to be scared, old man, 'cause you don't tell me where the Cruz bitch lives, I'm going to work on you with this thing."

Her eyes narrowed. She whispered, "Who?"

"Playboy. The one who tried to hijack me." Fighting the urge to run, his fingers flexing. "God*damn* I wish we had a gun."

She grimaced. "Back door."

He nodded, followed her down the same nice hallway in reverse, carpet patterns and sconces. Around a corner, down another length of hall. "We can get out to LaSalle through here." She pushed open a door, and they stepped into a sweltering loading dock. High ceilings, hard rubber floor, the smell of trash. Roll doors on one wall. He spotted an exit twenty feet away just in time to see it open in an explosion of light, white sun stabbing into the murky dimness. Saw a figure coming through, barrel-chested man in blue, heavy belt—shit, another cop—hands to his eyes, looking back at someone and saying, "Man, it's *dark* after that sun," and then Cruz pulled him out of the loading dock and back into the hallway.

They stared at each other. Trapped. From one direction gangbangers, from the other cops, and nowhere in between for them to hide, no alternate routes. The stairs and elevator were too risky—the geriatric doorman wouldn't hold off Playboy for long. But if they stayed here, the police would get them.

Jason grit his teeth and looked wildly around. Tried a door that looked like it led to a service closet, found it locked. Looked at a small decorative trash can, wondered if he could throw it. A trash can against a submachine gun. He shook his head. The door to the loading dock was in the center of the wall, and there was just enough space beside it that he could probably pack himself into the corner, hope the guy coming through didn't notice right away. Get the jump on him. Though he wasn't eager to swing at a cop, especially with gangbangers coming the other direction.

Footsteps echoed from the loading dock. They had seconds.

He looked at Cruz, saw the way she was assessing the situation, not frozen up but working it, and he felt a strange comfort in that, and then the idea hit and he yanked her into the corner by the door, putting her back against the wall and standing squarely in front of her, his shoulders spread as broad as possible, and then he said, "Trust me," and he kissed her.

At first her lips were stiff, resistant. Then they opened, her tongue fluttering soft against his, her arms wrapping around him as she realized what he was doing, how right it had to look, how passionate. And maybe it was the energy of the moment, but as the door swung open and he heard the heavy footfall of a cop behind him, he found that he wasn't having to fake the passion, that he was genuinely hungry for her, the spice of tea faint on her lips, the earthy smell of the sweat on her neck, the strength in the fingers gripping his back. She fit against him, and his nerves strained forward, quivering.

He was barely aware of the cop pausing behind him, could feel the tingling in the back of his neck. Then he banished all thought and concentrated on believing in the kiss.

The footfalls began again, softer on the carpeted hallway, one rough voice saying, "Goddamn, you remember what it felt like to kiss a woman that way?" A beat later, the other cop deadpanning, "Sure. Your wife, Saturday night," then both of them laughing, the sound of it receding as they turned the corner.

Jason couldn't say for sure, but he felt like she held the kiss the same slightly unnecessary extra half-second that he did.

He glanced down the hall to make sure they were gone, then stepped back, feeling suddenly naked now that he no longer touched the heat of her body, and she said, "Come on."

Through the doors to the dry heat and wet stink of the loading dock. He cracked the outside door a finger's breadth, risked a glance. The police cruiser was empty. He pushed the door open, and then they were walking down LaSalle, the 22 bus rumbling by, smell of exhaust and blinking tears against the brightness.

"That was close," he finally managed.

"Yeah," she said, and then laughed, not the good laugh from before, but one tinged with something thin and hollow. "I know one of those cops. I recognized his voice."

"Makes sense. Galway probably recruited from your team."

She shook her head. "He's not from my team. He's not even from my district." Her voice had a manic intensity to it. "The city is divided into five separate areas, and he works in a different one."

"But . . . that means—" He paused. "So other cops are coming after us, too?"

"Yeah," she said, and then said the exact words he was thinking. "How big *is* this?"

# CHAPTER 29
## Shoes

Jason was thinking about the way blood looked as it soaked into dust.

They were back in the car, heading east, just after noon but the sun already slanting down the backside of the sky. Chicago was far enough north that the sun never seemed to really peak, just sort of slid around the lip of heaven, even in the summer. That didn't cool it down any, though. The heat shimmers that rose off the Caddy's hood blurred sweating sidewalks: A churro vendor listlessly ringing his bell, white light ricocheting off glass storefronts, Tex-Mex music coming from the speakers of a Western-wear shop.

Over there, the dust'd been *everywhere*. Dust on the streets, dust in the air. Devil-dogging the heels of their boots, whomping out where a 95-pound shell slammed the horizon. When an ajaja settled on Baghdad, the sky would turn yellow with haze. Dust in the crack of their ass, dust in the cuff of their eyelids.

The broken street where Martinez died was powdered with ocher dust.

"Donlan," Cruz said.

"The head of detectives?"

"Yeah." Her voice sounded flat, and she spoke to the passenger window, not to him. "I don't want to believe he's involved, but if he is, that could explain the other cops. Even from a different area."

"You're saying he's got dirty cops all over the city?"

"Not necessarily. He's a powerful guy. If he gave the order, clean cops would try to get it done, too."

Jason nodded. Swallowed, his mouth dry with a memory of desert. "We should assume he's involved."

She seemed to wince, but said nothing.

"I guess we should get off the street," he said. "Any ideas?"

"It's up to me to come up with all the ideas?"

He glanced over, glanced away. A man was hosing down the sidewalk, the water sparkles of cascading sunlight. The light changed, and he turned north at random.

What now? A bar? Another motel?

Nothing sounded right. Besides, every time they tried to help themselves, they just dug deeper. The day Michael had died, Jason had been overwhelmed at the thought of facing just the gangs. Now that seemed parochial, their enemies had multiplied so many times. First, dirty cops with plenty of juice. All the clean cops, too. Galway, and the mercenary with the scarred face. And worst of all, the man with the heavy muscles and the cold eyes. Anthony DiRisio. An evil spirit in a cheap suit.

Anthony DiRisio, who had murdered his brother.

His fingers went white on the wheel. So much had happened in the last days that he'd hardly had a chance to think about Michael. To mourn him. Life had intervened most fucking spectacularly. He should have had days to think, to drink, to cry and punch holes in the drywall. To comfort Billy.

He heard Michael's voice in his head, saying, *Bang up job you're doing with that last one, bro. Thanks* so *much for taking care of my son.*

Jason glanced in the rearview, saw it was clear, pulled a clean U-turn.

"Where are you going?" Cruz asked. Saying *you*, not *we*.

"I need to see my nephew."

"Why?"

He looked over. "Because he's my nephew." He held it

for a moment, then spoke again, lighter. "Anyway, he's staying with a friend of mine. We can hide the car, figure our next move."

She just wrinkled her mouth and looked back out the window. She'd been like that since they'd left her apartment, sort of crumpled and inward-facing.

"Are you okay?"

"Gangbangers have a contract on us, my boss is in league with them, and I don't have a clue what to do about either of those things." She turned to him, stared a long time. "Am I okay?"

He shook his head. "There's something else."

"What do you mean?"

"That was all true before, but you weren't like this. You didn't get like this until you realized Donlan was involved. Is he that scary?"

She turned away.

A thought struck him. "Wait a second. Was it him?"

Cruz didn't ask *who?*, didn't say anything at all, which should've told him all he needed. But he dug anyway, like an idiot. "Donlan was the cop that you . . . the one you—you know."

She leaned forward, turned on the radio with a snap. The CD in the changer started where it'd been left, Pearl Jam's "Riot Act," that spoken-word song with Vedder saying how the haves have not a clue. She scowled, switched to FM, started spinning the dial.

"Look, I didn't mean to . . ." Jason trailed off. "I just didn't know, that's all."

"Yeah, well, now you do. Congratulations."

"You're *pissed* at me?" Paused. "You're pissed at *me?*"

"Oh for Christ's sake." Her voice loud. She turned to the window, said, "Pull over here."

"Why?"

She shot him a look, and he shook his head, eased the car to the side.

Cruz got out without a word, left the door standing open.

Stalked down the street. Was she leaving? He watched her throw open the door to a convenience store. The sun off the glass made it hard to see, but it looked like she was buying something. Jason glanced around, checked the rearview, uncomfortable to be just sitting here exposed. When he looked back at the storefront, she was already outside, hitting something against her palm, then stripping the wrapping off. Cigarettes.

She put one between her lips and cupped her hands around it in a practiced pose, the lighter flaring in one hand, the pack shielding the other side. She inhaled like she wanted to finish the smoke in one hit.

Her shoulders drooped, and she rocked her head back softly. Blew a long stream of gray. Smiled, and took another drag as she walked. He watched her hips swing. She looked good, relaxed, like after a day at the spa.

Cruz stopped by a trash bin, took a last inhale, then stubbed out the cigarette and tossed it in. Started for the car, made one step before something came over her face, her lips clenching, little frown wrinkles popping. She sighed, then turned and chucked the pack and lighter as well.

"Better?" he asked when she settled into the passenger seat.

She said, "Let's go."

She sounded pissed off in just the right way, and it made him smile.


Given everything that was happening, Crenwood seemed a strange place to be, and it had Jason's nerves jangling. Hell, less than a mile away was the Disciples house he'd bluffed his way into.

On the other hand, the last place anybody would look for them was the heart of enemy territory.

"A little further," Ronald said, and motioned with his fingers. The big man had answered Washington's door when they knocked, nodded at Jason, and listened patiently while they explained they wanted to park the Caddy out of sight.

Washington's garage was a squat structure separated from the main house by an alley, and the whale of a Caddy was a tight fit in the tiny garage. "Further. Stop."

Jason hopped out, turned sideways and held his breath to squeeze out of the garage. "Washington's car will be okay on the street?"

"That beater?" Ronald snorted, then tugged the garage door closed. He led them back to the house. "Dr. Matthews is in his office. It's a busy day, but I know he wants to see you."

"What's up today?" Jason stepped inside.

"The benefit. Mr. Kent giving a lot of bank tonight."

The layout still felt familiar, not from last week but from last lifetime, though now the kitchen had teenagers washing dishes and peeling potatoes, and what Jason remembered as the living room had been turned into a study area, with GED prep books spread on the table. On the couch an older Latino kid was repeating phrases to a younger one, his fingers tracing the words in an English primer.

It wasn't until Washington opened the door of his office that Jason remembered the other night, the words they'd exchanged. But the look on his friend's face made it damn clear that he was the only one who'd forgotten.

"Jason." Incongruously, Washington was dressed in a tuxedo, the tie unclipped and dangling, the cummerbund tight around a sagging belly. His expression was stern as Jason introduced Cruz.

In contrast, she smiled. "It's nice to meet you, Dr. Matthews. You do a lot of good out of here."

"Never enough."

"At least you're fighting."

Washington nodded. "We're trying." He gestured to Ronald. "Why don't you show Officer Cruz around?"

She caught the hint. "I'd love that." She gave Jason's hand a squeeze, a quick move that took him by surprise and left him smiling. The smile faded when Washington gestured him into the office and closed the door, like a principal calling out a teenager.

"Listen, about the other night." Jason sat on the couch. "I didn't mean the things—"

"Son, I'm going to ask you a question, and you better not lie to me."

The tone took Jason aback. "Okay."

"You lie to me and we're through, you hear?"

"Yeah, *okay*."

Washington leaned forward in his chair, elbows on his knees and eyes appraising. "Did you kill him?"

Kill him? Kill who? Jason stared. "What?"

"Did you?"

"No! Who?" He held his hands up and open. "I haven't killed anybody."

Washington narrowed his eyes, cocked his head.

"I don't know what you're talking about." He returned the stare unblinking. "I swear to you, I don't."

A long moment of silence. Then Washington nodded and leaned back. He sighed like he was blowing out the last of his breath. "All right."

"What's this about?"

"The head of the Gangster Disciples, man named Dion Wallace, was killed last night."

"*What?*" He flashed back to the gang crib, C-Note Wallace telling him there was a war going on. Yesterday afternoon. "What happened?"

Washington shrugged. "I don't know. But I know you and Ronald talked on the porch for a long time last night, and I saw murder in your eyes."

"I went to see him, but I didn't kill him." Jason ran through it, starting with his meeting with C-Note and continuing through everything that had happened since. Washington listened, fingers steepled imperturbably in front of him, betraying no emotion. Rage, frustration, even philosophy wouldn't have surprised Jason. But the apparent apathy made him talk faster, emphasize the points more. Finally, he asked, "Are you following me?"

"Perfectly."

"These guys are arming gangbangers. The same kids you're trying to help, they're setting against each other."

"Sounds like it."

"So how come you're so calm?" His voice rising a little at the end.

Washington shrugged. "You watch the news. Our last *governor* is being tried for corruption: Money laundering, illegal campaign contributions, hired truck scandals with possible Mafia ties. The *governor*. You think a couple of corrupt cops are going to stun me? This is Chicago."

"And so it's business as usual? You don't want to fight back?"

"Please." Washington sighed. "There are ways to fight that don't involve a handgun."

"Like what?"

"Like the way I'm doing it, or the way Mr. Kent is doing it. Man is using his money to make things better. He's giving something to make the world a better place, instead of taking something. You want to admire someone, admire him. Because as long as you're holding a pistol, you're a taker, not a giver."

"Yeah, well, I don't have half a million dollars laying around."

"It's not the money. It's the commitment to making things better." Washington reached for the ashtray on his desk, took a half-smoked cigar from within and lit it with a wooden match. "Commitment is something you might want to think about, son."

Jason felt a flush creeping up his neck, heat in his cheeks. "I *am* committed."

"To what?"

"To Billy! You wouldn't believe the things I've been doing, trying to find—"

"Uh-huh. And while you've been running around playin' Superman, what do you think your nephew's been going through?"

Jason's mouth fell open. He started to reply, then stopped

himself. Finally, he said, "You said that it would be okay if
he stayed here."

"It's fine with me. But it's not *me* you're hurting."

"What—look, it's not like I'm hanging out at the strip
club. I'm out there risking my life to protect him."

Washington nodded. "Being a soldier."

"Damn right."

"That's important to you, isn't it?"

"What am I if I'm not that?" The words came unbidden,
and surprised him.

"How about an uncle?" Washington's voice could've cut
granite. "It ever occur Billy needs that more than a soldier?"

Jason sighed. "I know. I *know*. And I'll make it up to him.
But first I've got to protect him."

Washington nodded, puffed his cigar. Blew a long stream
of gray smoke. "Thing is, it's not just the bad guys he needs
protecting from. Put yourself in his shoes. You're eight years
old and just had your father taken from you. Your *father*.
Don't you see? His sky is falling."

The vein in Jason's forehead thumped, and his mouth
tasted small and sour. He looked away. He didn't often think
about the day Dad left, mostly because for practical purposes
the guy had been gone years before he bothered to move. It
was something that Jason had always sworn to do differently,
if he ever had kids.

"You understand where I'm going?" Washington's voice
gentler. "What I mean by commitment?"

Jason nodded. "So what do I do?"

"Talk to him."

"But . . ." He fought a twisting in his gut. "What do I say?"

"How should I know, son?"


He found Billy in the dark corner of a sunlit room, laying on
the floor with his legs flung out, using a red crayon to draw
on a brown paper bag. His tongue stuck a flicker past his
lips, a wet snail. When he heard Jason's footsteps, the crayon
stopped moving and his body stiffened.

"Hey, buddy."

Billy didn't look up. He pinched the crayon harder, the tip of his finger bloodless, and started stroking fast, hard lines.

Jason took a tentative step forward. "What are you drawing?"

Silence. Jason felt an acid shudder in his gut, like he'd put away a pot of coffee. He had no idea what to say to an eight-year-old who'd lost his father. Hell, he had no idea what to say to an eight-year-old at all. He thought of Michael, could almost conjure him up amidst the dancing dust motes, his brother shaking his head. Jason sighed inwardly, thought, *Couldn't I just go back and break into the Disciples drug house again?*

But Washington was right. He had to be more than just a soldier.

If only he knew how.

"Are you mad at me?" Jason spoke softly. "It's okay if you are."

Billy hunched further over his drawing.

"I know how things must seem to you right now. How . . ." He faltered. "Confused you must be. And sad, too. It's okay if you feel like that. It's normal." He tried to do what Washington had said, put himself in the boy's shoes. At that age, how did you conceive of death? Did he understand he'd never see his father again? Or was that too big an idea?

Michael.

They would never again sit at the kitchen table drinking coffee through till dawn. Michael would never again greet him with a smile and a nod and a pint of beer. And Jason would never get to apologize for the way they'd left things, or to thank his brother for always being there, even during the times they wanted to tear each other's heads off. Loss was a cold stone aching in the center of his chest.

How much worse, then, must this be for Billy?

Jason squatted in the sunlight beside his nephew. A neat terminator divided his forearm into sunlight and shadow as he reached out, touched Billy's shoulder. Set his hand there, feeling the warmth of the skin, the motion of his breathing.

Just held the moment, the connection, trying to put into it what comfort he had.

"What's going to happen?" Billy spoke to the floor.

Jason sighed. *I don't know.* "Things are going to be okay."

"How?" The boy whirled, jerked back from his hand. "*How?*"

"Well . . ." The truth was that he had no idea. The truth was that all he'd done so far was make things worse. The truth was that there were people out there who wanted them both dead, and Jason didn't have the first clue how to stop them. But what he said was, "I'm going to find the guys who hurt your dad, and I'm going to make sure that they can't hurt you."

"Then what?" Billy's eyes were wide and wet. "What happens after that? Where will I live? Do I go to school? What *happens?*"

Jason stared at him. Right, he thought. Sure. The boy was eight. He wasn't concerned about gangsters. If an adult told him he was going to take care of something, Billy'd believe it. His grief would manifest other ways: anger, depression, fear of abandonment. With his father gone, the world he knew had ended. *Of course* Billy was wondering where he would live.

And it was a pretty good question.

Panic flashed through Jason, quick and hot as lightning. The thought had occurred to him a hundred times in the last few days, and every time he'd shoved it away, told himself he needed to focus on action, on finding out what was happening. But now it couldn't be denied any longer.

He was the only family Billy had left, and like it or not, he was responsible for the boy.

Jason felt his chest tighten. He wasn't ready. Not for anything like it. He could hardly take care of himself. To promise Billy anything would mean giving up everything. He'd have to make choices about his own life, stick to them. Pretend he was a sensible adult with his shit buttoned up, instead of a lost child nursing wounds only he could see, feeding the Worm he claimed to hate.

He cast about for something to say. Looked at the wall, the window, the sun, his eyes dancing. Coming to rest on the drawing in front of Billy.

"Can I see?" He reached for the paper bag, hoping for something to distract him, to distract them both.

The drawing had started simply: A door with a four-panel window on either side, and in front, a lumpy, out-of-scale tree. The same house drawn by generations of children, the lines rough and hesitant, a kid's clumsy attempt to conjure something from his mind.

But darker lines grew out of it. Horizontal and vertical slashes that framed boxes. Each connected, spouting from one another. Doors between them, and windows. A series of rooms, he realized, like a twisted mansion. Space piling on space, higher and further. An impossible, unwieldy labyrinth. A sorcerer's lair. And in the smallest room in a forgotten corner, lost in the maze, stood a stick figure with big hands and wide eyes.

Jason stared at the drawing, his fingers trembling. Stared at the red world Billy saw himself in. Not just lost.

Alone.

"I'll tell you the truth, kiddo." He passed the drawing back, then swung his legs out to lay on his belly beside Billy. "I don't know yet. There will be a lot of things we have to figure out. But everything will be okay. I promise." Realizing, as he said the words, that he meant them. That he would do whatever it took to make them true.

Billy wiped his nose with the back of one hand, unconvinced. "I was scared last night. You didn't come back."

"I know. I'm sorry." He reached out and picked up the crayon Billy had abandoned, twiddled it idly between his fingertips. "I was . . . well, I was trying to get the bad guys. If I could have, I'd rather have stayed here with you."

"You would?"

"Definitely." He nudged Billy with his shoulder. "You're my man."

They lay there in a silence a moment. The crayon's tip

had been worn to a broad spade, and Jason sharpened it with the edge of his thumb. The red wax jammed under his nail like blood.

"Uncle Jason?"

"Yeah?"

"Do you need to go to the hospital?"

"Huh?" He cocked his eyebrows. "Why do you say that, buddy?"

"My dad said that you were sick."

"Sick?"

Billy nodded. "He said that when you went to war you were okay, but that you came back sick." His eyes were egg whites sizzling in a pan. "I don't want you to be sick. I don't want you to die, too."

Jason stared at him. Opened his mouth, closed it. He could feel the Worm tensing inside of him, like it hoped to burst through his chest. When he spoke, his voice came out soft and measured. "Your dad's a smart man. I guess I did come back sick. But it's not the kind I can die from."

"What's wrong?"

"I'm not sure how to explain." He blew air through his mouth. "You know how sometimes you make a mistake and it's not a big deal? It's wrong, but nobody gets hurt. Like when you screw up a homework problem."

Billy nodded.

"Well, sometimes you can make a small mistake that *is* a very big deal. It can be something really simple," seeing the stranded ambulance, a target under skies of flame, "something that seems like the right thing to do. Except if things don't go the way you expect, something bad can happen. When it does, it's easy to feel like you're to blame."

"Something went wrong?" Billy's voice was just a little louder than a whisper.

*Martinez clutching his throat, blood squeezing through clenched knuckles.* "Yeah."

"It was your fault?"

"Well, what went wrong wasn't my fault."

"I don't understand." Billy stared at him. "It wasn't your fault?"

"Sort of. I made a mistake that let somebody else do something bad."

Billy wrinkled his brow. "But you said you were doing the right thing."

"I thought it was." Seeing the wounded Iraqi child in the back, his eyes wide and scared. "I was trying to save people's lives."

"Did you?"

*You killed Martinez,* the Worm hissed in his belly. *You took a twenty-year-old kid off mission against explicit orders, in an area you knew was full of insurgents and snipers. You killed him.*

"I think we might have," he said. "But my friend died, too."

"That's why you got sick?" Billy looked at Jason with the unblinking directness of a child.

"I—" He hesitated. Was it? He'd walled this part of himself off for so long. Hadn't questioned his guilt, hadn't let himself even look at it. And now that he did, he found things weren't as black and white as he pictured. Yes, Martinez was dead. But soldiers died. It was part of the job description. And dying to save the life of a child, that made you a hero, didn't it?

Jason pointed at the drawing. "Lemme see that again."

Billy passed it to him, confused. Jason peered at, made a show of holding it close to his face. "Yup. I thought so. You're missing something."

"What do you mean?"

Jason bent over the paper. Drew a vertical line with four diagonals branching off, topped by a circle with a mop of squiggly lines. A smile and big hands. Passed it back. "There, see?"

"You drew someone with me."

"Look familiar?" He flipped his bangs.

"Is that you?" Billy squinted at the stick figures, the tall one standing behind the smaller one, a hand on one stick shoulder.

"That's me, buddy." He smiled. "That's me." *Somehow.*

*I swear to God, somehow that's going to be me.*

Billy stared at the drawing, then back at him. Then he rolled over and threw his thin arms around Jason, squeezing like that was all that kept him from being swept away.

"Shhh." Jason whispered, little-boy smell strong in his nostrils, sunlight and sweat. A weird blend of emotions shivered through him: terror, sure, but also resolve. And something else, too. It'd been so long since he'd felt it that he almost didn't recognize it.

Pride.

"It's okay, buddy." Jason paused. "Everything is going to be okay." He stared at the ceiling, watched dust burn in a beam of light. Stroked his nephew's hair and made him promises, realizing that he had no idea how to keep them, knowing he'd give his life to.

And then he saw something he never expected.

# CHAPTER 30
## Pale and Sticky

The gun was made of purple plastic, and for a second, even before he remembered what it was and where it came from, Jason felt it tug at him like gravity.

"What the . . ." He trailed off, looked down at Billy. "Where in the world did you get that?"

Billy pulled away, looked up at Jason, then over to the nightstand. "Dad gave it to me. I lost it under the bush when I hid, but yesterday Ronald took me out to look for it." He looked suddenly guilty. "It's yours, though, right?"

Jason realized his mouth was open, so he closed it. Stretched for the Transformer, the toy his brother had gotten for Christmas in 1983, a robot that could turn into a gun. The toy he had lusted after for months, playing with it when Mikey wasn't looking, until he'd accepted his brother's dare to sprint across the El tracks and won it for himself.

It fit his hand so well he wondered if it was why real guns felt like home.

"It's . . . yeah, it used to be mine." He found himself smiling. "I wonder where it's been all these years."

"It was in the basement." Billy wiped his nose on the back of his hand. "Dad gave it to me. But you can have it back."

Jason laughed. "No, kiddo, it's yours."

Billy took the gun and began idly toying with it, folding and unfolding one component. "I wish . . ."

The beginning of the question made Jason wince, imagining all the things his nephew might be wishing. All the things he had a right to but could no longer have. In truth, he was scared to even know what the boy had in mind, but if he was going to be the man in the picture, the one standing by Billy, he may as well start here. "What do you wish, buddy?"

"I wish we'd never gone down there. To the basement." Billy spoke to the floor. "If we'd left instead, we wouldn't have been there. Everything would be okay."

Jason cocked his head, wondering if he was missing something. Down to the basement, was that code? Then he realized what Billy was saying, *Wham!*, like a million volts rattling up his spine. Was it even possible? Could it be? "Your dad took you into the basement the day the men came?"

Billy nodded. Jason straightened, put his hands on Billy's shoulders to stare him in the face. "I have to ask you a question. It's important. Can you think about it very carefully?"

His nephew nodded.

"Did he bring anything with him?" Jason remembering the last time he'd seen Michael, the guy fidgeting with that briefcase, moving it here and there. Never able to find a spot he seemed to feel comfortable leaving it.

Billy looked up and to the left. His tongue wormed through his lips as he concentrated. A long moment passed. Then, "Yes." He brightened like he'd gotten the right answer to a quiz. "He brought a bag."

"A briefcase?"

"Uh-huh."

Jesus. Could it be that simple? Could Billy have had the answer all along?

Of course he could. All he'd needed was for Jason to be around to ask. Being an uncle had just walloped being a soldier. *Umm, duh,* he heard Michael saying. *'Bout time you pulled your head out of your ass.*

He smiled at his nephew. "Thanks, kiddo. You're a genius."

"I am?"

Jason nodded solemnly. "Oh yeah." He ruffled the kid's hair, then stood and started for the door. He had to talk to

Cruz, let her know. And Washington. They had to start planning. Get the car out—

He froze, one hand on the doorframe. Took a breath, turned around.

Billy sat in the center of the room, right where he had been. His eyes were wide and one lip was trembling.

*Idiot.*

Jason walked back to his nephew, dropped to an easy squat. "I did it again, didn't I?"

Billy nodded.

"I'm sorry." He kept his head level with the boy's, trying not to be an authority figure. "I'll learn." He paused. "Will you help me?"

Billy sniffed damply, regarded him with sober eyes, and said, "Okay."

"Okay." Jason nodded. He hesitated, wondered how much to say. Then remembered how it had felt to do the right thing with Billy, how he'd felt the Worm loosen its grip. "That briefcase your father took to the basement? That's what the bad guys were looking for. That's why they came. Do you understand?"

Billy nodded. "Like in the movies."

"Yeah, pretty much. And before, I thought that they had gotten it. But now I bet your dad hid it. You with me?"

"Uh-huh."

"Here's the thing." He took a breath, made himself speak calmly, like there was nothing to be afraid of. "The bad guys, they still want that case. And they want to catch us, because we've seen them. They're very—do you know what determined means?"

Billy sighed.

"Right. Right. Sorry. They're very determined. They'll keep coming back."

"Why don't we go away? Somewhere they can't find us?"

It wasn't a bad question. Hell, it was one Jason had asked himself. But where would they go? Moving to a new city wouldn't do it. They could never be sure that Galway or DiRisio wouldn't decide it was too big a risk to let them be.

They'd end up living like criminals—running, dodging, hiding. "Well, we could. But they might keep coming after us."

"How do we stop them?"

Jason started to answer, stopped himself. "Well, what do you think?"

Billy sucked his lower lip into his mouth, his eyes moving down and around like the answer might be on the floor. Then, suddenly, he looked up. "The briefcase."

A warmth spread through Jason's chest, a weird feeling he'd never known. Was this what parenting was? Had Michael felt this way watching Billy tie his shoes or do crossword puzzles? "That's right, buddy. There's only one problem." He paused. "I'd have to leave you to go get it."

Billy's hand snatched his own, clung hard.

"It's okay. Take it easy. I want to stay with you. But I don't want more men coming after us, and I think the briefcase could make sure of that." He paused. "I think I should go. I think it will keep you safe. But I won't if you don't want me to." Jason squeezed Billy's hand, looked him in the eye. "It's up to you, kiddo."

He stared at the boy, this eight-year-old with his brother's face. Shoulders thin under the gray Army T-shirt. Skin pale and sticky with tears. Stared and wished for a magic wand, a bag of fairy dust, whatever it took to reverse time and give this poor boy his father back, his life back.

And then Billy said, "Okay," and let go of his hand.

# CHAPTER 31
**Dirty Clothes**

Anthony DiRisio stood in front of the windows, arms at his side. Hell of a view. The skyline to the south, Lincoln Park spilling east, beyond that, the lake, blue-gray water dotted with colorful sails.

Elena Cruz lived pretty good for a policewoman.

The jerkwad cops that had searched the place earlier had closed up behind them, but the lock on the door was junk. He'd jamb-popped it with his knife and strolled in.

The apartment was a sizable one-bedroom with curved brick ceilings and a Murphy bed that folded back into the wall. He pulled it out just for kicks and lay down, his shoes up on the covers, fingers behind his head. A faint girl smell lingered in her pillows. After a moment, he sat up, opened the night table drawer. An Ondaatje novel, *The English Patient.* He'd seen the movie, liked it all right. A tube of lip balm. A snapshot of a Hispanic woman with a moustache. A silver vibrator. He turned it on. The batteries were low, the thing barely humming. He smiled, turned it off, put it back.

The cops had been after evidence, bundles of hundreds or sacks of weapons. They'd have checked the toilet tank and tapped for loose floorboards, felt the pockets of coats and the seams of the sofa. DiRisio was hoping for something more abstract, something that hinted where she might be.

He worked steadily but swiftly. Skipped the bathroom, skipped the kitchen. There was a mound of dirty clothes on her closet floor. Her dresser contained folded shirts and jeans, a tangle of underwear. He held up soft thong-cut panties, Vickie's Secret, size small. A potpourri sachet made them smell like cinnamon. Nice. If Palmer was tapping her, he was in for a treat.

No diary, no appointment book, no day planner.

He moved to the living room where she kept her desk. Sifted through paper clips and pens. A silver half dollar. A small chunk of amber. A rabbit's foot. An abandoned network cable ran from the wall to the desk. Shit. The cops had her computer. He'd like to have gone through it.

"Where are you, honey?" Looked around the room. Opened a cabinet. DVDs, a board game. "Come to daddy." Checked the fridge. A couple beers, some mismatched takeout containers, a bottle of Sriracha, a lime that had seen better days, a quarter-inch of milk in a gallon jug. Not a homebody, then.

Something moved behind him.

DiRisio spun fast, dropping as he went, right arm swinging out in an arc, pistol leading the way.

An orange and white cat with green eyes stared at him over the SIG's dot-and-bars. The cat blinked. The cat yawned.

Anthony DiRisio smiled.

"Hi, kitty," he said. "Come here."

# CHAPTER 32
**Whiskey and Black Coffee**

The way the light from the window fell on him, Ronald could have been a statue, an ebony sculpture of an old-time railroad worker. The sun carved his muscles in sharp relief, hard swells that strained his shirt sleeves. A five-pound sledge dangled from one hand, the heavy head stained a soft ocher with rust. He stared out the front window with quiet concentration.

"Hey Ronald, you seen Cruz?"

The big man tore his eyes away from the window, glanced at Jason. "That the girl you came with?"

"Yeah."

Ronald turned back to the window. "Upstairs. Said she wanted to freshen up."

"Thanks." Curiosity pulled him over to stand beside Ronald. Out the window, on the sidewalk past the Lantern Bearers sign, Washington stood talking to a middle-aged white guy with salt-and-pepper hair and sweat marks on his crisp oxford. Beyond them afternoon sun glared off parked cars, and on the other side of the street lay the abandoned lot, tall grass swaying gently around the carousel he remembered from years ago.

"Okay," he said. "I'll bite. What's so interesting?"

Ronald gestured with his chin. "See that dude talking to Dr. Matthews? That's Adam Kent."

The name sounded familiar. He squinted. Medium build,

neat hair, nice clothes. But nothing notable about him. He didn't think he'd ever seen him before, but the name sounded familiar. Where had he heard . . . right. "The guy giving Washington half a million dollars at the party tonight."

Ronald nodded slow, his eyes locked outside.

"You curious what he looks like?"

"Nah. Seen him before. He's here all the time."

"So what?"

"Look at him, man." Ronald spoke without turning. "Dude can write a check for five hundred thousand dollars, just give it away. Got enough money that half a million don't hurt none."

"Nice of him."

"Yeah. It's just . . ." Ronald hesitated.

"What?"

"I mean, I walk by him on the street, I wouldn't even notice. Looks like any other white guy. I always thought having that much money, you'd look *different,* you know? Like a glow or something." Ronald shook his head. "Hell, a brother with that kind of money, he's wearin' a platinum dollar sign covered with diamonds."

Jason laughed. "Listen, can you do me a favor?"

Ronald glanced over, face impassive.

"Cruz and I are going to leave. Those guys that killed my brother, I think we know how to get them."

"'Aight."

"Thing is, I can't bring Billy along, but I'm worried about leaving him alone. I was hoping you could kind of, I don't know. Look in on him. Hang out with him a little. Let him know he's safe."

"I feel that." Ronald nodded. "Sure."

"He's scared."

"He don't need to be. Ain't nothing going to happen to Bills while I'm around."

Jason nodded, thanked him. Then he headed out of the front room toward the staircase. He stole a glance over his shoulder before he left; Ronald had turned back to the window and was staring out, shaking his head. Jason smiled.

He found Cruz in one of the upstairs bedrooms, the television on, the remote clutched in white knuckled fingers.

". . . the ongoing corruption trial of former governor George Ryan . . ."

He stepped beside her, but she didn't react. "Hey," Jason said. "Listen—"

"Shh." She held up a hand.

"In other news, the troubling story of a police officer suspected of murder."

He'd been reaching for her shoulder, but froze at the announcer's words.

"The body of Dion Wallace, a member of the Gangster Disciples street gang, was discovered last night after neighbors reported hearing gunfire. Police found Wallace dead in his West Crenwood home, shot twice in the head." The house onscreen was cordoned off with yellow tape, and police cars were parked around it, angled random directions. A mugshot of C-Note Wallace glared off the side of the screen. "Sources within the Chicago Police Department told NBC 5 that preliminary investigations indicate the murder weapon belonged to an Area One Gang Intelligence officer involved in an ongoing investigation of Wallace."

The image cut to a podium with a middle-aged man in a French-cuff shirt and a striped tie. The caption read, *CPD Deputy Chief James Donlan*. Donlan held up his hands to quiet a roar of questions.

"At this time, the Chicago Police Department is not willing to make any final judgments regarding this case. While she has been designated a person of interest, Officer Cruz has not been charged with anything. However, I also want to assure the community that the CPD takes any accusation of police brutality very seriously, and that a thorough investigation is already underway."

The image cut to a picture of Cruz in uniform, younger and with different hair. The announcer continued. "Officer Elena Cruz, a ten-year veteran with a distinguished record, was the first woman to serve on the elite Gang Intelligence team. However, there have been numerous recent complaints against Officer Cruz, who has been largely restricted from working the street. A coworker, speaking on condition of anonymity, described her recent behavior as 'erratic and prone to violence.' The whereabouts of Officer Cruz are currently unknown. Back to you, Don."

An anchorman with precise hair and a perfectly symmetrical face said, "We'll have more on this disturbing story as it develops." He turned, and the camera angle changed. "More than ten people have come forward with allegations of child sexual abuse by Father—"

Jason stepped forward and turned off the television. He turned to look at her, found her staring, a statue with trembling hands. "I'm sorry, Elena." She shook her head, lips pulled into a thin, hard line. She looked like she'd been kicked in the gut. The silence seemed loud, and again he said, "I'm so sorry."

She turned and walked to the window. Stared out at nothing.

He rubbed at his eyes. "Washington told me that Dion Wallace had been killed last night. I just didn't put it together." Jason remembered the guy by the river, Scarface. He'd made her drop her gun. "That's why there are cops after us. One of them used your gun last night to shoot Dion." He paused. "But how would they put it together so *fast*?"

"Donlan." Her voice was barely a whisper.

Right. Her one-time lover, the cop with plenty of juice. So it wasn't one kick to the gut. It was two. "God." He sighed. "And that 'anonymous source.' That would have been Galway." Three.

She didn't respond, and he moved behind her, put a hand on her shoulder. She flinched. For some reason that cut him.

"All my life," she said, "all I've wanted was to be a cop. I was good at it, too." She shook her head. "Damn it, I was a good cop."

"You still are."

"Don't." Her tone was pure contempt. "Don't patronize me."

"I'm not. You're still a good cop."

She laughed through her nose, a hollow and scornful sound. "No I'm not. I'm an assassin. I killed Dion Wallace. You know how I know?" She flung the remote to bounce off the hardwood floor. "I saw it on TV."

"Elena—"

"Stop, okay? Just . . ." She sighed. "Just stop."

He stood behind her, wanting desperately to say something that could make it better. Knowing exactly how she felt. He'd felt the same way walking out of the Administrative Discharge Board. Being a cop was as central to her as being a soldier had been to him, and now the bastards had taken that, too.

Without thinking, he spun her into a hug. She stood rigid as stone, and he just had time to wonder if he'd made a terrible mistake.

Then something in her snapped, and she buried her head in his shoulder, her hair in his face. Her hands wrapped around his back, squeezing at first and then turning to fists, beating against the muscles of his back, left then right then left. Jason took it without complaint. Just held her, felt her chest heave as she cried without a sound. He didn't murmur soft nothings, didn't try to tell her it would be all right. Just held her and let her spend her fury and frustration against him, let it break like waves on rock, until slowly the force diminished, and her fingers closed around his T-shirt, clutching at it as she shook in his arms. Just held her and stroked her hair and felt the warmth of her.

And when she was spent, he said, "I know how to beat them."

Cruz pulled back, looked up at him with wet eyes. "What?"

"Remember our mysterious caller?"

" 'The burned child fears flame.' " She sniffled, then took a step away, moving to hold his hands between them like they were dancing.

"We assumed that the evidence he gave to Michael was

gone. That Galway and DiRisio had taken it." He paused. "But what if we were wrong? What if Michael hid the evidence somewhere safe, safe even from the fire?"

She stared at him for a moment. "You mean—"

"Yes."

"And you know—"

"Yes."

The beginnings of a smile graced her lips. "Where?"

"Michael's bar. In a place they wouldn't have known to look. We can go get it right now. End all this shit. Make sure Billy is safe. Get your job back."

Her eyes narrowed. "Burn Galway and Donlan to the ground."

"Yeah."

"Yeah."

Her hands squeezed his, her fingers not the baby-soft girlskin he was used to. Hands that worked, that knew how to hold a weapon and grip a chin-up bar. He liked touching them. "What do you say?"

She smiled at him, then stepped forward and grabbed his neck, pulling his mouth to hers. He stood frozen, still able to smell the tears on her cheeks, but then her tongue parted his lips, menthol and spice in a soft dance growing harder. His body reacted, pulling her closer, the ridge of her pelvic bone pressing his hips, her body warm against his chest, warm and right and close. His hands tangled in her hair, and she gave a soft moan, and then they were stumbling across the floor to the bed, not breaking the kiss, hands flying everywhere, her back, his shoulders, the curve of her hips. When they reached the bed she pushed him, and he fell backwards. She was on him even as he hit, crawling onto his body, her hands fumbling at his belt, the brush of her fingers sending electric shivers up his spine, his cock straining at his jeans, her smell sexy and strong, and he could barely wait to pull the sweater over her head and kiss the triangle of cinnamon skin in the hollow of her throat, to yank her jeans and panties to her knees and slide inside her, feel her warm and sweet, a place to lose himself, to forget, to separate themselves from everything that was happening—

He reached for her hands and gripped them in his own, pulling them from the belt she'd managed to undo in no time at all. "Stop."

She froze, then leaned back, the crotch of her jeans rubbing his, a knowing look on her face, her voice whiskey and black coffee. "Stop, huh?"

He groaned involuntarily, bit his lip. Then shook her hands, pushed them away. "Stop. Seriously."

She cocked her head. "What's the matter with you?"

He was wondering that himself. "I just . . . this doesn't feel right."

"It doesn't *feel* right?" She raised her eyebrows. "You really know how to romance a girl."

"I don't mean that. It feels great. It's just . . ." He paused. "This doesn't seem like you."

She stared at him, something flashing in her eyes. "What the fuck do you know about me?"

"I'm just saying, I don't know, I don't want to end up with you thinking of me the way you think of him, of Donlan. Like a mistake, something you regret."

She pushed herself off him, shaking her head. Stalked over to the mirror and began to straighten her sweater, not looking at him, her voice venomous. "I don't need your protection."

"I know that." Things had gotten turned around. It had been clear in his mind, the idea that with her he didn't want to do the same old thing, just use sex as a conduit to forgetting, but now everything seemed jumbled. He sat up, sighed. Ran a hand through his bangs. "That's not what I meant."

"It doesn't matter." She turned her head back and forth, examining her profile in the mirror. She blew a breath, then patted her pockets, came up with a blister pack of gum. Popped one of the pieces in her mouth and chewed viciously. "We should go anyway."

"Listen—"

"I'll see you downstairs." Without a look back, she walked out the door. He could hear her walk down the stairs, the sound steadily growing fainter.

He sighed, flopped back on the bed, stared at the stucco shadows on the ceiling. "Shit."

# CHAPTER 33
## Shadows and Rain

It was only afternoon, but the light was fading against a sky bruised purple with the promise of storm, one of those summer squalls that settled in and turned day to night. Jason had the passenger's side window open, his elbow on the frame, arm out and planing. He'd tilt his hand down and his arm would dive, then point it up and his arm would rise. The hair on his forearm was struggling to stand, and he could smell ozone on the breeze.

"Worked out well," Jason said. "Washington's party being tonight, I mean. For him letting us use his car."

Cruz nodded, flipped the turn signal of the borrowed Honda.

"Of course, I wish we could go to the thing." Talking to fill the stony silence. Out his window the world moved past: A cell phone store, a closed hardware shop, a burnt-out two-flat plastered with posters. "Half a million dollars. Jesus, that's a lot of money. Wouldn't mind being able to write that check."

He glanced over at her, the way she drove staring straight ahead. Strong, independent, but something brittle in the pose as well. And why the hell not? One minute they're about to make love, the next he's pushing her away. "Look, Elena, I'm sorry—"

"Forget it." Her voice was calm.

"No, I mean it. That wasn't the way I planned—I mean, not planned, but you know, wanted, things to happen." He sighed. "It's just—"

"Forget it," she said. "It's not a big deal."

"Right," he said, feeling strangely sick. They rode in silence through electric air.

On the right they passed a school, brick, three stories, dark against dark skies. The bottom levels of the building showed clean spots where graffiti had been sandblasted. Opposite was a row of cracker-jack two-flats and a barren lot, fenced off and untended, the grass waist high.

"I wish we had a gun, at least."

"You keep saying that."

"I keep meaning it."

"You know the worst thing I learned," Cruz said, her voice abrupt in that change-the-subject way, "when I joined Gang Intel?"

He fought the urge to say, *That your partner was selling arms to gangbangers?*, afraid it would come off the wrong way. "What?"

"One of the best ways to gauge the power of a gang is to see how many schools fall on their territory."

"Seriously?"

"The Latin Saints, for example. Their area is pretty small compared to some of the others. And Hispanic gangs don't deal in narcotics as much, so they aren't as well funded. But you know what they have?"

"Schools?"

"Schools. Two high schools and a junior high. They recruit shorties right out of recess. Use the young ones to carry dope, money. Or to do shootings. They have a tattoo, a stick figure, and you gotta earn it. I stopped this kid one time, maybe sixteen, he had one the length of his forearm. I asked what he did for it, you know what he said?" She paused. "He said, 'A few things.'"

He didn't know what to say to that, let the moment stretch. Then, "This is Damen."

"I know." She braked at the stop sign. Looked at him, her eyes narrow. "You're sure it will be there?"

"I'm sure."

"Because this is an awfully big risk."

"I'm sure." *I have to be.*

She stared, the darkening skies hiding her features, all but a glint of lost light from her eyes. Finally she shrugged. Turned the corner.

Damen Avenue, just like three days ago. Had it been only three days? Three days since he'd turned onto the street with his nephew in his car, feeling smug and sure and looking forward to rubbing his brother's nose in his failings. Three days since he found the still-smoking horror that had been Michael's bar; three days since his brother's dream had turned into their nightmare.

Damen Avenue, just like before but nothing at all like before.

She stopped the car across from the burned hulk of the bar. The clouds had painted the streets twilight. The special in the window of the storefront diner was now a half-slab and greens, six bucks. He was rolling up his window as the first drops of rain plinked against the roof. They sat for a moment watching it begin. Heavy, pregnant drops that exploded on the hood of the car. Two, five, twenty, a hundred, and then hissing sheets that blurred the world. Lightning glowed behind them, followed by thunder like someone rolling heavy furniture across a wooden floor.

"Maybe," Jason said, "this is a good omen."

She looked at him sourly.

He opened the door and was soaked to the skin before he could close it. Mist rose from the blacktop, the day's heat steaming. Jason slicked his bangs out of his eyes, then popped the trunk, took out the old pry bar they'd borrowed from Washington's basement. Its heft was a comfort as they crossed the deserted street.

The police tape fluttered yellow, the only color he could see in this sudden purgatory. Beyond it lay the charred and bubbled ruins where his brother had died. The rain was already collecting in scorched hollows, sweeping loose ash into a black lake. Jason stared, feeling something like a head rush, his thighs weak and vision blurry.

His brother had died here. Right here, alone and scared.

Thunder cracked again, closer this time, and the rain lashed down harder.

"You want an engraved invitation?" Cruz stood with hip cocked.

"I was just . . ." He shook his head. "Michael was my older brother. He saved my butt so many times when we were kids." Rain beat goosebumps into his skin. "I just wonder if at the last moment, Michael was praying I would come save his."

Cruz softened, left the tape and stepped in front of him, her features traced by the light from the diner windows. She opened her mouth, closed it, then said, "Are you all right?"

He nodded, slowly. Tightened his grip on the pry bar.

She put one hand up to cup his cheek. Her palm was warm, and the ridge of her thumb fell tingling across his lips. She nodded toward the wreckage. "Come on. Let's finish this. For him."

He figured the first step was the hardest, so he made himself take it. Then he turned and held the tape up for Cruz. She started carefully through the debris. Her clothing was soaked, and ash clung to her pant legs as she wound her way into the center of the building. A few blackened steel girders supported a skeleton of the ceiling, and the darkness fell across her in patterns. She twisted the flashlight in her hand and a thin beam of wavering light fell on the ruined floor. "Where is it?"

Jason gestured with the crowbar, walked past her. "Back here." He climbed gingerly onto a pile of twisted lumber, testing to be sure it would hold his weight, then scrambled to where blackened bricks marked the entrance to the back room.

Rubble lay in scattered piles, chunks of brick and mortar. It took him a minute to get his bearings, and then he pointed. "There." A metal lip shone beneath a section of wall. He and Cruz each took an end and heaved, tipped the stone up and over to fall with a splash and a crack. The trap hatch was a scorched square of metal thirty inches to a side, with a ring in the center. The heat had warped the metal, and Jason didn't bother with the pull-ring. Instead he slid the crowbar into the crack and shoved. The metal shivered, but didn't give. He grabbed a chunk of brick and concrete, and pounded the bar in deeper. Then he took a breath and wrapped his hands on the cold iron bar.

Cruz squatted beside him, her hands above and below his, skin warm in the cold rain. He smiled, said, "Ready?", and then heaved back on the bar, his feet scrabbling at the rocky earth for purchase.

For a long moment nothing happened. Then with a pop like the top off a bottle of beer, the hatch gave, swinging back on bent hinges to crack on the stone, revealing a square hole silent as the grave. The first inches of steep metal Navy stairs faded swiftly into a play of shadows and rain.

Past that, nothing.

Jason set the crowbar on the stack of bricks. His bangs had fallen across his eyes again, and he slicked them back, hands trembling, though whether it was from effort or tension, he couldn't have said.

Down that hole was everything they needed.

Or nothing but ghosts.

He took the flashlight from his pocket, grabbed the lip of the trap hatch, and started down.

# July 9, 2004

*Jason sits on the ridge in full kit—desert BDUs, body armor, M4 carbine, spare 5.56 ammo, helmet with NODs, sidearm, Gerber knife, Wiley X ballistic sunglasses, first aid kit, gallon of water, sixty, seventy pounds in all—and watches the house burn.*

*Flame runs like water, spills in hungry shades of orange and yellow. The heat warps the world into twists and spires. Greasy black smoke pours out windows. The warmth on his face is a pulse, a brush of sun.*

*He has his iPod going, only the left earphone in, Bjork singing over shimmering tones that all is full of love, that you have to trust it, her dreamy voice a fantastical counterpoint to the angry roar and crackle of flame. Down the hill, Jones macks for the camera, rifle in one hand, a thumb jerking toward the flame, as Kaye frames the shot with the digital camera.*

*"I was talking to that guy," Martinez points, then pats an ammo pouch on his flak jacket, pulls a pack of Miamis, Iraqi knock-offs of Marlboro Reds. Lights one with a Zippo, takes a drag. "He told me the people lived here were Sunnis, that's why they got burned out."*

*"They work for Saddam?"*

*"Nah. Just Sunnis, somebody didn't want 'em around."*

*Jason nods, swatting at a fly buzzing his ear. He does a silent count of his men, Jones, Campbell, Kaye, Frieden,*

*Crist, Flumignan, Borcherts, Paoletti, Rosemoor, and Martinez, ten. "Too bad."*

*"Too bad for them, too bad for us." Martinez turns, holds the moment, then smiles. "Here we are without a couple of hot dogs and some long damn sticks."*

*All is full of love, all around you.*

# CHAPTER 34
## The Dark Below

Floating dust and the smell of fire.

Under chipped paint, the metal railing was cool. Jason kept a hand on it as he moved down the steep staircase, swinging the flashlight in arcs. The darkness was thick and hungry enough that the flashlight seemed only to make the gloom more oppressive. He pointed it like a blind man with a cane, sweeping the ground before him. Pipes and electrical conduit hung from scorched concrete. The air was thick with a smell of burned toast. Piles of junk and abandoned furniture loomed like the bones of giants.

Metal bonged, and he turned to see Cruz descending, outlined in pale gray light, rain seeming to magically appear around her, the drops bounded by the square trap hole. She had the crowbar in one hand and her flashlight in the other. Where their beams met, the spot seemed to glow with light against the greater darkness.

"The fire didn't reach it," she said. Her voice muted and hollow with subterranean acoustics.

"Went up, I guess," Jason said. "The ceiling is concrete."

She nodded, then frowned. "Shit." He followed her gaze. Shelves had been overturned, and piles of broken glass sparkled. Boxes lay open, their contents strewn in all directions. She sighed. "Galway and DiRisio must have checked here. They'd have had *hours*. If there was something to find, they'd have found it."

Jason nodded absently, seeing two basements. The one his flashlight illuminated, ruined and silent. And the one he and Mikey had sat in years ago. All afternoon they'd hauled junk out of the place, and when they were done, they'd collapsed on ladder back chairs. Listened to the Sox game and shared a bottle of Black Label that Michael had stashed, passing it back and forth, smiling.

"To the good life, bro." He barely whispered the words.

"What?"

"You from Chicago?" He started for the southwest corner.

Cruz followed, her footsteps seeming to come from all directions. "Yeah. Well, Cicero."

The chairs were gone, the radio was gone, but the radiator was right where he remembered it. An old stand-up job, maybe three feet high and the same across, a coiling rack of heavy metal jutting out of the wall. "Growing up, you ever hear about bars, speakeasies, I guess, that served alcohol during Prohibition?"

"Sure."

"This used to be one. Speakeasies survived by payoffs. Grease the wheels, get left alone. But," he squatted in front of the radiator, ran his hands over the cool metal, "sometimes even the ones that paid got raided. You know, so the city could make it look like they were cracking down on Capone and the rest."

"So?"

"So," he said, his index finger finding a metal rib, "owners realized they needed good places to hide things." Jason lifted the latch. There was a click as it locked upwards. He grabbed the radiator with both hands and pulled. It swung aside like a door.

Behind it lay a cast-iron safe, the face set even with the wall.

"No shit," she said, admiration in her voice.

"No shit. Michael loved all the little secrets in this place. He used to store a bottle in here just to have an excuse to open it." Jason reached for the handle, fingers tingling. He jerked down on the lever.

It didn't budge.

"Gimme the crowbar." He wedged it behind the handle, the tip braced against the floor. Took a deep breath and heaved. Nothing. He pictured DiRisio smiling down at Mikey. The last face his brother ever saw. Threw himself against the drop-forged steel, the veins in his neck popping, his arms shaking.

The handle didn't even shudder.

Jason stood, wound up, and hurled the crowbar. "Christ!" It arced through the air with a whir like a helicopter cranking up and smashed into something metal at the far end. The clanging echoed back loud. He felt tears of frustration gathering at the corner of his eyes. So close. They were so god-damn close. But what good was *close*?

The circle of light Cruz held on the radiator swayed and stretched, then narrowed as she knelt in front of it. One hand traced the face. "We can figure this out."

"Don't waste your time," he said, one hand rubbing his eyes.

"Look, it's a hidden safe. He probably didn't bother with a random combination." She sucked air through her teeth. "When's Billy's birthday?"

"Huh? April 2." He turned, hope springing sudden, and then equally suddenly quelled. "No, it won't work."

"Why?"

"The dial only goes to 50. He was born in '97."

She rocked back on her haunches. Twisted a curl of hair idly, fed the tip of it to her mouth. Then smiled. "You got twenty bucks?"

"Why?"

She reached for the dial, spun it three times, then stopped, spun it the other way, stopped, then once again. The latch swung with a quiet clank. She smiled. "April 2, 1997: 42-9-7. He combined the month and day, split the year."

He stared at her for a long moment. "I could kiss you."

"Open the safe. You owe me twenty bucks."

\* \* \*

The briefcase was a brown leather zipper bag, the kind lawyers liked. Soft and new-smelling. The same one he'd watched his brother worry over just days ago.

Jason stared at it. Hiding this briefcase had been his brother's last act.

Why had he done that? If he'd suspected men were coming for him, he wouldn't have waited, wouldn't have put Billy at risk. So it must just have been a precaution. Jason remembered how nervous his brother had seemed about the bag, how he'd moved it around. He must have stowed it so he could relax, know that it was in a safe place. And not just any safe place.

One where Jason would know to look.

The thought sent a chill dancing between his vertebrae, like Mikey had left it here as a message. A last request.

*I won't let you down, bro. Not this time.*

Jason reached in and grasped the briefcase handle. For a moment he imagined he could feel the warmth of his brother's fingers on the leather. Cruz held both flashlights, and a dim globe of light surrounded them, splashing a matter of feet before vanishing into the abyss. He could hear her breathing, soft and wet and more than anything, *alive*. Against it, the zipper sounded grating. He opened the briefcase slowly, hands shaking.

Inside sat a plain manila folder an inch thick. Legal-sized, and filled with paper. That was all.

Jason wasn't sure what he'd expected, but something more dramatic. He flipped the folder open. A document with the dense print of legalese. Beneath that, some sort of spreadsheet. Something else that looked like a manifest. He rifled quickly. Pages and pages of documents, data in rows and columns, cramped paragraphs, notes and letters. It was paper. Just paper. And yet someone had killed Michael for it.

He broke the stack into two piles, wordlessly handed one to Cruz. Then Jason Palmer leaned against the basement wall of his brother's bar and began to read.

The air was cool, and once the warmth of exertion gave way, he began to feel a chill. His fingertips were raw, the nerves close, and he could feel the texture of the paper, every wrinkle and bump. He turned pages slowly, let his eyes drink the information. When the cold had him shaking, he stood and jumped up and down, stamped his feet. Then sat and continued. Reading with care, like a scholar working with ancient manuscripts. Finishing one and returning to others he'd already reviewed. Assembling a picture, a page at a time. His hands were white with a delicate filigree of blue veins. He looked at details, compared them. Fit them together. Tried them like puzzle pieces: Did this match against that one? How about the other? The world narrowed to the dim glow of the flashlights, a circle of warm light floating in nothing. Just him and Cruz and this riddle. This last message from his brother.

There were a lot of documents, and they were complicated. He didn't rush. It took most of an hour. But even before he was finished, he understood. Understood why his brother was dead. Why his nephew was in danger. Why they were all hunted.

More than anything, he understood the problem was bigger than he'd dared imagine.

Cruz had finished first, and was staring into the darkness, her hair drying frizzy, a twist of it between lips. She pulled the hair from her mouth and said, "This can't just be Galway and DiRisio."

He set the paper down. "No."

"Do you think it means—"

"Yeah," he cut her off. "I think it does."

Cruz shook her head, rubbed her eyes. "Jesus Christ."

He listened to the soft steady patter of rain on the stairs. The violence of the storm had settled into an easy rhythm, the kind of soaking drizzle that could go all night. Normally he liked rain, but he found no comfort here, entombed in the dark below the spot his brother died.

"No wonder they killed him. This . . ." She shook her head. Blew air through her mouth. "So now what?"

"We got what we need. Let's go." He collected everything, rapped the stack against the floor to even the edge, and put the manila folder back in the briefcase.

After the sepulchral darkness of the basement, the world above seemed huge and wild. Climbing the ladder, he had an eerie feeling that something had changed. That he was coming out the trap hatch a different man. He stood to one side and offered Cruz a hand, and she took it. They picked their way across the rubble, the rain soaking clothes that hadn't dried from the last time.

"Who do we take this to?" Cruz asked.

"No one."

"Huh?"

"We don't *take* it anywhere." He stepped over a charred beam. "We stay out of sight. Just make copies, and send them to everyone."

She smiled. "NBC 5, for one."

"Yeah. The *Tribune*. The *Sun-Times*."

"The mayor. Fast Eddie Owens."

"Fast Eddie Owens . . ." He had an image of a sun-faded poster, a campaign ad. It had been in the front window of Michael's bar. "The alderman? Why?"

"This is his district, and he's an anti-gang crusader. He's even backing a budget proposal to upgrade the equipment of cops on the street, buy digital cameras and PDAs. I won't bore you with details, but believe me, it would make a huge difference." She stepped gingerly onto the sidewalk and began digging in her pocket. Came out with the keys and went around to the driver's side of Washington's Honda. "And he's not part of the police department."

"Good by me. Hell, let's send it *everywhere*." His head buzzing. Thinking of the documents he'd read in a darkness beneath the world. Just words, just paper and ink. But more, too. Blood. Lives. All being manipulated with a sheer and brutal pragmatism that left him sick inside.

But at least it was almost over. They had what they needed to end it. Jason opened the passenger side door, the air inside stuffy with the smell of Washington's tobacco. He tossed the briefcase in the back and brushed off what dirt and ash he could from his clothes.

He was just about to sit down when his window exploded.

# CHAPTER 35
## Mean and Close

His body moved before his brain caught up. Jason whirled, saw a car screaming toward them, something low-bodied, a dark shape cutting the rain. A strobe of lights flared from the passenger side, and as he dropped he processed the image, someone shooting at them with a submachine gun, a drive-by, he was in a goddamn drive-by, and as he realized that, fivesixseven holes ripped in the door beside him, the fire-cracker rattle of the gunblasts arriving just afterward, the bullets traveling faster than the sound.

He heard an engine turning over, looked to see Cruz cranking the key. Jason threw himself into the passenger seat as Cruz slammed the car into reverse, the Honda whining like a toy as it rocketed backward. The sudden motion had him scrabbling for a grip, and he got a hand against the dash just as the rear window blew in spiderwebs of broken glass. Cruz's lips were moving but he couldn't hear what she was saying, and then the Honda slammed into something solid, a bone-crunching jerk he felt in his teeth, the impact of metal on metal, a screeching sound that pitched him back into the seat, neck whiplashing, the angry slippy hum of tires against wet concrete, momentum slamming shut the passenger door, and then Cruz threw it into drive and spun the wheel and stamped the accelerator, and they were moving again, the Honda leaping forward gamely, a rattling from behind like they were dragging the bumper or muffler.

His head hurt, and he realized he must have hit it against something, maybe the dash. Cruz kept mumbling to herself as she squinted out the windshield, foot jammed all the way down on the gas. The world blurred and shifted, lights running like melting wax, and for a moment Jason wondered if he'd hit his head harder than he thought. Then he realized it was water streaming down the glass, the rain, and he said, in a voice that sounded calmer than he would have expected, "Wipers."

She reached for them with her left hand, and he could hear what she was saying now, Hail Mary, full of grace, the Lord is with thee, blessed are thou among women, the wipers starting now, shick-shock, their pace steady and fast and metronomic, her words timing to them.

*Get it together, man. You're a soldier. What's your goddamn situation?*

The sit rep was that they were streaking north on Damen, the wind howling in the passenger window, where a few scraps of safety glass clung stubbornly to the frame. Turning, he could see headlights through the splintered back window. Someone chasing them. He couldn't say who, though he'd seen the car. Low and fast-looking. A Mustang, a Charger, something like that. Something that would be able to smoke a '94 Honda. Her ramming maneuver had bought them a little time. But unless she'd been able to take out a tire or bend an axle, it wouldn't be enough.

"Holy Mary, Mother of God." Cruz's voice was settling now, not the panicked mumbling of before. Her eyes flicked to the rearview, narrowed. "Hold on."

Jason reached for the seatbelt, clicked it into place as she yanked the wheel to the right, a hard, sliding turn on streets slick with rain and grease. The back fishtailed, skidding around, and then she hit the gas again, the vector overwhelming the spin as they charged east. The street was ghetto-residential, sagging houses drooping toward cracked earth, rusting fences, weeds shining damp in gardens of broken glass. Battered cars lined both sides of the street, shit, all facing toward them, which meant they were going the wrong direction down a one-way street. The rain had driven people off the street to their porches, and Jason heard angry yells. Someone threw a bottle wrapped in brown paper, the glass smashing in their wake.

Behind them, headlights spun around the same curve, slid too far, side-slammed into a parked car. Jason watched, willing the car to flip. It didn't. Another set of headlights came in behind.

"There's a second car," he said.

Cruz nodded, her knuckles white on the wheel.

He'd have given a finger for a weapon. He felt helpless, Cruz driving, him riding shotgun without a shotgun. More flashes exploded behind them, but didn't seem to hit anything.

A hundred yards ahead, headlights glowed. An oncoming car. The street was too narrow for them to pass. It would trap them.

"Elena—"

"I see it." She stayed on course, running straight, the accelerator to the floor. There was a cross-street between them and the oncoming car. A northbound street, Racine he thought. It was a toss-up whether they could get there first. A horn shrieked from the oncoming car. Behind them, the Charger was gaining fast. Jason gripped the armrest. Angry yells poured in the Honda's broken windows. A couple years ago a white delivery driver had accidentally hit a black kid in this neighborhood. The crowd had pulled him from his car and beaten him to death before the police arrived. Jason watched the headlights grow larger, the distance disappearing.

Then they reached the corner and Cruz yanked the wheel left in a full-speed turn. Centripetal force threw him against the seatbelt. Tires screamed on asphalt. Jason had a glimpse of the terrified eyes of the driver of the other car, a Buick, and then they cleared it by inches.

He swiveled to look behind in time to see the Charger slam into the Buick. The squealing horn died, replaced by the nails-on-chalkboard sound of metal tearing. Glass cracked and popped, and headlight beams swam wildly up the sides of rotting houses. Then the Charger flipped to its side and surfed a trail of sparks out of sight.

Jason let himself breathe again.

They were heading north, the Honda's four cylinders as close to roaring as they were likely to get, a clank coming from the engine that he didn't like. Fifty blocks up, Racine was a lovely residential street of hundred-year trees and million-dollar graystones. But on the south side it twisted between abandoned factories and weed-filled lots strewn with black garbage bags. The rain covered everything with a greasy film.

"We made it," he said.

Cruz nodded, blew air through her lips. Didn't even slow for a red light. Shipping containers packed dark parking lots under broken warehouse windows. They hit a bump that knocked loose glass from the broken rear, the green pieces glowing eerily under dingy streetlights. Jason tried to picture where they were on his mental map. They'd made distance on the empty streets, probably putting them at the south end of Bridgeport. There weren't any headlights behind them. With luck, the second car had gotten tangled up in the accident. At very least, it would have to reverse and circle around.

Cruz eased up on the gas, letting the Honda drop to fifty. She took one hand off the wheel, flexed it, the knuckles popping, then did the same with the other.

"Nice driving, Officer." He smiled, postcombat shakes hitting now, that goofy energy. "They teach you that at the academy?"

She laughed, a nervous sound. "Jesus."

"Mary," he said. "You were saying Hail Marys."

"I was?" She shook her head. "Didn't even notice. Haven't said a Hail Mary since I was sixteen."

"I guess somebody was listening."

"Guess so." She put on her blinker for a left turn onto Thirty-fifth.

"Where are you headed?"

"The Stevenson. Put some distance."

He settled back into his seat. From the expressway they could get most anywhere, then wind their way back to Washington's place at leisure. The light at the lonely corner ahead was green. He could see the darkness of the river just west of them. The windshield wipers thunked back and forth, strangely comforting.

They were almost through the turn when the Escalade jack-hammered into them. The Honda rocketed forward, spinning, the back wheels lifting. The spiderwebbed rear window exploded, fragments of safety glass raining in sparkling slow motion. There was a blur of headlights, flashbulb bright. The world spun like a carousel. Through the windshield he saw the pitted and scarred landscape of some kind of construction site swing by, replaced by a flash of the truck that had rammed them, then a metal railing and yawning darkness. He felt a sick slippy sensation as the Honda hit the guardrail, half bending it and half bouncing over it, and briefly they hung in a fantasy of flight, wheels spinning over nothing.

Then black water rushed up to meet them.

The impact slammed Jason against the seatbelt, his head snapping forward, white stars flaring. The front of the car plowed water up in a shimmering arc lit by one unbroken headlight. He just had time to wonder if the water would be cold before it started pouring through the shattered windows.

It was.

He gasped for breath, shook his head, dazed. Felt like he'd been hit by a linebacker, the wind yanked out of him, vision darting and narrow. He fumbled at his seatbelt as the Chicago River rushed into the car, the water sheened with oil.

Beside him, Cruz moaned.

Jason looked over, saw her sprawled across the steering wheel, blood trickling from her forehead. Her fingers fluttered like she were waving away bugs.

"Elena?" Water was coming in at an unbelievable rate, gushing over the side of the car. He tugged at his seatbelt, fingers unwieldy. The release button seemed stubborn, and it took a moment to realize he was pressing the wrong side. "Are you all right?"

She moaned again, straightened slowly. In the heat of the chase, she hadn't had time to buckle her seatbelt. Her eyes were wide and unfocused, her bangs wet. He leaned over and the car reacted to his movement like a tipping rowboat. The water had filled to seat level. The windshield cracked in lightning ripples.

"Elena. Let's go!" Her eyes seemed to spin glassy in her head, then she blinked, long slow blinks like she was focusing. She nodded at him.

Free of his belt, Jason scrambled half over his seat, splashing in the back for the briefcase. It was too dark to see, and the angle hurt his head, blood rushing in to make the world pulse. He bumped something, lost it, reached again. Found one leather edge jammed under the seat. The briefcase must have slid under and gotten wedged in the impact. He leaned over, breath coming hard, tugging.

Cruz moaned, and he looked over to see her with her head back on the steering wheel. Dark blood ran down her cheek. She lay there like she were taking a nap.

"Elena!" He made his voice snap. "We have to move."

She stirred, then slumped again.

The windshield creaked from the pressure of water. If it gave, the car would go like a brick.

He was bent over the seat, the edge of the briefcase in one hand. He yanked at it, and it gave a little, but then stopped. It was wedged on something, the handle probably caught. He could get it. He was certain. It wouldn't take a minute.

The windshield creaked again. Cruz had stopped moving.

Jason cursed, then let go of the case and leaned across her. With fast cranks he lowered her window, the water pressing against it hungrily, slopping in. She gasped at the cold, eyes widening. The Honda made a sickening groan and lurched forward. A crack rippled across the windshield like ice on a lake.

Jason grabbed the passenger side window frame, chunks

of safety glass poking dull into his hands, and hauled himself out to belly-flop in the oily water. The headlight below him lit the river like a polluted swimming pool. He took a breath and dove, his eyes closed against the murk. Counting, one, two, three, four, frog-legging down and over. Then surfacing slow, one hand above to make sure he didn't hit the bottom of the car. When he felt air he kicked hard and came up alongside her door.

She stared at him, blinking like she was surprised he was there. The Honda shuddered, the entire hood submerged, three-quarters of her window underwater. He grabbed the frame with his right hand and with his left leaned in for her, clamping his arm in a crude hug under her shoulders. "Come on," he said. "I need you to help."

She blinked, shook her head, then nodded. Her hands found the window frame, white fingers clenching the edge. He tugged at her, planting his feet against the side of the car, the traction of his sneakers lending purchase. She steered herself out the window, body slipping through. He had her most of the way out when the windshield gave. Water flooded in, yanking the car downward. He kicked frantically, one arm slung around her, terrified she would get caught and tug them both to the bottom.

And then she was clear, and he was on his back, pulling her in a lifeguard cradle through inky water.

The Honda canted up, only the crumpled trunk sticking out of the water, already beginning to sink. Iridescent bubbles streamed around it.

"Are you okay?" He kicked backwards. The eastern shore was closer, so he headed that way. There was hardly any current; this section of the river was really a channel, used for shipping.

"I'm dizzy," she said.

"Can you kick?"

Her legs began to scissor. It was wobbly at first, but grew stronger as they moved.

Jason looked up to the bridge twenty feet above. From this angle he couldn't see much, but an Escalade was a big vehicle. If it were there, he should have been able to spot it. Maybe they'd continued on, not wanting to linger near the accident. The corner had been deserted when they'd gone over, but surely other cars would have come soon.

An Escalade. Until now, he hadn't had time to process what that meant.

The east bank of the river was lined with scrub trees, their branches festooned with plastic bags and rotting sneakers. A sludgy, organic smell surrounded them. The channel walls were vertical concrete three feet high. He looked at it, then at her.

"I'm okay," she said.

He let her go cautiously, and she tread water with one hand on the wall. Jason took a breath, ducked underwater, then kicked hard, flinging an arm up to catch the lip of the breakwall. He brought his other to join it, then pulled himself up, the concrete scraping against his body. A thin ribbon of trees bordered the construction site he'd seen before the car went over. Heavy equipment was parked fifty yards away, and mounds of dirt screened them from the road.

He lay on his belly and extended an arm for Cruz. Water sluiced off her as he hauled her out, her feet scrabbling against the concrete.

When she was safely on dry ground, he flopped down on his back. He hurt in a hundred places, and his breath came hard. But they had made it. He stared up at the sky, the rain cool and cleansing. Clouds hid the stars. Cruz lay beside him, panting. Her upper arm touched his, and the warmth felt good. He lay still, not thinking and enjoying it.

Then Cruz jerked upright. "The briefcase."

He shook his head.

She stared at him. "You were reaching for it. I remember."

"It was caught." Jason sat slowly. He ran a hand through his hair, brushing twigs. "Under the seat. I couldn't get it in time."

Her eyebrows knit. "It had everything to save your life, and Billy's. You needed that briefcase." City light reflected off the clouds to paint her profile, and he saw something like understanding dawn there. "But I couldn't move."

He didn't know what to say, so he said nothing at all.

Cruz stared for a long moment. Then leaned forward to bring her face close. Her hair was matted and wet, and she had a leaf stuck to her neck, but she glowed anyway. "Thank you," she said.

"You would have done the same."

She smiled. "Don't believe it." Then she kissed him, her lips cool, her tongue sweet, and he felt something loosen in him. The Worm giving ground, and he realized that whatever else happened, whatever this thing between them turned out to be, he hoped he didn't screw it up the way he screwed most things up. He prayed that if it did end wrong, at least let it be a *new* screwup. A screwup that came of reaching for something more. Maybe even of daring to be responsible to someone else.

Then he heard a voice he recognized.

"Y'all kissing on each other after climbing out of the Chicago River?" Playboy sounded mean and close. "That's just *got* to be love."

# CHAPTER 36
## Trust

Full circle.

The first time they'd met, Playboy had been smiling and armed as he took Jason by surprise. Now here they were again, a few days later, history repeating itself yet again. Like a little kid making the same joke over and over: Not that funny the first time and worse with each repetition.

"Stand up *real* slow." Playboy wore a black track suit made of some shiny material. The Cadillac necklace gleamed from his chest, and in his right hand he held what looked to Jason like a Ruger P90, chrome over black. Behind him stood two men: a tall, skinny guy who kept shifting on his feet and a stocky muscle-man with tape across his nose. The wrestler Jason had hit with a car door. Full circle.

Jason took his hands from Cruz's hair, held them out at shoulder height. Twisted to get a leg underneath, then rose up straight and easy. His eyes drank the landscape, looking for any advantage. The only cover were the mounds of rain-spattered dirt behind Playboy, sloping ten-foot hills that hid the street beyond. He thought of diving for the river, but it was no kind of cover at all. It was only in movies that bullets didn't hurt once you hit the water.

"You a pain in my ass, know that?" Playboy shook his head. "Most people, they'd have called it a day after goin' off the bridge. Couldn't believe when Curtis," gesturing at the tall one, "said he saw y'all swimming for shore. But then, you a soldier, right?"

"Yeah," Jason said softly. "That's right."

"I feel that." He gestured with the pistol. "Toss your strap."

"Huh?"

Playboy rolled his eyes. "Your gun. Drop your gun."

"I don't have one."

The gangbanger raised the Ruger to point at Jason's face, the black hole of the barrel sure and unblinking. Jason stared back. "I don't."

"What'd you do with my Beretta?"

"DiRisio and his crooked cops took it from me."

Playboy's eyes narrowed at that. "DiRisio, huh?"

"Yeah. Same guy who hired you to grab me. Same guy who killed my brother."

Wind stirred leaves in the reedy trees along the water's edge. Playboy stared at him another moment, shrugged. "That was a nice gun."

"You want to give me the one you're holding, I'll buy you a new Beretta." Trying to play cool, just like the first time they'd met. To keep tensions from escalating. All the while, his heart vibrating against his ribs.

"Don't think so." Playboy gestured at Cruz with his free hand. "Stand up, sister."

Cruz started to rise, made it halfway, then staggered. Her legs went wobbly, and she moaned and fell. Tried to catch herself, her hands tangling up with her ankles. Jason lunged to help her, moving without thinking. She'd seemed stronger a minute ago. Standing up must have been the problem. "I think she might have a concussion."

"Yeah?" The voice bored.

"She's not part of our business."

Playboy snorted. "Man, pick your bitch up."

Jason's fingers tingled, that old battle rush. He knew then, knew with certainty. Playboy was here to execute them.

Jason had seen it more times than he could count. Mass graves and abandoned bodies. Hands tied or cuffed, two in the head. Sunnis at first, but before long plenty of Shi'as, too. Regular folk, mostly, caught up in a war they hadn't chosen to fight. Victims of political rivalries, or kidnappings, or plain evil luck. Caught beneath the wheels of circumstance and shredded like dolls.

But knowing Playboy's intentions didn't change anything. They were alone in a wasteland, unarmed, and damn near helpless. Jason grit his teeth and put an arm under Cruz's shoulder, lifted her slowly to stand. Her weight was awkward. Her right arm flopped behind his back, and it seemed heavy the way it hit him.

Playboy regarded them from five feet away, the gun sideways in a gangster grip.

"You're holding your weapon wrong," Jason said.

"That a fact."

"Yeah. The recoil is going to throw your aim off. Hell, a big .45 like that, you might end up punching yourself in the face."

"Want to bet," rocking the hammer back with his thumb, "whether it'll work or not?"

Icy water flowed through Jason's veins. This couldn't be the way. He hadn't walked beneath Middle Eastern suns to die on the banks of a shitty river. Hadn't found Cruz just to die with her. "Why are you doing this?" Fighting for time, his eyes darting.

"Mother*fucker.*" Playboy's voice a chipped razor. "You really asking after what you did?" He stepped forward. "C-Note was like my brother. He and I been tight since we was shorties. You shoot the man in his *bathrobe,* and got the nerve to ask me why I'm doing this?"

"I didn't kill C-Note."

"Yeah, and my black ass is mayor." Playboy's eyes burned. He stepped forward, the gun level with Jason's eyes. "I loved that man. Not ashamed to say it. *Nothing* I ain't prepared to do to get those that killed him."

"We're not them." Anger powered the truth in his voice. Bad enough to think of losing now, when they were so close. But to die because of the handiwork of his brother's killer? The irony was too cruel. "It was DiRisio killed C-Note."

"A man staring down a gat'll say anything to survive."

Cruz moaned and sagged like she were losing consciousness. Her head flopped on his shoulder, and Jason tightened his grip on her. As he did, he felt her hand tap his back again. There was something weird about it. He looked over at her, expecting to see dilated pupils, pale skin, the classic signs of shock and concussion.

Instead, from behind the wet hair that screened her eyes, she winked at him.

"You know what?" He turned back to Playboy. "You're right."

Jason moved fast, a quick lunge sideways. Brilliant fire exploded in front of him, the bullet ripping the air where his head had been. In the sudden glow he saw the other two gangbangers scrabbling at their waists, guns coming up, and then Cruz stepped forward and pressed a small automatic pistol under Playboy's chin.

"Don't believe the movies," Cruz said, her posture straight and her voice steady. "This is a Glock 27. It'll fire *under* water. Our little swim won't even slow it down."

Playboy stood frozen, his gun arm out, pointing at nothing. Jason locked the gangbanger's arm with his right hand and twisted the Ruger free with his left. He sighted down the barrel at Playboy's soldiers. They had weapons up, the taller one swinging the gun back and forth between Jason and Cruz.

In the silence, Jason could hear the rain patter on the river. Tension tightened his shoulders, made his muscles sing. The twitchy one was making Jason nervous, swiveling back and forth between him and Cruz. "Curtis. You look like a man making a decision. But stay cool for a second. I just want to talk."

The tall man didn't say anything, but stopped swinging the gun.

"Now," Jason said, hoping his voice didn't betray his tension, "it would be the easiest thing in the world for us all to open up right now. We could all die here, beside this shitty river. But if we do, nobody gets any satisfaction. You know why? *Because we didn't kill C-Note.*"

"You say so." Playboy's eyes were half-closed, like he couldn't be bothered with the situation.

"Think about it, man. Who set you on me in the first place? DiRisio. And I'll bet you he was the one said that we killed C-Note, wasn't he?" Playboy's eyes confirmed it. "I thought so. How'd he know a thing like that? The cops hadn't even left the scene, he knows what's going on?"

"Street knows what it knows."

"Does the street know that DiRisio is also selling hardware to La Raza and the Latin Saints? You didn't think you were the only ones getting some of his love, did you? He's arming your enemies."

Playboy shrugged. "Says you."

"You want proof?" Jason gestured to the river. "Go for a swim. It's in the back of the car you drove off the bridge. We were going to use it to take DiRisio down."

"Not just him," Cruz said quietly. "A dirty cop, too. Tom Galway. He works gangs."

"That a fact."

"It is." Jason stepped forward. "They killed your boy, then sent you to finish us before we brought them down. Hell, this way they don't even have to get their hands dirty. You've been conned, man. We all have."

Playboy narrowed his eyes, then reached into his pocket. Cruz pushed the Glock harder into his neck. He looked down at her with a bulletproof smile. "Easy." Took his hand out slowly, turning it up to display a pack of Pall Mall Menthols and a green Bic. Pulled out a cigarette and lit it casually, using both hands, like he were chilling in a club instead of standing on the bank of a polluted river with a pistol at his throat. "Saying that's so. What then?"

"We're going to go take care of him."

Playboy shook his head, blew smoke. "Can't let you two walk out of here."

Cruz laughed. "You're not letting us. We're walking. The question is whether you are."

Playboy shrugged. "Ain't afraid to die."

"I believe you," Jason said. "But I also think you're not

stupid. DiRisio killed your friend. He's equipping your enemies. He's just as much a problem for you as he is for us. But
he's got connections, so you can't take him on directly. We
can. Him and a dirty cop." Jason shrugged. "There's no angle
to killing us."

"Unless y'all are lying to me."

Something tightened in Jason's chest. This would be the
most dangerous part. "You're right. After all, a man will say
anything when he's at gunpoint." He swallowed hard, then
slowly lowered the Ruger. Lightning raced up his thighs. He
locked the safety, then, adrenaline shaking the world, spun
the pistol butt first and held it out to Playboy. "So we're clear,
I don't like you, man. But you're not my enemy, and I'm not
yours."

Cruz looked at him wild-eyed. "What?"

"It's okay, Elena. Let him free." Jason kept his eyes locked
on Playboy's. "Go ahead. It's not a trick."

The gangbanger looked at the gun, looked at Cruz. She
had her teeth clenched, the line of her jaw hard. She seemed
unsure. He didn't blame her, but she could still blow it.

"Elena." Jason spoke softly. "I need you to trust me."

She stiffened. He could see her wrestling with it. Then,
slowly, she stepped away. Kept the gun in her hand, but lowered.

Playboy's eyes moved back and forth between them. His
lids were narrowed, but not in the half-asleep pose he'd been
affecting. He reached up slowly and took the pistol.

"I'm giving you this because I want you to know that we
aren't lying." Jason spoke quietly. "We didn't kill C-Note."
His heart was pounding. The safety would slow Playboy
down enough for Jason to tackle him, but his friends were
the real problem. Jason was counting on them following
their boss's lead. If they didn't . . .

Playboy took a last drag on the cigarette, then flicked it
away. He held the gun at his side, his arm loose. Tilted his
head up so the rain ran down his shaved skull. "And you're
going to take care of DiRisio."

"And Galway. And everybody in with them."

"If y'all are playing me—"

"You're a general now," Jason said. "You got a hundred soldiers standing behind you. We know what happens if we play you."

The man nodded slow. "Guess that's so." He tucked the Ruger into the back of his pants, and Jason started breathing again.

Then the wrestler cocked his pistol. "Fuck *that*. Let's take care of business." Beside him, Curtis nodded, his gun aimed at Jason's chest. Cruz brought her Glock back up, holding it beautifully, two hands, legs spread in a target-shooter stance.

"Nah. Man's got a point. Besides," and Playboy smiled a thin, brutal smile, "not like we can't find him again. Him and his little nephew."

Jason felt his lips twitching, fought the urge to close his hands into fists.

The wrestler said, "I say we—"

"I ask your opinion, motherfucker?" Playboy glared at him. "Man, I've had crotch lice got more brains than you, you're going to tell me what to do?"

"No, but—"

"But what, *bitch?*"

The wrestler straightened at that, his nostrils flaring. Glared at Playboy, a hard look between hard men. If this went wrong, Jason knew, then things were going to get ugly. Bullets flying, everybody shooting at everybody, who knew who'd get hit.

Finally, the wrestler looked away. "It's your world."

"Goddamn right. It's my world." Playboy held the stare for a moment, then turned to Jason. "So we're clear, I don't much like you either." The gangbanger reached in his pocket, pulled out his cigarettes. Shook one out slow, held it to his lips, fired it up with the Bic. "But keep your end of this, and we 'aight."

"You come after me or mine again, we're going to mix it up."

"Do right, I won't have to." In the distance, a siren wailed.

Playboy glanced over his shoulder. "Now. Do yourself a favor and don't be leaving for a bit. I see you coming after us, might be I take that the wrong way."

Jason nodded.

Playboy turned and walked away, his cross-trainers carving trenches in the soft mud. Curtis and the wrestler followed him, walking backwards with guns out. Jason stood with his skin vibrating until they were out of sight.

Then he heaved a sigh. "Jesus."

Cruz stared at him. "How'd you know that would work?"

"Playboy thinks he's a soldier. Long as we had the upper hand, he couldn't back down. But if we're two soldiers talking about a mutually beneficial arrangement, well, that's different."

She shook her head. "Boys. You're all just little boys with guns."

"You only figuring that out now?" Jason shook out his shoulders. Felt that familiar lightness, relief and tension mingling. The siren grew closer. Dealing with Playboy had only been a distraction. They still had their real work ahead of them. And now they didn't have the evidence to make it safe.

*One step at a time, soldier. That's how the march works.*

"Speaking of guns," he said, and stared pointedly at her. "For two days I've been wishing we had one, and for two days you've been awfully quiet about yours."

Cruz shrugged. Hiked up one pant leg, then bent to strap the Glock into the ankle holster she'd slipped it out of while pretending to faint. When she straightened, a smile tugged at one corner of her lips.

She said, "I'm working on my trust issues."

# CHAPTER 37
## Toys

The boy was playing with the gun, and the sight twisted something in Washington.

Billy leaned against a heavy oak bureau that had been in the room as long as Washington could remember. He was hunched in the classic hiding position, plastic pistol held in both extended arms. Rain lashed the window in blinding sheets, and yellow headlights rolled slowly by. Billy tracked them with the gun, steady and slow. Pulled the trigger: once, twice, then threefourfive. "Gotcha," he muttered, and swung the pistol back.

*It's just a toy, old man,* Washington reminded himself. *Can't take everybody's toys away.* Still, it bothered him to see it. He couldn't put his finger on why, exactly. Maybe just seen too many boys with real guns in their hand. He rapped on the edge of the doorframe. "How you doing, son?"

"Okay."

"What are you up to?"

"Just playing." Billy left the window and sat on the edge of the bed. "This used to belong to Uncle Jason. See?" He held it up.

Washington leaned down to read the inscription on the handle. It would have been easier to bring the pistol to his eyes, but he didn't want to touch even a toy gun. Maybe ridiculous, maybe not. Recovering alcoholics didn't tell themselves they could drink light beer. Not if they wanted to stay recovering, at least. "This says *Michael* Palmer."

"I know, but it's scratched out. Uncle Jason won it from him." Billy held the gun in both hands. "Maybe when I grow up I'll be a soldier like he was."

The knot inside cinched tighter. "Maybe."

Billy looked up at him, head cocked. "You sound funny."

"I don't like guns."

"Because they're dangerous?" Billy said it with the mocking insouciance of a child.

Washington sat on the edge of the bed, hearing that old cold song of twisting metal. The siren song that had roared through him sure, pure, and sweet all those years ago. Like always, it tugged at him, urged him back. He sighed, cocked his head. "I remember being your age thinking how much fun all that stuff on TV looked, people shooting each other. But it's only on TV that it's that easy. Most of the time you can't just shoot the bad guy."

"Why not?" Billy's eyes were earnest. "If you know they're bad, I mean?"

"Well, for one thing, that's not easy to know." The rain fell steady and slow, drenching the world. "Some that seem one way are really the other. Ronald used to be a bad guy. Me too."

"*You* were a bad guy?"

*A roar, and a hot punch against his hand. The boy with the cauliflower ear spinning, slow, a last pirouette, eyes already dying.*

*A debt that could never be repaid.*

"Yes," he said quietly. "Yes, I was."

Billy chewed his lip. "What if somebody is *really* bad, though? Not like you or Ronald, but *really* bad?"

Washington could hear the question under Billy's words, understood that he was asking about the people who had murdered his father. And part of him wanted to say that you still couldn't make that kind of decision. That people changed, that you could change them. That good could always be reclaimed from evil. But he didn't want to lie to the boy.

"I don't know, son. I don't have an answer for you. I just know I don't like guns."

Billy nodded slowly.

"But," Washington said as he stood, "that don't mean you can't play with your toy. Though right now, we got more important things to worry about. Like getting you dressed for tonight. You need any help?"

"Nuh-uh." Billy set the gun on the bed and went over to the closet. "I know how to do it."

"You sure?" Washington straightened his bow tie in the mirror. He'd delayed renting a tux until the last minute, but he had to admit, he was enjoying wearing it. "I'd be happy to make you look as dapper as I do."

Billy shook his head, pulled the plastic garment bag out. "You got that upside down."

"Hmm?" Washington glanced down. "What?"

Billy pointed at his belly. "That thing."

"The cummerbund?" He'd slung it the way that made sense, ruffles pointing down, kind of a sleek look. "I don't think so."

"Yup." Billy nodded firmly. "It's supposed to go the other way, with the things up. It's to catch crumbs."

Washington laughed through his nose. Kids. "Crumbs, huh?"

"Uh-huh. The guy at the store told me so. And there are holes in the pocket, too."

"Holes?"

"For pulling your shirt down."

Bemused, Washington slid his hands in his pockets. He didn't plan on taking fashion advice from an eight-year-old, certainly not on a tuxedo—

Damned if there weren't holes in there.

# CHAPTER 38
Soldiers

It was never a good sign when you could smell yourself.

Cruz forced a smile for the bus driver, doing her best not to look like a crazy woman. Judging by the way the guy wrinkled his nose, it didn't work. Her hair was matted, her face dirty and bruised, blood scabbing a thin tear where her forehead had hit the wheel. Her skin itched with something she'd rather not think about, and her jeans and summer sweater had been two days dirty *before* they'd gone in the river.

"Quite a storm, huh?" she asked, and swiped her CTA card. A thin trickle of brown water poured from her wallet to spatter on the floor.

"Sure," the driver said, and looked away.

They walked down the bright aisle. A couple of girls in hospital scrubs, an elderly man asleep with his mouth open, two laughing teenagers, a frazzled mother of four. This far south, a light-skinned Latina and a white guy would normally catch stares, but now everyone found a reason to gaze elsewhere, afraid of catching whatever madness infected them. Only the children looked, eyes like saucers. Shivering in her wet clothes, she took a seat in the back row, where the engine's heat penetrated. Jason remained standing, fingers clenched white on a pole. Though he wasn't moving, he gave off the vibe of a man pacing angry circles. There was something in his posture that scared her a little bit; not *of* him, but *for* him. "What are you thinking?"

He shook his head.

"The war?"

Palmer's cheek twitched. He stared out the black windows.

She shrugged. Her head and neck throbbed, and she wasn't in the mood to play Twenty Questions. She could see the skyline to the east, the lights of the Sears Tower lost in glowing cloud. Tiny reflections of the city burned in every drop of water on the window. "You know, you surprised me back there. Letting Playboy go."

"I wanted to waste him." He shook his head. "When I think of him in Michael's house, talking about killing Billy."

"I wouldn't have let you."

"That wasn't what stopped me."

"What did?"

He paused. "He was a chess piece." He sat down beside her, bangs falling in wet clumps across his forehead. "Killing him, it just . . ."

"Wouldn't have made any difference?"

He nodded, staring straight ahead.

"We're screwed, you know."

"Yeah."

"Maybe . . ." She scratched at the back of her neck. "Maybe it's time to look at leaving."

"Where?"

"I don't know. Rent a cabin somewhere. Get out of sight."

He shook his head. "You were on the news, remember? You run, it's all over."

"I didn't mean me."

He gave her a measuring sort of gaze. She met his eyes. Even with all the grime, he looked good, a strong jaw, nice features, something boyish in his energy. For a long moment, he just stared. Then he took her hand, weaving his fingers through hers. Sighed. "They never caught the sniper."

"What?"

"The one who shot my friend." His voice was thin and soft. "I remember that day so well. Scarlet sunset, broken concrete, the brown eyes of the kid in the ambulance. But I can't—I just—I don't know where the sniper was. He could have been on a rooftop blocks away." He shrugged. "I picture him sometimes, try to imagine what he looked like, what he thought when he squeezed the trigger. A man about to get lucky with a thousand-to-one shot. He would have thought of himself as a soldier too, I guess. Defending his country. Sometimes I think everybody sees themselves as soldiers."

She traced the rough pads of his fingers.

"You want to know the real reason I didn't tell anyone about what happened? Because I'm afraid of the questions." His nostrils flared, and his tone changed. "No, not even that. Not *questions,* plural. One question. The obvious one." He turned to look at her. "You know the one?"

She said nothing.

"Sure you do. The question is how in the world did I get discharged for what happened. Yes, I took my men off-mission, and that's not good. But I was a noncom, a squad leader. We're expected to react to changing situations. That was my job. And losing a man, well, it's tragic, but Martinez was shot by insurgents. Maybe I made a questionable call, but it wasn't negligent or malicious. So how would that get me discharged? I mean, you're a smart woman—didn't you wonder?"

She tried to keep her face noncommittal. "Maybe a little."

"There you go."

"Do you *want* me to ask?"

He moved his teeth like he were chewing gum. Held the silence. Then, "I used to tell myself that it was my lieutenant's fault. That he didn't back me. But that's not true. The truth is I fell apart."

"What do you mean?"

"I froze up. Couldn't stand the possibility of losing someone else under my command. I'd dream about Martinez, and then when I had to take the squad out the next morning, I'd be a wreck. A walking panic attack. I'd abort a mission for the tiniest reason, or no reason at all. Hell, I even managed to start drinking, which isn't easy in a Muslim country. It's not like the old days, privates sucking dope through their ri-

fle barrels. I got scared of the responsibility, and I got self-
ish." He sighed. "And it put lives at risk. I *deserved* to get
discharged. It was the right call. *That's* the truth."

She opened her mouth, closed it. A thousand possible answers paraded past her, and none sounded right.

"I know what you're offering to do," he said. "And I appreciate it. But I'm not quitting. I can't."

"I'm not saying—"

"It's not you." He shook his head. "I messed up so many
things. Not just in the war. I've been running from responsibility all my life. Hell, if I'd taken a little more responsibility
for Michael, he might still be alive."

"There's no reason to believe that."

"I think there is. Anyway, it doesn't matter. I'm tired of
dodging what I know needs to be done. I owe better to myself. To Michael. And I damn sure owe more to Billy."

The bus hit a bump in the road and set off dull firecrackers
behind her eyes. With ginger fingers she explored her forehead. The skin felt tender and swollen, warm meat. She didn't
remember hitting the steering wheel, didn't even remember
the car falling. Just the impact that threw them, and then the
water, cold, cold, her head throbbing and Jason gone. That had
been her first thought as she started to pull herself together—
a complete lack of surprise to find him gone.

Then he'd appeared at her window and pulled her free,
and in the process sacrificed the thing he needed most.

"Okay," she said.

"Okay?"

"Let's do it." She put all her meaning into her eyes. The be-
trayals, and the jokes, the loneliness. The months—years—of
not letting anyone in, not being able to. It was a lot to convey
with a look, but sometimes words murdered ideas.

He held her gaze, then smiled slowly. "Okay."

Outside the bus windows, neon burned, advertising
taquerías and Currency Exchanges. The drizzle was letting
up. "So what's our plan? We're back where we started."

"Not quite. We know what's happening now."

"But it doesn't do us any good. Without evidence, telling

the media won't make a difference. They'll just see us as crazies."

"What about the alderman?" Jason rubbed at the stubble on his chin. "You said he's a good guy."

She shrugged. "What are we going to do, just march into the alderman's office and tell him what we saw?"

He stared at her like she'd said the secret password, a strange light in his eyes.

"No," he said. "Not his office."

# CHAPTER 39
Crazy

"Make yourself at home," Jason said, pushing open the door. His studio was as he'd left it, the blinds open and bedding tangled. The cereal bowls still sat on the table where he and Billy had left them after breakfast. He saw a flash of his nephew grinning about being allowed to leave the plates on the table, instead of having to wash them and put them in the dishwasher like he did at home.

"You sure it's safe?"

"I doubt they know where I live. It's month-to-month, cash. Like I said, dodging responsibility."

She nodded, looked around. "It's nice."

"It's a hole," he said. "I rented it when I came back. I wasn't sure I was staying in Chicago."

"Where would you go?"

"There's the rub." He dropped the keys on the table, plugged his cell phone in to charge. "Bathroom's that way. I'll see if I can find a clean towel for you. And we need to get you some clothes if we're going to pull this off. Something swank."

"They'll be watching my apartment."

"You have a girlfriend, someone who can lend you some things?"

Cruz cocked her head. "My friend Ruby lives over in Wicker Park. She made me wear a fuchsia bridesmaid's dress with dyed-to-match shoes for her wedding. I figure she still owes me."

"Can we borrow her car?"

"So long as I don't tell her what happened to the last one."

It ambushed him when he opened the closet.

Cruz had let him shower first, saying she wanted to take a bath while they waited for her friend. He'd felt kind of awkward, not sure if he should close the door or what. Whatever had happened in the river, and on the bus, it had changed things between them. Bound them together. Door closed, he'd decided. But not all the way.

In the shower he'd scrubbed hard, the soap stripping off what felt like half an inch of grime and sweat. Stepped out reborn, knotted a towel around his waist, and opened the door. Elena had smiled as she breezed past him, and run a hand along his bare stomach. She'd drawn a bath, humming something, a high, sweet song, and he'd thought how he might not mind hearing it for a long time.

Then he'd opened his closet and the garment bag had ambushed him.

His clothing was orderly, T-shirts and jeans neatly folded on the shelves, socks and underwear in bins below, dirty laundry in a basket in the corner. The rod held two pairs of slacks, a windbreaker, his suit, three stray hangers, and the garment bag. He hadn't touched it, or even looked it, since he'd hung it there months ago. It was like he'd developed a localized blindness that screened it out.

The plastic felt cool. Jason carried it to the bed. Set it down like a priest laying out his vestments.

The creases were still razor sharp. Ribbons hung on the left breast, above his marksmanship pin—sharpshooter, not expert, which had bothered him as an NCO—and below the combat infantry badge. His sergeant's chevrons were stitched on the sleeves. Behind the jacket were two pale green oxfords, the trousers, and a black tie.

He hadn't worn his Class A Dress Uniform since he'd

walked out of the Administrative Discharge Board, the words "other than honorable" ringing in his ears, his mouth dry and craving bourbon. He'd finished his truncated deployment in BDUs, packed his ruck, and hopped a plane to Kuwait, then Germany, then Atlanta, and finally Chicago. Only to arrive home and find the same kind of war raging in his old neighborhood. The same murky alliances and lust for power, the same lies and obfuscations, the regular people caught in the crossfire.

He ran his fingers along the fabric. It felt right. He'd gone in the closet intending to wear his suit. But what was a suit to him?

After all, he didn't have to be in the Army to be a soldier.

Jason knocked on the bathroom door and told Cruz he was going for food, then took the fire stairs to the street. His uniform drew nods from the guys hanging out on the corner. He nodded back, walked past the payday loan place to the Italian beef restaurant.

"Two combos, wet and spicy."

"Fries?"

"With cheese." The smell of grease set his stomach rumbling.

He took the bag of carryout, two cans of Coke, and an inch-thick stack of napkins back to his apartment. Moved the cereal bowls to the sink, wiped the kitchen table, and set out the food. He thought about fixing a drink, decided he didn't want one. Couldn't afford it, anyway—exhaustion had drained his limbs, and whiskey wouldn't help. He heard the bathroom door open, and then Cruz stepped out.

"Holy shit," he said, his mouth hanging open.

"Ruby came by while you were gone. You like?" She wore a dress of thin fabric, black with scarlet roses. The material clung to her, tracing the soft curve of her breasts, the swell of her pubic bone. Makeup concealed the bruise on her forehead, and she wore her hair twirled up and held in place with something that looked like chopsticks, revealing a graceful neck and collarbone.

"You look amazing."

"Thank you. You look pretty good yourself, soldier. Want to see the best part?"

"That isn't the best part?"

She held up a black clutch purse, smiled coquettishly, and withdrew the Glock 27.

He burst out laughing. "Come on. Let's eat." He held a chair for her, and she sat demurely. The whole situation felt surreal, a tiny time-out against a mad world, and he decided to enjoy the minutes they had. Sat beside her at his crummy kitchen table, poured her a Coke as if it were wine. "We have several specials tonight. First, Freedom Fries Velveeta: select portions of potato lovingly boiled in two-day-old grease and smothered with yellow. I also recommend the combo, a Chicago classic: spicy sausage nestled in a Kaiser roll, topped with two inches of Italian beef, dipped in au jus, and crowned with pickled hot peppers. The use of fingers is advised."

"Mmmm," she said, reaching for her sandwich. "I love a man who knows how to treat a lady." She took a bite and chewed languorously, her eyes fluttering closed. "I don't think I've ever tasted anything this good in my life."

"It's like camping. Everything tastes better if you have to work for it," he leaned forward to keep the hot grease off his uniform.

"I'll keep that in mind next time I'm escaping a sinking Honda."

They attacked the food, the two of them in formal dress eating junk food under fluorescent lights. He finished first, and leaned back to watch her, her fingers shiny with grease, a smear of cheese on her lips. When she finished, she crumpled up the wax paper, then set to sucking her fingers one at a time. "You know, this plan . . ." She paused, took a sip of Coke, holding the cup with her palms. "Well, it's not a plan."

"More like a prayer," he agreed. "Got any better options?"

"No. But even all cleaned up and looking fine, I'm not sure he won't think we're crazy."

He shrugged, took a napkin and scrubbed his fingers. "Maybe. But we can tell the alderman exactly where to look.

You said he's a good guy, tough on crime, big on his district. This should matter to him."

"If he believes us."

"If he believes us." He tossed the napkin in the garbage, leaned back in his chair. Had the flashing urge to suggest they call the whole thing off, spend the night in bed instead. Not even sex, he realized, feeling the aches in his body. Just sleeping. "Speaking of crazy, some day, we get through this, I might do something else crazy."

"What's that?"

He smiled. "Ask you on a date."

# CHAPTER 40
## City on Fire

Their timeout was over.

Jason could feel it in his chest. Breathing was a conscious activity, something he had to remember to do. Whatever cosmic force had conspired to give them a few stolen moments of peace and animal comfort, it had moved on.

The Swissôtel was a fifty-story glass triangle wedged between the Chicago River and Lake Michigan. It was above his pay grade, but he'd heard it was nice: panoramic views, modern décor, a penthouse pool. None of which mattered a damn to him right now.

What did matter were the three squad cars parked in the front circle, twenty feet away from them.

"What did you expect?" Cruz asked. "It's not just the alderman. This is a two-hundred-dollar-a-plate benefit. These people are the aristocracy. Helping the unwashed is one thing; eating with them is another."

"Where will the cops be?"

Cruz stared out the windshield of their borrowed car, a Taurus with a bad case of the shakes and a yellow-ribbon bumper sticker that read, *I support empty gestures.*

"Uniforms in the lobby, probably a few plainclothes upstairs."

Jason nodded, energy speeding his pulse, sharpening his

vision. "Look, last chance. This is the only way I can see to get Billy free of this. I have to do it. But you don't."

Cruz leaned over and kissed him, a soft play of lips, more comfort than sex. When she broke the kiss, she kept a hand against his cheek, her eyes close. For a moment they shared a look. Then she said, "Game on, soldier."

Game on.

He got out of the car, closed the door. Tension shivered up his spine, but he kept his face calm and smiling. A valet took the keys in trade for a ticket Cruz tucked in her purse. Jason straightened his uniform with a gentle tug, then extended his arm. Together they walked into the lobby.

The décor was Upscale American Hotel: muted paisley carpet, polished mahogany, yellow light rising from brass sconces. Artfully arranged couches in beige and gray, occupied by guests in expensive shoes. An attractive blonde concierge stood at one end of a marble counter.

Three cops stood at the other end.

They wore Chicago-blue over tactical bulletproof vests, the hardware making them barrel-chested. Radios, cuffs, ammo cases, and key chains all hung on their belts, but all Jason could see was the sidearm each carried. He stopped inside the door, turned sideways, his body blocking their view of her. "You know those guys?"

She snuck a furtive look past his shoulder. "No."

He nodded, his eyes scanning the lobby. Trying to look like the kind of man who belonged at a charity dinner. The son of a prominent businessman, just pausing to talk to his date. There were two more cops standing by the enclosed fireplace near the entrance.

Cops in front, cops behind. He could feel his heart in his throat, even as he reminded himself that there was no way they were the target. The cops had to be routine security, just assuring that an event attended by a political figure went off smoothly: no wackos, no former employees with a grudge. All Jason had to do was keep cool.

His eyes fell on a brass stanchion with a sign atop it:

BENEFIT DINNER FOR THE LANTERN BEARERS
EDELWEISS SUITE
43RD FLOOR

"Okay," Jason said, and started walking. Cruz fell in alongside him, her arm still tucked through his. "What we're doing here is hiding in plain sight."

"Right."

"No one will be looking for us here."

"Right."

"We're just going to stroll past them."

"Right."

Jason's muscles were tense as he moved. The smile plastered on his face felt forced, the same rigid skeleton expression he had in snapshots. The cops were calm, but not lax. Their eyes watched the crowd. The tallest, a jowly guy with a mustache, looked at Jason.

*Run,* his body screamed. *Do it now.*

Instead he made himself flash a bare nod, then turned to look at Cruz. Said, "I hope we aren't too late for dinner. I'm starving."

She didn't miss a beat. "I'm sure they'll have something. I just hope we have a better table this time than last."

"Do you think the alderman will still be there?"

"Oh, I hope so. I'd really like to meet him."

They came close enough to smell the aftershave on one of them, something lemony and cheap. Jason concentrated on lifting his feet and putting them down, on his inane conversation with Cruz.

Then they were past, and he took a deep breath. The air was cool and clean. He cocked his eyebrows at Cruz, shook his head barely. They'd made it. He led her toward a bank of elevators, the doors shining like they were polished twice a day. With a soft tone, one opened in front of them.

"Hey." The voice came from behind, gruff and loud.

Cruz tightened the grip on his arm. He kept walking, fighting to keep the pace steady.

"Hey! Hey you."

The elevator slid shut in front of them. Jason's throat felt swollen as he turned around. The tall cop stood behind him, one hand resting on the butt of his gun. Jason thought he might be able to jump him, get a punch in and make a run. Kevlar did nothing against a fist. He started to speak, lost it. Coughed, then made himself say, "Yes?"

The man stepped closer. He had thin brown hair and wore the lemon aftershave. His fingers tapped on his sidearm. He looked at Cruz, then back to Jason. Narrowed his eyes slightly.

Then he said, "I just want to thank you for what you're doing," and extended his hand. For a second Jason didn't understand what he meant, how this cop he'd never seen before could possibly know what they were doing.

Then he remembered the uniform. Relief flowed through him like warm water. "Thank you, Officer. That means a lot to me." He took the cop's hand, shook it firmly.

"Are you back for long?"

"For good, I think."

"I'm glad to hear it." The man hesitated. "No matter how you feel about the war, we all owe you guys a debt. The country said go and you went. You've made us very proud."

Jason felt a surge of absurd gratitude. "Thank you."

"Anyhow, don't mean to keep you folks." Another ding sounded, and a different elevator opened. The man raised an arm to hold it open, and gestured them in like a doorman. "Have a good night."

"You too, officer." Jason pressed the button for 43. He could feel one eyelid wanting to twitch in a nervous tic, and rubbed at it. As the doors closed, Cruz slumped against the back wall of the elevator. "Jesus. Thought we'd had it there."

Jason nodded, flexing his shoulders to release the tension. Modest beeps marked floors as the elevator rose. "You said there will be more upstairs?"

"Probably."

"Will they know you?"

"Doubt it. I know a lot of the tactical guys in Area One, but the Loop is Area Four. But—"

"You were on TV. I know." He shook his head. "We'll

keep it quick and low profile. Just get in, find Washington and the alderman, go from there. Simple."

Cruz looked as dubious as he felt. *Sure. Just waltz past plainclothes cops, convince a guy who thinks I'm suffering post-traumatic stress to extend his voucher to the most important politician in the room, then convince the alderman, without a shred of evidence, to undertake a crusade that will set the city on fire.*

*Simple.*

Jason pushed the thoughts from his mind. Replaced them with an image of goofing off in Lake Michigan, he and Mikey linking arms in a cradle for Billy to stand in, counting three, two, one, and then heaving together, the boy arcing a dozen feet, his legs bicycling, water trailing prismatic behind whoops of joy.

The elevator doors slid open. Jason counted three, two, one, and stepped out.

The buzz of conversation hit first, a hundred voices talking and laughing. A short hallway opened to a banquet room dotted with circular tables. White linen, half-empty wine glasses, bright floral centerpieces. Beyond burned the lights of Navy Pier, the Ferris wheel turning in slow circles.

Ronald stood out in the crowd, towering above millionaires that looked at him with the frosted smiles of zoo-goers dubious about the security of the cages. Jason caught his eye, and the big man moved to meet them. His tux pants were two inches too short, and the fabric strained over his biceps. "Thought y'all were going over to that bar."

"We did."

"Get what you need?"

"Yes and no." He grimaced. "Mostly no. How's Billy?"

"Good. Last I saw, little man had discovered the buffet."

Jason's head snapped fast. "He's *here*?"

Ronald shrugged. "You axed me to keep an eye on him. Where's he gonna be safer—in a roomful of rich white folks, or alone back at the house?"

For Jason's money, Billy would be safest locked in a small room with armed guards outside it, but he saw the point.

"Yeah, all right. How 'bout Washington? You know where he is?"

"Holdin' court, I expect."

"Thanks," Jason said. "When this is all over, I hope you'll let me buy you a beer."

The big man shrugged. "You can buy me two, you want to."

The crowd was in that state of upscale levity born of single malt before dinner and pinot noir during, and as Jason wound his way through, people smiled at him, nodded. A woman raised a champagne flute in salute. He had chosen the uniform because it felt more natural than a suit, but he was starting to wonder if the trade-off in visibility was worth it.

"You're a celebrity in that thing."

"Sure," Jason said. "Everybody loves a soldier. These folks just don't like their sons to become one. You see him?"

"No."

Beside the swinging service doors was a dead zone. Jason stepped into it, scanned the room, an eye out for Billy. The crowd was mostly white, with a handful of Hispanics and African Americans. Everyone was dressed the same, and for a moment it seemed vaguely funny, all the world-makers in uniforms of their own. Then, through a break in the crowd, he spotted Washington, arms up in preacher pose, talking to a good-looking black man with a broad smile. "Got him." He squinted. "And I think that's the alderman he's with."

As he started over, he felt his heart quicken, a lifting in his chest. His mouth was dry, his words gone. Everything he cared about depended on the alderman believing them. Jason had an image of Billy splashing down in Lake Michigan, the way the kid would always rocket to the surface in an explosion of bubbles, saying, "Again, again!" He thrust that aside, too.

Washington saw him coming, and a shadow rippled over his face. He stopped in the middle of a sentence, one arm out like he were holding a metaphor. "Jason." Not sounding happy to see him. His eyes flicked up and down Jason's uniform. "I didn't expect you tonight."

"I didn't either." Jason turned to face the alderman, suddenly unsure how to begin.

"Ahh, Alderman Owens, this is Jason Palmer. He's . . . ," Washington paused, ". . . an old friend of mine."

The alderman hit him with a friendly grin. "What's a respectable soldier doing hanging around with a reprobate like Washington?" They shook, the man's grip firm. "This is Daryl Thomas," he said, gesturing to the man beside him. "He's my right hand and my second in command."

"This is Officer Elena Cruz, with the Chicago Police Department." Saying her name felt like a risk, but he needed her to lend credibility to what he had to say.

"Officer Cruz," the alderman took her hand in that horizontal handshake. "It's a pleasure." But something stirred in his eyes, like he were trying to remember details he'd recently heard. "What brings you out tonight?"

A dozen approaches flashed through Jason's mind, then vanished just as quickly. There was no strategy to follow here. He had to just tell the truth, to tell it as fully as he knew how, and to pray that it was enough. "You do, sir."

"Oh?"

"I need five minutes of your time."

"I'm always available to constituents, especially friends of Washington's. Call the office tomorrow, ask for Daryl. He'll make sure you get set up with an appointment next week."

"I'm sorry, sir. I wasn't clear." Jason straightened his shoulders and put his hands behind his back to stand at something like attention. "I meant I need your time right now. This second."

Washington put a hand on his shoulder. "Maybe this isn't the best—"

"Sir, this is a matter of life and death." Jason didn't risk looking away from Owens, but his thoughts were on Washington. *Stick with me, old man. Trust me.*

The alderman had the amiable hesitancy of a man expecting a punch line. "Life and death?"

"Yes."

Owens and his assistant shared a look. "I have to admit, I'm curious, Mr. Palmer. What's this about?"

There it was. The simple question, and there was a simple answer to match, a simple, dirty answer. The one they'd discovered in the basement of Michael's ruined bar, in the darkness beneath the city. An explanation for everything: His brother's murder, the hunt for Billy, the gang war, all of it. An answer written in blood and shadow.

"Money, sir. It's about money." He paused. "It's about men who are willing to do anything for money. And they're doing it in your district."

"Jason, what are you—" Washington's voice was thin and nervous.

"I'm sorry." Jason turned to face his mentor. "I'm sorry to do this here, tonight. And I know we've had our disagreements lately, and I understand your side of things. But I'm looking you in the eye and I'm telling you, *this is the truth*. This is why Michael was murdered."

Washington stared at him appraisingly. The moment stretched, and Jason found himself aware of tiny details, the mismatched angles of hairs in Washington's mustache, the smell of cooling steak permeating the room, the chamber music barely audible under the crush of conversation. The older man hesitated, then nodded slowly.

"Murdered?" Owens spoke softly. "Sergeant Palmer, if this is some sort of joke, I'm going to be very disappointed."

"Sir, believe me when I tell you that I've never been more serious in my life."

The alderman nodded, the motion businesslike and sure. "Then you best go ahead."

Jason took a breath. Words were all he had, but they such a small thing when set against blood. And the debt of blood here ran higher than he could say.

"A few days ago, my brother was murdered in your ward." He raised a hand to forestall sympathy. "Two men came to the bar he owned. They were looking for something, and when he wouldn't give it to them, they killed him."

"What were they looking for?"

"Do you live in Crenwood, sir?"

The alderman looked cagey at the change of subject. "Yes. Halsted and Sixty-first. Aldermen have to live in their districts."

"There's an El station near there."

"About two blocks south. What does this have to do with—"

"I grew up on the south side, but I had a few friends who lived on the north. I'd ride the El up to see them, and it was like going to Oz." He remembered staring at all the clean, bright buildings. No graffiti, no gangs. "My friends' parents liked living in the city because they were close to work, restaurants, shops, you know. All the usual reasons. After I left, I'd always wonder why Crenwood looked so different."

"The north side tends to be college-educated, with white-collar jobs and higher household income. That means better schools, more business, more community resources." The alderman shook his head sadly. "It makes sense, but can you imagine a world where the *lower* income neighborhoods got more support and better schools?"

Jason smiled. Felt himself liking this guy. "That'd be a better world than this one. Because I agree—those are the neighborhoods where people want to live. I'm not an expert, but as I understand it, that's why when it became popular to live in the city again, people chose neighborhoods like Lincoln Park and Old Town. And when they got crowded and prices went up, folks started to push further out, into Wicker Park and Lakeview and Andersonville. Neighborhoods that were still rough around the edges, where they could afford a flat or a carriage house, a place to raise their children. Developers came in, and then retail, and everything got nice and safe. Now the same thing is happening in Bridgeport and Rogers Park."

"Gentrification is a thorny issue." He sounded bored.

"But it's an opportunity, too, right? The trick is being ahead of the game. You need to buy before the neighborhood hits. If you really want to make money, you do it somewhere other people weren't even looking."

"I suppose." Owens glanced at his watch.

"Mr. Alderman," Daryl Thomas nudged his boss. "You should probably work the room before people start to leave."

Cruz looked at Thomas with her eyes narrowed, but Jason didn't have time to wonder what it meant. "Sir, wait—"

"Sergeant Palmer." Owens put a hand on his shoulder. "I assure you, this is a problem I've put a *lot* of thought into. And I'd love to hear your take on it. But why don't we talk another time, when we can really roll up our sleeves?"

"Because if you don't listen right now we may not live to see you again."

Owens paused, stared over the edge of rimless glasses. "That's a little melodramatic, isn't it?"

"Ask my brother." Jason spoke softly.

The alderman's smile curdled. "Sergeant, I'm sincerely sorry for your loss, but I'm not sure where this is going. Are you saying your brother was killed because of some sort of real estate scheme?"

"Yes. And not just him." He took a breath, then launched into it. "Sir, someone is using every means possible to lower property values in Crenwood so they can buy it up against its eventual gentrification."

Owens gave him a long look. His eyes searched Jason's. Then he broke into laughter.

"I'm serious, sir."

"So am I." Owens chuckled. "This is *Crenwood* you're talking about. Do you know how low property values are already?"

"I do." Cruz spoke firmly. "Sir, I've worked Crenwood for a dozen years. It was always poor, but it used to be a solid neighborhood of working families. Now it's a war zone. And honest people who wouldn't have dreamed of selling a decade ago are taking fifty cents on the dollar."

"Getting worse is in the nature of things." But the alderman stroked at his chin, his eyes narrowed. "Who are these alleged people?"

Jason grimaced. "We know some of them, sir, but not all of them. We've been over legal documents, real estate contracts, shipping manifests, documentation of holding companies. There weren't any personal names, but there was plenty to trace everything back to a source. That's what the men who killed him were looking for." He didn't mention that they didn't have the evidence anymore. One step at a time. Get the guy onboard, then he could tell the whole story. "And they came after us, too."

"What happened?"

"They ran our car into the river." He kept his gaze level.

"Ran your car—"

"Into the river. Off the Thirty-fifth Street bridge. That's how Officer Cruz cut her head." He gestured, and she pulled her bangs aside to show the bruise, still visible under makeup. "We can take you there if you'd like, show you where we went over."

The alderman hesitated. "You said these people are using every means to drive prices down. What does that mean?" Jason felt a thrill of hope. The alderman had said *these* people, not these *alleged* people.

"Mr. Alderman, what I'm about to tell you sounds far-fetched," Cruz said, her voice soft but steady. "Sir, the people behind this are fostering a gang war in Crenwood. They're keeping the Gangster Disciples and the Latin Saints at each other's throats. Then they're torching specific properties and laying the blame at the gangs' feet. And to make sure that the war stays hot, they're arming both sides. Last night we watched two of these men sell submachine guns to a group of Latin Saints."

"Submachine guns?" The alderman's eyes widened. A faint sheen of sweat lit his brow. "Who was selling them? Who are you talking about?"

Cruz hesitated. Jason met her eyes, thinking, *Moment of truth.*

"One of them was an arms dealer named Anthony DiRisio," Cruz said, speaking slowly. "And the other was a police sergeant named Tom Galway."

The alderman stared at her open-mouthed. The noise of

the party continued, but it felt far away. Jason's fingers tingled, and spiders climbed his spine. He could see every face in the room. Rich men with sagging bellies, taut-skinned women wearing jewelry that cost more than he'd made in a year of soldiering, all talking and laughing and making deals in slow motion, a twisting dance of flesh and intent.

"This doesn't make any sense." Owens looked back and forth between them.

"It does if you're the right kind of person. If you're rich and want to get richer and don't care about the people in your way."

"But why Crenwood? With the gangs, the violence, the blight, we're hardly the next Lincoln Park."

"Not the next, no. But Chicago is getting full. People keep moving in from the suburbs, and the hot new area to buy keeps pushing outward. It's mostly gone north, but that can't last forever. Besides, there's another reason." Jason saw someone move in his peripheral vision, spun in time to see two men embrace, slapping each other on the back. Jumping at shadows. "It's why I asked where you live."

Owens squinted at him, his hand stroking his chin. "The El."

"Exactly. All the places I've mentioned, the ones that gentrified, they were on the train lines. Like those friends I used to visit. Their parents wanted to live in the city, but it's a pain to drive to work. Traffic is brutal and parking is expensive. So people want property along the mass transit lines. And once all the neighborhoods on the northbound trains are too expensive or too far—"

"The South Side will start to look like prime real estate. And if someone had pushed property values low enough to buy a lot of land, especially around the trains, they'd make a heap of money." The alderman turned to look out the window. The lights of Navy Pier burned parti-colored, the edges shimmering where they met the water. He folded his hands behind his back and stood straight, staring into the night.

"If what you're saying it true, then a lot of innocent

people are being hurt." Owens turned back around. "And if it's not, you're asking me to commit political suicide. Accuse a CPD sergeant of arming gangbangers? Start digging into real estate records for the whole ward, hounding investors, maybe even donors?" He shook his head. "I'd be making enemies I couldn't possibly take on."

Jason's pulse beat his forehead as he watched the alderman make up his mind. And why not? Who were they to him? Nothing but strangers with wild theories.

"Sir—" He opened his mouth, willing the words to come. Not sure what they could possibly be, what could make a difference. Realizing that if he didn't say the right thing, right now, he was going to fail Michael one final time.

"Edward." Washington had been so silent through the last few minutes Jason had almost forgotten he was there. Now, seeing the man straighten, he felt a flush of panic. Washington looked at Jason, then at Cruz, and finally over to the alderman. "Sir, you're wasting time."

*Oh god.* Jason scrabbled for words to stop him.

"How's that, Dr. Matthews?" Owens's face was unreadable.

"Because you listened to all of that."

"Wait a sec—" Jason started to interrupt.

Washington ignored him. "You listened to all of that, and you're not doing anything about it yet."

Jason's jaw dropped open.

Washington paused, and when he spoke, it was in the rich voice of a lecturer. "Edward, I realize you don't know Jason Palmer, and that must make it hard to believe what he's said. But you know me." Washington put a warm hand on Jason's shoulder. "And I'm telling you that his word is all you need."

The party still swirled around them, but for Jason, the world had come down to this single minute. His chest swelled, and his vision went swimmy around the edges. He could feel the rush of blood in his veins, the stickiness of his palms.

Then the alderman nodded. He spoke slowly, saying, "All right, Washington. All right." He turned to Jason. "I'll need all the details you can give me."

Jason wanted to throw his head back and whoop. They'd

done it. Maybe their luck was finally changing. He gave Cruz a giddy smile.

Only she wasn't looking at him. Instead, she stared the opposite direction, her mouth open. "What?" He followed her gaze to the entrance of the room.

And realized their luck wasn't changing at all.

# CHAPTER 41
## Family

The first reaction was fear, an animal panic that made the air hum and buzz, that slowed time, the world gone languid as his instincts screamed for flight.

The second was the copper taste of murder in his mouth. A primal rage, a desire to beat and smash and kill.

Fingers clenched white, stomach loose and warm, Jason stood rooted, staring at the man in the doorway.

An evil spirit in a cheap suit, only this time Anthony DiRisio wore a tuxedo over heavy slabs of muscle. Five o'clock shadow and thin black hair, a nose too large and bent slightly sideways. He stood at the entrance, his eyes scanning the crowd, moving slow and precise. A predator's gaze, working right to left.

"Mr. Palmer?" Owens asked, one eyebrow high.

Jason shook his head, yanked himself out of his stupor. Turned so his back faced the door. "DiRisio." He grimaced. "He must have been watching my apartment after all, and followed us here." Something nagged at him, a detail he couldn't put his finger on. It felt important, but refused to clarify. Maybe something he'd seen on the drive over?

"The arms dealer? Here?"

"Yes. Mr. Alderman, we have to get my nephew and get out of here."

"Your nephew?"

"My brother's son. He's here." Jason clenched his lips,

risked a quick glance over his shoulder. DiRisio had vanished in the crowd. "Sir, we have to go. Can we continue some place more private?"

"All right." Owens looked at his second, who frowned. "Daryl's right. I should probably say a few good-byes. It will look strange if I don't. Twenty minutes?"

Jason nodded. "Fine. Where can we regroup?"

"My car is in the service garage. A black Towncar. But how will you get past your man?"

"We'll figure something out."

The alderman smiled. "I'm glad a soldier is on the job." He turned to Thomas. "Let's make the rounds quickly, shall we?"

Jason watched them go. He'd done it. Joy bubbled up within his chest, and he turned back to his friends. Cruz grinned a hundred-watts worth. Washington put a hand on his shoulder. "Good work, son. I'm proud of you." He looked Jason square in the eye. "Your brother would be, too."

Something swelled in Jason's chest, something fluttery and luminous, and he felt the muscles of his cheeks pull into a too-wide smile. He held out a hand, and Washington took it, then pulled him into a hug. The familiar tang of Old Spice filled his nostrils, a safe, comforting smell. He wanted to linger, to laugh and toast their success.

But DiRisio was out there.

Jason stepped back, grimaced. "I'm sorry, but we should—"

"I know, son. Go."

Jason squeezed his shoulder, touched Cruz's arm, the skin soft and warm, and then he stepped into the thick of the crowd. Where would Billy be? The air had the recycled smell of a too-full party, cut by the chaotic tinkling of women's laughter. There weren't any other children around. It was too crowded for DiRisio to try anything, or at least he hoped so. Still, he wouldn't feel better until he found his nephew. He started for the buffet, where Ronald had last seen Billy.

But there was no sign of the boy. He felt his heart quicken. He couldn't risk calling out. DiRisio could be stalking this same ground. But where would the boy be?

Then he had a thought, and dropped to a squat. A small pair of shoes were barely visible beneath the table. Jason parted the tablecloth. Billy looked up, his smile blooming like a flower. He wore a tuxedo and a clip-on bow tie. Now in robot form, the Transformer wreaked havoc on a landscape of baguette slices and gouda cubes.

Jason's heart climbed his chest, buoyed by a wave of pure warmth. If this was what responsibility meant, he could get used to it. "Hey, kiddo."

"Uncle Jason!" The boy leaned forward and threw his arms around Jason's neck. "I missed you."

"Me too." He tousled Billy's hair. Part of him wanted to crawl under the table with him, but there wasn't time. Soon, though. They were almost finished. "We gotta go, buddy. You ready?"

Billy nodded, released his arms, and climbed out, carrying the toy by one robotic arm. Jason stood, trying to at once scan the room and remain inconspicuous. At least DiRisio didn't know Billy was here. He kept to the fringe of the crowd, moving against the windowed walls.

Ronald stood in the corner, Cruz beside him, her features drawn with worry. She brightened when she saw him. Jason spotted Washington, nodded toward the others, and he joined them.

"Now what?" Cruz had moved so her back was to the room. "Out the front door?"

Where would DiRisio be? Jason put himself in the other man's position. "No. He doesn't know we spotted him, and the crowd is tough to move through. His best bet would be to watch that door."

"So what then?"

A harried server pushed past him, balancing a tray of desserts. He saw Cruz looking at it, met her eyes, both of them smiling. "Let's go."

The servant's entrance was marked by a set of swinging kitchen doors. Beyond lay a bright white hallway, the lush atmosphere of the ballroom replaced by rubber-mat floors and fluorescent lights. A row of six-foot service carts held the remnants of dinner, half-eaten steaks in pools of béarnaise, abandoned vegetables. Two Hispanic guys in spattered aprons and hairnets leaned against the wall, laughing at something. They froze as the doors opened. One of them said something in Spanish, then, "Bathroom other way."

Cruz pulled her badge from her purse. *"Policía."* The men looked at one another nervously, and she let them. *"¿Dónde está el elevador?"* The larger of the two waved down the hall. She nodded curtly.

The service elevators were built for functionality, with worn linoleum floors and scuffed walls. The five of them stepped aboard, gestured away a pretty maid who started to follow, pressed the door close button.

Jason leaned against the back wall. Let himself breathe. They'd done it. Somehow, against all odds, they'd done it. He felt a smile creeping onto his face, and a weird sense of lightness in his limbs. He looked up to find Cruz smiling, too. That good smile, the one he liked.

"Come here," he said, not caring that the others could see.

One side of her lips curled higher than the other. "You."

They met halfway.

"Why aren't you coming home now?" Billy looked up at him with guileless eyes.

"I will soon, buddy. We're almost done."

"Did you get the, the uh—"

"Briefcase?" Jason glanced in either direction down the empty hall. They'd gotten off on the second floor rather than ride it all the way to the kitchen. "Yeah, we did. Everything's under control, buddy. You're going to be okay."

"What about you?"

Jason smiled. Dropped to one knee. "I'm going to be okay, too."

"That's good." The boy sounded tired. "So you'll be home soon?"

"Very soon."

"Good." Billy hesitated. "Will you come to see me when you do?"

"Sure thing. But you'll be asleep."

The boy shook his head, looked at the floor.

"You having trouble sleeping, buddy?"

Billy nodded.

"Bad dreams?"

"Uh-huh." Billy's voice little boy earnest.

Jason felt the weight of the moment. An everyday moment of fatherhood, the kind of thing Michael probably had dealt with effortlessly. But Michael was gone now. It was up to him.

"You know what you do?" Jason put one hand out, took the Transformer from Billy, started to fold it. Surprised to find his muscles remembered exactly what to do with his long-ago toy. He turned it into a gun again, and passed it back to Billy. "Take this to bed with you. No bad dreams will come near you then."

"That's silly. You can't kill a nightmare."

Jason laughed. "Maybe not. But I bet you feel better anyway." He stood up, looked at Washington. "You'll watch out for him?"

The man nodded. "We both will." He took Billy's hand. "Ronald's probably got the car pulled around—you ready to go see him?" Billy nodded and let Washington lead him away. Jason stood and watched them walk away. Felt a tug in his chest.

"You okay?" Cruz touched his arm.

He nodded. "Just realized I have a family." He turned to her. Smiled, and kissed her again. She returned it, her lips soft with promise, not the fever of earlier, but something lasting, the kind of kiss that might go for years. Finally, he broke it, glanced at his watch. "We better get moving."

In the lobby, men and women waited with valet tickets, or kissed cheeks in final good-byes. A table of tourist chicks sat sipping Cosmos and playing at *Sex and the City*. The uniformed cops were gone; he supposed they'd probably been clocking overtime.

"What if DiRisio came down?" Cruz asked.

"He couldn't be sure we would come through the lobby.

My bet is he's still watching the ballroom exit, hoping to bottleneck us." Jason had a twinge of that same feeling he'd had upstairs, something about DiRisio that didn't fit. Shook it off and stopped to study a fire evacuation map. "Looks like the service garage is this way."

The volume turned down with every step away from the lobby. They passed a restaurant, the air heavy with the smell of french onion soup and filet mignon, and took a side corridor to a door marked "Employees Only."

The garage was dreary, the buzzing sodium lights draining color. Several panel trucks were backed in against the wall, followed by rows of staff cars, Hondas and Fords, most a couple of years old. The air was stale with old exhaust and cigarettes.

The alderman's car sat twenty feet away, beside a delivery truck. The Towncar was running, a trickle of exhaust rising from the tailpipe. Lightly tinted windows screened the interior, but he could make out a man in the rear seat. "Right on time," Jason said. They started toward the car, Cruz's high heels clicking on the concrete. "Let's get this over with, get home. I could sleep for a week."

Jason opened the car door and leaned in, opening his mouth to say hello.

In the splinter of a second it took to process the man pointing a gun at him, a thin face marked by a white ridge of scar tissue, it hit Jason what had been nagging at him.

Anthony DiRisio had been wearing a tuxedo. If he'd followed them here, where would he have come up with a tux?

Then something hard and heavy cracked his skull, and the world shivered into night.

# CHAPTER 42
Fucker

Back in the desert.

The street was winding and filled with children. They laughed, wrestling, tumbling in the dust, all almond eyes and shining smiles. But beyond them he could hear a noise, a humming, crushing sound, something coming closer. It was death, he knew that, and he yelled, tried to warn them. The children wouldn't listen, none of them would *listen,* even as it came around the corner, a juggernaut of creaking metal treads and armor plates the color of disease, spitting gouts of flame in a tide of red and yellow. The children played, never looking at the machine drawing closer, this terrible engine that had its own momentum, that ruined everything in its path. Martinez was in the street, too, the children squealing with delight as they climbed on him and over him, and he hummed a single steady note as he stared at Jason, hummed it as the flames reached him, hummed it as fire ate the world, hummed a single droning note like the end of everything.

Then the car hit a bump, bouncing Jason Palmer's head against the window it lay on, and he came to, the hum transformed into the buzz of tires, the vibration of glass against his ear. His eyes opened, bleary, swimming, too wet. The car seat fabric. Headlights through the glass. His hands, in front of him and touching at the wrists.

Voices.

It came back in a flash, and he closed his eyes, head and

heart racing. Pain blossomed with consciousness, a throbbing flower with roots unmaking his brain. It was worse with his eyes closed, color and shape playing against the darkness as they passed other cars, nothing to focus on but creeping scarlet pain.

Voices again, from the front. "I'd like to get there tonight, Grandma."

"Don't be an idiot. We can't afford to get pulled over."

"Why not? You could chat with them, you know, bullshit about the job. Pretend you're still a cop."

"Fuck you."

Jason's skull was filled with concrete. He was in a car. Slumped on the right side. The men in front of him were talking. Bickering. His body hurt, every crack and divot in the road ringing up through his temples, and his hands were bound together. Zip-tied, by the feel of it; his hands bloodless and numb. There was something warm leaning against him. Warm and heavy and soft.

He waited for the next set of headlights to pass, then risked opening his eyes a slit.

No.

It was Cruz. He could just make her out in his peripheral vision. Her eyes were closed, but he didn't see any obvious wounds. Whoever had taken him out must have done her just as fast.

Pain had come first. Now anger followed. He cherished the burn, the black powder heat. Owned it, bank up the fire inside. He was going to tear someone's head off. He owed Cruz that much. He could lunge forward, try for the wheel. Or if he could get his arms up and over one of their heads, he could—

*Stop.*

The voice in his head was familiar, but it wasn't his own. It was Mikey's.

*You aren't clearing a room, rifle in hand and squad at your back. You're dizzy. Unarmed. Your hands are bound. Go easy, little bro. Think. Figure out what you're fighting. I'm depending on you.*

*Billy is depending on you.*

Jason took as deep a breath as he dared. Closed his eyes to focus, then opened them again, looking forward this time. He remembered Billy's description of the men he'd seen murder his father: one big, muscular and balding; one slim and normal-looking, hair black and gray.

Anthony DiRisio sat on the right. Thinning hair and hard jaw, the casual weight of working muscle. An air of cold menace. Calm, cracking jokes as he rode shotgun. The driver more nervous, his fingers tapping the wheel, his shoulders tensed. His hair was black giving way to gray. Galway, Cruz's old partner. A cop gone to murder and worse, but not used to it yet. Not comfortable.

So two. And when he opened the car door he'd seen a third guy, the gunman with the scar across his cheek, the one he'd dumped in the river down by Lower Wacker. He must be in another car.

Through slit eyes he couldn't see much out the window, just the lanes of a highway, some construction barriers. The rain had stopped, but drops on the window spun onrushing headlights into stars. Lonely street lights, and beyond them, trees. They'd left the city behind. Suburban houses still peeked through, but Jason could only assume they were headed out to some quiet rural woodland where two shots in the head wouldn't be heard.

All because of the alderman.

*Fucker.* He'd played the good man, the JFK Democrat, smart, dedicated, considerate.. Talked with conviction about the flaws in the system, the worm in the apple, when all the time he'd been describing himself. Christ, the guy had listened as they parroted his plan back to him.

That was why DiRisio had been there, why he'd been in a tux. It hadn't been for Jason and Cruz at all. He'd been there because he worked for the alderman. He was the fixer, the lethal hand of darkness.

"This is a waste of time," DiRisio said. "Let's just clip them and dump them in the river."

"He wants to talk to them." Galway tapped his fingers on the wheel.

"A washed-out soldier and a cop wanted for murder. Nobody'd miss them." He paused. "Though that partner of yours is a peach. You ever get a taste?"

Galway turned to stare at DiRisio. He had a stern profile, craggy and unblinking, and he didn't look nervous anymore. "You're a piece of shit. You know that?"

DiRisio laughed. "Pots and kettles, my friend."

"I'm a cop. You're not my friend."

"You got that half right."

Jason tuned them out, hearing Galway's words again. *He wants to talk to them,* the cop said. The alderman wanted them alive for some reason. Which meant they weren't on their way to an execution field after all. So long as they had value, they wouldn't be killed. Questioned, beaten. But not killed.

And so long as they were alive, there was time. Time to get his bearings, time to seize an opportunity.

Time to make them pay.

It was a thin thread of hope, but Jason clung to it as the car rolled into darkness.

Somehow, someway, he would make them pay. Even if it cost his life.

A rich man's neighborhood. Garish houses set back from the road, fronted by wide swathes of rain-black lawn. The mansions were all different styles, English manors to Greek revivals, but they were united in a single characteristic: All were bordered by fences. Some dressed up their intentions with decorative stone, others played honest with spiked metal, but the message was universally clear.

Stay away; the world belongs to us.

They'd been heading north on the Edens, that much he'd been able to catch from a highway marker. He had no idea how long he'd been unconscious, and hadn't been able to see their exit, but he guessed they were in Kenilworth, maybe

Highland Park. Big-money neighborhoods, the kind where you told people you lived there, they whistled soft, wondered privately what you pulled down.

Jason remembered the alderman saying how he had to live in his district. There wasn't a more polar opposite of Crenwood than the street they rolled down. Owens probably owned some piece-of-shit ranch, had his mail delivered there, put the address on election forms.

The hum of the tires slowed, then they turned left into a driveway, smooth blacktop leading to a high stone wall. Headlights splashed across a heavy metal gate. A car pulled in behind them, the light dazzling after the dark. Galway opened his window, punched a button on an intercom. They sat in silence a moment, then the gate swung ponderously open, revealing a curved driveway snaking up to a large house, boxy and bright with glass. The driveway was fifty yards of white gravel that cracked and popped as they rolled. Galway pulled in along the front steps, killed the engine. Jason closed his eyes, lay still. The silence was loud enough to hear his pulse beat in his ears.

"How are they?" It was Galway's voice.

"Fine. Palmer's been awake for awhile."

"You've got to be—" Interior lights flashed on, painting Jason's eyelids pink-orange. He could hear the seat in front of him creak, Galway turning around. "He doesn't look awake to me."

"He is. Right, Jason?"

There didn't seem to be any point in pretending. He opened his eyes to see Galway's cowboy face staring at him over the seatback.

"How did you know?" Galway glanced over.

"His breathing changed." DiRisio spun, a smile beneath his lopsided nose. His gaze was unreadable as a cobra's. "Why don't you go see if he's ready. I'll watch them." For a moment it looked like Galway was going to argue, but then he opened the door and stepped out.

The engine ticked softly in the summer heat.

"So." DiRisio said softly. "Alone at last, right? Just two

soldiers." He looked down at Jason's uniform. "The Class A's are a nice touch. I always hated the things, but you look good."

"You killed my brother."

"Yes." DiRisio stared back. "I did."

Jason grit his teeth. Fought to master it. He made himself look out the window. He'd been flexing his fingers slowly ever since he woke up, and the feeling had come back, sharp pins and needles. It wasn't ideal, but it would have to do. He wormed his way upright. Cruz slid off his shoulder, her head rolling to one side. The way she flopped like a doll fed the fire within. Jason flexed his shoulders, feigning stiffness, then brought them down with one elbow resting against the back seat. "I figured a fuck like you would just shoot us, dump us in an alley."

"Now see, that hurts. What did I ever do to you?" DiRisio raised a finger to his temple. "Oh, that's right. I crushed your brother's windpipe and watched him flop to death on a dirty bar floor."

Jason threw himself forward, thrusting off his elbow for leverage, zip-tied hands stabbing forward, fingers out and spread to spear DiRisio's eyes. The big man reacted with startling speed, leaning back, left arm coming up in a wave that caught Jason's attention, something like a block. He started to adjust for it, keeping his momentum going, only somehow now there was a pistol in DiRisio's other hand, the black eye pointing straight at Jason's forehead. Like it had appeared there by magic. Jason checked himself, caught his hands on the back of the seat.

"Easy, Sergeant." DiRisio's finger was inside the trigger guard and gently tensed. "The boss wants to talk to you. Which means I'd just as soon not kill you yet. But you pull something like that again, I might change my mind."

Jason grimaced, then eased himself back.

"Here's something you better understand." DiRisio thumbed the safety and made the SIG vanish. "You've been a pain in the ass. I respect that. But I haven't gotten much sleep the last few days chasing you around, and I don't like fancy parties. So don't irritate me. Because when it comes time for you to go, it can happen fast," he snapped his fingers, "or real damn slow. And not just for you." DiRisio's eyes flicked over Cruz. "We clear?"

Jason turned, looked out the side window. Clenched his jaw. His hands shook, and he concentrated on willing them to stop. On battling the icy spiders climbing his spine and the crackling rage in his belly. Thinking of Mikey, laying on the floor of his bar, eyes bugged and hands desperate at his throat.

"Attaboy. Just sit and hate me real quiet like."

The house door opened, and Galway walked out. The gunman with the scar had been smoking a cigarette on the porch, and flicked it away as Galway joined him. The two men spoke briefly, then Galway strode over and opened the door, his sidearm in his right hand.

"Come on, Palmer. Man wants to see you alone."

"No." He slid his feet under the seat in front of him, tensed his muscles. He could do this much, at least.

"I sound like I was asking?"

"I'm not leaving her with this psycho." He kept his voice calm. "You want to waste me, waste me. But I'm not leaving her alone with him."

Galway sighed. "Jesus Christ."

"Relax, tough guy." DiRisio smiled. "I'll take Palmer in, you see to her."

Galway looked at Jason, who nodded reluctantly. He didn't think Galway would mess with Cruz. Besides, he didn't have much choice. DiRisio opened his door and got out, the car rising on its shocks as his weight left. He opened the rear door, jerked his SIG, and gestured with it.

Jason climbed out of the car, his muscles stiff and screaming. Took a moment to stretch his arms upward. Putting his thoughts in rigid order. Strength and discipline. Whatever lay inside the house for himself, he could take it. Maybe he'd even earned it, mistakes he'd made: Martinez, the Worm, Michael. But Cruz hadn't, and neither had Billy. If the last thing Jason did was save their lives, well, he could die with that.

That was what soldiers did.

"Move."

Jason started up the path. Scarface leered at him, then fell in with DiRisio. The front door to the house was open, framing an inviting foyer painted in creams and tans. Silver-framed mirrors and colorful rugs, a staircase winding up. As he stepped in, Jason risked a glance over his shoulder. The men stood four steps back; out of reach, but too close to miss a shot. Professionals. Jason glared, then continued, the foyer giving way to a high-ceilinged living room. Supple leather chairs, low-slung coffee table, abstract art reflected in pale hardwood floors. A faded red door decorated with Asian characters was set in the far wall, and DiRisio told him to knock.

"Yes." The voice was muffled.

Jason reached for the door handle, willing his body ready, welcoming the old familiar tingle in his fingers. This was as good a spot as any. He visualized the move: open the door, hurl himself through, use the momentum to slam it behind him. It would only hold off DiRisio for a fraction of a second, but that should be enough for Jason to make a play.

Maybe the last of his life.

# CHAPTER 43
## Deep

She swam in some deep fuzzy place, the surface of consciousness rippling above. There were sounds, and someone touching her, but she didn't want to open her eyes. Wanted only to sleep, to plunge back into the abyss.

"Wake up, Elena." A man's voice, close. Jason? The voice was correct, she realized. She should wake up. There were important reasons.

"Come on, wake up."

Things to do. They were in trouble. They had to tell—

She gasped, and her eyes flew open. She was in a car, the backseat, side door open, humid air thick as soup, a shape leaning in the door, a man, one hand propped on the seat, the other reaching. Her purse. The gun was in her purse. She tried to check the seat next to her, found that her hands were bound. The man touched her arm, and she moved without thinking, caught his wrist and twisted, bent it back, spinning her body for leverage.

The man yelped, dropped to his knees. Fumbled at his belt.

Came up with a gun.

"God*damn*it, Cruz!"

She recognized the voice now. "Galway." She stared down the barrel of his gun, let go of his hand. Looked around. She was in the back of the Towncar. Last thing she remembered was hearing footsteps coming fast, turning, seeing a shape colliding with her skull. They'd walked into a trap. "Motherfucker."

Galway snorted. "Sure." He held the gun steady, his finger outside the trigger guard. Good form, prevented accidents but wouldn't slow him down.

"Where's Jason?"

"Inside. Let's go."

"Inside?" Her head was clearing enough for her to know what that meant. The alderman. "He wants to talk to us? Why?"

"You'll need to ask him. Come on, now." His voice was firm but not harsh. "Slide out of the car. Slow."

She didn't want to, but didn't see a choice. She moved gently, taking the opportunity to scan for her purse on the floor. Praying they'd just tossed it after her, not checked it out. But there was no sign of it.

Cruz spun her legs out of the car, awkward and overdressed in the formal attire. Her heels spiked the gravel. Galway backed up a step or two, the pistol out, watching her carefully. She stood up, then suddenly went swimmy, black spots dancing in front of her eyes. Scrabbled at the car roof, found it wet, her bound hands sliding, thighs trembly, the spots multiplying, the world dark, then shit, she was falling.

Strong arms caught her. Her head screamed to attack now, that he couldn't at once prop her up and have the gun trained on her, but her body was shaking, blood thumping hot and heavy. Two serious blows to the head in one day. What were the odds. She closed her eyes, concentrated on deep breaths. This close, she could smell Galway, his familiar cologne like woodsmoke. How many times had she smelled it, rolling with him through Crenwood, bullshitting and philosophizing, listening to him talk about his life, his divorce?

Galway guided her hands to the car door, helped her get a grip, then stepped away as her vision cleared. "Christ, Elena." He shook his head. "Why did you have to get involved?"

"It was my case."

"And I told you how to close it. Would it have been so bad to put everything on a waste like Playboy? Just let one job go? So *what* if he didn't kill Palmer? You know Playboy has more than one body on his resume." He shook his head. "I never wanted you to get caught up in this."

"It was my case," she repeated.

Galway snorted. "Yeah."

Her vision had steadied, and she looked around. A house, shit, a mansion more like. Boxy Bauhaus-knockoff nestled under ancient oak trees. The air was fetid with the smell of growing things.

"You feeling better?"

She looked at him, the stern face now wearing thin, in need of a shave, with pits under his eyes and a faint twitch to his lip. The pistol at his side, like he just happened to be holding it. "Why are you doing this, Tom?" He didn't reply, and she took a careful step, then another. Her strength seemed to be returning, though pain was coming with it, a deep ache sloshing between her temples. "Was it money?" The high heels were the wrong choice, near impossible in the wet gravel. She stepped to the lawn, turned to face him, bent a knee to hike a leg up and undo the strap of one shoe. "I know you've got bills, your son. But I never would have figured you to go bad."

He shook his head. "Quit stalling."

She dropped the shoe to the ground, put her bare foot in the wet grass, bent her knee to work on the other. "There were always rumors. That guy shakes down pimps, this one freelances for a dealer, the other steals cash from crime scenes. But it was always lousy cops waiting out their pension. You, you're a great cop. What happened?"

"Elena, look." The lights from the porch framed his shrug in silhouette. "I'm sorry you're mixed up in this. I really am. But cut the true confessions crap, okay?"

She tossed the other heel. "Are you really going to shoot me? Your partner?" She took a step toward him, bound hands low, not threatening. "I know you've done some bad things, but are you willing to go that far?"

"I haven't shot anybody." He spoke quickly.

"What about down by the river?" Maybe guilt would shake him. "You shot at me then."

"No." His voice firm. "That was DiRisio. I saved your life. He would have hit if I hadn't stopped him."

Hope flared in her chest. Maybe they could work this out yet. "You see? I knew you were still police." She took another step. "Let's figure this out together, cop to cop. There's got to be a way out."

"I wish," he said, and brought the gun up to shoulder height, the barrel at her torso. "But I saved your life once already."

She stiffened, the backs of her arms cold, goosebumps breaking out on her shoulders. Overhead, a wisp of gray clouds parted to reveal a tarnished silver moon.

"You want to know what it was? You really want to know?" His eyes flashed, and he flexed the fingers of his gun hand, tapping them against the grip. "I got *tired*. Tired of hauling in fourteen-year-old kids for murder counts. Tired of trying to track down their parents, finding Mommy three sheets at eleven A.M. and Daddy ten-years gone. Tired of standing over different teenaged corpses on the same corners. I mean, that corner at Fifty-fourth and Damen, you know how many bodies we had there last year? *Five*. On one worthless corner. Kids dying over ten feet of cement in front of a gas station." He paused. "I used to believe that we could change things on the street. I used to think the work *meant* something. But it doesn't. We're not cops. We're zookeepers. And I got tired."

"So you figured you may as well make a buck?" She didn't even try to keep the acid from her voice.

He shook his head. "That's not why."

"But there was money."

"Of course there was money. But it wasn't *why*. I did it because . . ." He blew a long breath, looked around, as if the words he needed were over her shoulder. "One night I stared at the mirror and asked myself if the world wouldn't maybe be a little bit better if somebody burned Crenwood to the ground and rebuilt it with a Starbucks on every corner and a nice private school. If we forgot 'political correctness' and 'giving everyone a fair shot' and just got rid of the assholes. And if we had to hurt a few people to do that, well, they were already so busy hurting each other I couldn't see the difference."

In the silence that fell she could hear the faint patter of water dripping between the oak boughs. She supposed she ought to be horrified at what he'd said, but she'd been a cop for too long. He hadn't said anything they hadn't all thought at one time or another. No way around it, prowling war-zone streets day after day. She couldn't refute him without lying, couldn't agree and remain true to herself. So finally, she just said, "Don't do this."

Galway stared with sad Irish eyes. He looked like an up-scale drunk, one of those dissipated men that spent their afternoons in hotel bars. "It's too late. I'm in too deep." He shook his head. "Besides, I tried to keep you clear. I told you how to fix it. I practically begged you to stay out. You ignored me. There's nothing I can do now."

"Tom—"

"Let's go," he said, and something in his expression told her he'd made up his mind. She grit her teeth, turned around, started for the house. The gravel was rough and wet against her bare feet.

"You know," she said, "somebody sent that evidence. Whoever it was, they're going to try again. You may not be able to stop him next time. And if that happens, you think the alderman is going to go down alone?"

"The alderman?" He sounded amused. "Look around you. This house ran four, five mill. You think he can pony that? And all the property in Crenwood, even cheap, it adds up. Owens doesn't have that kind of cash. And he doesn't have the brains to come up with a plan like this. Hell, without that assistant of his, I doubt Alderman Owens would know how to lace his Stacy Adams."

She paused, turned. Perplexed.

"Elena, we don't work for the alderman." Galway spoke slowly, like he was explaining to a child. "He works for us."

# CHAPTER 44
Seethe

Jason froze midlunge, forward motion checked by surprise. He'd only seen the man behind the desk once before, but it hadn't been five hours ago. Seen him from Washington's living room, standing beside Ronald, the two of them staring out the front window at a man who could give away a half million dollars and not miss it. "You're Adam Kent."

The man behind the desk narrowed his eyes, looked past Jason to DiRisio. "Did you—"

"Of course not." DiRisio's voice was calm. "He's a smart kid. I told you that."

Kent nodded, sighed. "Ah well." He unbuttoned his tuxedo jacket, soft and expensive looking, not the shiny fabric of a rental.

*Jesus. He was at the party, too.* And on the heels of that, *Of course he was. He* threw *the party.*

Jason's mind whirled. It didn't make any sense. This guy had given Washington all that money to *save* former gangbangers. And at the same time he was arming them, setting them against each other? Burning out houses and buying up property?

Kent gestured to a chair. "Mr. Palmer. Have a seat."

Jason hesitated, then started forward, eyes scanning. Studying the battlefield. A large office. Padded chairs fronting an open fireplace big enough to park a car. August, the rest of the city gasping and sweating, and Kent had a fire battling his air-conditioning. In the center of the room lay an elegant desk of pale wood fronted by three angular chairs, the lines modern and uncomfortable. Jason spotted his cell phone and wallet along with Cruz's purse, sitting on the center of the desk. Behind it stood French doors leading to the backyard, the darkness outside dotted with landscape lighting.

He sat on the edge of his chair, watching DiRisio and Scarface take up guard positions. After a moment, Kent came around the desk to lean against the edge, his posture casual and friendly. He looked like a bank manager. Medium jaw, plain features, salt-and-pepper hair. Ronald had nailed it: You'd walk right past him on the street, never think a thing.

Then Kent crossed his arms, blew a breath and said the last thing Jason expected. "Mr. Palmer, I owe you an apology."

If the man had screamed and raged, Jason would have been prepared. If he'd made threats of torture, promised pain beyond bearing, he would have been ready. But this, this left him speechless.

"First, I'm sorry for the way you were brought here. The circumstances demanded it, but it's a bit crude. Which leads to my second apology." He laced his fingers in a gesture of contrition. "I am so very sorry for what happened to your brother."

Jason's mouth fell open.

Kent continued. "Anthony is overzealous. All I asked him to do was *talk* to your brother. The last thing I want to do is hurt people like Michael. It's bad for business."

Jason looked back and forth, feeling like he was racing to keep up. Scarface looked at him impassively. DiRisio picked at something in his ear. If what his boss said bothered him, he didn't show it.

"Business?" Jason could feel the heat rising in his cheek. "You mean inciting a gang war for profit? Burning a neighborhood?"

"Yes." Kent's voice was matter-of-fact. "Look, when a house is infested with termites, you don't put up new drywall. You tear it down and start over."

*This* man gave Washington a half million to help gang-bangers? Then the last piece clicked into place. It made sense, in a twisted sort of way. "I get it."

"What's that?"

"Why you helped Washington. You borrowed a play from the CIA. Because you're a white guy from the suburbs, and all of Crenwood looks the same to you. You need on-the-ground intelligence. Right?"

Kent nodded. "Washington is a good man, and I'm happy to help him help those boys. Especially since that also means I can learn everything I need to know."

"*Help him?*" Jason sputtered. "You used him to commit murder."

He shook his head, sucked air through his teeth. "No. 'Murder' is an emotional word. It's petty, and small. You may not like my methods, but I'm building something. When I'm done, Crenwood will be a safe neighborhood, the kind of place people want to raise kids. And yes, before you bring it up, of course I'll make a lot of money in the process. But the world will be better. I'm a businessman and a pragmatist, but I'm not a monster. I don't even have a moustache."

Jason narrowed his eyes. "Okay."

"Okay?"

He remembered Cruz on the river front. "A friend of mine taught me that as long as someone's got a gun on you, the correct answer to anything is 'okay.'"

Kent laughed. "I see your point. But I want your full attention."

"Believe me, man. You've got it."

"Fair enough." Kent glanced over to DiRisio, gave a quick nod. DiRisio made the gun vanish, then left the wall and moved to stand just behind Jason. "Now," Kent continued, "you have something I need."

"You really think I'm going to give up my nephew?"

"Your nephew?" A bemused smile played on Kent's lips. "What would I want with him?"

The skin of Jason's shoulders crawled. "But the gang-bangers, and DiRisio—"

"We're all looking for what I wanted." Kent leaned forward. "The papers, Mr. Palmer. All I want are the papers your brother had, the ones you told the alderman about. You give me that, we're done."

Jason stared, fighting to keep a straight face as the gears clicked. Remembering the party, how he'd hedged with the alderman, not explicitly telling him the evidence had been destroyed because he didn't want to shake the guy's trust. The alderman had reported back to Kent, who now believed Jason had his brother's files.

All Kent wanted was something Jason didn't have.

"You're saying that you'll not only let me walk out of here, you'll leave Billy alone?" He put as much scorn into it as possible.

"Absolutely. That's all we've wanted all along," Kent said. "Mr. Palmer, I realize you don't like me, and I understand why. But the truth is that I don't bear you any ill will. For you, this is a personal matter. But for me, it's just business. I'm in the middle of a very complicated financial venture. Your brother got involved when he shouldn't have. He wouldn't listen to reason. I didn't kill him for pleasure any more than I brought you here to show off my evil plan."

"Okay."

"All right. You're hurting and I can't change that. But listen to what I have to say." Kent ran a hand through his hair. "There's no *advantage* to killing you. Without evidence, there's nothing you can say that could hurt me. *Nothing.* I have a lot of money, and a lot of people eager to do me favors. What do you have? A history of petty theft and an 'other than honorable' discharge from the Army." He shrugged. "I'm sorry, but you're outmatched. So let's keep it simple. Give me what I want, and I'll give you back your life."

Jason felt sick. Wrong as it was, the man was right. But he also believed Jason had something he didn't.

"Look," Kent said, "this is a one-time opportunity to save the lives of your nephew and your lover. To watch Billy grow up. It's a good offer. Take it."

Jason sat back in his chair, met Kent's eye. The guy looked sincere, but that was like gauging the intentions of a crocodile. Still. Much as Jason wanted to doubt, Kent made sense. They were out of plays. Going to the alderman had been a last-ditch hope. If Kent let them go, there really *wasn't* anything they could do to hurt him.

Which only made his anger seethe hotter. Just like in the war, the real players were invulnerable. People talked about the immovable object and the unstoppable force. But the real story belonged to the people caught between the two. People like his brother.

" 'A complicated financial venture,' eh?" Jason shook his head. "You realize you're talking about people? You're killing them, burning their homes, ruining their neighborhoods. To make money. Just another rich white guy who can't get enough."

Kent snorted. He stood up, went around the desk, dropped in the chair. "It's not love that moves the world, Mr. Palmer, and the only color that matters is green. Black, white, brown, who gives a shit? It's about rich and poor. I'm very rich, so I win. You can spout coffeehouse crap all you like. But first decide whether you'd prefer to die tonight or to see your nephew grow up."

*Think, goddamn you. Think.* He looked away. Grit his teeth and tugged at his wrists. The zip-tie was unyielding, and his fingers thick and heavy. Every fiber of his body screamed to fight. To stand and make a move, to throw himself at Kent or DiRisio. He'd lose, but he'd go out fighting. A soldier's death. Not this terrible choice.

Not having to make a deal with the man who murdered his brother.

If he agreed, and Kent was honest, they'd be free. He could watch Billy turn nine, have another porch-lit drink with Washington, explore the thing between him and Cruz. And even if Kent decided to kill him, at least Billy would be safe. With the evidence gone and the witnesses dead, there would be no reason to come after the boy.

Kent spoke softly. "I know you hate me, Mr. Palmer. But you're a smart man. So do what you have to do. Tell me where those papers are." He ran long fingers through his hair, then laced them behind his head.

Sometimes you had to fold the hand. Jason dropped his head, stared at his lap. *Forgive me, Michael. I tried.* He opened his mouth to speak.

And saw Kent's gesture again. Running his hands through his hair.

"The big one was bald," Billy had said two days ago, sitting in the sunlight of Jason's apartment, telling a story that tore him apart. A story of two men that had come into the bar and killed Michael. One balding and big. The other thin and plain-looking, with black and gray hair.

And he realized that no matter what he said, Kent would never stop hunting his nephew.

DiRisio had been one of the guys in the bar. He'd bragged about it. The other man they had just assumed was Galway.

But Adam Kent's hair was also black flecked with gray.

# CHAPTER 45
Breaking Point

"It was you." The words came as a snarl, an animal roar. His mind screamed at him to stop, to slow down, but his anger had control. "Mother*fucker*." He started to lunge from his chair, willing to give it a shot now, knowing it didn't matter. That there was no deal. No hope.

Something slammed into the base of his neck, at the right-hand side. The whole world went watery. He struggled through it, his legs out of his control and far away, the weight enormous. His body told him it couldn't move. He moved anyway. Moved for Michael, and for Billy. Moved even though it was impossible.

Until DiRisio hit him with another open-hand chop at the other side of his neck, and his legs just gave.

Agony shot through his body, lightning bolts and pyrotechnics, the Fourth of July behind his eyeballs. He felt a hand in his hair, yanking, and then he was falling back into the chair. Landing heavy, his arms flopping useless in front of him.

"Don't kill him." Kent's voice was firm, none of the soft sell he'd been peddling.

"He's fine." DiRisio's voice seemed to echo and warp. "I hit the pressure points behind his carotids. No permanent damage."

Jason closed his eyes, fought for breath and balance. He

felt like his center of gravity was doing flips. Gagged and coughed. Struggled. *Get control. Do it* now, *soldier.*

Deep breaths. Visions of melting ice, faint blue that washed everything away. That countered the fire in his head.

He opened his eyes. Hate like hundred-proof liquor raged through his veins. "It wasn't Galway in the bar. It was you."

Kent gave him an amused look. "Your brother had evidence that could have derailed everything I'd been working on. It might even have been enough to prosecute me. *Me.*" He shrugged. "A business arrangement that important I'm going to see to personally."

His body rubber, Jason struggled to rise.

"Oh, for Christ's sake." Kent's cool slipping, finally. "Sit down. We can shoot you without giving you your wish."

Jason glared at him, his hands pulling useless at the ziptie. "My wish?"

"To die." Kent smiled at him. "That's what you want, right? I know all about your discharge from the Army. I know what you've been doing since. And I know that if your nephew hadn't been holding you back, you'd have let yourself get killed already. Well, guess what? Tonight's your lucky night." He buttoned his tux jacket and turned to DiRisio. "Let's end this costume drama, shall we?"

DiRisio jerked his head at Scarface. The man pushed off the wall and padded out the door.

What was this? Something he hadn't anticipated. Then he realized. Cruz. They were going to use Elena against him.

He bit his lip till he tasted blood. All right. It was time to get dying. When she came in, they'd make their play. Go out in a blaze of glory and end this thing before anyone else could get hurt. Frankly, he welcomed it.

But when he looked back, it wasn't Cruz framed in the doorway.

Billy's eyes darted and his skin glowed feverish. He held Washington's hand so tightly both their knuckles were white. The old man wobbled on his feet, a trail of blood running from his temple.

"No." The word slipped from Jason's mouth. His chest

felt like it was in a vice, and liquid fire burned in his bowels. "No."

"I'm sorry, son." Washington sounded tired. "They came out of nowhere. Ronald tried to fight, but—" His voice tightened.

"Uncle Jason?" Billy's voice was ribbon thin. "What's happening?"

The trust in his voice tore like fishhooks. Jason stared. His lover and his father and his brother and his nephew, all of whom he'd failed to protect.

*Liar.* It was worse than that. He hadn't just failed them.

He'd doomed them.

None of this would have been happening if he'd just left well enough alone. If he'd simply gotten the boy out of danger, instead of pretending he was a soldier, chasing the monster in hopes of slaying it. Running from his home may not have been much of a life for Billy, but at least he would have been alive. But now . . .

He realized that Billy was staring at him. He forced his hands to stop shaking. "It's okay, kiddo. Everything will be okay."

DiRisio chuckled.

"Bring them in." Kent gestured. "The woman, too."

Scarface put a meaty hand against Washington's back and shoved, sending him staggering into the room. Billy clung to his hand, his eyes lasered on Jason's. Scarface followed, a gun held to Cruz's side. The mercenary guided them to a leather couch against the wall. Washington sat stiffly, Billy close beside him. Scarface dumped Cruz on the far side, her arms zip-tied in front of her. Last in the door was Galway, his face drawn and pale.

"Don't do this." Jason said it softly. "Please."

Kent sighed and leaned back. "You know what I want."

Truth time. "I don't have the evidence anymore." Said it fast and sure, staring Kent in the eyes. "We found it in the basement of Michael's bar. But Playboy came after us as we left. They drove our car into the river. We couldn't get the briefcase out in time."

"That's not what you told the alderman."

"I didn't tell him I had it, either. I just sort of hinted at it."
He kept his gaze perfectly level. "I wanted to win him over,
and I was afraid if I told him the truth, he wouldn't listen."

Kent slowly ran a tongue around the inside of his lip.
"You're sure of that?"

"I swear to you." Sweat soaked his body, and his skin felt
tight enough to tear.

The fire's flickering light cast dark pits across Kent's
eyes. His hands were folded in his lap, one finger tapping a
metronome beat as he weighed Jason's words. Finally he
shook his head. "I need to be certain." He sighed, then nodded at DiRisio.

The man made the SIG vanish, then reached into the
pocket of his tux pants, came out with something. With a flick
of his wrist, he snapped a four-inch serrated blade open, then
winked at Jason.

Jason closed his eyes and took a deep breath. *Michael, I
need you. Give me strength. Please.* Kent would want him to
scream loud and long and tell the same story every time. He
couldn't pretend he was somewhere else, couldn't try to think
of his body as meat. He would have to embrace the pain, let it
push him past his breaking point. It was the only way to make
them believe.

But when Jason opened his eyes, DiRisio wasn't leaning
over him.

He was by the couch.

With Billy's tiny arm in his hand.

# CHAPTER 46
## Pinwheels

Despite the sickness in his legs and the pain sloshing in his head, he fought to his feet. Scarface came off the desk, raising his pistol. Jason didn't care, wouldn't let a little thing like dying stop him now.

Then he saw DiRisio touch the knife to Billy's soft wrist. A tiny motion could open the boy's arm to the bone. Jason stood trembling ten feet away, a gulf that may as well have been an ocean, and watched DiRisio smile at him.

His mind raced and darted. A thousand plans and possibilities stampeded past, none of them enough. He could pick up tiny details, Cruz's awkward posture on the sofa, half up, half down, locked in place the same way he was. Washington's face screwed into a wince, his hands reaching sideways. Billy's eyes bugged white, the tension in his shoulder from the angle DiRisio twisted.

A thin ripple of silver dancing along the ridged blade as it pushed into flesh.

*"Stop!"*

The voice came from behind, an order that ripped the air. A voice as a weapon, a cop's voice. Galway.

DiRisio froze, the knife just breaking the skin of Billy's arm.

"Stop." Galway spoke again. "Stop this now."

Jason craned his neck back to look at Galway, the weary face with its sagging jowls and stern chin. His suit was rumpled, hair unkempt. He looked a hundred years old. No match for a monster like DiRisio, a trained and eager killer.

The moment hung, delicate and pregnant. Finally, Kent said, "Tom, why don't you go have a cigarette?"

Galway shook his head. "When it was just bangers dying, I could live with it. They would have killed each other anyway. But I never should have let you murder Michael Palmer. And I won't let you do this. Not to a child."

DiRisio's eyes narrowed. "You're going to stop me?"

Everything seemed stuck in amber. Emotions flickered across Galway's face: fear, guilt, responsibility, disgust. Then he drew his gun with a whisper of metal on leather, and said, "I guess I am."

Jason looked over at Cruz, saw her staring at her partner, the tiniest of smiles playing on her lips.

"I understand how you feel," Kent said, voice honey. "This is more than you signed on for. And you know what? No problem. You want out, fine. I'll even give you the bonus we discussed, enough to put your son through grad school. But for now, be reasonable. Turn around, walk out the door."

Galway didn't answer. Just rocked the hammer back and steadied his aim. Scarface held his own gun level on the cop's chest. Jason dared a step forward.

DiRisio's eyes beamed hate like a wave of heat. He looked back and forth between Scarface, Kent, and Galway. Finally, he shook his head and pulled the blade from Billy's arm. Jason let out a breath he didn't realize he'd been holding.

"Okay, Tom." DiRisio straightened. He folded the knife, then slid it into his right pocket, a metal clip holding it in place. His eyes were flat and unreadable as he raised his hands to chest level. "You win." He turned to Scarface. "Drop your gun."

Galway glanced over at the other mercenary. Just a split second. A tiny twitch of his eyes. But in that moment, Jason saw DiRisio gesture with his left hand, a flamboyant sort of wave.

"Look out!" Jason threw himself at Scarface, knowing what was coming.

DiRisio's first shot took Galway in the arm, the impact a hammer blow, spinning him. The second bullet punched his chest. A third and fourth rode the echo of the second.

Jason didn't wait to see him fall. He barreled into Scarface, using his momentum as a weapon. The mercenary started to twist, but Jason threw a knee, and the connection bent his opponent over just as Jason jackhammered his bound hands up as hard as he could. He felt something snap in the mercenary's neck, saw the muscles around his eyes go limp.

Then everything exploded. The world fell to fragments, sight and sound out of sync. Snippets of scenes flickered past his eyes.

Cruz launching herself off the couch toward him.

Galway's face framed in a flash of sodium white, teeth clenched and chest blooming red as he fired a wild dying shot.

The bullet cracking drywall like the finger of an invisible giant.

DiRisio turning with a funhouse grin, weapon raised, sniper eyes.

Scarface falling, drooping like a child's doll, his weight and mass a lead blanket.

Kent rising behind the desk. Shirt impeccably white.

The dark hole of the SIG, a chasm he could lose himself in.

Billy squirming on the couch.

Jason's hands fumbling for the gun Scarface held, the grip slick, his hands slow, so slow, he could see the pistol dropping, knew that he wouldn't make it.

DiRisio's finger tightening on the trigger.

A blur of pale skin and brown hair connecting with DiRisio's arm. Oh God. Billy, trying to help.

Fire jerking sideways.

DiRisio's snarling growl, mouth wide and feral. Left hand reaching for Billy's neck.

Down, down, Scarface's gun falling, rebounding off the polished hardwood as Jason dove for it.

DiRisio plucking Billy off the couch and tossing him like a pillow. All fifty pounds of the boy flying, his hands spinning wild pinwheels as he tumbled through the air.

Billy's head connecting with the wooden back of a chair. His body falling.

No.

No.

No!

With a final shove, Jason threw Scarface away from him and stretched for the gun with his bound hands. The grip was sticky. He jerked it upwards, realizing even as he did that he was too late, that DiRisio had him. He stared at the man who had killed his brother, wanting his last emotion to be hate, waiting for death even as he tried to fight. Wondering if he would hear the bullet.

An explosion.

DiRisio spun sideways. His left arm flew to his shoulder. The SIG-Sauer slipped from his right in slow motion. He staggered, and another blast tore a hole in the wall where his chest had been. With a growl he gripped the edge of the doorway and threw himself out of the room.

Not understanding, Jason turned.

Elena Cruz stood perfectly straight, arms together in front of her. A ribbon of smoke drifted from the singed corner of her clutch purse.

# CHAPTER 47
## The Whirlwind

His first thought was that he'd never loved someone so much as he loved her in that moment.

His second thought was for Billy.

"Watch him!" Jason gestured at Adam Kent, who stood stunned and blinking behind his boxy desk. Cruz whirled, and he raised his hands high.

Jason scrambled across the floor, stepping over Galway's ruined corpse, the cop's vacant eyes staring at the ceiling. He found Washington already cradling Billy, hands stroking his hair. The old man's face was a mask of pain, and as Jason forced himself to look down, his mind was full of horrors, a cracked skull, the boy's face cyanotic blue. But though his eyes were closed, Billy's breathing seemed steady.

"He's okay," Washington rasped without looking up. "Just a cut, maybe a concussion. I don't know." His hands shook on the boy's pale shoulders.

Jason rose, the gun in his bound hands. Fire pumped in his veins. DiRisio. This time he would pay.

Kent's eyes grew wide as Jason stalked to the desk. "Mr. Palmer, I assure you, I wouldn't have hurt—"

Jason silenced him by raising the gun. "Scissors."

For a moment Kent just stared, but then his mind caught up. "Sure," he said, and reached for the desk drawer.

"Slowly."

The millionaire gently slid open a drawer and removed a

pair of black handled scissors. Jason held his arms out, the gun level at Kent's belly. "Cut the zip-tie."

Kent glanced at him, at Cruz with her gun steady on his head. With exaggerated care, he slid one blade of the scissors under the tie and clamped down until the plastic broke.

"Now hers." He covered Kent while the man freed Cruz.

"Galway?" She asked, her voice cracking.

Jason shook his head, and her eyes narrowed. He stared at her for a moment, probably only a second, but it felt much longer. He was at once exhausted and jittery, every cell humming, and he let it all show in his eyes. All the pain and rage, his retinas playing a movie of Billy flying through the air. Looked at her and let her know what he was going to do.

Gave her a chance to stop him.

When she didn't, he nodded and turned for the door. Behind him he heard Cruz ordering Kent to sit down. Jason's fingers tingling with energy and the return of circulation. He paused for a moment and looked back at the scene: the slow spread of crimson from Galway's body, Scarface unmoving in front of the desk, Cruz with Kent locked dead to rights. And on the floor, Washington holding Billy, and crying.

He knew that somewhere out there, DiRisio waited. A guy like that, he wouldn't quit, not now, not over a shoulder wound. And remembering how fast he moved, the joy he took in killing, Jason wasn't sure he was a match for the man, even now.

It was ironic. Kent hadn't been wrong about him. For months, he'd half-chased death. Flirted with it. Teased it. Now that he had reasons to live, he had to gamble his life. He owed it to them. To Washington, a man of peace dragged into violence. To Ronald, killed or wounded trying to protect a boy that wasn't his. To Galway, who had turned out to be a cop after all. To Michael, who had dared dream of a better world. And to Billy, the only true innocent in the whole mess.

With the weapon in front of him, Jason stepped out the door, a soldier hunting an evil spirit in a cheap suit.

\* \* \*

Cruz knew what Jason planned to do. In that long moment he'd stared at her, he'd told her as clearly as if he'd said the words. With that look he'd asked her permission to kill Anthony DiRisio, and she'd given it.

She supposed as a cop she ought to feel bad, but couldn't find it in herself.

"Put your hands on the desk." She cracked her voice like a whip, and Kent complied quickly. It made her sick to look at him, his former rich man's arrogance replaced by a pasty, nauseous expression. His eyes darted from body to body, the reality of costs right in front of him, no longer items on a spreadsheet. "I didn't know it would be like this," he said, his voice thin.

"Shut up," she said. "Don't move. I don't care if you're just trying to scratch your nose. Your hands leave that desk for a *second,* I'll blow you away." The words felt silly, something from an action movie, but they had the intended effect. Kent went rigid as a statue, palms flat and fingers spread.

Eyes still on him and gun up, she took four cautious steps back, feeling behind her with her feet to make sure she didn't trip. When she reached Galway's body, she stepped over him so that she could look down without letting Kent out of her peripheral vision.

Her partner lay on his back. He'd been hit at least three times, two in the chest, and he lay in a spreading lake of blood. His mouth and eyes were open, and his service weapon lay a foot from his hand.

An ache rippled through her. *Goddammit, Tom. A day late and a dollar short, again.* She thought of his son, Aidan, seventeen years old and sullen, but with his father's bright eyes and sharp mind. He would go to college, get a job, marry, raise kids of his own, but he would never be able to say he knew his father. A man who had made mistakes and taken the easy path. Who had been, at times, a bad man, and at other times a hero. Who could only be defined, like everything else, in shades of gray.

She glanced quickly at Kent, who hadn't budged. Then she dropped to a squat and used her free hand to close Galway's eyes. Good and bad were for angels to judge. Here on earth, she could at least give him a little dignity.

"Officer Cruz!" The urgency in Washington's voice yanked her to her feet, let her know something was wrong. At first she assumed Kent was moving, and raised the Glock quickly, eyes staring down the barrel. But the millionaire sat exactly where she'd left, his face white and hands flat. She looked over to Washington.

And saw Billy convulsing in his arms.

Jason took careful steps, weapon up and sweeping. The motion was familiar. How many hundreds of times had he moved this way? How many rooms had he cleared, how many desert streets had he walked point? Though the pistol he'd picked up felt different than his M4 carbine, the principle was the same.

The living room was bright with lamps and catalog furniture. An open arch led to a darker room, and he quickstepped along the wall to stay out of the line of fire. Felt the beat of his heart, the sweat on his sides. The old fear. Back in battle.

He took a breath and then swiveled around the corner. A long table with one tall metal candlestick on it, ornate chairs on both sides, a giant hutch in the near corner. Dining room. Beyond it another door, probably to the kitchen. He tried to remember the size of the house, to place the room in context. He guessed there were maybe five or six more rooms on the ground floor. Best to clear them before tackling the upstairs. He'd be exposed on those steps.

Jason moved forward, pulse throbbing in his forehead. Stretched out a hand for the kitchen door and pushed it slowly, concentrating on the room ahead.

Behind him, the doors of the hutch parted silently, and a dark shape unfolded from it.

Cruz sprinted the few steps to where Washington knelt. The boy seemed to be in an epileptic fit, his hands and legs twitching, head jerking.

"What happened?"

Washington stared up at her, his eyes burning panic. "I

don't know. He just . . . started. Maybe the hit to his head.
Do you know what to do?"

She grimaced, then dropped beside the boy. "Here," she
said, and held the Glock out.

Washington jerked away as if burned. "No, I—"

"Look, just point it at Kent, and if he moves, pull the
trigger."

"You don't understand—"

Billy made a long strangled gasp. His face was beginning
to color. "There's no time." She shook the gun at him.
"Come on!"

Reluctantly, Washington reached for the weapon. His lips
curled like something was rotting in his mouth, but he raised
the gun and pointed it in Kent's direction, and that was all
she cared about right now.

Her mind scrambled to remember her first-aid classes.
What were you supposed to do? First, don't move him unless
he was in a dangerous area. The thought would have made
her laugh under other circumstances. *Focus, dammit*. Okay,
second, get him off his back. She reached down and put her
arms beneath the boy's shoulder, feeling the play of tiny
muscles as she rolled him onto his side. It was coming back
now. Clear the airway. She had a vision of her instructor
telling her never to do it by grabbing for the tongue. Instead,
pull the chin out with two fingers behind the corner of the jaw
to force the tongue forward. Cruz fumbled to get one hand
beneath the boy's head, the other on top.

Billy's choking gasps gave way to a slick, wet wheeze.
The flailing of his limbs eased, then quieted. She held his
head in place as his breathing calmed. Beside her Washington
laughed, and she turned to find him looking at her and Billy,
pure joy in his eyes, and she reflected that back at him, feeling a flush of happy relief unlike anything she'd ever known.

Until she heard Adam Kent say, "Washington, I'm going
to have to ask you to put down that gun."

He heard the sound before he felt the impact, and it saved his
life. Jason threw himself sideways, one arm coming up to

shield his face, the other whipping the gun around. The metal candlestick that should have split his head cracked his forearm instead, a sudden nova of pain rocketing up the nerves as his fingers went numb and loose. He saw, rather than felt, the gun fall free, and for a split second it seemed to hang in defiance of gravity, time stopping long enough to allow him to admire the intricate perfection of the world, the faint trace of light silhouetting the barrel, the hatchwork of the grip.

Then Anthony DiRisio jerked the candlestick in a blurring backhanded blow, and this one Jason didn't dodge, the metal catching him in the mouth, gut-sick shiver as it connected with his teeth, white and black stars, and he was falling backwards. His arms tagged the wall, lost purchase, and then his tailbone slammed to the floor, barbed wire and broken glass scraping up the inside of his spine. Everything went wet and zoomy.

"You," Anthony DiRisio said, "are a pain in the ass. But you aren't much of a soldier." Jason had a sense of motion above him, growing closer. Then a weight on his chest. DiRisio was straddling him, knees along his sides. Leaning closer. "Kind of funny," he said, as he lay the candlestick across Jason's throat. "You get to die the same way your brother did." His right shoulder was bloody, the arm flopping, but he pinned that end of the candlestick to the ground with his leg and used his left hand to push down the other side.

The sudden pressure of the metal against his trachea made him gag. Jason gasped for breath, nothing coming, just nothing, like sucking on a cueball. Suns burst behind his eyes, and his hands flopped. He tried to buck, but DiRisio's muscles were iron, and he had leverage. The candlestick ground deeper. The killer rocked forward, his face only inches from Jason's, the individual stubble of five o'clock shadow visible on his cheeks. He smelled sour, coffee and sweat. Jason tried to get his right arm up to push against the metal bar, but it was numb and clumsy from the blow.

*I'm sorry, Michael.*

Then a thought. Right arm. That meant something. What? Colors flashed behind his eyes.

Right arm. Right hand.

Darkness flowed in the edges of his vision.

Right hand pocket.

He fumbled his left arm up against DiRisio's hip. There.

Jason yanked the folding knife out of DiRisio's pocket and flicked it open. The man turned, sensing something wrong, the pressure off Jason's throat and a rush of air coming in, but Jason didn't stop, just swung his arm up as fast and hard as he could and buried the blade in the side of the monster's neck.

DiRisio's eyes bulged. He jerked back, his good left hand scrabbling at his neck, his right flopping at his waist. Blood fountained as he fell off Jason's body, crabbed backwards, his legs flying. A choking wheeze became a rattle, and then his hands started to twitch, and he collapsed with the handle protruding from his neck.

Jason pulled himself away, coughing. The pain in his throat was living fire and the air gasoline, each breath making it worse. He leaned against a wall, watching the room spin, waiting for it to slow.

And as it did, he remembered something he'd told Billy earlier. Despite the pain, he found himself smiling. He'd have to tell his nephew he'd been wrong.

Turned out you could kill a nightmare after all.

The gun felt wonderful in Washington's hand, and he hated himself for it. It rewound the clock thirty years, turned him back into an animal, a dog that bit out of fear. A killer listening to the old cold song of twisting metal. And yet, the song sounded so very much like home that when he heard Kent order him to put the gun down, he couldn't tell if he was relieved or angry.

Kent stood beside an open drawer, a snub-nosed revolver pointed at them. The pale face and shaking hands that had lulled Washington to relax, to let down his guard enough to check on the boy, they were gone. In their place was his former unflappable confidence, the slightly cruel sneer. *All war is deception.*

Beside him, Washington could feel Officer Cruz tense

like a bowstring. She still had her hands on Billy's head, a pose that reminded him of religious iconography, the Blessed Virgin healing a wounded child. But he knew better than to expect spiritual aid.

After all, he'd made only one vow in his life, and he'd broken it. And now they lived in the shadow of the gun. He wasn't surprised. It was a lesson he'd learned early and hard. Pick up the gun and you live forever in its shadow.

Sow the wind, reap the whirlwind.

"I said," Kent's voice firm, "put it down."

But then, what option had there been? He could explain the engineering of the Roman aqueducts, but couldn't save the boy's life. Different books. Yet he could hardly sit and watch him die. Not for a principle. Certainly no principle was so crucial it justified the death of an innocent child. At the end of a day, wasn't that what defined a principle?

Washington stood, the weapon steady in his hand.

"What are you doing?" Kent asked.

Surely no hard and fast rule applied in every situation. Or if one did, it stated that it wasn't acceptable to stand by while an innocent boy died. Or to allow a man who attacked children to go free.

And the sting of betrayal. He'd *believed* in this man. Needed to believe in him, to believe that there were other ways to fight.

He took a step forward.

"Freeze, goddammit." Kent cocked his pistol, held it in shaking hands. "You're a man of peace, remember? You swore you would never pick up the gun again."

Washington nodded. "I guess I was wrong, Adam." Then he squeezed the trigger, just as he'd done thirty years ago. Just like then, there was a roar, and a hot punch against his hand.

Kent's shot came a fraction of a second later, the gun jerking as he staggered back, face wild and confused. His jaw fell open. A red flower bloomed against the starched white of his shirt. He stared at it, blinking. Then his legs gave and he went down like a drunk, the pistol falling from his fingers. In the end, he died the same as anybody else.

Washington waited till he was sure Kent wouldn't get up before he fell down himself. Fire in his chest, cold in his belly. Long overdue. An old debt, now paid.

He heard Officer Cruz but he couldn't see her. Felt her rip open his shirt, press hard. She was yelling, telling him not to give up.

He smiled at her misunderstanding.

From around either side of the darkness he took to be her, he saw a strange glow. Like someone stood behind her with a flashlight. He squinted. It was odd. He couldn't bring Officer Cruz into focus, but somehow he could clearly see shapes standing on either side.

Two young boys. One was Billy, on his feet and breathing easy. The other was a smiling black boy about the same age. Who was it?

The boys each took one of his hands, Billy the left, the smiling boy the right. Their touch flooded him with peace like warm rain.

And just before he died, he saw that the smiling boy had a cauliflower ear.

# *August 25, 2005*

*They wait for him inside. Alive and dead, they wait.*

*He heard the shots. Somehow knew what to expect, even as he forced himself to his feet, even as he staggered through the living room, hand tracing one wall.*

*The living. Cruz, her arms a mess of gore as she labored over Washington. Billy on his side, eyes closed, breath steady.*

*The dead. Scarface, Kent. Galway.*

*And Washington. Jason knows even as he watches Cruz press on his chest, as he watches her try to save him. He can tell by the strange little smile on his friend's lips.*

*More than he's ever wanted anything, Jason wants to lie on the cool hardwood floor and close his eyes. Rest and let this all fade away.*

*Instead he looks around. Flashes of Baghdad, the inside of a café after a suicide bombing, chunks of drywall and wood, fist-sized holes in the walls. The glass doors to the back are spider-webbed and gaping. One of the chairs has been knocked into the fireplace, and the stuffing burns with a hungry green flame that casts flickering shadows.*

*Perfect.*

*He walks to the fireplace, bends to grab the protruding leg of the chair, a wave of heat washing red over his face. Carries it to the drapes on the rear wall and touches them. The fire leaps like a child.*

*He goes to the sofas. To the bookshelves. To the ornate chairs and the hardwood bar. Touches them all, and everywhere he touches, fire is born.*

*He leaves the chair leaning against a wall of photographs and framed newspapers. Adam Kent cutting a ribbon on his company's new offices. Adam Kent shaking hands with the Mayor. Adam Kent looking somber next to an article describing his IPO.*

*The car keys are in Galway's pocket. Jason kneels by Cruz, still bending over Washington, and touches her shoulder. She looks at him through a wet veil.*

*"Let's go," he says.*

*She swallows, and nods, face lit by fire. She lifts Billy, cradles him.*

*He takes Washington. It isn't easy, but he doesn't want it to be.*

# CHAPTER 48
## Lantern Bearers

Jason made sure the door was locked. Double-checked it.

Then he walked through Michael's bedroom, his fingers tracing objects his brother had touched. The soft worn texture of the comforter. A pair of running shoes, the soles scuffed bare. A bureau of polished mahogany. He went in the bathroom. Shaving cream and a razor, a comb with strands of hair stuck in it, half-empty shampoo bottles. He looked in the closet, opened dresser drawers. Shirts neatly folded, underwear jammed in. A tin holding spare change. A couple of loose pictures:

Michael and Lisa coming home from the hospital with baby Billy wrapped up like a burrito.

Billy wearing a McDonald's crown and tearing open a birthday present, his face lit from within.

Jason's mother, that scowl she always got when you pointed a camera in her direction, but a smile in her tired eyes.

The teenaged Palmer brothers at the lakefront, circa 1992. Cheeks sunburned, hair wild. Michael's arm around Jason's shoulder.

Jason took the photo to the edge of the bed, sat down. It was cool to the touch, and there was a thumbprint along the edge, like Michael had paused on it himself. Jason put his own thumb there, felt something straining inside his chest. Started to fight it, reminded himself that was why he'd come up here. Glanced again at the door to make sure it was locked.

And finally let go.

The sobs came hard, long brutal tugs at his innards. He bit his fist to fight the noise, but let the tears run free, rocking back and forth, his feet on ground his brother had walked, his head and heart far away. Let himself remember the afternoon the photo had been taken. The heat of the July sun on his face and shoulders. The way he'd been vaguely embarrassed to be at the beach with his mother, to be posing for a picture. The girls in the background, soft brown spirits of a lost summer. The waves forever frozen in the image, one just breaking, white foam and sand grit, and behind it another, and another, on into an endless blue sky.

He cried for all the things he'd done wrong with Michael, and all the things he'd never get to do right.

But he also cried for all the moments that had been perfect.

And he cried because finally he could.

Eventually, he stood up. Put the photos back in the drawer. Went to the bathroom and took off his dress shirt. Ran cold water, splashed dripping double handfuls on his face, then borrowed his brother's razor to shave, doing it slowly and carefully. Toweled off and looked in the mirror. Put his shirt back on, thumbing the buttons slowly, then reknotted his tie.

He would mourn again. He would cry again. All his life, he supposed. But now someone else needed him more than he needed himself. Practicing his smile, he unlocked the bedroom door and went downstairs.

Cruz was in the kitchen, talking on the phone. He tapped his wrist, and she nodded. Behind him, footsteps echoed down the stairs. His nephew looked fragile in an Izod shirt and slacks. Tendrils of purple and yellow marked his forehead. His concussion had messed with his short-term memory, as they often did, and Billy couldn't remember anything later than sitting under the table at the party, smashing cities of hors d'oeuvres with the toy that had been his father's, and then his uncle's, and now his.

Strange to think it, but in an odd way, DiRisio had done Billy a favor.

Billy stared up at him with wide eyes. Michael's brown eyes.

"Hey, kiddo. How you doing?"

"Okay." Billy said, shuffling his feet awkwardly.

"It's okay to feel sad." He knelt in front of his nephew. "I do."

Billy bit one lip. "Me too." The boy looked at him like it were a headache, like Jason had a pill that could make it go away. He felt that old panic, the instinct that had sent him running most of his life. The one that saw responsibility the way other people saw an onrushing train. He had an urge to ruffle the boy's hair and then go fetch the car.

Instead he took his hand. "You know what your dad would say when I was sad, though?"

"What?"

Jason leaned forward, motioned Billy closer, then closer still. When the boy's face was only inches from his, Jason dodged in, his face moving fast, planted his lips against Billy's neck, and blew a raspberry against the soft skin. Billy shrieked and squirmed, wriggling away, smiling, his hands furiously wiping his neck. "Gross!"

Jason smiled back. "I always thought so."

"I got your package." There was anger in Division Chief James Donlan's voice. "I know you're pissed at me, but this is a lousy way to play."

"My package?" Cruz switched the phone from one ear to the other.

"Real estate contracts, shipping manifests, payroll logs, bank account info for Tom Galway, Alderman Owens, some guy named Anthony DiRisio. It'll take the lawyers weeks to backtrack it all. And with Adam Kent involved, what was already a major news item just got escalated to the story of the damn century. Bitchy of you, Elena."

"What are you talking about?"

"Christ and all his spotted saints. I'm talking about you sending this to every news outfit in the city."

"I didn't send any packages." She felt like she was half a step behind. "I know what you're talking about, but the copy I had ended up in the river. Is there a mailing label?"

He paused, and she heard the rustle of papers. "Huh. No. No postmark. It must have been hand-delivered last night."

She closed her eyes, rubbed her temples. Score another point for their mysterious informant. Stories of the gun battle and fire at Adam Kent's house had been all over the news. The media had been having a field day broadcasting theories as to how a CPD sergeant, two known mercenaries with extensive criminal records, and one of Chicago's wealthiest men all ended up dead in what they dubbed "The Millionaire Massacre."

Someone must have decided they wanted the truth out there. She could understand Donlan's ire. It was a PR nightmare. Dirty politicians, dirty cops, and a forced acknowledgement of the seriousness of the gang problems ripping apart the South Side. All heightened by a lurid whiff of conspiracy. The story would dominate dinner tables and bar rooms for a long while to come.

She tried to feel bad about it, but the feeling just wouldn't come. "Sounds like you've got your work cut out for you."

"You don't have any idea," he said. "I'm slated to be fed to the media this afternoon. But first I have to explain to the superintendent how such a colossal fuck-up happened on my watch."

"Yeah, well, cue the violins," she said. Jason walked into the kitchen, straightening his tie. He smiled at her, tapped his wrist where a watch would be if he wore one. She nodded. "I have to get going."

"Wait." She heard a creak like Donlan's chair leaning back, and could picture him in his office, broadcloth armor and a bleached smile, the smell of Dunhills. "You were there, weren't you? At the Massacre."

"I don't know what you're talking about."

"I could always have you arrested and questioned."

"I could always bring a libel suit against the department for labeling me an assassin in the press."

He paused, then heaved a sigh. "Look, I'm sorry. For everything, I mean. What happened between us, and afterwards. And for dropping your name on TV. I didn't have a choice."

"I think you did."

"Okay. I deserve that. I know things got messed up. But I still consider you a friend. And one hell of a cop."

She twisted the phone cord around her fingers. "That would mean more if I didn't think you wanted something from me."

"Don't be like that."

Cruz said nothing, content to wait him out.

"Okay, fine, you win. I'm a prick, all right? Yes, I want something." His breath heavy. "This whole thing, it's a mess, and there's no upside to it. But if you were involved, we could position you as a hero. The undercover cop who busted an arms ring and helped stop a gang war. That turns it around, makes this into a great story."

She laughed. "You're asking me to bail you out?"

"The department, not just me. There's no reason to get personal or political here."

It finally snapped, the last strand of affection or respect for him. She smiled to see it go. "Remember our breakfast the other morning?"

"Of course."

"Like you said then, this is Chicago. Everything is political."

"Wait—"

"Listen very closely, James. I have something I want you to hear."

She hung up.

The ceremony was hard, but it was nice, too. The minister had known Michael and Washington both, and described them with humor and warmth, telling stories of projects they had worked together, of their unflagging devotion to the community. Jason had tipped him a hundred to play "Hallelujah," the Jeff Buckley cover of the Leonard Cohen song, one of Michael's favorites. As the notes rang over the speakers, Jason closed his eyes and saw his brother smiling behind the bar, saw Washington smoking a cigar, a book on his lap.

Afterwards, they went to what had been Washington's house. With the money from Kent, he and Ronald planned to convert it into a full-time gang recovery center. Jason didn't think he'd stay on to run the thing, but he owed it to his brother and father to finish what they had started.

Ronald moved through the room slowly, his arm in a gigantic cast. "That's the fourth time I been shot," he'd told Jason earlier. "Wish these dudes would get it through their heads I ain't going nowhere." He clapped his good arm around the shoulders of friends and former gangbangers. The tension that usually filled the house was gone. Today all were united in loss.

Boys and men ate chicken casserole off paper plates and drank Kool-Aid and beer. They traded sad nods and somber stories. The Oscar kid took Jason aside and told him how Michael had helped him get his driver's license, taught him on his own car, so that Oscar could take a job out in Melrose Park. Billy moved amidst shopowners and former killers, school teachers and cops. Someone put on music, and Ronald set out a box of Washington's cigars. The air turned blue.

Jason shook hands and listened to stories, nodded and smiled. Realizing again how little of his brother he had known, how he'd seen only a certain side. But realizing also that the side he'd seen was one that others hadn't.

To them, Michael was near sainthood, a guy who fought for his neighborhood at his own expense, larger than life. Jason was the only one who knew that his brother could also be a hot-tempered, arrogant prick. There was something sweet in the knowledge. He loved his brother all the more for knowing him to be human.

"You okay?" Cruz handed him a beer, opened one of her own.

"You know what?" He smiled at her. "I think I am."

She smiled back, took his hand. They stood for a moment, then she glanced at her watch. "It's time."

They took the backstairs up to the bedroom where they'd almost made love. The memory hit them both at the same time, funny and awkward and sweet. Cruz turned on the television, tuned it to local news.

Whoever had sent the documents to the media had poured blood in the water. The reporters were smiling sharks, savaging anyone who talked to them. James Donlan squirmed, his politician's smile faltering as he repeated over and over that he couldn't discuss details, that a full investigation was pending. The mayor's press secretary read a brief statement promising consequences of the highest order. Footage of Kent's mansion played, the boxy lines cracking under the weight of fire, smoke punching out windows, smoke knocking down walls. There was a photo of Adam Kent in a tuxedo, and though the anchor stopped short of directly accusing him, she did say recent evidence suggested he may have been involved.

Cruz said, "This is the most beautiful thing I've ever seen," and he laughed.

The anchor continued. New documents implicated Alderman Eddie Owens in the scheme. The mayor was said to be personally disappointed. There was footage of the alderman with his hands in front of his face, scurrying into a black Towncar. Jason wondered if it was the same one.

The image cut to the alderman's right-hand, Daryl Thomas, the man they'd met at Washington's party. He stood behind a podium giving some sort of a speech, distancing himself and the rest of the administration from the alderman's actions.

Cruz shook her head.

"What?"

"I don't know. There's just something so familiar about that guy."

The anchor said that while formal elections would be scheduled, Daryl Thomas would be taking over aldermanic duties in the meantime. The anchor riffed on Thomas's qualifications: BA from Chicago, MBA from Northwestern, ten years in local politics. Strong connections to industry and big business. Respected in the community.

The screen kicked back to Thomas talking, his arms out.

"This is the kind of moment that defines a city. We can either collapse under the weight of scandal, or we can pull together and rise above it. But what we can never do is forget. Just as the burnt child fears the fire, so must we be ever vigilant against corruption and cronyism . . ."

There was more, but Jason didn't hear it. He and Cruz were too busy staring at each other with their mouths open.

The evening was hot, and the smell of exhaust lay heavy on the porch. Jason set his hands on the railing and leaned against it. Stared across to the abandoned lot, the tall grass painted ocher by the setting sun. In the middle of it, Billy sat on the carousel. A recovering gangbanger pushed it for him, the metal squeaking and grinding, and Jason could hear laughter from here.

"How you holding up?" Ronald eased the screen door shut behind him.

"People keep asking me that." He shook his head. "Okay, I guess."

Ronald nodded. They stood and looked at the evening. A car rolled by, a low-slung custom Mustang. Bass rattled the windows. Two men sat inside, nodding slowly to the beat. They wore blue bandannas and hard expressions, hitting Jason with their best thousand-yard stares. He met their eyes, feeling tired inside. Worn down.

"You know what started this whole thing?"

Ronald nodded. "That woman cop, Cruz, she told me."

"A power play. That's all. The man in the number two seat wanted to move up, so he scraped together a file on his boss's sins, and sent it to someone else so his hands stayed clean."

"Maybe he just wanted to stop something he saw goin' on."

"Nah. If that was all, why not blow the whistle himself?" Jason shook his head. "Funny thing is, I saw all this before. I saw it in Afghanistan and I saw it in Iraq. Everybody fighting to cut out their little piece of the pie. Their politicians, our politicians. Contractors and CEOs, mullahs and warlords and generals. Sometimes they did it with a document, sometimes with a bullet. But win or lose, the people playing the game never got hurt like the regular people in the middle."

Ronald shrugged. "Don't know about Iraq, but that sounds 'bout right for Chicago."

"I just . . ." Jason straightened, held his arms out. "I don't know. I just wonder what the point is. Of everything we've done. Taking down Kent and the alderman. It's been three days, and already there's a new alderman that's smarter and more ruthless. And there's probably a new Kent out there, too. So what was the point?"

Ronald turned, leaned against the railing. Patted his pockets, found two cigars. He handed one to Jason, bit the end off his own. "Remember the other night? That story Dr. Matthews told?"

"The Lantern Bearers." Jason nodded.

"He told that story before, lots of times. Truth is, I was kind of like you. Not sure I really got the point, you know, dying to light a lighthouse." He fired his cigar, spat a scrap of tobacco. "Now, though, I think maybe Dr. Matthews was saying that you can't get rid of the darkness. I mean, it's darkness, right? It's gonna fall. But still, you fight against it." He turned, gestured with his cigar. "Besides, even if it ends, ain't the day something to see?"

Jason snapped a match, held it to the end of his cigar, then took a drag and blew smoke into the evening air. The sky burned crimson and yellow. Behind him he could hear the noise of the memorial, the buzz of talk. The somber phase had passed, and now there was laughter and the clink of glasses. Someone had changed the music, soul with a good backbeat. He glanced through the screen, saw Cruz on the impromptu dance floor. Their eyes locked, and her lips formed a slow, sweet smile full of promise. They stared for what seemed like a long time before she winked and returned to swaying with the Oscar kid.

Jason raised himself up on tip-toes and breathed the night air, and with every breath it was as though he were letting something go. As if the Worm that had been eating him alive had gone to dust, and he was letting it out one exhale at a time. He had the feeling that when it was gone, this beast of guilt and shame and fear that had possessed him, when it had abandoned his chest for good, it would leave room for something else.

He didn't know what, exactly.

But he looked forward to finding out.

# AUTHOR'S NOTE

"Crenwood" doesn't exist.

In the year I spent researching and writing this book, I frequently wrestled with whether or not to use an actual neighborhood. I didn't need to make one up; poverty, gangs, and violence are very real problems, and while Crenwood is imaginary, it is closely based on a particular South Side area. However, in the end, I decided to rename it out of respect for the people who live there.

Also, because this is a novel rather than a sociological study, I significantly simplified the number and size of gangs. While a story must revolve around a small group of characters, real gangs have no such limitation. If you ever want to blow your hair back, try Googling "MS-13." If we don't make some changes as a society, and I mean quick, we're in for a world of hurt.

For narrative reasons it is sometimes necessary to create bad cops, and the rules of human nature assure that they occasionally exist in life, too. But in my experience, the vast majority of police are good people working a hard job, and getting paid too little for it.

Finally, as Winston Churchill said, "We sleep soundly in our beds because rough men stand ready in the night to visit violence on those who would do us harm." No matter how we feel about the war, the administration, or the policy, we owe our soldiers a debt of gratitude.

# ACKNOWLEDGMENTS

I used to think that writers worked alone, sweating out their vision with nary a word to another human. Happily, I was wrong. This book wouldn't exist without help from a number of people.

Any author who doesn't first thank their agent clearly needs a new agent—or at least doesn't have mine. Deepest thanks to Scott Miller, a good friend and a remarkable advocate. Onward and upward, bro.

While most books have one editor, I was lucky enough to draw two, both among the best in the business. Ben Sevier said he loved it but that it could be better and gave me fourteen pages detailing how. Marc Resnick chimed in with stellar suggestions that took it to the next level, then shepherded the result with fierce energy, guarding and guiding the book for a year. If it were up to me, their names would be on the spine as well.

My sincerest gratitude to all the folks at St. Martin's Press, a publishing house of the first order, peopled by some of the most passionate and talented individuals I've ever met. Special thanks to Andy Martin, Matthew Shear, Sally Richardson, George Witte, Matt Baldacci, Dori Weintraub, David Rotstein, Christina Harcar, Kerry Nordling, and Lauren Manzella.

Assistant Director Patrick Camden of Chicago PD News Affairs and Commander Nick Roti of the Gang Intelligence

Unit both had enormous patience for a barrage of foolish questions. A particular thank you to officers Dave Trinidad and Joe Perez, two cops who ride the front lines—and who lent me the bulletproof vest to join them. Finally, a shout-out to my friend Officer Jason Jacobsen, LAPD firearms instructor, South Central gang cop, and former Army Ranger, who gave me a mountain of material and corrected some embarrassing errors.

I'm also grateful for the expertise of Captain Robert Brechtl, an investigator with the South Bend Fire Department; Tim Cummings, a veteran with a keen eye for all things Army; and Dr. Vince Tranchida, New York City medical examiner.

When I couldn't figure out what happened next, when I had backed myself into a corner, when I was losing hope on the thing as a whole, my good friends Marc Paoletti, Michael Cook, and Joe Konrath took turns saving my butt with hours of beer and brainstorming. Thanks, boys.

I'm fortunate to have the finest, most tolerant group of early readers out there. Thanks to Jenny Carney, Tasha Alexander, Dana Kaye, and Pete Boivin for not flinging the manuscript across the room. And a special cheers to Brad Boivin, who gave me the hint about Jason's character that brought the whole thing together.

As always, my friends kept me going—yeah, y'all in Atlanta, too—and for that, I'm eternally grateful.

I owe more to my family than I will ever be able to repay. Mom, Dad, Matt: you guys are the reason.

Finally, love and thanks to my wife, g.g. I'm a novelist, but I don't have the words.

Read on for an exclusive excerpt from
Marcus Sakey's next novel

# GOOD PEOPLE

Available at book retailers everywhere

When the smoke alarm started shrieking, Tom was reading in the den again, and again she was locked in the bedroom. Same house, different worlds. They both had their escapes.

The suddenness of the alarm made him swing his feet off the desk, the chair rocking forward as he did. It was a sound he associated with cooking more than anything else—Anna was a great chef, but their ventilation was for shit, and whenever she pan-seared something, she ended up smoking them out of the kitchen and setting off the alarm.

But tonight's dinner had been cans of Campbell's nuked and eaten separately. The remnants of his beef stew were cold in the bowl, alongside a novel, the spine cracked so the book laid flat.

Once the panic faded, he realized that the sound was different, muted. Like it was coming through walls, he thought, and on the heels of that, realized that it must be from their tenant's apartment. The ventilation on the first floor wasn't any better than theirs.

Tom sat back down, pinching the bridge of his nose. Muted or not, the screech wasn't helping his headache. One of those lingering mothers that hung behind his eyeballs. When he moved them, it felt like something tugging at his optic nerve, a cold nauseous ache that made him want to close his eyes. While he was at it, open them to find himself somewhere else. Somewhere warm, with a soft breeze and a

hammock. Maybe the smell of the ocean. Sometimes he pictured Anna with him, lying against him: The old Anna, the
old him, fresh and in love, before their dreams became a burden. Sometimes he didn't.

He sighed, took a sip of bourbon, and turned back to his
book, a novel about twenty-something American expatriates
living in Budapest. They were looking for themselves, and
for their fortune, and they were beautiful, and so heartbreak-
ingly young it hurt to read not because Tom couldn't believe
he had ever been that age but because he couldn't believe he
wasn't still. In that secret center that he thought of as himself,
he was in his mid-twenties, astride the intersection of freedom and responsibility. Old enough to know who he was and
what he wanted, but young enough he didn't owe anybody or
need to get up twice a night to take a leak. A good age.

He planted elbows on either side of the book and rubbed
sore eyes. Mid-twenties . . . D.C., the apartment in Adams
Morgan, a second-floor unit above a bar-and-grill. He'd still
been harboring dreams of being a novelist, worked in the
evenings to the smell of hamburgers drifting in the open window. Anna had her own place, but slept at his most of the
time. They'd thrown a Halloween party one year, and she'd
gone as an abstract painting, naked except for a flesh-colored
bikini and swirls of fluorescent body paint. When they'd
made love that night, the paint smeared the sheets with flowers, and she'd laughed about it, thrown her head back and
laughed that good laugh, then wrapped her painted arms
around his back and rubbed color onto him.

He took another sip of bourbon.

There was a tentative knock at the door. He said, "Yeah,"
and Anna stepped in. She wore cotton pajamas and no makeup.
Her eyes were round and puffy.

"Do you hear that?"

The smoke alarm was perfectly clear, but he fought the
smart-ass remark, and just nodded. "Bill's, I think."

"It's been going for a while."

"Just a minute or two." Even as he said it, he realized that
this wasn't like an alarm clock, something to ignore. Stood

up. "I guess you're right." He stepped past her, tracing one hand along her hip as he did.

She fired a tired smile at him. "You want me to come?"

"Nah. Go back to bed." He walked the creaking hardwood hall to the kitchen and grabbed the keys to the bottom unit. He and Anna had fallen in love with the building the moment they'd seen it: A brick two-flat, almost a hundred years old, in Lincoln Square near the river. The neighborhood was great, safe and full of families, and the house backed up to a park they had imagined taking their own children to someday.

Of course, the building ran two-hundred grand more than they'd anticipated spending. But renting out the bottom floor let them swing the house payments, more or less. *More or less: The modern way.* Tom opened the front door and started down the steps. *Mortgaging the present to afford the future.*

The smell of smoke pulled him from his reverie. "Shit." He hustled down, yelled over his shoulder. "Anna!" The door to the foyer stuck, and he yanked hard to open it. Behind him he heard her footsteps, but didn't stop, just stepped into the narrow vestibule. A trickle of gray slid beneath the door to Bill Samuelson's apartment. Shit, shit, shit. Tom banged on the door, feeling silly, like the guy was going to hear knocks but not the smoke alarm. He fumbled with the keys, trying one and then another before he got the deadbolt open. Tried to remember everything he'd learned about fire. *Touch the door*, he thought, *see if the flames are on the other side, if you're going to feed them oxygen.* But the wood was cool. Anna stepped behind him.

Tom twisted the knob and cracked the door. The front room was a haze of smoke, the aftermath of a rock concert. The alarm screamed panic. "Hello?" He couldn't see any flames, so he opened the door all the way and stepped in. The room was spartan, just a battered easy chair and a big television propped on a particle-board entertainment center. A halo of swirling yellow clung to the top of the lone lamp.

The décor reminded Tom that he was in another man's apartment, but he pushed the thought aside. This was *his* house, *his* building. Damned if he'd let it burn to uphold courtesy. He quickstepped down the hallway. The smoke grew thicker and darker. He pulled the hem of his shirt up over his mouth, sucked hot air through it.

The kitchen overheads drilled tunnels of shifting light. Tom could sense heat before he saw flame, primitive instincts feeding dread as he moved toward the stove, where spikes of yellow and green danced. The flames wrapped a blackened teakettle, cloaking it in fire, and for a split second he imagined that the kettle itself was burning, and then he realized that the fire was coming from the gas jets. He lunged forward, spun the knob to kill the gas, feeling the fire like a wave of heat. Nothing happened, and he realized the gas wasn't the source, that the fire came from below and around the metal ring. Months of dribbled grease had caught and pulsed with a sweet black smoke. The wall behind the stove was blackened.

"Shit," Anna said from behind him. "Does he have a fire extinguisher?"

Tom threw open the cupboard beneath the sink. The air was clearer down here, and revealed cleansers, a couple of half-empty liquor bottles, but nothing useful. He stood. There was a mug on the counter beside a jar of Sanka. He could fill it with water . . . wait. Better. The dishwashing hose. Tom stepped to the sink, spun the water on, then reached for the gun.

"No!" She had to shout over the alarm. "Grease fire."

*Grease fire, grease fire, grease fire.* Right. Water would just spatter it, send flying blobs of burning oil in all directions. What the hell did you use for a grease fire?

Anna was answering the question for him, pushing past to open the doors of upper cabinets. Canned soup, pasta, a box of Girl Scout cookies. Teas and coffee. Spices with the price tag still on. A ten-pound sack of flour, blue letters on white paper, the top rolled down and rubber banded. She pulled it from the shelf, knocking glass bottles to clatter on the counter. The flames had spread to a second burner. She snapped off the band and opened the sack, then leaned closer to the fire and dumped it, thrusting the bag like she was flinging water from a bucket. An avalanche of powder poured out over the stove, the wall, the counter. The flames sizzled as the flour hit, and then with a *whoomp* were buried beneath mounds of white. Particles rose in the heat, spinning and dancing like dust motes.

Tom felt his breath whistle out, realized he'd been holding it. The world seemed suddenly strange, that post-panic moment when things returned to normal. For a moment they just stared at each other, then Tom said, "Good thinking."

"*What*?" Shouting.

Tom spotted the alarm mounted above the entry to the kitchen. He stretched to spin it off the wall, then yanked the battery. The shriek died without a whimper. He turned back to her. "I said, good thinking." He looked at her and broke into a smile. "Casper."

She stood with the empty bag in her hand, her face and hair coated white. For a moment, she looked puzzled, then saw her arms dusted with flour and began to laugh.

He laughed too, and waving his arms to clear the smoke, stepped over to the stove, preparing himself for the damage. Aligning expectations: the fire had been constrained to the stove, thank god. It would be totaled, the microwave above it as well. The back wall would need fresh drywall, and the whole kitchen would need a coat of paint. He expected all of those things.

What he didn't expect was to see, amid mounds of flour piled like snowdrifts, five neatly banded bundles of hundred-dollar bills.